D1046655

Primary Target

An Owen Allison Mystery

Books by John Billheimer:

The Owen Allison Series

The Contrary Blues (1998)
Highway Robbery (2000)
Dismal Mountain (2001)
Drybone Hollow (2003)
Stonewall Jackson's Elbow (2006)
Primary Target (2019)

The Lloyd Keaton Series

Field of Schemes (2012)
A Player to Be Maimed Later (2013)

Nonfiction

Baseball and the Blame Game (2007)
Hitchcock and the Censors (2019)

Primary Target

An Owen Allison Mystery

John Billheimer

The Mystery Company
Bryn Mawr, Pennsylvania

PRIMARY TARGET

Copyright © 2019 by John Billheimer

This is a work of fiction. All the characters and events portrayed in this book are fictitious, and any resemblance to real people or events is purely coincidental.

All rights reserved. No part of this book may be used or reproduced in any manner whatsoever without written permission except in the case of brief quotations embodied in critical articles or reviews.

Published by The Mystery Company, an imprint of Crum Creek Press
www.crumcreekpress.com

First Edition: September 2019

Cover art by Jocelyn Chuang

Hardcover ISBN: 978-1-932325-59-1
Paperback ISBN: 978-1-932325-57-7
Ebook ISBN: 978-1-932325-58-4

For David Bauer

"His life was gentle, and the elements so mixed in him that nature might stand up to all the world and say, this was a man."

Shakespeare, of course.

David would recognize the play,
and this dedication is for him.

ACKNOWLEDGMENTS

Every work of fiction reflects some matters of fact. As always, I am indebted to a number of people who helped me get a few facts straight. These include Bob, Dan, and Dale Lewis for pharmaceutical details; Howard Sussman and David Fitz-Patrick for insights into the potentially harmful effects of insulin injections; and the clerks at the Raleigh, WV, County Courthouse, for patiently acquainting me with the practice of early voting and the procedures for challenging suspect votes. Any blame for misstatements in these matters belongs to the author.

In the interests of sharing the blame, I once again wish to acknowledge the contributions of the Wednesday Night Wine Tasting and Literary Advancement Society, whose members help to keep me upbeat, upstanding, and up-to-date. The West Coast contingent of this quasi-elite group includes Sheila Scobba Banning, Anne Cheilek, Mark Coggins and Ann Hillesland, while Sheila York contributes a sharp editorial eye from the East Coast.

Finally, I wish to thank my publisher, Jim Huang, who has been a strong supporter of my work ever since my first mystery found its way into print.

PART I

SUICIDE OR MURDER?

O'DAY'S DAYS

ALBANY — *Here in upstate New York, the presidential nomination that appeared to be a shoo-in for Missouri Governor Sam Halstead has turned into a photo finish. A last-minute flood of campaign ads for California Senator Jason Davison have put young Davison neck and neck with old pro Halstead in next Tuesday's primaries. Davison victories here and in Pennsylvania would leave both men with roughly equal numbers of pledged delegates and put the nomination in the hands of voters in next month's primaries in Indiana and West Virginia.*

Tom O'Day, for the New York Herald Dispatch

1

BUYING LANDSLIDES

Owen Allison was running late for a 9:30 meeting with Sheriff Thad Reader. The battery in his mother's fifteen-year-old Chrysler had died, and he had jump-started it with his Saturn's battery, one of the few remaining features of his own car that still worked. The Saturn's transmission had gone bad two months earlier. He couldn't afford to repair it, but he didn't need to right away, since his mother's Alzheimer's had progressed to the point where she no longer drove. It would make sense to sell off one of the cars, but in their current condition neither had the resale value of week-old bread.

The Chrysler's air conditioning hadn't worked for two years, and all its windows were open in an attempt to ward off the heat of the April morning. The car labored around the curves of the meandering West Virginia road, which followed a shallow creek bed lined with middle-class homes showing signs of wear and deferred maintenance. Missing shingles, cracked concrete and flaking paint were common. But the surest signs of the state's declining economy were the card tables decorating many of the porches and yards. Cluttered with pots, pans, and other household goods, the tables sat under jerry-rigged clotheslines hung with discarded shirts, dresses, and jeans. All parts of a perpetual yard sale.

With the economic downturn, the county's accident investigations were just about the only source of income for Owen's consulting business. All the more reason for being on time instead of ten minutes late, he thought as he pulled into the Barkley town square.

Public buildings bordered three sides of the square. The domed courthouse stood on the north side, flanked on the west by a red brick building that housed the sheriff's office and on the east by the library, which had a half-dozen homeless scattered on its steps waiting for the ten o'clock opening. Their numbers seemed to be increasing. The economy and the opioid crisis threatened to give new meaning to West Virginia's "Panhandle State" nickname. On the south side of the square, the welfare office, which had expanded into the space once occupied by a movie theater, shared space with a beauty parlor, discount shoe store, and four boarded-up storefronts.

The parking spaces in front of the courthouse and welfare office were full, but there was plenty of room in front of the county office building. Owen found a shady spot reserved for VISITORS, rolled up the Chrysler's windows, and retrieved his tan sport coat from the passenger seat. He got out, and as he pulled on his jacket, he glanced up at the flags on either side of the courthouse dome. The state flag bore the image of a farmer and a miner atop a red ribbon with the state motto, *Montani Semper Liberi*. Owen remembered the translation from his childhood. Mountaineers are always free. Well, not always, he thought. Not any more. Maybe they ought to replace the farmer and the miner with the image of a pair of faded overalls draped over a makeshift front-porch clothesline. He slammed the car door and started up the stone steps to Sheriff Reader's office.

The overhead fan in Thad Reader's office was not quite as effective as the Chrysler's open windows in dispelling the morning heat. Reader sat behind his desk in full uniform, but the balding man in the nearest visitor's chair had already abandoned his jacket for rolled-up shirtsleeves. Both men stood when Owen entered.

A scowl had caused Reader's glass eye to cloud over like a fogged-up windshield. Worried that his lateness was the cause of the scowl, Owen immediately apologized. Reader waved off the apology and gestured toward the visitor, saying, "Owen, you remember Tom O'Day, don't you?"

Owen nodded and extended his hand. "Of course. You were down here covering the Caldwell case a couple of years ago."

O'Day's face widened into a broad, engaging smile as he shook Owen's hand. He was at least four inches taller than Owen's six feet, and his shoulders were slightly stooped from years of leaning down to talk to shorter listeners. "You guys did yourselves proud on that one."

Reader returned to his swivel chair and motioned for the other two men to sit as well. "With our primary coming up, Mr. O'Day wanted to talk to us about election fraud."

"That so?" Owen said. That explained Reader's scowl. Election fraud had been an explosive issue with the sheriff even before it became a nationwide political football.

"Well, West Virginia does have a colorful history when it comes to elections," O'Day said. Unaware that he was juggling dynamite, the reporter set about demonstrating that he'd done his homework by tracing the last sixty years of the state's long history of shady election practices. He started with the 1960 primary that Joe Kennedy bought for his son Jack and ended with the Texas convict that polled forty-two percent against President Obama in the 2012 Democratic primary. In between there were episodes of cemetery voting, ballot-box stuffing, incumbent kickbacks, and ballots that passed from hand to hand like square dancers doing a right-and-left grand.

Owen watched Reader drum his fingers through the litany of electoral abuse. Finally, the sheriff leaned forward so far that his swivel chair squealed and raised his hand. "Mr. O'Day, if you want us to work with you again, you shouldn't start by insinuating that the entire state is overrun with election fraud."

"It's a little more than insinuation," O'Day said. "It's historical fact."

"Well, none of what you're talking about happened on my watch," Reader said. "The convict vote was unfortunate, but there was nothing illegal about it. The man paid his $2,500 filing fee to get on the ballot, and the voters did the rest. As to your other historical facts, they either happened long ago or downriver, or both. The Kennedy primary is ancient history, and those corrupt officials you're talking about are in jail a couple of counties southwest of here."

"It might not be your county, but it's your state," O'Day said. "And you can't deny it has a rich history of vote buying and stuffed ballot boxes."

"That's history," Reader said. "It's my job to see it doesn't repeat itself in next month's primary."

"It's next month's primary that brings me down here," O'Day said. "If Jason Davison wins the New York and Pennsylvania primaries this month, and it's looking like he might, he'll catch up with Sam Halstead and the winner of your primary in May could be the presidential nominee. The stakes will be high, and you'll be overrun with reporters."

"You among them, I assume," Reader said.

O'Day took a copy of a magazine story from his briefcase and laid it on Reader's desk. "Both of you should have been pleased with the story I wrote about the Caldwell case. I gave you full credit for recovering over $150 million in embezzled funds."

Reader nodded toward Owen. "That was mostly Owen's doing."

"Well, it happened on your watch, sheriff," O'Day said. "And I'm guessing my write-up helped you win your last reelection campaign."

"Didn't hurt," Reader said.

"I thought you did a nice job," Owen said. "For an outsider, you got most of the facts right. I did think you could have eased up a little on the word 'hick.'"

"I was just quoting my sources."

"Mr. O'Day," Owen said. "I can count on one hand the folks around here who'd use the word 'hick.' And none of them would use it talking to a New York reporter. So why don't you just tell us what you're after here."

"Can we talk about next month's primary, then?" O'Day asked. "If I'm right about the candidates coming in neck and neck, the eyes of the nation will be on you. Your primary hasn't been so important since Kennedy beat Humphrey here in 1960. And I see a lot of parallels between that primary and the one you've got coming up."

Reader stroked his neck, causing his jaw to jut out at the reporter. "And just what parallels are you finding between today and something that happened over half a century ago?"

O'Day showed no sign that he sensed the challenge in Reader's voice. "Well, for one thing, your primary was decisive. The winner went on to the White House. For another, rumor has it that young Jason Davison's at least as randy as Jack Kennedy. And finally, you've got a politically savvy Daddy Bigbucks who wants to buy the election for his son. Let's face it, back in 1960 Joe Kennedy bought out the state for his boy Jack."

"I wouldn't say he bought out the state," Owen said. "Just kind of rented it for a day."

The reporter smiled. "No matter what face you put on it, he bought enough votes to put his son over the top."

"He bought just enough votes," Owen said. "Jack Kennedy used to joke about it. Claimed he got a telegram from his father saying, 'Don't buy another vote. I won't pay for a landslide.'"

O'Day tapped the briefcase on his lap. "That quote's the title of one of the books I've been reading."

"I've read it," Owen said. "It's not bad, but it could have used a better editor. The author said everything at least twice."

"One of the things he says more than twice is that votes are still up for sale in this state."

"Let's just hold it right there," Reader said. "I agreed to invite Owen in and have this little talk with you because I appreciate the help your article gave me in the last election. But this talk of parallels between today and 1960 is getting a little out of hand."

Reader held up his index finger. "First place, my politics are purely local. I don't much care whether Davison or Halstead winds up on the presidential ballot. Second place, I'm an officer of the law. Vote buying is a felony, and I won't countenance it in this county." He closed his fist and bounced it on his desktop. "So you'd best tread pretty careful when you talk about buying

15

votes in next month's election. You got something to say, I want to hear some facts. Not just something you might have read somewhere."

O'Day flipped open a spiral notebook. "Everything I have read about West Virginia elections indicates the only thing that's changed since 1960 is the price of votes. Back in Kennedy's day, people were offering half-pints and sawbucks for votes. Today, a vote can cost as much as twenty dollars."

"Got to allow for inflation." Owen smiled and stroked his beard. "A half-pint will probably still buy a vote, though, depending on the brand. But a sawbuck sounds a little high for a presidential vote back then, wouldn't you say, Thad?"

"Does sound a mite high," Reader said. "First election I ever voted in, this'd be back in '72, five dollars was the going rate for a vote for sheriff. President would have been a lot less, around a dollar. 'Course, back in 1960, they could have overcharged an out-of-stater like Kennedy."

O'Day arched his eyebrows in an exaggerated show of incredulity. "You're saying a vote for sheriff cost more than a vote for president?"

"It's a practical matter," Reader said. "Down here, the sheriff's office comes with a lot of perks. He can hand out jobs, fix traffic tickets, and take it easy on your teenage offspring. President's too far away to do any of that. And even if you made the trip to D.C., you'd have to stand in line behind lots of fat cats who donated big bucks to his campaign."

O'Day jotted down a few quick notes. "That sheriff/president comparison is exactly the kind of insight I need for my column. But it sounds like you're saying the sheriff's job is up for sale."

"No more than the president's," Owen said. "But we could be jerking your chain a little."

"If you're going to be reporting down here, you'd best develop an ear for that," Reader said.

O'Day was not deterred. "According to the Charleston Mail, vote buying is still a seasonal business down here." The reporter flipped back a few pages in his notebook. "The paper claims it 'puts a little zip in the economy every two years.'"

16

Thad Reader scratched under his glass eye and fixed the reporter with a glare from his good one, a glare that Owen had seen crumble hardened criminals. "Write this in your book. There's no vote buying in this here county. Not on my watch." He jabbed a finger at the reporter's notebook. "Period. End of story."

The reporter shuffled through his notebook pages. "Then your county must be the exception that proves the rule. In the last several years, the sheriff and more than fifty public officials in Mingo County have been jailed for voter fraud and corruption."

"Don't you dare compare us with Bloody Mingo." The sheriff's chair squealed as he leaned forward to face O'Day. "I'm not saying that vote buying isn't a problem in a lot of the counties south of Route Sixty. But you Northerners have got no cause to feel superior. Here in West Virginia, elections are rigged the old-fashioned way: one vote at a time. Up north where you come from, fat cats buy votes by the bushel full. A slug of TV spots here. Saturated radio ads there. Newspaper editorials every day. And who knows how much foreign hacking. Seems to me our way's a lot more democratic. Although I'll grant you, the way it's been done down here must seem a little quaint to you big-city reporters."

O'Day shook his head. "If the primary race stays close, you're about to be overrun with big-city reporters. Half of them think *Deliverance* was a documentary. They'll come in expecting to find a barefoot, inbred, and ignorant third-world country. On a slow news day, they'll file stories featuring vote buying, opioid overdoses, welfare cheats, strip mining, poverty pockets, and roadkill recipes."

"That's a pretty grim picture," Owen said.

"I can't control it, but I can help you counter it," O'Day said. "I know you two guys are good and competent. When the reporters swarm in, give me a little access. Plug me into your loop and I'll plug you into mine and help polish your image in the national news."

Reader was quiet, then responded with a tight, grim nod. "All right. We'll keep you in the loop. On one condition. If your digging turns up any evidence of vote buying in this county, any evidence at all, I'll trust you to bring it to me. Then stand back and I'll give you plenty of fodder for your stories."

The reporter closed his notebook. "It's a deal."

The sheriff extended his hand across the desk. "In that case, I think we're done here."

As soon as the reporter had gone, Reader managed a thin smile and said, "He's already got his mind made up. Red Davison is going to buy the election for his boy Jason. That's the story O'Day wants to tell. He'll dress it up with some prime examples of election fraud and tombstone votes. It's not hard to find those if you know where to look. And he's already looking at Mingo County."

"So how do you turn it around?"

"Well, like I told O'Day, vote buying's a felony. So I'll let it be known I'll prosecute it to the full extent of the law and then make a few arrests to show I'm serious. I can't be everywhere, though, so I need people I can trust to help out." Reader paused and looked at Owen. "You, for instance. You got some time between now and election day?"

"I'm available. And I need the work." Owen smiled at his own understatement.

"Then you've got it. We'll need to find poll watchers and people to watch the poll watchers. And make sure nobody tampers with the absentee ballots and the no-excuse votes."

"What's a no-excuse vote?"

"Fancy name for an absentee ballot. Except you don't need to be absent on election day. The state will let you turn in your ballot any time during a fifteen-day period before the election. Makes it easier to get out the vote. Trouble is, it makes it easier to rig the outcome too."

"Why's that?"

"Bigger window of opportunity for the fixers. Instead of concentrating all their efforts in a single day, they've got two weeks to find the weak spots in the system and attract customers."

"It should be easy to find customers," Owen said. "On my drive in, half the front yards along Paw Paw Creek had card tables packed with price tags on pieces of people's lives. If you're selling grandma's brooch or grandpa's watch, along with your own pots and pans, it's got to be pretty tempting to put your vote up for sale as well."

"It's against the law," Reader said. "And it's counterproductive to boot. Think about every group you've ever been a part of, from your kindergarten class to your tennis team. How'd you like to pick the group leader by weighing wallets?"

Owen smiled. "We've seen enough examples of that to know there are better ways."

"Hell, a random game of 'rock, paper, scissors' is a better way. Some fellow once said it would be better to be governed by the first two thousand names in the phone book."

"I think I've heard something like that," Owen said. "I think the guy who said it was named Aaron."

Reader laughed. "'Course, the first two thousand names in a West Virginia phone book are likely to be kinfolk."

Owen didn't laugh. "That's exactly the kind of joke you've got to stifle around people like O'Day."

"What the hell, I'm a native. I'm entitled to joke about family trees that don't branch much. Like blacks using the n-word. But I'm just jerking your chain," Reader shrugged. "Like I told O'Day, if you're down here for any length of time, you'd best develop an ear for it. You're right about the pull of poverty, though. We're dealing with double-digit unemployment down here, and twenty bucks for a vote can be mighty tempting to somebody who's out of work." Reader barked out a short laugh. "Hell, there's just too many weak spots in the system. It's no wonder voter fraud is practically a cottage industry in this state. But I don't need to tell you that. You were born here."

"I may have been born here, but the first time I ever voted here was four years ago when you were re-elected. I left the state to go away to college and did most of my voting in California."

"Compared to West Virginia, elections must be pretty clean out there."

"Not much buying and selling on Election Day. There's the same problem you pointed out to our reporter friend, though.

19

Both parties buy votes by the bushel with TV ads."

"No law against that. With all that time you spent in California, though, you must have a fix on this fellow Davison."

"Not really. He came on the scene after I left the state. Won his Senate seat after a term in the state legislature. But his dad was governor when I lived there. Got rich at it. Ruined my consulting firm by voiding the award of a big contract we'd won and giving it to a crony."

"Everybody's saying his daddy's money has been a big factor in his recent surge. So you probably don't hold too high an opinion of the younger Davison."

"Like I said, I don't know much about the son. In my experience, though, the turd doesn't fall too far from the asshole."

Reader laughed. "That sounds like something I would say."

"I'm sure you will, next chance you get."

"No. I'd have to pick my spots. It's a little crude, even for me. But it's good to know you're not bitter."

"His father cost me my business. And my marriage. Why on earth would I be bitter?"

Reader's questions about Owen's time in California brought back a flood of memories as he negotiated the winding roads back to the home he shared with his mother. Ten years ago, he'd been living happily with his wife Judith in Palo Alto, operating a small business with two partners, consulting in risk analysis. When Governor Davison's interference caused their business to go belly-up, he'd taken a stopgap job with the Department of Transportation in Washington, D.C. But Judith wouldn't leave her Palo Alto law practice to join him, and their marriage couldn't survive the separation.

Owen's job with the federal government couldn't survive either, in large measure because of his impatience with bureaucracy. He'd always worked for himself, with no more than a couple of partners. If you needed something, you just walked down the hall and asked for it. Even in all the time he'd lived on government contracts, he'd dealt mostly with the same people, sometimes for years. There was freedom in that. And accountability. And that freedom and accountability disappeared once he was inside the Washington, D.C. beltway.

When family problems and a mine disaster took Owen back to West Virginia, he stayed in the state to help nurse his widowed mother through the onslaught of ovarian cancer and the early stages of Alzheimer's. While acting as a caregiver, he opened a one-man consulting firm and found sporadic work reconstructing accidents, analyzing mine failures, and helping Sheriff Reader with criminal investigations. The work was good when it came, but it hadn't been coming fast enough to cover his expenses, which continued to grow as his mother slipped deeper into dementia.

Looking back over the last decade from the vantage point of his early fifties, it was easy enough to blame his recent string of failures and money worries on the rigged bid that had doomed his California consulting business. Much too easy. As a risk analyst, he knew enough about the vagaries of chance to realize that his marriage might have failed even if his business hadn't, and that he probably would have spent the last two years in West Virginia nursing his mother whether or not his business and marriage had failed.

The road straightened and fed into the cul-de-sac that held his childhood home. Even before he opened the front door, the smell of freshly baked bread told him his mother was probably having one of her good days.

He found his mother leaning over a card table in the living room, playing Scrabble with her primary nurse, Trish Elkins. Another sign that she was having a good day.

Ruth Allison smiled as Owen entered. "Come on in, George," she said, nodding toward a folding chair. "Join us for a game."

Owen didn't take the fact that his mother called him by his older brother's name to be a bad sign. That mix-up had been a regular occurrence even before Alzheimer's had made heavy inroads.

"It's Owen, Ruth," Trish corrected.

"Why, my goodness, I know that. He's my son after all. We can start over, can't we, hon?"

Owen pulled up the folding chair and sat at the table. "Don't bother starting over. Just pass me some fresh tiles."

Trish Elkins counted out seven tiles and scooted them across the table to Owen. She was a strong-boned nurse from the heart of coal country, almost as tall as Owen, but with broader shoulders and a face that fell just short of being beautiful.

One of the few benefits of living in a poor state during an economic downturn was that household help could be hired at affordable rates. Owen paid Trish just a little more than the minimum wage, and did the same for a neighbor lady who also helped with the housecleaning. So long as Owen worked at home, he'd managed to cobble together round-the-clock care, but it was obvious that the future would require more of Trish's nursing presence.

"How'd your meetin' with that there reporter go?" Trish ran her hand through her dark red hair and arranged her tiles to form the word SHINE on the Scrabble board. Her speech patterns never failed to startle Owen. Trish was a caring, competent nurse and an attractive woman, but her diction and elocution sounded like something out of a handbook for redneck comics.

"Went pretty well," Owen said. "He thinks whoever wins West Virginia's primary is likely to be the presidential nominee. Wanted to get a little background on the state."

"Seen me an ad for this fellow Davison on the TV," Trish said. "He's a lot more handsome than the other guy. Looks like a president. That won't hurt him none."

Owen sorted his tiles. "Warren Harding looked like a president. He may have been handsome, but he was the worst we ever had. Daniel Day Lewis looked like a president in *Lincoln*, and all that took was a little greasepaint and a prosthetic nose."

"Let's hope Mr. Davison has other presidential qualities besides his looks," Ruth said, laying down tiles to spell out MASHINE.

"Machine," Trish said, casting a warning glance at Owen. "That's a right fine word, Ruth. Your play, Owen."

Owen took his cue from Trish and played his tiles quickly without challenging his mother's word. When he had interviewed caretakers, Trish had been his first choice, but he'd acquiesced to a recommendation from the administrators at the local hospital where Ruth had volunteered when she was healthy. The hospital's choice had been a woman with perfect diction who coddled his mother, slathering her with baby talk and slacking off on her exercise regimen. When Owen heard her address Ruth as "Oopsie Tootems" while skipping her morning walk, he replaced the hospital's choice with Trish Elkins, who had proven to be a marvel. Trish reinstituted a rigid exercise routine and treated his mother like an adult, discussing current events and playing Scrabble, rummy, and a variety of card games like euchre and honeymoon bridge during the afternoon and evening.

After two more rounds of play, Ruth stared at the Scrabble board and said, "M-A-S-H-I-N-E," spelling it out. "That's not a word. Who played that word?"

After a short silence, Owen said, "You did, mom."

"I most certainly did not." Ruth looked to Trish for verification. "That's just not a word."

Trish responded with a non-committal shrug.

"Well, if I played that mess of letters," Ruth said, "why didn't one of you challenge me?"

"I misread it, mom," Owen said. "I thought you'd spelled out M-A-S-H-I-N-G."

"My momma stopped raisin' fools when she met the local minimum," Trish said. "I know better than to challenge you two sharks at this game."

"You're both lying to me." Ruth pounded her fist on the table so hard the Scrabble tiles jumped. "If we're playing the game, let's play the game. No, by heaven, let's not play any more." Ruth swept her hand across the board, scattering the game tiles. "I won't be treated like a sick old lady, and I won't be coddled. I've had quite enough of that."

Trish stood and put a calming arm around Ruth. "It's my fault, hon. I should have known better."

Owen had seen other sudden outbursts as Ruth's disease progressed, but he was still stunned by their ferocity. "Next game, mom, I'll challenge every one of your words. I promise."

Ruth shook her head. "Won't be a next game." She seemed to relax into Trish's enveloping arm. "At least not tonight."

Trish helped Ruth to her feet. "Let's call it a night." Ruth seemed disoriented, but she followed the nurse's gentle prodding toward the staircase. "There's a turkey sandwich on the sideboard," Trish said over her shoulder as they started up the stairs. "Fresh bread, fresh bird."

Owen retrieved the sandwich, grabbed a Stella Artois from the refrigerator, and took his laptop to the kitchen table to check on his emails. Nothing in the way of business opportunities. A few companies he'd bought things from back when he could buy things kept reminding him they were still around. As he scrolled down, he found an email from Ray Washburn, one of his former partners in Tranalytics, the California consulting firm that had folded when Governor Davison torpedoed them. Washburn had stayed in California and was retired now. His IRA had survived better than Owen's, partly because he'd had a longer time to build it up, and he was now in his late sixties. Washburn had forwarded an email from their third partner, Dan Thornton. Thornton had retired to upstate Washington at the same time Owen had moved east, and the two had had little contact since their business folded. Washburn's only comment on the forwarded email was, "Further proof there is no God."

After apologizing to Washburn for being out of touch, Thornton's email rambled uncharacteristically, mixing reports on his day-to-day activities with a litany of health problems that included limited mobility, incontinence, foot maladies, and a cognitive disorder that left him unable to concentrate. He'd lost contact with friends, rarely left the house, stopped seeing his neighbors, and had to discontinue an interview with a newspaper columnist doing a simple businessman profile when he couldn't remember anything about Tranalytics but its name.

An interrupted interview appeared to be the least of Thornton's worries, as he went on to list serious financial problems that included significant medical outlays, an underwater home mortgage, and devastating losses in his retirement account. The email meandered on, as Thornton mixed his fears for the bleak future his wife Theresa could face as a widow with half-hearted jokes about food stamps and homeless shelters. He closed by asking for suggestions and signing himself as "A dim shadow of your former Tranalytics partner."

Owen read the email over three times, sick at heart. Dan Thornton had once had one of the most incisive minds he'd ever known, particularly in financial matters. It was hard to believe that mind had composed the rambling, discursive email whose listing of disasters made Owen's own problems seem insignificant. He couldn't believe he'd spent the better part of his drive to and from the sheriff's office feeling sorry for himself. After all, he had an unmortgaged roof over his head, even if it was his mother's, and work that he could still take pride in, even if the jobs were few and far between. And his chief physical complaint was a lack of speed on the tennis court, a malady his doubles partners would claim was nothing new.

Owen read Thornton's email a fourth time, trying to find a ray of hope or a way to help. When none occurred to him, he picked up his phone and dialed Ray Washburn in Palo Alto. Washburn and Thornton had started Tranalytics together, and he'd always been closer to his founding partner than to Owen.

Washburn answered his phone on the first ring, saying, "I was just going to call you."

"That email from Dan is just about the bleakest, most devastating thing I've ever read," Owen said. "Do you think there's something we can do to help?"

"I don't think so," Washburn said. "I just got a call from Theresa. Dan seems to have taken his own life."

2

A GOOD DAY FOR A FUNERAL

There was a time when Owen had thought you could blindfold him, fly him to any airport in the U.S., remove the blindfold, and he could tell you where he was just by looking at the people, the view, and the terminal architecture. Now he wasn't so sure. The view of snowcapped Mount Rainier on the flight into Seattle was a dead giveaway, but the airport itself, with the security lines inside and the beehive parking structure outside, could have been anywhere. As he stood waiting beside a baggage carousel, though, the steady drizzle outside and the variety of raingear inside, ranging from clear plastic foldaways to belted Burberrys, coupled with the robust, healthy faces streaming out of the secure area, just felt like the Emerald City.

He scanned the stream of arriving faces for the one that would always jolt him. His ex-wife Judith finally appeared, trailing a red roll-aboard suitcase behind her. Her pace quickened when she caught sight of him, and she hurried into a hug, dropping the suitcase handle as she wrapped her arms around him.

They broke the embrace and Owen recovered the suitcase, took Judith's arm, and headed toward the parking structure. "Been waiting long?" Judith asked.

"Just long enough to rent a car."

"How far is it to Bellingham?"

"GPS says a little over ninety minutes. Plenty of time to make the memorial service."

"I still can't believe Dan would commit suicide."

"Neither can Theresa."

"Of course not."

"No. I mean she doesn't believe it was suicide."

"He left the motor running in his garage. Does she think it was an accident?"

"Hard to see how it could have been. Ray Washburn says there was a hose leading from the exhaust to the passenger window."

"Did he leave a note?"

"I don't think so. Theresa wasn't very coherent the two times I talked to her."

They arrived at the maroon Camaro Owen had rented and he hefted the red suitcase into the trunk. Judith slid into the passenger seat and sat sideways, staring at Owen. "But if it wasn't suicide or an accident, that doesn't leave many options."

"I pointed that out to her."

"What did she say?"

Owen turned on the ignition. "She kept breaking down on the phone. I couldn't follow what she was saying. She finally made me promise to talk to her after today's service."

"Why you? What does she think you can do?"

"She remembered I had some police connections up here from my research days with Tranalytics. And the Caldwell case was national news. She and Dan read about it in the Seattle paper."

"It's been over ten years since you had a research contract up here. And your police contacts then were with the highway patrol, not local law enforcement."

"I promised to listen. What else could I do?" Owen edged the car out of the parking structure and the gray spring rain enveloped them. "If anything, she's likely to need legal help."

"Why do you say that?"

"Dan mentioned it in an email to Ray before he died. He had a lot of problems. Physical, mental, financial."

"I just can't imagine any problems big enough to drive the man we knew to suicide."

"Neither can I."

"I'll talk to Theresa. Maybe I can help with any legal issues."

"Be good if you could." Owen glanced over at his ex-wife. There were wisps of gray in her brunette bangs, and a hint of crow's feet at the corners of her hazel eyes. But it was hardly a stretch to tell her, "You look great."

Looking straight ahead, she smiled and said, "Thank you." Then, after a long pause, "I'm seeing someone."

They were words he'd dreaded, but they didn't really surprise him. Like a doctor's unhappy verdict on a lump that had been too long neglected. "I guess I've always hoped …"

"It's been over ten years, Owen."

"I've had mom to look after."

"Ten years and half a continent."

"It's not Jack Fucking Davis, is it?"

"That was over a long time ago."

Owen stifled the urge to say, "While we were still married," and instead said, "He's still senior partner?"

"Yes, we still work together, and yes, he's still married."

Didn't stop you before, Owen thought. But he said, "Tell me about this new guy."

"His name's Allen Bennet. He's a trademark attorney. A widower."

"Any children?"

"Two teenagers. A boy and a girl."

"You'll make a good mother."

"It hasn't gotten quite that far yet."

At least that was something. He didn't want to hear any more. "Well, anyhow, I'm happy for you." There was a time when he could have put more feeling into those words. He'd been in a relationship himself, a few years ago, and he remembered hoping that Judith could find the same satisfaction. But the group that had looted the Caldwell bank had left several victims in their wake, and the woman he'd loved had been one of them.

The roadway gave him a chance to change the subject. "The bridge we're coming to collapsed about five years ago."

"That's comforting."

"It crosses the Skagit River, which empties into Puget Sound. An oversize truck took out one of those triangular steel girders above us. Driver made it across, but the bridge collapsed behind him."

"Was anyone hurt?"

"They fished three or four drivers out of the river, but no one died."

"Funny how talk of my relationship reminded you of a collapsing bridge."

"I think it was the other way around. I bid on the job of analyzing the failure. Lost out to a local firm."

"That has a familiar ring to it."

For a few miles the only sound in the car was the drumming of rain and the squeak of windshield wipers. Then Owen pounded the steering wheel and said, "God damn Red Davison."

"Oh, stop it," Judith said. "It wasn't only Governor Davison's bid-rigging cronies that did you in."

"What do you mean?"

"You know what I mean. Dan wasn't bringing in his share of the business."

"I guess he was starting to decline even then. We just didn't see it."

"And you wouldn't knuckle under to Santa Clarita and change a couple of sentences in your light-rail report."

"It was more than a couple of sentences. They wanted me to double the ridership projections."

"It cost you a lot of business. And they built the system anyhow."

"That's right. They built the system anyhow. It cost twice as much as they estimated and the ridership didn't even come up to the levels I projected, let alone the levels they wanted to see in the report. It's bankrupting the city."

"So, in the end it didn't matter what you wrote in your report."

"It mattered to me."

"Still, you didn't have to move all the way to D.C. when Tranalytics folded."

And you didn't have to stay in Palo Alto, Owen thought. "The government work was steady. I was tired of living from proposal to proposal."

"I warned you, though, that federal bureaucracy would drive you crazy. It didn't take long for you to get into trouble."

Owen smiled. "But you bailed me out."

Judith returned his smile. "More than once."

"We were a good team." He tried not to emphasize the past tense, but there it was.

"Yes. We were."

This time Judith changed the subject. "The scenery is beautiful. So lush and green."

"That's why they call Seattle the Emerald City."

"So it's got nothing to do with Oz."

"I'm guessing they waited until L. Frank Baum's copyright had expired."

The rain stopped briefly, and they could see the sun reflected off Mount Baker. Then it resumed as quickly as it had stopped, dappling the waters of Puget Sound.

Owen restarted the windshield wipers. "A good day for a funeral."

The funeral service was held in a compact red brick church nestled in a valley at the foot of Mount Baker. Owen and Judith arrived a half-hour early to find Dan Thornton's wife, Theresa, standing in the narrow entryway, protected from the rain by a gray-shingled canopy.

The new widow stood tall and erect, with jet-black hair that was swept back in a severe bun and framed a brow marked by deep furrows that made her once-beautiful face look like a farmer's field at planting time. She held Owen and Judith's hands as she listened to their expressions of sympathy, then clasped Owen's right hand in both of hers and said, "I must talk to you. You will be coming to the house after the service, won't you?"

"Of course," Owen said.

"I just know Dan couldn't have done what they say he did."

"It certainly doesn't seem like him," Owen said.

Two more mourners came up the church to the narrow

30

entryway and stood behind Owen and Judith. Theresa released Owen's hand. "I just want to thank you for coming. Both of you. As a pallbearer, Owen, you should sit in the front row, beside the coffin. Of course, you should go with him, Judith. It's so good to see the two of you together."

"I'm together, but she's still a little flaky," Owen said. It was an old family rejoinder that popped out automatically whenever anyone asked if the two of them were together, but it added two more furrows to Theresa's forehead.

Judith gave Owen a disgusted look, grabbed his arm, and hustled him into the church and down the center aisle to the front pew, where they joined Ray Washburn and his wife, Sandy. The four of them talked in low tones as more mourners filed into the church. The only other attendees Owen recognized were Dan's two grown sons, seated in the front row on the other side of the aisle. The small church was not even half full when the black-robed priest, followed by two young altar boys, entered from the sacristy and began the funeral mass.

The funeral service hadn't changed much from the days when Owen was an altar boy. In those days, he'd been struck by the impersonal nature of the service, with the parish priest repeating the same homilies regardless of the identity of the departed. Old or young. Male or female. Cancer case or accident victim. All received the same parting words.

He was surprised to hear today's priest mouthing the same familiar platitudes, as if Dan Thornton had been no different from the occupants of the coffins Owen had seen lowered into the ground forty years ago in West Virginia.

There was one significant change from the funeral masses of Owen's youth. Before signaling the pallbearers to carry the coffin to the waiting hearse, the priest turned to the congregation and asked if anyone had special memories of the deceased that they would like to share.

Ray Washburn rose, walked to the lectern, and delivered a moving personal tribute that traced his friendship with Dan Thornton through their years as business partners. In Owen's experience, the problem with most such extemporaneous eulogies was that the speakers talked more about themselves than the deceased, but he felt that Washburn avoided that pitfall to paint an accurate portrait of his former partner.

When Washburn had finished, the priest asked if anyone else would like to share their memories of Dan Thornton. From her seat beside her two sons, Theresa Thornton turned and looked hopefully around the congregation. When no one stirred, the priest repeated his request and looked a little embarrassed by the lack of a response.

Judith dug her elbow into Owen's abdomen. "For heaven's sake," she whispered. "Do something."

Owen rose unsteadily, telling himself he just had to remember to limit the use of personal pronouns. Then he clutched the lectern and began, "I knew Dan Thornton first as an employee, then as a partner, and finally as a friend." Damn, he thought. There it is right up front. The dreaded "I" word.

"He had four passions in his life," Owen continued. "His wife, his children, his work, and the Chicago Cubs." The Cubs reference got a few smiles and nods from the congregation. "We spent many hours arguing whether his Cubs or my favorite American League team, the Indians, had the more futile history." Watch it. Two more personal pronouns. Stick to Dan. "Well, that argument is ancient history now that both teams have made it to the World Series recently. Dan used to be vulnerable in fantasy leagues because he would load up his teams with Cub players, whether or not they could carry their weight. That strategy doesn't look so foolish anymore. But his love of the Cubs was the only place he ever let his passion overcome his judgment. He had one of the most precise, objective minds I've ever known. He left an indelible mark on his family, the research community, and the world at large. He will be sorely missed."

There. A strong finish with a minimum of personal pronouns. He released the lectern and looked down at Judith, who was smiling and nodding. It had been a long time since he'd seen that smile.

The few mourners who accompanied the hearse to the cemetery fit under a sagging twelve-by-twelve canopy that collected rainwater in its folds and released it in rivulets at opposite corners. The readings over the coffin were the same ones Owen remembered from his youth, and the homilies were just as impersonal.

After the coffin had been lowered, Owen used his suit jacket as an umbrella to protect himself and Judith as they slogged through the wet grass to their car for the drive to Theresa Thornton's home.

The Thorntons' two-story wood frame house was set high enough in the foothills to have a view of both Mount Baker and Bellingham Bay. Theresa sounded half apologetic as she handed Owen a glass of Cabernet and said, "It's nothing like what we had in Atherton, and we paid a little too much for it, but it's home."

"It seems quite comfortable," Owen said. "And the views are fantastic."

"If the rain clears by sunset, you'll really see something." Theresa touched his arm. "Let me attend to my hostess duties, and then we really must talk."

"Whenever you're ready," Owen said.

Theresa had arranged a series of photographs of Dan on the walls of their dining room. Grouped chronologically, they started with his Boy Scout days and stretched through his working life. Dan playing baseball. Dan skiing. Dan rooting for the Cubs. Dan and Theresa on their wedding day. Dan and Ray shaking hands in front of their first Tranalytics office. Dan, Owen, and Ray receiving a professional award. There was only one photo from Dan and Theresa's days in Washington, which looked as if it had been taken when they moved into their current home.

Owen looked at the array of photographs, talked briefly to Dan's brother and two sons, then chatted with Judith and Ray and Sandy Washburn until Theresa Thornton beckoned to him from the hall doorway.

He followed her downstairs to a family room where the large cavity in a floor-to-ceiling entertainment center dwarfed the tiny portable TV sitting in it.

"The Hi-Def TV had to go," Theresa explained. "Along

with a lot of other luxuries we couldn't afford."

"I'm sorry," Owen said.

"The house should have gone too, but we would have taken too big a loss." The furrows in Theresa's forehead deepened as she grimaced. "These were supposed to be our golden years."

"You said you didn't believe Dan committed suicide," Owen said.

Theresa sighed. "He couldn't have. For one thing, he was a devout Catholic. And for a devout Catholic, suicide is a guaranteed one-way ticket to hell."

"If he was such a devout Catholic, why didn't today's priest know him better? His talk was general enough to cover half the population."

Theresa grimaced again. "That wasn't our parish priest. Our pastor takes an old-fashioned view of suicide. He refused to conduct the service. As far as he was concerned, there was no hope for Dan's soul. I had to shop all over Washington for a caring radical alternative."

"Stories like that have made me a lapsed Catholic," Owen said.

"You don't go to mass anymore?"

"I go with my mom from time to time during the winter. Most other Sundays, though, I'm on the tennis court. But we should be talking about Dan, not about me. What else makes you think he wasn't a suicide?"

"His life insurance. Suicide voided it. He knew that. His insurance payments were the one bill he kept current. He wouldn't leave me destitute. We talked about it. Over and over."

"But wasn't he having health problems?"

"Oh, God, yes. That's why we talked so much about his life insurance. He had so many problems. That speech you made today. I thank you for it. But Dan was nothing like the man you described. You wouldn't have recognized him. Not at the end. He couldn't concentrate. Had mental lapses. Fainting spells. I couldn't let him drive alone. He even had to wear a diaper. A diaper! And his feet were so swollen he could hardly walk."

Owen thought Dan's condition would be a powerful

argument for suicide. But he didn't say so. Instead, he said, "The way the hose was arranged, it couldn't have been an accident. If it wasn't suicide, there's only one alternative left. Did Dan have any enemies?"

"The past few years, he's been practically a recluse. He wasn't alert enough to make friends, let alone enemies. You saw how empty the church was." Theresa shook her head. "But there was no note. That's a positive sign isn't it? Don't most suicides leave notes?"

"No." Owen hated to keep contradicting her, but he'd looked up the statistics. "Less than forty percent actually leave notes."

"Oh. So that's not much of an argument. But there are the files. The missing files."

"What files?"

"We rented a small unit in one of those storage operations on the outskirts of town. Filled it with furniture, old pictures, business files. Stuff from Atherton that wouldn't fit here. I went there two days ago to get some old photos of Dan for the display upstairs. But someone had been there before me. The unit was packed full, but whoever was there had moved furniture to clear a narrow path to the file cabinets against the rear wall. When I looked in the file cabinets, one drawer was practically empty. It had held old Tranalytics files. From the early years."

"Is there some chance the drawer was never full?"

"None. Those file cabinets were jam packed when we moved them into storage. Dan hated to throw anything out, but I made him dispose of anything he couldn't fit into three file cabinets."

Owen smiled at the thought of Dan weeding his business files. "I can't throw anything out either. But maybe Dan took the files himself."

"He never went there without me. He didn't trust himself to drive alone."

"Did he have any use for the files that you know of?"

"Well, a man from the local newspaper, the Guardian, was interviewing him about his career. They do a weekly column on famous local residents. As you might guess, the bar on what passes for famous is set pretty low. Anyhow, the man came to the house for the interview, but Dan had one of his attention lapses and had to cut the meeting short. Dan was really embarrassed. He just couldn't remember anything about his work at Tranalytics. He told me he kept apologizing and offering to finish the interview at a later date."

"Did he ever finish the interview?"

"Not so far as I know."

"And the files aren't somewhere around your house?"

"I couldn't find them anywhere. They'd be hard to miss. There was almost a whole drawer missing."

"Maybe he turned them over to the reporter."

"I doubt it. Dan's old files would have been much too detailed for the kind of interviews running in the Guardian."

"Did you check with the reporter?"

"No."

"Well, we can do that at least."

"Would you do that? His name's Alex something. Alex ... Matthews. And there's something else I'd hoped you might check out. Would you talk to the local sheriff? He's convinced Dan killed himself. But you and I know he wouldn't have done that." Theresa clasped both of Owen's hands in hers. "Would you do that please? I wouldn't ask, but I know you've had experience with law enforcement."

"It's pretty limited. I've helped my own county sheriff with some cases, but they've mostly involved topics I know something about. Mine failures. Car crashes. I don't have much experience with suicides."

"You solved that one case about the missing banker and the fraudulent paintings. It made the Seattle papers. Dan and I were so tickled to see your name."

"That may not mean much to your local law enforcement. How did they seem when they talked to you?"

"They made up their minds pretty quickly that it was suicide."

"Who found the body?"

Theresa seemed to collapse inwardly, like a balloon leaking air. "I did. God. It was awful. I'd come home from work and opened the garage door. All that smog and stench. And Dan in the middle of it." She began trembling so badly that Owen put his arm around her. "I just can't talk about it. Please. Won't you just talk to the police?"

"I'll stay over a day. Talk to the reporter. Take a look at the storage unit. See what I can find out from the police." He didn't want to raise her hopes too high, so he added, "I'm afraid I can't promise much more than that."

"Oh, God. Thank you. That will be such a help." Theresa smoothed her black dress and ran both hands along her swept-back hair. "I must look like a mess." She turned and started up the stairs. "I've got to get back to the guests. Thank you so much."

Owen climbed the stairs to the reception, corralled Ray Washburn and Judith, and recounted the conversation he'd just had with Theresa.

"I told Theresa I'd stay over tomorrow and talk to the sheriff. Can you see that Judith gets to the airport?" Owen asked Ray.

"Of course," Ray said. "But from what you've told us, it doesn't sound like there's anything to suggest Dan didn't kill himself. He may not have left a suicide note, but that email he sent me was well on its way to being one."

"I'm glad you agreed to stay over," Judith said. "It can't hurt to follow up with the local law. Even if all you do is help set Theresa's mind to rest."

"I don't know that she'll ever come to terms with it," Owen said. "But that business with the missing files does sound a little fishy." He turned to Ray. "Can you think of any records from Tranalytics early years that would be worth stealing?"

Ray shook his head. "Nothing comes to mind. But we all salvaged our own files from those years. I'll take a look at mine when I get home. See if anything pops out at me. You should do the same."

Owen checked his watch. "There's still time for me to call Thad Reader. He's the sheriff I work with back home in West Virginia. Maybe he can grease the skids a little with the local law here in Bellingham."

Owen used the downstairs phone to leave a message for Thad Reader and noticed a stack of local newspapers on the shelf next to the phone table. He called the number on the Guardian masthead and asked to speak to Alex Matthews. The operator put him through to Matthews' voice mail, and the message on the phone stunned Owen. He hurried back upstairs, took the tray of coffee mugs Theresa Thornton was carrying out of her hands, set them on the kitchen table and asked, "Didn't you tell me it was a male reporter who interviewed Dan?"

"Yes. Is something wrong?"

"I just called the Guardian. The Alex Matthews who writes the 'Local Notables' column is a woman."

3

A HUMAN PINCUSHION

"I get that a lot," Alex Matthews said. "I show up for an interview and people do a double take because they're expecting a man. It would help if the paper printed my picture next to my column."

Owen wondered whether a picture would really help. The only thing about the thin, elderly columnist with close-cropped gray hair that signaled her gender was her high-pitched voice, and that wouldn't show up in a photo.

Matthews propped her black tennis shoes on top of her desk and leaned back against the edge of her cubicle. "Week or so ago, a guy called in who just refused to believe I wasn't a man. Got him so flustered he hung up. Never did find out why he called." She smoothed the creases on her pant legs. "But you, now. You're just the opposite. The minute you found out I was a woman, you wanted to see me."

"I guess it must have seemed that way," Owen said. "Someone claiming to be Alex Matthews of the Guardian interviewed a friend of mine at his home recently. But that Alex Matthews was definitely a male."

"Not that I couldn't use the help, but there's barely enough salary here for one person. Was this imposter running a con of some sort? What did he want from your friend?"

"That's not clear."

"Did your friend give him money?"

"Not so far as I know."

"What did your friend think this ersatz reporter wanted?"

"That's not clear either. My friend committed suicide shortly

39

after the interview."

Matthews's feet left her desk for the floor and her chair back snapped forward. "My God."

"The interview was evidently quite upsetting. I wanted to make sure neither you nor the Guardian was connected with it in any way."

"Of course not." Matthews paused. "But that doesn't mean the Guardian might not be interested. It sounds as if you could have quite a story there. What was your friend's name?"

"Dan Thornton."

Matthews frowned and pursed her lips. "Not a name I recognize."

"This caller you talked about. The one who was so frustrated to find out you were a woman. Did he give his name?"

"No. You think it might have been your friend?"

"How long ago was it?" Owen asked. "Can you pinpoint the date?"

Matthews opened a leather-covered datebook and flipped backwards through the pages. "I remember I was working on a piece about Chihuly. That would mean the call came in about nine days ago. Right about lunch time."

"Three days before Dan died. Would there be a record of the call?"

"I didn't take any notes. And the paper gets so many calls, any record of the incoming phone number would have been wiped out at least a week ago."

"If it was my friend, the call record could still be on his phone."

"Of course. And if it was your friend that called me . . ."

"Then he knew his interviewer was an imposter. Which could shine a whole new light on his death."

Theresa Thornton leaned forward to examine the numbers slowly scrolling on the screen of her laptop. "Here it is," she announced, stopping the scroll. "Dan did call the Guardian office. Three days before he died. Just as you expected."

"So he knew he was dealing with an imposter," Owen said.

"But I thought the interviewer had finished his job," Theresa said. "Dan kept watching for the finished result in the Guardian."

"Didn't you say Dan was unhappy about not being able to recall whole patches of his Tranalytics career? Maybe he thought of something that seemed important enough to report to the interviewer. Or maybe he'd had some suspicions that the interviewer wasn't genuine and was trying to check him out. Did you say you'd actually met the guy?"

Theresa shook her head. "No. The one time he visited the house, he was leaving just as I got home from work. I saw him get into his car and pull away."

"Would you be able to describe him?"

"I'm just not sure. It was raining. He seemed big. And broad. And he was wearing a black slicker." She spread her hands in front of her, palms outward. "It didn't seem important at the time."

"He was after something that was important enough to him to risk being caught impersonating a Guardian reporter. Maybe Dan figured out what it was he was after."

"Something in our storage unit. The missing files."

"It's time to go out and look at the files that aren't missing," Owen said. He nodded toward the laptop. "But first, let's print out all those phone numbers, going back at least two months. Maybe one of the numbers Dan called put him in contact with the phony reporter."

Theresa said very little on the drive to the Thorntons' rented storage unit. Most of what she did say was some variation on the theme "Why didn't Dan tell me about the imposter?"

"He probably thought he could handle it himself," Owen said.

"He was at a point where he couldn't even handle his own bodily functions. Anything he tried with the phony reporter was bound to turn out badly."

"That would have been hard for him to know, and even harder to admit," Owen said. "And if he did think there might be some danger involved, he wouldn't have wanted you anywhere nearby."

"The fool." Theresa sighed. "The bloody fool."

The rental unit was a twenty-by-twenty orange concrete room at the end of a block-long row of similar rooms. Theresa unlocked the roll-up door and Owen helped her lift it to reveal storage boxes piled floor to ceiling against the two side walls, flanking an array of furniture that included two dining-room tables stacked with the legs of the table on top pointed skyward like a long-dead farm animal, a swaybacked leather couch, two chipped chests of drawers, at least a dozen ladder-backed chairs stored seat-to-seat, a disassembled brass bed, and two easy chairs outlined beneath protective sheets. A thin film of dust covered everything in the unit, and scuff marks on the floor showed where the swaybacked sofa had been moved aside to open a narrow path to three metal file cabinets against the back wall.

Theresa pointed to the swaybacked sofa. "That sofa had been moved recently. That's how I knew Dan had been here without me."

"Dan or somebody else," Owen said, following the narrow path to the metal filing cabinets. The lowest drawer of the middle cabinet was still slightly ajar. Half of its contents were missing. According to the label on the drawer, it should have held TRANALYTICS RECORDS, 1977-1995. Owen knelt and examined the files that remained.

"Everything from 1985 to 1995 appears to be missing," he said. "Judging from what's left, that includes time sheets and expense reports as well as project files." He stood and dusted off his slacks. "Hard to know why anyone would want old time sheets. Whoever it was must have been in a hurry and grabbed everything from that time period."

"Doesn't seem like much for so many years," Theresa said.

"Dan, Ray, and I split the files among us," Owen said. "Dan took most of the administrative records, since that was what kept him busy back then. But you say none of the missing files have turned up at your house?"

"Not in any obvious places. I haven't conducted an all-out search. Unless Dan went to some pains to hide the files, though, it looks like they're all missing."

"We passed some sort of watchman's booth on the way in," Owen said. "Is there always somebody sitting there?"

"Somebody's been there every time I've been here," Theresa said. "Usually it's the owner."

"Maybe he can tell us something."

They drove Theresa's Volvo back to the booth at the entrance to the storage area. The occupant, a squat, balding man wearing a black T-shirt that barely covered a bulging belly, recognized Theresa and left his station to talk to them, introducing himself to Owen as Otis Wilcox. As Owen shook hands with Wilcox, Theresa said, "We were wondering if you'd noticed any activity in our unit over the past month or so?"

Wilcox's face clouded. "Why? Is something missing?"

"Nothing of any great value," Theresa said. "But a few things had been moved around, so it was hard for me to find what I was looking for."

"Reckon your husband might have shifted some of the contents," Wilcox said. "He was here about a week ago."

"I didn't know that," Theresa said. "He rarely comes here without me."

"I know, ma'am. I almost didn't recognize him. He was driving a smart-looking yellow Mercedes convertible that I'd never seen before."

"We usually don't bring the convertible out here," Theresa said. "There's just not much space in it for hauling things in and out of storage."

"Well, I never would have recognized your mister if he hadn't slowed and waved," Wilcox said.

"Was he alone?" Owen asked.

"Why, I don't rightly know. The convertible top was up and from where I sit, up high, like, I could only see the driver's head."

"Do you happen to remember what day you saw him?" Owen asked.

"About a week ago. Believe it was Tuesday. Day after my day off."

"That would have been the day he died," Theresa said.

"Your husband passed away, ma'am?" Wilcox said. "I'm

so sorry. I didn't know."

"It was an accident," Theresa said. "At home. He fell asleep and left the gas on."

"But that's awful," Wilcox said. "He was always a real gentleman with me."

"We'd be most grateful for anything you can recall about his last visit," Owen said. "It might help us track down the missing items."

"I thought you said nothing was missing."

"Just some papers," Theresa said. "Things that would help me remember him."

"I've already told you everything I can recall," Wilcox said. "That was sure some sweet ride he was driving."

"Well, you have my number," Theresa said. "Please call me if you think of anything more."

As Theresa pulled through the exit gate, Owen said, "Everyone remembers that old yellow Mercedes."

"Buttercup," Theresa said. "It wasn't in the best of shape. Dan rarely took it out anymore. And never without me. But he must have used it to get those files just before he died."

"And handed them off to someone," Owen said.

"Or had them taken from him," Theresa said.

Owen's cell phone rang and the screen identified Thad Reader as the caller. "I just called the office of Sheriff McDonald in Watcom County to vouch for you," Reader said. "Praised you for your work on the Caldwell case. They sounded skeptical, but I told them you'd do in a pinch. That should at least get you in the door."

"Thanks for the ringing endorsement," Owen said.

"I made up the part about your being okay in a pinch. Got a call from our friend O'Day this morning. He's trying to curry favor by sharing a rumor that a local rest home has been ordering absentee ballots for its residents."

"Anything wrong with that?"

"Rumor has it the rest home is filling out the ballots without ever bothering the residents. O'Day thinks he can get us a sample. We can check it out when you get back. You expect to be there much longer?"

Owen glanced over at Theresa. He realized he didn't have much hope that his visit to the local sheriff would turn up anything useful. "Not much longer. Thanks for your help with the local police."

"See you soon," Reader said.

Owen hung up and turned toward Theresa. "Sounds like it's time for me to visit the local law. That was the sheriff I work with in West Virginia. He says he's greased the path to his counterpart up here."

"Greased paths can be tricky," Theresa said. "Careful you don't slip."

The tall, rawboned deputy's nametag read WILLIAM LEE. He shook hands with Owen and said, "Sheriff's down county today. But he says I'm to give you any help you want."

"I appreciate that," Owen said. "I'd like to see your files on the Thornton suicide."

"Sure thing." The deputy ushered Owen into a spare, pale green interrogation room, then left and returned with a loose-leaf binder and a file box. He placed the box on the lone table in the center of the room, handed the folder to Owen, sat down across from him, and asked, "What's your interest in this case?"

Owen opened the binder. "The deceased was a friend. I told his widow I'd look into it."

"Well, I've got to tell you, I've never seen a more likely suicide. Hose pulled right through the car window. Victim with money problems and enough health issues to fill a medical text."

Owen scanned the first-page summary with the victim's identity, relevant dates and times, and the signatures of the investigating officers, one of whom was William Lee. Then he flipped to the second page of the binder and wished he hadn't.

The second page displayed an eight-by-ten photo of Dan Thornton behind the wheel of his Mercedes convertible. Owen blanched. If it weren't for Thornton's name on the spine of the binder and the first-page summary, he never would have recognized his friend. The face behind the wheel was nearly skeletal, and his sparse hair was a lifeless white, instead of the full yellow-blond pompadour that had always been Dan's trademark.

Owen's dismay must have shown in his face, because the deputy said, "Don't see too many of these, I guess."

"Never a friend," Owen said. "And not a lot of strangers recently. Since catalytic converters came in, it's gotten harder and harder to use car exhaust to commit suicide. Not enough carbon monoxide in the exhaust gases."

"But your buddy had an old seventies Mercedes, still producing all the monoxide a man could want."

"You see many suicides like this up here in Washington?" Owen said.

"Not many. Like you say, they dropped off when catalytic converters came in."

"Reason I ask, don't you think it's a little strange my friend would be wearing his seat belt?"

"Force of habit, I guess," Deputy Lee said. "We're a 'click-it or ticket state.' Maybe he didn't want to be facing a fine if he botched the job."

Owen ignored the deputy's comment and flipped past the photo to read the narrative on the next four pages. When he finished, he said, "So there were fingerprints on the driver's side of the car, but none on the passenger's side."

"There was nobody with him in the car."

"But his wife usually rode with him when he took the car out. His illnesses made him too unreliable to drive alone."

"Car had been professionally cleaned recently," the deputy said. "Like as not, they would have wiped down both of the front seats."

"And I see there were no fingerprints on the duct tape that bound the hose to the exhaust."

"No. But your buddy's prints were all over the hose."

"It was his hose."

Deputy Lee just shrugged.

"It was Dan's duct tape, too. Wouldn't you expect his prints to be on it as well if he wrapped it around the hose?" Owen was

46

starting to believe it might not have been a suicide.

"What? You think somebody might have given your buddy a helping hand?"

"It's been known to happen."

"Not this trip. All the signs point to suicide. Depressed victim. Poor health. Home mortgage under water. Hose hooked to the exhaust. Definitely not accidental, so you'd be talking murder. Where's your motive?"

Owen filled the deputy in on the phony interview and the missing files.

"So your buddy gives a stack of old business files to somebody who's not quite on the up-and-up," Deputy Lee said. "Nothing there shouts out murder to me."

"Got to admit it's fishy, though," Owen said. "Raises a few questions."

"Got any answers?"

"Not yet. But I will." Owen turned the binder page to the autopsy report and photos. He would have preferred to skip the photos and go straight to the supporting text, but with the skeptical deputy staring at him across the table, he felt as if he had to examine each photo thoroughly.

"All these needle marks," Owen said. "Abdomen, shoulder, thigh."

"Man was a human pincushion," the deputy said. "Abdomen was where his wife gave him insulin shots. When he did it himself, he used the thigh. Shoulder was where he got flu shots, antibiotics, antidepressants, and anything else he needed. He kept four or five doctors busy. Appointments two or three times a month. Sicker than a kindergarten full of snifflers."

Owen pointed to a page of the autopsy report. "You check these drug traces against his medical prescriptions?"

"Man had enough pills to stock a corner pharmacy. He was doped up, but there was nothing in his blood that wasn't either legal or on his list of medications."

"And the skin color is consistent with carbon monoxide poisoning."

"Cherry red. Just like the textbook says."

Owen lifted the lid of the file box the deputy had brought to the table. "What's in here?"

"Victim's clothes. We told his widow it would be okay to come and pick them up."

"So you're closing the investigation. You're convinced it's suicide."

"Hardly see how it could be anything else."

Owen removed a gray windbreaker from the box and smoothed it out on the table. "Got a magnifying glass somewhere around here?"

"Not going to go all Sherlock Holmesy on me, are you?"

"My eyes aren't what they used to be," Owen said.

The deputy left the room. By the time he returned with a magnifying glass, Owen had spread a brown-checked Pendleton sport shirt and a white T-shirt on the table alongside the windbreaker.

Owen took the glass from the deputy and bent to examine the T-shirt.

Deputy Lee watched the progress of the magnifying glass and said, "Nobody wears undershirts anymore."

"Nobody you know, maybe," Owen said. "It's a generational thing."

Owen finished examining the T-shirt and ran the glass carefully over the sport shirt and windbreaker as well. When he'd finished, he stood and said, "All right. Look at this."

He put two fingers inside the right sleeve of the windbreaker, spread the fabric, and handed Deputy Lee the magnifying glass. "Look closely," Owen said. "You'll see a tiny pin prick."

The deputy squinted through the glass. "Yeah. I see it. So what?"

"That pin prick lines up with tiny holes just below the right shoulder of the sport shirt and T-shirt. I'm guessing those holes were made when somebody shoved a syringe through the clothes while Dan was still wearing them."

Owen reclaimed the magnifying glass. "Since that's not the way Dan's wife or doctors would have administered medicine, I'm thinking you ought to check the fabric around those holes to see if there are any traces of whatever went through in the syringe."

4

CLOSE ENOUGH FOR GOVERNMENT WORK

Watcom County Sheriff Jim McDonald had returned from his trip and was back in his office the next morning, along with Owen and Deputy Lee. "All right," the sheriff said, cupping his hands around a steaming cup of coffee, "run this by me again. You say there were tiny holes in the dead man's right shirt sleeve?"

"That's right, sir," Deputy Lee said. "Mr. Allison here found them."

The sheriff ran his hand over his smooth bald head. "And how did we miss these holes the first time around?"

"They were pretty small, sir," Lee said. "You needed a magnifying glass to see them. And the only one that really showed up was the one through the windbreaker."

"The windbreaker was a synthetic fabric," Owen said. "But the shirt was a pretty loose weave. It hid the hole pretty well."

"And where did you get the magnifying glass?" the sheriff asked.

"From my office, sir," Deputy Lee said.

"So you left this man alone with the evidence?" the sheriff said.

The deputy frowned. "Your instructions were to give him everything he wanted."

"I certainly didn't expect you to contaminate the chain of evidence," the sheriff said.

"Wait a minute," Owen said. "Are you suggesting I created those holes? I would have had to put on the undershirt, then the shirt and windbreaker to make sure the holes lined up. And then take them all off before Deputy Lee got back with the magnifying glass."

"You could have just guessed the location of the holes," the sheriff said. "It wouldn't have been too hard. Especially if the only clear hole was the one in the windbreaker."

"I'd have to guess at the location of any punctures in the dead man's arm as well," Owen said. "But why would I do that?"

The sheriff spoke slowly, as if he were explaining something to a small child. "It looks for all the world as if your friend committed suicide. If that's the case, his wife can't collect any insurance. If it's not suicide, though, that money goes straight to her."

"You talked to my local sheriff, Thad Reader," Owen said. "Didn't he vouch for me?"

"He spoke quite highly of you." Sheriff McDonald paused. "Unfortunately, nobody vouched for Sheriff Reader, and I don't know him personally. But what I do know about West Virginia sheriffs is that those jobs tend to go to the highest bidders."

"Oh, for Christ's sake," Owen said. "Have a look at the clothes yourself. In the meantime, I'll get you some references for Sheriff Reader."

"That won't be necessary. The damage is already done. The evidence has already been contaminated." Before Owen could respond, the sheriff turned to Deputy Lee. "Where are the clothes now?"

"I sent them to the lab for analysis."

"Who's doing the work?" the sheriff asked.

"I got Jess to do it. He did the original autopsy. Said he'd have something this morning."

The sheriff turned back to Owen. "So if Jess doesn't find anything and the clothes come back clean, will you be satisfied your friend was a suicide?"

"Not necessarily," Owen said. "If it was a syringe that made those holes, and if it went in cleanly, there might not be any residue on the clothes."

The sheriff rubbed his right shoulder. "Don't think I've

51

ever gotten a shot where the nurse didn't keep a cotton swab handy to dab away the excess. Situation you're imagining, with somebody jabbing your friend unexpectedly, I'd think it would be hard to pull off a clean shot."

"There's other evidence besides the windbreaker," Owen said. He told the sheriff about the phony interviewer, the missing files, and the lack of fingerprints on the duct tape joining the hose to the car exhaust.

"Wouldn't call that evidence, exactly," the sheriff said. "Missing files and fingerprints seem more like a lack of evidence. And nobody saw that interviewer fellow but the widow, who stands to profit if the death wasn't suicide."

"Sounds like you've got your mind made up," Owen said.

"Preponderance of evidence points to suicide," the sheriff said. "That's the way we saw it, that's the way we called it. Take more than a random pin prick to get me to reopen that case."

The door to the sheriff's office opened, and a man entered carrying a black garment bag over his shoulder.

"Jess," the sheriff said. "We were just talking about you." He nodded toward the garment bag. "You got results, you could have just called them in. No need to air our dirty laundry in person."

Jess swung the garment bag off his shoulder. "I thought I'd better come in person. This case has been bothering me ever since I did the original blood work." He laid the garment bag on the sheriff's desk and fixed Owen with a quizzical stare.

"Jess Conway, this is Owen Allison," the sheriff said. "He's the fellow who found the pinholes."

Jess shook Owen's hand and said, "Nice work. You with law enforcement?"

"I consult some on investigations in my home state."

"Where's that?"

"West Virginia."

"That's enough chitchat," the sheriff said. "What did your tests tell you about those clothes?"

Jess smoothed out the garment bag. "There was insulin residue on the right shoulder of the undershirt. That could

52

explain something that's been bothering me."

"Explain what?" the sheriff asked.

"Postmortem showed the victim's blood sugar level was below ten," Jess said. "It didn't seem quite right. But all the signs pointed to carbon monoxide poisoning."

"But if someone had given him an overdose of insulin…" Owen said.

"With his blood sugar that low, man would have been damn near comatose," Jess said.

"How much insulin would it take to drive his blood sugar that low?" Owen asked.

"Hard to say exactly, but lots more than his usual dosage. It didn't register with me until you found those holes, but then I did some experimenting." Jess took Dan's windbreaker from the bag and put his hand inside the left sleeve at the cuff. "The ordinary diabetic's needle wasn't big enough to leave a noticeable hole in the windbreaker. It took an eighteen gauge needle to make a hole the size of the one in the right sleeve." The ball of Jess's forefinger showed through the hole he'd made in the left sleeve.

"Big needle, big syringe, big dose," Owen said. "So whoever was in the passenger seat waited until Dan pulled the car into the garage and then jabbed him with the needle."

"Could have worked that way," Jess said. "But there's at least one problem with that scenario."

"What's that?" Owen asked.

"No matter how much insulin he took on, the victim wouldn't go under right away."

"Even if the victim were as weak as Dan Thornton?" Owen said.

"Even skinny as your friend was, it would take at least ten to fifteen minutes to knock him out with insulin injected through the shoulder," Jess said.

"So someone would have had to hold Dan down," Owen said.

"Were there signs of a struggle?" the sheriff asked.

"Bruise on the victim's left wrist showed up in the autopsy. With all the other evidence, I didn't think anything of it." Jess looked at Owen. "Then when you raised the issue, I took another look at the car."

"What did you find?" the sheriff asked

"The carpet on the driver's side had been ripped up pretty bad. Lots and lots of heel marks."

"What about the driver's seat?" Owen asked.

"It's an old car. The leather seat was damn near threadbare with a couple of long cracks. The cracks had been there for some time, but had lengthened a little recently."

Owen tried to dispel the image of Dan Thornton kicking out against the driver's well of the Mercedes. "So it sounds like the passenger surprised Dan with the needle, then climbed over and held him down until the insulin did its job."

"Could have happened that way," Jess said. "Your friend was weak and belted in. Would have been tough to fight off a bigger man."

"Then when the insulin put Dan under, the guy rigged the hose and pumped in the car exhaust," Owen said.

"The insulin alone might have done your friend in, but I guess the killer couldn't be sure of that," Jess said.

"Or couldn't wait around the garage any longer to find out," Owen said.

The sheriff lowered his head into both his hands. "Press could have a field day with this. Already got a phone call from some woman at the Guardian. Going all Woodward and Bernstein on me." The sheriff lifted his head and looked at Owen. "I suppose that was your doing."

"Alex Matthews. Yes, I contacted her. It was her name the phony reporter used. That's how I knew he was bogus."

"Little pissant weekly, and the woman accused me of a cover-up." The sheriff's head jerked upward. "Told me I wasn't doing my job."

"I certainly didn't tell her anything about the evidence," Owen said. "Didn't know anything about it when I met with her."

"Woman already had her story written. 'Out-of-towner comes in and hangs a murder sign on a corpse we listed as a suicide a week ago. Intrepid Guardian reporter shines light on cover-up.'"

"Leave me out of it," Owen said. "Just tell the press the lab results were delayed and you weren't sure about the cause of death until you saw them."

"That's pretty close to the truth," Jess said.

Owen smiled. "Close enough for government work."

"What's already been reported?" the sheriff asked.

"The newspaper obituary just cited carbon monoxide poisoning. It didn't mention suicide," Owen said.

"Funny thing is," Jess said, "if the killer hadn't strung out that hose to make it look like a suicide, we would have written it off as one. Or at least as an accidental death."

"You're convinced it's murder," the sheriff said. "But there's still a problem with the chain of evidence."

"Forget that," Owen said. "Even if I'd brought in a big syringe and made the holes myself, it still wouldn't explain Dan's blood sugar levels."

"All right. I'm convinced. We've got a murder on our hands and a killer running loose." The sheriff sighed and turned to Owen. "What's your take on what went down?"

"Here's one way it makes sense," Owen said. "The killer wanted the files Dan had taken from Tranalytics. He lied about working for the newspaper to get Dan's confidence and locate the files. Dan must have tumbled to his act, strung him along, and took him to get the files he was after out of storage. Then something went wrong. Maybe Dan confronted the guy on the way back from the storage unit. Maybe the guy just didn't want any loose ends."

"Seems like your friend would be taking an awfully big risk," the sheriff said.

"When Dan was healthy, he was always proud of his physical abilities," Owen said. "Maybe his mind was writing checks his body couldn't cash. In any case, he'd have no reason to expect anyone would be willing to kill for those files. I mean, what could possibly make the thirty-year-old files of a defunct consulting firm worth a man's life?"

"You tell me," the sheriff said. "What was in those files?"

Owen shrugged. "Damned if I know."

"Not much to go on," the sheriff said. "Will you be sticking around?"

"No. I can't. I've got to get back to West Virginia. State has an election coming up." Owen raised his eyebrows in the sheriff's direction. "There's votes to be bought and sold."

"I was out of line," the sheriff said. "I had no business suggesting such a thing."

"That's all right," Owen said. "There was a time not too long ago when your crack about vote buying would have been close to the truth."

The sheriff loosed a short laugh. "Close enough for government work, anyhow."

Ray Washburn and his wife Sandy stood with Owen and Theresa Thornton in Theresa's living room watching the sunset spread a gold glow over the rim of Bellingham Bay. "My God," Washburn said. "I mean, my God, you figured it out. From a few pinholes. And the cops agreed with you."

"I had the coroner's report backing me up," Owen said.

Sandy Washburn patted Owen's shoulder. "Way to go, Owen. That's cause for celebration."

"At least now I know Dan didn't kill himself," Theresa said. "But it won't bring him back."

"Oh. I'm sorry, Tess," Sandy said. "I take back what I said about celebrating."

"That's all right," Theresa said. "I know what you meant. There's a little wine left from the wake. I'll go get it."

While Theresa busied herself in the kitchen, Owen said, "I gather Judith got off all right."

"We took her to the airport," Ray said. "She needed to get back to her practice."

"Of course." Owen realized he was sneakily proud of what he'd pulled off and would have liked to toast his success with his ex-wife.

Theresa returned with four glasses of red wine on a silver tray. She distributed the glasses and proposed a toast. "To

Dan. And the happier place he's in." They clinked glasses and repeated, "To Dan."

After a drawn-out silence, they all found places to sit and Owen said, "The police will want to talk to you, Theresa. You're the only person besides Dan who saw the phony reporter."

"Of course," Theresa said. "But it was only a passing glimpse."

"They'll want to take some fingerprints from your house, too. Wherever you think Dan might have met with that man the first time. He probably wouldn't have been wearing gloves then."

Theresa's lips stretched into the start of a thin smile. "Thank God I've neglected my housekeeping chores since I've been working."

The sun had vanished, but there was still enough light to reflect the slate blue surface of the bay below. Ray Washburn set his wine glass on the coffee table. "I just don't understand what could have been in those files that was worth killing for."

"We've got to face the fact that the killer may not have found what he was looking for," Owen said. "Dan only had one-third of the Tranalytics files."

"That's a happy thought," Ray said. "So you think he might come after us next. Or me, at least. I was the partner of record during the time covered by the missing files."

"But I came on board midway through that period," Owen said. "And the three of us split the files evenly, depending on what each of us had worked on."

"You both need to be careful," Theresa said. "Don't talk to strangers."

"We both need to go through our files," Owen said. "Carefully. With an eye to anything that might be embarrassing or incriminating."

Ray rose and walked to the bookshelves next to the TV console. "Dan's got a batch of our old reports right here. We can start there."

"I think we can assume we won't find anything in our published reports," Owen said.

"What makes you say that?" Sandy asked.

"They're already a part of the public record," Owen said. "Distributed far and wide. Be impossible for anyone to track down every copy."

"So which of our jobs might have attracted his attention?" Ray said.

"I know what I was working on back then," Owen said. "The motorcycle accident study was the first job I tackled when I came on board. Then there was lots of work with the Highway Patrol. Drunk driving campaigns. Special enforcement evaluations. And that mobile phone study."

"We ought to destroy those mobile phone files ourselves," Ray said. "That's one of the few jobs we really blew."

"I thought that job went pretty well," Sandy said.

"So did we, at the time," Ray said.

"I wouldn't say we blew it, exactly," Owen said.

"What would you say?" Sandy asked.

"Mobile phones had just hit the market," Owen said. "Manufacturers claimed that using them in a car was no more dangerous than tuning a radio. The Highway Patrol wanted to know just how dangerous they might be. So we set up a simulation."

"If you can't solve it, simulate it," Ray said.

"We ran drivers through a simulator and reported that dialing a mobile phone while driving really was no more dangerous than tuning a radio," Owen said. "Problem was, both of those actions were more hazardous than anyone realized."

"Which we told them," Ray said. "We wanted to take the study further and track actual accident data, but the client didn't think that would be worthwhile."

"Their reasons for pulling the plug seem silly now," Owen said. "It was the mid-eighties, and they thought an accident study would be biased because only rich people with bigger, safer cars had mobile phones back then. Now, of course, everybody and his teenage daughter has a cell phone and it's pretty clear they're a driving hazard."

"Like I said, we ought to gather up every one of those old mobile phone reports and burn them ourselves," Ray said. "But what about the job Governor Davison did us out of? I've still got that recording of the call from his fixer giving us advance notice that they wouldn't be awarding us the contract we'd already won. And asking us to sub to his firm on the rebid."

"That was so disgusting," Sandy said. "And you had the recording as evidence."

"We mined that seam once without any luck," Owen said. "We gave the state a copy of the recording and they whitewashed the dirty dealing with an internal investigation that never saw the light of day."

"All the same, I'm going to pull out that recording when I get back home," Ray said. "Evidence of a rigged bid and a rigged investigation could still embarrass Davison. And his name's back in the news nowadays."

"It's the son that's making news, not the ex-governor," Owen said. "Speaking of which, I haven't had a chance to check. What happened in yesterday's primaries?"

"Davison and Halstead are neck and neck," Sandy said. "They're both setting up shop in West Virginia."

"Then I better get back home before the buying and selling starts," Owen said.

PART II

CAMPAIGN CHICANERY

O'DAY'S DAYS

CHARLESTON, WV—*Jason Davison's lavish spending in the New York primary has won the delegates he needed to pull even with Governor Sam Halstead in the race for the presidential nomination. That leaves the decision up to voters in next month's primaries in Indiana and West Virginia. The latest polls rate both states as toss-ups, with Halstead a slight favorite in Indiana, and Davison currently nursing a narrow lead in the Mountain State.*

Tom O'Day, for the New York Herald Dispatch

5

MAKING IT EASY

Owen slid into the passenger seat of Sheriff Thad Reader's patrol car and asked, "Where are we headed?"

"Davison headquarters in downtown Barkley," Reader said. "Our friend O'Day has passed along what looks to be a fraudulent ballot. Election's more than three weeks off and the shenanigans have already started."

"And you think the Davison camp is behind the shenanigans?"

"That's what I want to find out." Reader glanced over at Owen. "Anything come of your meeting with that Washington sheriff I talked to?"

Owen filled Reader in on the faked suicide investigation.

"I think you missed your calling," Reader said. "Maybe you ought to come to work for me full time."

"I don't know," Owen said. "Seems like having your job depend on West Virginia voters is even more chancy than having it depend on winning government contracts."

"Well, we're about to talk to some folks who are trying to get in touch with those voters."

Reader pulled into a NO PARKING zone in front of a boarded-up storefront. The store next door was festooned with a huge red, white, and blue banner announcing DAVISON FOR PRESIDENT. Posters with the candidate's picture decorated the windows of the campaign headquarters and had been plastered on the windows of its boarded-up neighbor as well.

Reader and Owen stopped to admire a sleek black Harley

Davidson CVO Road Glide custom motorcycle parked in front of the campaign headquarters. "Pretty slick," Reader said. "Reckon it would cost about half my salary."

Owen paused at the door of the headquarters. "This was a Woolworth's five-and-ten when I was growing up. Couldn't imagine the town without it then. Now it's like it was never here."

Inside, the former five-and-ten throbbed with activity. Phone lines and electrical cables linked a dense network of desks holding laptops, phones, pamphlets, stacks of paper, and cans of soda. No desk was unoccupied, and a few were shared by two workers. Owen guessed that the average age of the campaign workers staffing the desks couldn't be more than twenty-five.

A blonde receptionist at the desk nearest the door rose as Owen and Sheriff Reader entered. The nametag jutting from a lavaliere in front of her pink cashmere sweater said "HI! I'M BETTY SUE." Both the nametag and the sweater were designed to be read from across the room.

The receptionist echoed her nametag by saying "Hi. I'm Betty Sue," and then asked, "Can I help you?"

Reader stepped in front of Owen. "I'm Sheriff Reader from Raleigh County. This is my deputy, Owen Allison. We're here to see Linton Barney."

"Is he expecting you?"

"Not if he hasn't broken any laws," Reader said.

Betty Sue appraised the two men with deep blue eyes that may not have seen it all but were learning fast. "I'm sure he hasn't. But I'm sure he'll want to see you anyhow. I'll just let him know you're here." She picked up her desk phone, punched a button, and announced their presence. After a brief pause, she smiled, hung up the phone, and said, "I'll take you right back."

The two men followed her to a back room that must have been a storage area for whatever business followed Woolworth's. Metal shelves along two walls held pamphlets, rolled posters, and boxes of campaign materials. A green chalkboard and a map of West Virginia with color-coded counties hung from a third wall, while the fourth wall had a large one-way window that looked out on the campaign workers.

Two men stood checking photo proofs at a long metal table in the center of the room. Betty Sue introduced them as Linton Barney and Harrison Marcus. Barney was the shorter of the two, with slick black hair showing flecks of gray and a fitted blue suit that looked to be hand tailored. Marcus was older and solidly built, with a neatly trimmed goatee that framed a face as hard as chiseled rock. The men totaled two smiles between them, but only because Barney's perfect teeth had enough wattage for a smile and a half. Marcus's pursed lips were tightly closed and seemed to fight against any deviation from the horizontal.

Barney kept his eyes on Betty Sue through the one-way window as she sidestepped other workers and returned to her desk. Then he turned his smile on Owen and Sheriff Reader. "And how can I help you gentlemen?"

"Just stopped by to say hello." Reader gestured toward the activity in the campaign room. "I must say I'm surprised and impressed by the size of your operation."

"We're covering all the counties south of Route Sixty from here." Barney nodded toward the wall map. "Roughly half the state."

"I was also surprised and impressed by the size of the campaign contribution I got from you yesterday," Reader said. "Wanted to drop by, thank you, and make sure there was no mistake."

"Mistake?" Barney said.

"You are aware that I'm running unopposed in this primary?"

"We know that." Barney smiled. "But you will be opposed in the November election."

"You folks will be long gone by then," Reader said. "I wanted to make sure you don't expect anything in return right now."

"Treat it as you would any campaign contribution," Barney said. "We're new to this state. Not quite sure how things are done here. The contribution is our way of introducing ourselves."

Reader looked at the wall map. "There must be twenty counties south of Route Sixty. You introduce yourself to every sheriff by giving them two thousand dollars?"

"Not every one," Barney said. "But a few were especially

important to us. Your county was one, since we're setting up shop here. We wanted to get to know you."

"Well, I'm not complaining, you understand. But if all you wanted was to introduce yourself, wouldn't a simple handshake have been more economical?"

Barney extended his hand across the metal table. "We can do that too."

Reader shook the extended hand. "Pleased to meet you."

"And we're pleased to meet you."

Reader unzipped the black document holder he was carrying under his arm and withdrew a long sheet of paper encased in a glassine envelope. "You may not be so pleased after you see this."

"What is it?" Barney asked.

"It's an absentee ballot," Reader said. "One of my constituents gave it to a reporter, who passed it along to me."

Marcus, who had yet to say anything, moved closer to examine the piece of paper.

"It was delivered to my constituent's father, who lives in a nursing home," Reader said.

"Sounds like a good way to make voting easier for shut-ins," Barney said.

"Notice how it's marked for a slate of your party's candidates," Reader said.

"Glad to see it," Barney said. "Is there something wrong with that?"

"It was delivered with those candidate choices already marked," Reader said. "That's making voting a little too easy."

"Are you sure about that?" Barney asked.

"My constituent was there when his father opened the ballot," Reader said.

"Who delivered the ballot?" Marcus asked.

"Don't know that. My constituent's father has Alzheimer's."

"Why come to us?" Barney asked.

"Your candidate's name is at the top of that slate. The box beside his name is checked."

"This is certainly not something we know anything about." Barney looked to Marcus for confirmation, and Marcus responded with a grunt and a curt shake of his head.

"Look," Reader said. "I know there are lot of preconceptions about West Virginia elections. Everybody thinks money rules. And it did, once. Kennedy bought the presidency here in 1960. Rockefeller spent twelve million winning his senate seat in 1984. And right now Mingo County's jails are filled with public officials who got caught with their hands out."

Reader tapped the absentee ballot. "I can understand why outsiders think candidates and voters are both up for sale. But I'm here to tell you, vote buying is a felony. And if I catch anyone doing it in my county, I'll arrest them. I don't think you'd want that to happen to your candidate."

Marcus narrowed his eyes. "Are you saying we can stop it from happening?"

Reader held up the ballot. "If you're responsible for this, you damn well better stop it from happening. But if what you just said was a subtle way of asking whether a bigger campaign contribution would get me to look the other way, then you're just a step away from arrest yourself."

Barney waved his hand to clear the air. "I'm sure that's not what Harrison was asking."

"I'm sorry if I wasn't clear," Marcus said.

Reader returned the ballot to the document holder and zipped it shut. "Then I think we understand each other."

"I hope so," Barney said. He gave Reader his business card. "This number should reach me directly. If I'm traveling, and you need immediate help, you can contact my assistant, Miss Gardner, who showed you in. You can pick up her card on your way out. Thank you for stopping by."

Reader turned to leave, but Owen said, "Mr. Marcus, I believe we've spoken before."

"I'm afraid I don't recall your name," Marcus said.

Owen handed the man a business card. "You worked for your candidate's father when he was governor of California. I had a consulting firm there, Tranalytics. You called to give me some bad news about a state contract."

"I'm sorry," Marcus said. "I just don't remember."

"I remember Tranalytics," Barney said. "You guys did that motorcycle crash study years ago. Sent guys right to the accident scene. It was the best bike safety study I've ever seen."

"Nice of you to say so." Owen nodded toward a black motorcycle helmet on one of the storage shelves. "Is that your Harley outside?"

"That's my baby," Barney said. "Do you ride?"

"No," Owen said. "Investigating all those accidents scared me off. I feel much more secure with four wheels under me."

From the doorway, Reader said, "Time to get four wheels under you right now."

On the way out, the two men stopped by Betty Sue Gardner's desk to pick up her business card. As Owen pocketed her card, he said, "I'm curious. What does Mr. Marcus do for the campaign?"

"His official title is campaign advisor. I believe he served Jason's father in the same capacity."

Owen shrugged. "He seemed standoffish. A little hard to reach."

Betty Sue smiled. "I can't speak to that. He usually travels with the candidate and stays in the background. It's unusual for him to be here alone. If Mr. Marcus wasn't forthcoming and there's some specific information you want, I'd be happy to get it for you."

"I'll remember that," Owen said. "Thanks for the offer."

As Reader pulled his patrol car away from the curb, he said, "That Betty Sue made me wish I was fifty again."

Owen laughed. "Believe me, fifty's no picnic. Did you notice she called the candidate Jason?"

"Who would you rather vote for? 'Jason' or 'Mr. Davison?'" Reader shook his head. "Those guys are too young to run the country."

"They're no younger than JFK was."

"That's what I mean. You know, my generation never had its shot at the presidency. They jumped from Bush senior and the World War II crowd to draft dodgers like Clinton and Bush junior. Viet Nam vets need not apply."

"Kerry and McCain came close."

"Close only counts in horseshoes and hand grenades. It's death in politics and poker."

"Think you could have done a better job than the draft dodgers?"

"Couldn't have done worse. What was that business there at the end between you and Marcus?"

"He's the guy that got the contract Governor Davison took away from us. Left his job at the Transportation Department to take it. We've got a recording of him calling to say they were going to void our award and offering us the chance to take a subcontract with his group."

"But you didn't take his offer."

"Hell no. His call was so blatant we couldn't believe he was serious. We thought it might be part of some sting operation. Besides, it was illegal for him to leave a government agency and take a job from them right away."

"Sounds more like West Virginia than California. How'd he get away with it?"

"Damned if I know. The department turned a deaf ear to our protests. I've always figured the governor put the fix in."

"He said he didn't remember you." Reader glanced over at Owen. "Had you ever met him before?"

"No. We just talked on the phone that one time. He'd been a fixer for Governor Davison. Our contract was just a payoff. He must have gotten so many he didn't remember screwing us."

"Oh, he remembered you all right. He was lying about that."

"How do you know?"

Reader flicked his glass eye with his thumbnail. "I've spent the last forty years learning to recognize when people lie to me."

"What did you do for the first twenty-five?"

"Believed whatever anyone told me. Got a purple heart and a glass eye to show for it."

Owen spent the afternoon looking through precinct-by-precinct results from the previous presidential primary for possible signs of fraud and got home that evening to find a message asking him to call Ray Washburn. As soon as Ray answered, Owen said, "I was going to call you anyhow. Guess who I met today?"

"No idea."

"Who's the biggest asshole we encountered in all the years we had a business?"

"That covers a lot of ground. Can you be more specific?"

"Harrison Marcus. He's helping out with Jason Davison's primary campaign."

"Holy cow. Did he remember you?"

"He said no. But the sheriff I was with thinks he was lying."

"Well, you're right. He qualified as Asshole Number One. No contest."

"Do you still have that recording of him?"

"That's why I was calling you. We just got back from Washington to find out our garage burned down last night. That's where I kept all my business records. Including our recording of Marcus's phone call. The fire inspector thinks it was arson."

6

IN HARM'S WAY

It took Owen a few seconds to absorb the news. "My God. First Dan's records, now yours. It certainly stretches the boundaries of coincidence."

"It's no coincidence," Ray Washburn said. "Someone is after our old records."

"But burning down your garage seems a little extreme."

"Not so extreme as what they did to Dan."

"I mean, why not just break in and take them?"

"They evidently tried that. Something set off our alarm the night before the fire. Neighbors say the police responded right away."

"So the alarm must have scared them off, and when they couldn't break in they just burned the garage down."

"We're just lucky the garage wasn't attached to the house."

"How'd they know you kept your records in your garage?"

Washburn let out a long breath. "That's the scary part. They called Janie."

"Why would they call your daughter? She wasn't more than ten years old at the time they seem to be interested in."

"Since she's become a stay-at-home mom, I let her use the Tranalytics name for her consulting work. It was easier than forming a brand new company. If you look up the local number for Tranalytics, it's hers."

"Was the caller a man or woman?"

"A man."

"When did he call?"

"Almost a week ago."

"So it was after Dan's death."

"There was no way for Janie to make the connection. At the time, we all thought Dan had committed suicide."

"What did the guy want?"

"To talk about some past Tranalytics work. Mentioned a few of our jobs. When Janie heard that, she gave him my phone number and told him he'd have to contact me."

"That's the last thing he'd want to do."

"Maybe. Maybe not. We were still in the dark about Dan. Anyhow, Janie said he seemed to want to go on talking to her. He asked her how much trouble she thought it would be to unearth back records on some of our older jobs." Washburn paused. "That's when she told him all the records I kept were in my garage and I was such a pack rat that she was pretty sure I could locate anything he wanted."

"Not any more," Owen said. "Did he mention any specific studies?"

"A few. The ones Janie recognized were the mobile phone and motorcycle crash studies."

"Those two fit the time period covered by Dan's missing files. But they came well before the rigged bid and incriminating phone call."

"So you don't think he was after the phone recording?"

"Who knows? He must have given Janie a name."

"Henry James."

"Well, at least he's not illiterate. What about a phone number?"

"Janie asked for a number in case I wanted to contact him. He gave her one, but it turned out to be a dud."

"Phony name. Phony number. Man's just too clever for us. A regular criminal mastermind."

Washburn cleared his throat and then said, "From where I sit it's not funny."

"Didn't say it was. What number did he give you?"

"I told you, it was a dead end."

"Humor me. What was the number?"

Owen could hear paper rustling at the other end of the line. Then Washburn said, "916-704-1212."

"Sacramento area code," Owen said.

"But it's a phony number."

"Think about it. If you were making up a phony phone number, wouldn't you start with an area code you knew was valid?"

"So the guy's based in Sacramento. Or close enough to be familiar with its area code."

"Or maybe he's just done business with the state. Either way, he's not so clever as we thought." Owen paused. "We can assume a few other things, too. The guy's after something we generated in the late eighties or early nineties. And it's not something he needs to see or copy or use as evidence. He's happy just to blow it up."

"So as far as he's concerned, he's accomplished his mission."

"That depends on whether he knows I'm holding a third of the records. Would Janie have told him that?"

"I don't even think she knows it. But I'll ask her whether your name came up."

"Even if she didn't know it, Dan did. And there's no way of knowing what he told the guy. He obviously trusted him for a while."

"So there's somebody loose who wants something you may or may not have."

"And he may or may not know I might have it," Owen said.

"But so far he's killed Dan and burned down my garage to get whatever it is. He knows you and you don't know him. If I were you, friend, I'd be extra careful the next few days. Stick close to your buddy the sheriff and don't talk to any strangers."

"I won't," Owen said. "At least not until I figure out what this guy is after."

Owen hung up and dialed a number he knew by heart. He realized he hadn't been dialing it often enough recently, and wished he had a different reason for dialing it now.

Judith answered on the third ring. "Owen. Theresa told me you convinced the local sheriff Dan wasn't a suicide. You're my hero."

He smiled at the sound of her voice. "That's been my aim in life. Sorry I took so long to make the grade."

"No need to apologize. If you called to gloat, you're entitled."

"Much as I'd enjoy basking in your admiration, I had another reason for calling."

"That sounds vaguely ominous."

"It is. Or could be. Ray Washburn just called me. Someone burned down his garage when he was in Washington."

"The way you say that, it wasn't an accident."

"It wasn't. That's where he kept his Tranalytics records. Evidently Dan's killer didn't find what he wanted in Dan's files and went on to Ray's."

"And you're worried you're next on the list."

"You and me both, I'm afraid."

"Do you mean we're both worried? Or we're both on the list?"

"Well, I don't think you need to worry about being on anybody's list. But I'm afraid I may have put you in harm's way."

"How? Didn't you take all your records with you when you left for the feds in D.C.?"

"Only the most recent." He started to tell her he'd assumed they'd be getting back together, but thought better of it. "I left the earliest records at the house."

"Then they're still here. In the crawlspace."

"That's good. Or bad, depending on how you look at it."

"Bad how?"

"The years through the early nineties are the records he took from Dan. Evidently he didn't find what he wanted. And he probably doesn't know whether it all burned up at Ray's. I've got some of those files, but some are in the crawlspace."

"But he'd have no reason to look here. Nobody knows the boxes are here except us. And I'd forgotten all about them."

"Out of sight, out of mind." Like me, he thought. "But you're sure no one else knows?"

"No one."

"Then I'd like you to do a couple of things. First, make copies of everything that's in the boxes and express the originals to me. Then lock the copies away somewhere you're never likely to be. I know it's a lot to ask. But I want to have some backup in case the originals are lost in transit. And I don't want you anywhere near the copies once you've sent me the originals."

"If it will help catch Dan's killer, I'll copy them in longhand and hand-carry everything to you."

"That won't be necessary. Although the personal delivery option does sound enticing."

"I'll bet you say that to all the girls."

"No. I don't. But I will say something else to you. I'll tell you what Ray told me. Be careful. And don't talk to strangers."

"Half my clients are strangers when they walk in my door."

"Well, if any strangers ask you about those files, run and hide. Then call the cops and me. In that order."

"I'll keep you both on speed dial."

The next morning, Reader summoned Owen to his office. "We confronted the campaign about the pre-marked ballot yesterday. Time to see what the Shady Acres folks have to say."

"I've been thinking about that," Owen said. "They're likely to deny any knowledge of the ballot and clam up. Why don't I go alone as a civilian looking for a home for my mother? See what I can learn about the place and their procedures."

"Sounds good to me," Reader said. "I'm close enough to retirement so that those rest homes give me the creeps."

The brochure for the Shady Acres Care Center was dotted with photos of smiling elderly faces that looked happy to be a part of the assisted living community. Far too happy for people standing in the shade of IV trees, Owen thought while waiting at the center's reception counter. And far too diverse for the local population.. Most likely professional models paid to pose for the camera.

A starched woman wearing a badge with the name Ramona over the title MANAGER came through a pair of swinging glass doors beside the reception counter and introduced herself to Owen, saying "I understand you're looking for a caring environment for a loved one."

"That's right," Owen said. "My mother. She has Alzheimer's."

"Has she been diagnosed?"

"Oh yes. She's somewhere between Stage Four and Stage Five."

"So, mid-stage. Where does she live now?"

"At home. She'd much prefer to stay there, but I travel a lot on business and, well, home care is becoming a little too expensive."

"I quite understand. It's a problem we hear about every day." She led Owen back through the swinging doors and down a long beige corridor. "Let me show you some of our assisted living quarters."

As they walked, Ramona kept up a steady sales pitch with phrases like "five-star rating" and "round-the-clock care" that Owen recognized from the brochure. But the residents using walkers and wheelchairs to navigate the corridor while tethered to IV trees wore blank, staring looks that had nothing in common with the smiling brochure faces.

Ramona stopped in front of a door at the far end of the corridor, announcing, "This is a typical single-occupant unit." She opened the door to a room that would have been spacious for hotel accommodations, but a little cramped for living quarters.

"I don't know," Owen said. "Mom's used to having the run of a two-story house."

"But you said she required supervision," Ramona said. "And we do have a nice garden on the grounds, along with common facilities and structured activities led by professionals trained in Alzheimer's care."

"I'm afraid Mom's not much for structured activities." Owen raised his eyebrows and cocked his head toward the saleswoman. "You know what she is really interested in, though? The election coming up in a month. I'm going to be out of town then. Do you have people who take your residents to the polling place?"

"We could do that. What we usually do, though, is help

our residents fill out requests for absentee ballots. We do that for quite a few of our people. They like to stay active in the community, and we like to help them."

"What a good idea," Owen said. "How many residents do you have here?"

"We have rooms for fifty, and we're nearly full right now."

"And what percentage would you guess actually vote their absentee ballots?"

Ramona looked at Owen as if he'd just asked an intimate question, but she said, "Oh, nearly all of them. I'd guess at least ninety percent. As I said, our people like to stay involved. I'm sure your mother would have no trouble making friends."

Owen thought he'd better ease up on the voting questions. He shook his head and backed out of the room. "I don't know. I'm afraid Mom would feel cooped up in a space that small."

"We do have a few two-room units," Ramona said. "They're all occupied right now, but one should open up soon. I could let you know when it does."

"That would be nice," Owen said. "How much would one of those units cost?"

"A hundred and twenty dollars a day, or thirty-five hundred a month. If you give me a card, I could let you know when the next one opens up."

Owen fished a business card out of his wallet and handed it to Ramona. "I didn't realize you had daily rates. So Mom could just sort of try out the facilities. See how she likes them."

"Well, yes, she could. But it usually takes at least a month to get a good feel for what we have to offer." She looked at Owen's card. "What's a failure analyst?"

"I investigate car crashes, mine cave-ins, bridge failures, things like that. Do a lot of expert witness testimony."

"And you say it involves a lot of travel?"

"More than I'd like."

Ramona started to put the card in her pocket, but stopped and said, "You didn't tell me your mother's name."

"It's Ruth. Ruth Allison."

"And she lives with you at this address?"

"Oh yes. It's the first home I remember."

"So she is registered to vote."

"As I said, election campaigns have always been a passion of hers. But I'm afraid she's getting so forgetful she won't be able to enjoy them much longer."

Ramona wrote Ruth's name on the back of Owen's card. "We're here to help with problems just like that."

Owen started to leave, then stopped and took an envelope from his pocket. "I'm afraid I forgot to mail this. Is there a mailbox nearby?"

"Just leave it at the front desk. There's a basket there for all our outgoing mail. The postman picks it up around five o'clock."

"Thanks," Owen said. "I'll do that."

Ramona smiled. "You keep in touch now, y'hear?"

"Oh, I will," Owen said. "I promise."

"I can't say whether they're doing anything crooked," Owen said after describing his rest-home visit to Sheriff Reader, "but it wouldn't be hard for Shady Acres to control the vote of every one of their patients. All they have to do is order absentee ballots by mail, fill them out, and either forge the patients' signatures or get them to sign their own somehow."

"What if a few patients have ordered their own ballots?" Reader asked.

"All letters go through the main desk. The staff will know if patients mail in orders for their own ballots. Then all they have to do is deliver the ballot they've already ordered."

"Probably wouldn't try to mark those in advance."

"But who knows what they might do later. All the ballots would come back through the main desk."

Reader shrugged. "So we know what they might do. That's a far cry from knowing whether they're actually doing it."

"Be easy enough to figure out after the fact. Just get the names of their patients and find out how many cast absentee ballots. Then ask those patients whether they remember voting."

"Trouble is, half their patients probably can't remember breakfast."

"Woman I talked to guessed that ninety percent of their residents vote. That's way better than the percentage for the population at large."

"You're forgetting Mingo County," Reader said. "They voted a hundred and six percent of their population last election."

"A hundred and six percent of the registered voters?"

"No. A hundred and six percent of the entire population."

"Must have had one hell of a 'Get Out the Vote' campaign."

"To get back to your rest home, though, if the going price for a vote is really twenty dollars, somebody there could be pulling in close to a grand just for rigging the absentee ballots."

"But how do we find out whether they're actually doing it? And, if so, who's paying?"

Reader scratched at his chin stubble. "I'm the sworn law officer here. Let me ponder that. Meantime, why don't you put your math education to work figuring out which of our precincts might be letting ghosts vote."

"I've been looking at the last election results. Just so I'm clear on the rules, long as you haven't been dead more than five years, you're still entitled to cast your ballot. Right?"

The sheriff leaned forward in his chair and arched his eyebrows as if Owen had asked a foolish question. "You're thinking of Mingo County. Over there, the recently deceased are allowed to vote in the next five elections. 'Round here, we only give the departed five days to exercise their franchise."

Owen had set up a spreadsheet on his laptop and started entering data on registered and actual voters from the last election when his phone rang. It was Trish Elkins, his mother's nurse. Her voice was uncharacteristically rushed. "Owen, you better get your butt home right away. Your mama's really upset."

"Did something happen?"

"I don't know. I can't get it out of her. I've never seen her carry on like this. She's used up her ration of hissy fits and has started in on conniptions."

"I'll be right there."

Trish Elkins had a steadying arm around Ruth Allison when

Owen came into the living room. The two of them were standing, and Owen hadn't seen such a grim look on his mother's face since he'd left the liquor cabinet a quart low when he was fifteen. At that time, Ruth had been brandishing a willow switch. At least now her hands were empty.

Ruth's head and voice shook with anger. "You sit right down, young man. Sit down this instant."

"Mom, I'm over fifty years old."

"I don't care how old you are. You've got some explaining to do."

Owen sat in a ladder-back chair and looked to Trish for help, but the nurse's face was impassive. "What's this all about?"

"I just got a call," Ruth's voice was still trembling, "a call from the Shady Acres Care Center. They told me a two-room unit had just opened up."

Owen felt a mixture of relief and concern. "Mom. That call wasn't about you."

"The woman knew my name," Ruth sputtered. "She said she was sure I'd be happy there."

"Oh, God." Owen took a deep breath and started to explain. "That room wasn't for you…"

"Oh. Are you thinking of moving out, then? You might at least have warned me."

"No. No." Owen held up his hand feebly, as if he were trying to stop six lanes of rushing freeway traffic. "I went there for Sheriff Reader."

"The sheriff is much too young to need a rest home," Ruth said.

"Please," Owen said. "Just sit down and let me explain."

Trish led Ruth to the sofa. When they were both seated, Owen explained that he had gone to Shady Acres pretending to be a customer because the sheriff suspected that the operators were forging their residents' names on absentee ballots.

When he'd finished, Ruth leaned forward and leveled a trembling finger in Owen's direction. "Son, I raised you to be an honest person, and it's gratifying to me to know that I can still tell when you're lying. But it's a little embarrassing to

80

realize you do it so poorly."

"I dunno," Trish said. "That story sounds just loopy enough to be true."

Owen sighed. "Mom, I grew up in this house. I know Dad helped build it. I know how much it means to you. I know you want to spend the rest of your days here. Believe me, I'm doing everything in my power to make that happen."

Ruth returned her accusing finger to her lap. "Well, another surprise like today and we'll both get our wish. Because my days will end right then and there."

Trish laughed and hugged Ruth.

Owen smiled and relaxed. Then he had a thought he later wished he'd kept to himself. "Look. I know this is going to sound funny in the light of what we've been talking about. But how would you like to spend a week at Shady Acres? Sort of like a vacation. You could take advantage of their programs and help out the sheriff at the same time."

Ruth's brow furrowed. "What are we talking about?"

Trish released Ruth from her hug. "Oh, Owen."

Ignoring Trish, Owen pressed on. "I mean, you could get to know the other residents. Find out what's really happening to those absentee ballots."

Ruth looked puzzled. "No. I mean, what are we talking about?" Then her face went blank, as if someone had flipped an invisible switch.

Trish took Ruth's arm. "It's okay, darlin'. You've had a hard day."

"A hard day," Ruth repeated.

Trish helped Ruth to her feet. "Maybe it's time for a little nap."

"A little nap. That would be nice," Ruth said as Trish led her up the stairs.

Owen followed them to the stairway, feeling helpless.

Trish returned after a few minutes to find Owen still standing at the foot of the stairs. "Really, Owen," she said. "You just spilled a bucket load of worry and hurt on your mom today. How could you even think of putting her in harm's way?"

81

The image of Ray Washburn's garage burned its way into Owen's brain. "Actually, I was trying to get her out of harm's way."

7

THE PEOPLE WHO COUNT

Thad Reader looked up from his desk as if Owen had been speaking in tongues. "You want your mother to do *what*?"

"Take a room at Shady Acres. Something's going on out there. As a resident, she might sniff it out."

"Your mom's got mid-stage Alzheimer's."

"That's why she's perfect for the job. They'll never suspect her."

"They don't have to suspect her. Even if she does learn something, there's a good chance she'll forget it. And any defense attorney would have a field day if we tried to use her as a witness."

"We'd have hard evidence in the form of rigged votes. And we'd have the riggers dead to rights."

"With your mom's mind the way it is, it's bound to be a hit-or-miss proposition at best. She might blurt out what she's there for without thinking. Even if her mind were sound, we'd be putting her body at risk."

"Actually, I'm trying to reduce the risk to her well-being." Owen told Reader about the murder of Dan Thornton and the burning of Ray Washburn's garage.

When Owen had finished, Reader fixed him with a stare from his one good eye. "So you figure because you're the partner with the remaining files, you're next in line."

"It stands to reason. It's like there's a bull's-eye on me and mom's house."

"And there was, what? About a week between the first

partner's murder and the second partner's garage burning?"

"Less than a week."

"Both your partners were contacted about their files. Has anyone contacted you?"

"Not yet."

"You let me know if they do. You can't expect to handle something like this by yourself." Reader pulled a black loose-leaf account book out of his top desk drawer and flipped to a tabbed page. "What does Shady Acres charge?"

"Hundred and twenty a day."

"That's roughly the price of a hotel anywhere but here." Reader tapped the black account book. "I've got a travel budget I rarely use. How's about I stake your mother to a week at Shady Acres?"

Owen didn't try to hide his surprise. "That would be great. I hadn't expected that."

"Have you given any thought to what your mom might do inside that place?"

"Order an absentee ballot. Act forgetful. Keep her eyes open. Make friends with the other residents. Ask them about their votes." Owen opened his hands, palms outward. "I'm afraid I don't have anything more specific than that."

"I'll work with her on specifics. Be good if she would keep a journal to help her remember things and give us a written record. In the meantime, what about you? Should we put your house under surveillance? Maybe install an alarm system?"

"It was an alarm system that sunk Ray Washburn. When they couldn't get in, they burned down his garage. I think instead of trying to keep them out, I'll just invite them in. Leave all the doors and windows open. Transfer the bull's-eye from my back to the front of my file cabinet. Let them have all the files I've got. After I've copied them, of course."

"You're saying the best defense is a white flag?"

"I'm pretty sure I don't have whatever they're after at home right now. The files they took from Dan covered the earliest years I kept, and I left those with Judith."

"So should we be trying to protect Judith?"

"There's no way they could know she has some of my old files. She didn't know herself. Now that she does know, she's going to copy them and ship me the originals."

"But if you let these guys come and go as they please, you might never find out who killed your friend."

"I've thought of that. A friend of mine in Utah has developed tiny cameras he uses for traffic surveillance. I'm going to borrow some and hide them around the house. When I'm finished, there won't be a mouse fart that goes unrecorded."

"Sounds like mouse farts are likely to be the least of your worries. In the meantime, why don't you plan on spending more time on my payroll wearing your uniform. Whoever's after you might think twice about messing with an officer of the law."

"Fine with me."

"You can start your uniformed duties tomorrow afternoon. Davison's people have informed us he'll be attending a rally during the shift change at the Mason Hollow Mine. They'd like to have a few deputies there for traffic control. Likely there'll be a few election fixers there as well, so you can acquaint yourself with the enemy."

"Why would you expect election fixers to be there?"

"This is the candidate's only public appearance in our county. It's a badge of honor for any locals with the money to buy or sell votes to be seen with him."

"Sort of like a political endorsement," Owen said.

"Makes the locals feel important. Like they're a part of the team. Legitimizes the whole operation. And it's good for morale."

"Theirs or the candidate's?"

"Both. Shift change is at 3:30. Get there an hour early in case you need to help with traffic control. Don't forget to wear your uniform. Better leave it at home when you check your mom into Shady Acres, though."

Ramona, the Shady Acres manager, opened the door to the two-room apartment and stood aside to let Owen and his mother enter. Ruth took one look, sniffed, and said, "I've got more room in my spare bedroom at home."

Ramona answered Ruth's objection by marching through the living room and opening a sliding glass door leading to a flagstone walkway that wound through a narrow flower garden. "Our garden area gives you more space. It's quite lovely out here."

Ruth stuck her head through the open door and brought it back quickly, making a face as if she'd tasted sour milk. "And a wall around it so I don't wander off. Honey, I'm leaving a way bigger garden that I've tended all by myself most of my life. And if I want to wander, by God, I'll wander."

"Mom," Owen said. "It's just a trial. One or two weeks. To see what it's like."

"Humph," Ruth grumped. "What's next? Trial euthanasia?"

Ramona stepped between Owen and Ruth. "Our aim here is to maximize the comfort of loved ones experiencing memory loss."

"Honey," Ruth said. "If I had any loved ones left, I wouldn't be here."

"Mom," Owen said. "That's not fair."

"Fair. Don't talk to me about fair." Ruth stepped around Ramona to face down Owen. "How many times have I had to clean up after you? You've always taken the easy way out. First divorce. Then the bottle. You're turning me out, but I didn't turn you out when we found you drunk in that sleazy motel."

"Mom. That was George you pulled out of the motel." To Ramona, he explained, "George is my older brother."

Ruth looked at Owen as if she were trying to place his face. "Well, I got the divorce part right, anyhow. You shucked your wife and now you're shucking me. Just too busy to attend to your responsibilities."

"Mom. We don't need to go over all this again. I'm traveling on my job. I can't be home to take care of you."

"It's always something, isn't it? When you were a boy you were too busy watching TV and playing games to help out around the house. Now you're still too busy. Going here. Going there. Too busy to take care of your own mother. Didn't get me to

86

Mass last Sunday. Won't be back in time for the election. That'll make the first election I've missed since I turned twenty-one."

Ramona stepped back in between Owen and Ruth. "Well, now, Mrs. Allison, we can help with both those issues. Every Sunday, we run a shuttle from here to Saint Vincent's Church. Both masses. And we'd be happy to help you order an absentee ballot."

"Would you do that, hon?" Ruth turned to Owen. "Why didn't you think of that?"

Owen shrugged. "I guess it never came up."

Ruth turned away from Owen and addressed Ramona. "Maybe you're right, hon. Maybe you folks here at Amnesia Acres can take better care of me than my loved ones."

"It's Shady Acres," Ramona said.

"Of course it is, hon," Ruth replied.

Ramona handed the apartment keys to Owen. "I'll let you get settled. You can find me at the front desk if you have any questions." She smiled the smile of a clock-watcher at quitting time and left the room.

"She seemed happy to leave us," Owen said. "I don't think there's a chance in hell they'll suspect you really want to be here."

"Well I don't want to be here. So it isn't hard to leave that impression. But that's the idea isn't it? At least that's what your friend the sheriff advised." Ruth took a blue book from her purse and showed it to Owen. The embossed title read MY RECIPES. "And they'll never suspect I'm taking notes in the back pages of my recipe book."

"You're doing just fine," Owen said. "That was a nice touch, pretending to confuse me with George."

"It comes with the territory." Ruth returned her recipe book to her purse and stared at her son. "And just who are you again?"

The Mason Hollow Mine opened onto one of those deep Appalachian canyons whose surrounding ridges limited available sunlight to eight hours a day. At 3:30 in the afternoon, shadows had already engulfed half of the mine's parking lot as night-shift workers started to arrive in their pickups. The lot was shaped like a flattened football with the mine entrance at the tip. Next to the entrance, a growing pile of coal glistened in the dwindling sunlight.

A crane loader worked to keep the pile from spreading by scooping up the coal and dumping it into a lineup of twenty-five-ton dump trucks headed for local power generators. Plumes of black dust rose as each bucketful of coal rumbled from the maw of the loader to the beds of the waiting trucks.

A growing crowd of spectators milled around the opposite end of the parking lot, staying as far as possible from the loading operation. Half the crowd found seats on rows of wooden benches lined up in front of the three aluminum trailers that served as the office of the Mason Hollow Mine. The middle trailer bore a white banner with red and blue block letters announcing WVA WELCOMES JASON DAVISON. A van from the Huntington TV Station WSAZ-TV had parked next to the trailer farthest from the mine entrance.

Owen and Sheriff Thad Reader leaned against Reader's patrol car, which he'd parked at the entrance of the lot to ensure that none of the arriving spectators blocked the access of the arriving and departing coal trucks.

"Well, we're doing our bit to control traffic," Owen said. "Maybe you ought to acquaint me with the local branch of the election fixers' union."

Reader pointed to a thin, balding man wearing a loosely knotted yellow necktie around the collar of a short-sleeved white shirt. He stood with a foot propped on one of the wooden benches in front of the middle trailer. "There's Checkbook Charlie Chapman. He's one of the biggest fixers south of Route Sixty."

"Why do they call him Checkbook Charlie?"

"One of his first big elections, he ran out of cash and started writing checks to buy votes. Made it pretty easy to track him down."

"Did he do time?"

"Couldn't even convict him," Reader said. "He claimed he was only paying off losing election bets with all those five-dollar checks. The folks that cashed those checks weren't going to claim any different, and a few of the jury members didn't see anything wrong with buying and selling votes anyhow."

"So he's still at it."

Tom O'Day, the reporter from New York, joined Owen and the sheriff. "I see you pointing out Checkbook Charlie."

Reader grunted. "No visible means of support, but he manages to buy a new car after every big election."

O'Day shielded his eyes against the dying sunlight to squint across the parking lot. "Well, you know what they say. 'It's not the people who vote that count, it's the people that count the votes.'"

Reader laughed. "Who said that?"

"Most people give Josef Stalin credit, but I doubt he ever said it."

"Not likely," Owen said. "He never got this far south."

Second-shift miners continued to arrive in their pickups. A few went directly inside the trailer nearest the mine entrance to clock in, but most found someone in the crowd to talk to. O'Day wandered off and intercepted one of the arriving miners, a wiry older man with a handlebar moustache and a Cincinnati Reds decal on his pock-marked helmet.

A varooming noise split the air as Linton Barney's Harley rounded a tree-lined curve and pulled into the parking lot. The passenger sitting behind him dismounted, took off her full-face helmet, and smoothed her blonde hair over the shoulders of her black leather jacket. It was Betty Sue Gardner, the receptionist from Davison's local campaign office.

Reader nudged Owen. "Woman looks even better in leather." They both watched as Betty Sue exchanged her helmet for a packet of papers Barney took from a satchel on the back seat of his Harley.

A long black limousine followed the Harley into the parking lot and Barney hurried to open the door for Jason Davison. The candidate emerged wearing a yellow hard hat and a dark blue business suit. He acknowledged the cheers of the crowd by raising both hands above his head and clasping them together like a winning prizefighter.

The mayor of Barkley followed Davison out of the limo and shook his hand as press photographers, TV crews, and spectators with cameras moved in for close-ups.

Tom O'Day worked himself free of the camera crowd and rejoined Owen and the sheriff. "First class photo op."

"You must have a cameraman in that throng," Owen said.

"Oh, yeah," O'Day said. "It's what passes for news nowadays."

Two aides popped the trunk of the limo, brought out a large wooden box labeled LEVER BROTHERS, and placed it upside down in the middle of the parking lot.

"It's an honest-to-God soapbox," Owen said.

"Man has spared no expense to get the details right," O'Day said. "Right down to the hard hat he's not going to need."

The two aides brought a step stool from the limo and placed it so the mayor could climb onto the soapbox. At the same time, the first group of six miners from the day shift emerged from the mineshaft riding a rail car. Grimy and soot-faced, they blinked against the dwindling sunlight and milled around the mine entrance, which looked to be about half their height. At the same time, fresh night-shift workers lined up to ride the rail car back into the bowels of the earth.

As the night-shift miners disappeared underground, the Barkley mayor finished his introduction of the candidate and stepped down so that Davison could replace him on the makeshift platform. The candidate raised both hands to silence the crowd and the loader filling the waiting trucks stopped as well, leaving a bucketful of gleaming coal poised in midair.

"I just came by today to let you all know I'm a friend of coal." The candidate mushed "you all" into "y'all" in an attempt to mimic the local twang. "More than half of the energy in this country and ninety percent of the energy in this state comes from coal, and I have nothing but admiration for you men who spend your days underground reclaiming that energy from the earth."

"And women," shouted an androgynous soot-faced miner leaning on a rail car. "Don't forget us gals."

Davison stopped, startled, and stared at the shouter. After a pause that lasted a little too long, he smiled and repeated, "and women." Then he continued, "You men and women mine the coal that makes the steel that makes our country strong. And if you elect me, I promise to see that you keep on with your noble and necessary efforts."

The crowd cheered, and Davison, seemingly still shaken by the interruption, reemphasized his friendship with coal and repeated his commitment to noble efforts a few times before settling into a string of election-year platitudes promising new directions and economic growth. He finally closed to another round of applause and invited the audience to ask questions.

"A mistake," O'Day said. "He's not too good at give and take. Mostly all he knows is take."

"I thought you gentlemen of the fourth estate were supposed to be impartial," Owen said.

"Just watch and listen," O'Day said.

One of the soot covered day-shift miners spoke up first. "When my daddy and granddaddy mined coal in these here hollers, there was over a hundred thousand of us miners in this state alone. Now we're down to fifteen thousand. How come is it that everyone else gets the coal while us miners get the shaft?"

The crowd laughed and applauded.

"Well, my friend," the candidate said. "Inside that shaft you just came from there are machines that do the work of ten men. That's the main difference between your grandfather's day and today. I'm afraid that's progress. And we don't want to stand in the way of progress now, do we?"

"Condescending asshole," O'Day said.

"But I'll tell you this," Davison continued. "If I'm elected president, no out-of-work miner will ever have to worry about where his next meal is coming from or whether his children can get affordable health care."

"Don't want no handouts," the questioner said. "Just want to work."

Davison looked around quickly for another question and took one from the night-shift miner with the Cincinnati Reds decal on his helmet that had been talking to Tom O'Day. "Seen you on the TV a couple of nights ago," the miner said. "You was talking to a bunch of tree huggers in Charleston. Didn't sound like no friend of coal then."

Davison launched into another lecture. "We are all custodians of the earth and have the obligation to leave it in a better state than we found it. That may mean making concessions and following rules so that we mine coal in a socially acceptable fashion. But it doesn't mean I'm not a friend of coal."

His answer silenced the crowd and the Barkley mayor stepped forward, pointed at his watch, and said, "I'm afraid that's all we have time for. The candidate has to leave for his next engagement."

A wave of relief swept over Davison's face. He stepped down from his platform and began shaking hands with spectators as he worked his way back to the limousine. A few of the spectators earned a photo with the candidate as well as a handshake. Checkbook Charlie was one of those who got both a photo and a handshake, but Owen couldn't tell whether the candidate had sought him out or Charlie had simply pushed himself forward.

As the candidate waved a final goodbye and the driver opened the door to his limo, Betty Sue Gardner picked her way through the crowd and handed him the papers she had brought from Barney's Harley. Davison took the papers, put his hand on her shoulder as he bent to whisper in her ear, and then guided her into the limo.

After the limo left, the remaining members of the night shift ducked onto the rail cars that took them into the darkness of the mine and the crowd began to disperse. Linton Barney threaded his way through the departing crowd, walking his Harley to Reader's patrol car, where the sheriff was keeping the access road clear for the loaded coal trucks.

"Quite a show," Owen said as Barney approached, raising his voice to make himself heard over the noise of the coal loader.

"Jason has a way with crowds," Barney said.

And evidently with receptionists as well, Owen thought, looking at the empty helmet dangling from the rear seat of Barney's motorcycle.

"I think I told you how much I admired that motorcycle crash report you turned out with Tranalytics," Barney said. "I was wondering if you still had any copies around your house."

A warning alarm jangled in Owen's nervous system. "I'm afraid I'm down to my last copy. It came out a long time ago and turned out to be pretty popular."

"I'd be happy to copy it," Barney said. "Maybe I could stop by your place and pick up your original while we're still here in West Virginia. I'd get it right back to you."

"No need to do that," Owen said. "I still get requests for it every couple of months. Why don't I just have it scanned and email it to you."

"That would be great." Barney pulled a business card from the breast pocket of his leather jacket and handed it to Owen. "I'd really appreciate it. There's no hurry. Just scan it whenever you get a chance."

"No problem." Owen pocketed the business card.

Barney strapped on his helmet and started off with the departing spectators.

Owen was suddenly aware of Reader's stare. "Did you hear that?" he said to the sheriff. "Man wanted to know about my Tranalytics files."

"Sometimes a request for a report is just a request for a report," the sheriff said. "Didn't you tell me all your reports are a part of the public record? That can't be what your garage burners are after."

"But he wanted to know if I kept my files at home. Ray Washburn warned me to watch out for anyone who asked about my files." Owen stared after Barney's departing motorcycle. "Funny thing, I kind of liked that guy. I feel like Michael Corleone must have when he figured out that his old friend Tessio had gone over to the other side after the Godfather died."

"Michael Corleone had Tessio whacked," Reader said. "You're not thinking about that, are you?"

"No, but I sure don't like thinking about becoming a whackee, either. I'm going to order some tiny surveillance cameras as soon as I get home."

"I'll have my patrols keep an eye on your house until your cameras come," Reader said. "Maybe even after they arrive."

"Appreciate it."

The sun finally disappeared behind the western ridge, leaving the entire hollow in shadows. As the last of the stragglers left the parking lot, Tom O'Day rejoined them and said, "Sam Halstead was here last week and didn't draw anywhere near that many people. Came in a jeep and went underground with the night shift."

"Sounds like you really are rooting for Halstead," Owen said.

"I'm just sayin' Halstead came in a jeep and went underground. Actually needed his hard hat. I'd be willing to bet he gets more votes from the miners than that limousine liberal we just listened to."

"At least neither of the candidates are promising to eliminate jobs for coal miners," Owen said.

"They're a dying breed," O'Day said. "I just heard your governor boast that the state has more Ph.D's than coal miners."

"If things keep on the way they're going," Owen said. "Between automation, accidents, and the EPA, it won't be long before the state'll have more governors than coal miners."

O'Day smiled, pulled a windbreaker on over his short-sleeved shirt, and followed the stragglers across the parking lot. As he left, Checkbook Charlie emerged from the center trailer, followed by Shady Acres' Ramona and two men Owen didn't recognize.

Owen nodded toward the group of four. "Like O'Day said, it's the people that count the votes that count. That's the manager of the Shady Acres Care Center with Checkbook Charlie."

Reader raised his pocket camera and snapped a picture of the four people standing under the JASON DAVISON banner. "Don't know the other two, but they won't be peddling votes in this county. Not any more. Not on my watch."

The four subjects stared across the parking lot at Reader, who responded with a friendly wave.

Ramona stared a few seconds longer than her companions before they all dispersed to their cars.

Oh, God, Owen thought. We may have learned something by seeing Ramona with Checkbook Charlie, but she's just learned at least as much by seeing me in uniform. Have I just blown Mom's cover?

8

CANDID CAMERAS

As soon as Owen got home from the political rally he called his friend Ken Kaylor in Utah. An inveterate tinkerer, Ken had designed thumbnail sized cameras with transmitters for firemen's helmets years before the TV networks thought of putting them in catcher's masks. He made Owen think of Q, James Bond's armorer and gadgeteer. The difference was that Ken had a sense of humor.

When they had worked together on the West Coast, Owen had often visited Ken in his workshop, where his white apron was always as spotless as the tools arranged neatly in labeled drawers and on wallboard hangers. It was the way he pictured him now, even though Ken had retired two years ago to be near his grandchildren.

After catching up on their personal lives and business gossip, Owen asked, "Do you still have those tiny cameras we used when we were trying to count auto passengers in high-occupancy vehicle lanes?"

"They're around somewhere. You know I never throw anything out."

"I need five or six."

"You know, no matter how many you string out, you're never going to get the hundred percent accuracy the highway patrol wants. There's always going to be a baby too low to spot or a kid asleep on the backseat out of camera range."

"I'm not going to be looking into cars. I'm trying to record a burglary."

"Then maybe you want one of those home alert systems that respond to any kind of trouble."

"No. I don't want to stop these guys. Just photograph them in the act."

"Sounds to me like you're unclear on the concept."

"The people I'm worried about are after some old business records that don't have much value to anyone else. But they can get nasty if you try to stop them."

"How nasty?"

"The last person they visited tried to stop them with an alarm system. When they couldn't get around it, they burned his garage down." Owen decided not to tell Ken they'd probably killed Dan Thornton. "So I guess it's only fair to tell you your cameras could be at some risk."

"Well, it's only fair to tell you those cameras have been out-of-date for a few years. You can get smaller, more accurate models right off the internet."

"Yeah, but then I'd have to read the instructions. I've used your gear before. I know how to set it up and what to expect." And based on past experience the price was likely to be much more reasonable, Owen thought.

"What the hell," Ken said. "Right now they're just gathering dust. Same deal as last time?"

"I pay the freight and take you out for dinner and drinks the next time we're together? I'd be a fool to turn that down."

"There's still time to ship the cameras overnight. I'll get them off right away. You be careful, hear?"

"Don't worry. I'll get them back to you in working order."

"The cameras are replaceable. *You* be careful."

As promised, the UPS delivery containing Ken's cameras and monitor came the next morning. The minute they arrived, Owen set about creating hiding places for the cameras. First he built a false back that fit inside the rural mailbox at the head of his driveway and punched a hole in the rear of the mailbox so that a surveillance camera lodged between the false back and the hole would have a clear view of his driveway, lawn, and front porch. Then he installed a camera in the light fixture over the front door and unscrewed the fixture's bulb so that the light wouldn't give away the camera's location.

At the rear of the house, he placed cameras in the eaves over the garage and at the base of a rhododendron plant near the back door. Inside the house, he installed a camera in an empty Quaker Oats box on the kitchen counter with a view of his office door and hid the last camera in a hollowed-out dictionary on a high bookshelf overlooking his office file cabinet.

Owen made sure that Ken's monitor could record views from each of the cameras and then hid the monitor under a laundry bag on the floor of his bedroom closet. He wanted to be able to watch the monitor upstairs at night, but didn't want to leave it out where any intruders might stumble across it.

Rigging the surveillance cameras took Owen well past lunchtime, and he was just starting to fix himself a turkey sandwich when he got a call from Thad Reader.

"Owen, one of my deputies just found your mother wandering the streets, pretty disoriented, about a mile from that rest home you put her in."

"How the hell could that happen?"

"We need to find that out. Right now she's here in my office. She recognized the deputy's uniform and asked for me by name, so he brought her here."

Owen shoved the turkey fixings back into the refrigerator. "I'll be right there."

Ruth Allison sat in Thad Reader's swivel chair while Reader and a deputy whose nametag read BLATT perched uncomfortably on either side of the sheriff's desk.

"Owen, honey," Ruth said as Owen entered the office, "I was just telling the two sheriffs here that the residents of that place you've got me in have about as much interest in politics as a class of held-back kindergartners."

"Never mind that for now," Owen said. "What are you doing outside of that place?"

"Why, I just went for a little walk. You know how much I like to walk after a big lunch."

"So you left there on your own?"

"Of course."

"But didn't anyone try to stop you?"

Ruth spoke slowly and patiently, as if she were explaining something to a small child. "I just waited until nobody was at the front desk. They never saw me leave."

"But then she couldn't find her way back," Reader said.

"Well, I don't rightly recall ever being in that part of town. There were some pretty gardens there, though." Ruth smiled at Deputy Blatt. "And this nice young man found me and brought me here."

"Shady Acres must not realize she's gone. At least they haven't called me. Did you notify them?" Owen asked Reader.

"Not yet," Reader dismissed Deputy Blatt and said, "I thought this would be a good chance to learn what Ruth here found out about the residents' voting habits."

"They're practically non-existent," Ruth said. "Yesterday I had to argue with everyone in the TV room to get to watch any part of the political shindig at Mason Hollow Mine. They cut the speeches off after five minutes so they could watch *Jeopardy*. Half the women there have crushes on Alex Trebek. It must be some kind of age thing."

Reader laughed. "Show Owen what you wrote in your recipe book."

Ruth took her book from her purse and turned to an earmarked page near the back cover. "I've been trying to talk to all the residents without being too obvious. So far I've only found four who show the least bit of interest in voting." She held up the book and pointed to a page with notations in her minute handwriting. "I've written down their names on these pages so I won't forget them. The two names on this left-hand page would vote for Davison. See there's a D at the top of the page. The opposite page is labeled H, because the two names on that page would vote for Halstead. All four of these people have already ordered absentee ballots."

She turned to a page covered with nearly twenty handwritten names. "But look at this. These people don't have the least bit of interest in voting. Half of them didn't even know there was an election next week." Another page held about ten names. "And here's a list of patients in the critical wing. They don't mingle with the rest of us, so I can't be sure they won't get their own absentee ballots. But they've all got bigger worries than an election outcome."

"So anytime the vote count shows a ninety percent turnout for the residents, which happened in the last primary, a good number of the votes must be bogus," Reader said.

"Hell," Owen said, "judging by the folks mom's been able to talk to so far, a fifty percent turnout would be suspect."

"Well, I haven't met everyone yet," Ruth said.

"We'll get you back there so you can do that," Reader said. "You're doing a fine job of canvassing."

"I'm not sure it's a good idea to send Mom back," Owen said. "Ramona saw you and me together at the Davison rally. They may suspect she's a plant."

"You know, I certainly wish I were faking my spells and memory lapses," Ruth said. "But I'm not. And the staff is professional enough to see that."

"Suppose they do suspect there's a connection," Reader said. "They might get more cautious and either quit altogether or fake fewer ballots. Or they might get more clever and outsmart us somehow. Either way, we're no worse off. And there's a good chance we'll either stop them or catch them."

Reader called his deputy back in. "Phil, why don't you drive Ruth back to Shady Acres. Make it look like you drove straight there after picking her up. Take it easy, and Owen and I will try to get there about the same time in separate cars from separate directions."

Owen and Reader followed Ruth and Deputy Blatt out to the parking lot. Owen held back a little and said to Reader, "There's at least one alternative you didn't mention. If the Shady Acres people suspect Mom's a plant, she could be in some danger."

"I don't think so," Reader said. "These guys are penny-ante grifters who only suit up once every four years. They're not hardened criminals. If you take your mom back to your place, though, she's likely to be in more danger from whoever it is that's after your business files."

"I finished installing surveillance cameras just before you called," Owen said.

"That's good," Reader said. "But I'll still have my men keep an eye on your house."

Ruth waved from the front seat of Deputy Blatt's patrol car as he pulled out of the parking lot. "When we get to Shady Acres, you should play the outraged loved one," Reader said.

"That won't be hard," Owen said.

"I'll make firm but threatening noises myself," Reader said.

"Maybe you shouldn't be there at all," Owen said.

"They've already seen you and me together. We can't undo that. Let's take advantage of it. Make them see that they could suffer if anything happens to Ruth."

Owen took a roundabout route but still arrived at Shady Acres at the same time as Ruth and Deputy Blatt. He followed the two of them into the Shady Acres reception area, where he marched ahead of them and strode up to the reception desk, demanding to know "What the hell's going on here?"

Ramona looked up from the reception desk, startled.

"I got a call from the sheriff's office telling me they've found my mom wandering the streets alone." Owen leveled an accusing finger at Ramona. "But no word from you at all. Did you even know she'd gone missing?"

Ramona answered the question with a shocked stare, looking from Owen to Deputy Blatt and back again.

"That's right ma'am," Deputy Blatt said. "I picked her up on Jefferson Street, about a mile from here."

"I didn't . . .I mean . . ." Ramona focused her stare on Ruth. "Ruth. When? How?"

"Don't try to blame my mother for this," Owen said. "I expect you and your staff to maintain some vestige of security."

"Ruth," Ramona said. "How did you get out of the complex?"

"I just went for a little walk," Ruth said. "It's no big deal."

"It most certainly is a big deal," Owen said. "My mother had no idea where she was wandering. She could have been seriously hurt."

"I'm very sorry," Ramona said. "Nothing like this has ever happened before. Ruth, help me out here. This can't happen again. How did you get away?"

Ruth's shoulders slumped. "I'm sorry. I just can't remember."

Owen had never seen his mother so seemingly defenseless. He couldn't tell whether she was acting or not, but she looked as if she needed support, so he put his arm around her. "It's all right, mom. You didn't do anything wrong."

"Well, all's well that end's well," Ramona said. "We'll be serving dinner in an hour. Ruth, you look as if you need to freshen up. And the rest of us need to get back to work."

"Before you get back to work, I've got something I want to say." Thad Reader stepped forward. Owen hadn't seen him come in, and he stepped aside to give the sheriff a clear path to Ramona and the reception desk.

"For those of you that don't know me, I'm the sheriff of this county. And instead of getting back to work," Reader said to Ramona, "maybe you better call the rest of your staff out here to listen to me."

Ramona whispered to the nurse at the reception desk, who disappeared through the set of swinging doors that led to the main living quarters.

"Now I shouldn't have to remind you," Reader said. "That this here institution needs the permission of this county and the state of West Virginia to go on operating. And I assure you that those permissions are not lightly given."

Owen still had his arm around his mother, clasping her right shoulder with his right hand. Reader moved to the two of them and covered Owen's right hand and Ruth's shoulder with his own massive left hand. "Now I've known this good woman since I was a child," Reader said.

Owen knew Reader was exaggerating, but no one dared to challenge him.

"Since I was a child," Reader repeated. "And it pains me to see her in this condition. But it pains me more to know that she isn't getting the care she needs from this institution."

Several white-coated staff members came through the swinging doors to join Ramona behind the reception desk.

"So I'm here to tell you right now that I'm taking a personal interest in the care you all give this woman." Reader squeezed Ruth's shoulder through Owen's hand. "If Ruth here has any complaints about your food... if the soup is too cold or the service is too slow... I will shut down your kitchen."

Reader raised his right hand and extended a gnarled index finger. "And if she suffers so much as a scratch while she's here, I will close your infirmary."

Reader shook his raised hand. "And if my office ever finds this woman wandering our streets alone again. Just once." He wiggled his extended index finger for emphasis. "I will close down your entire operation."

Reader dropped his right arm to his side and scoured the assembled Shady Acres staff with his one good eye. "Have I made myself clear?"

"Quite clear," Ramona said.

Reader took one step backward and touched the tip of his Mounties hat. "Good. Then we can all get back to work."

Ramona came out from behind the reception desk and took both of Ruth's hands in hers. "I'll see you to your room and help get you ready for dinner."

Owen watched Ramona lead Ruth back into the living quarters and followed the sheriff out the front door. "Can you really make good on all those threats?" he asked.

"Hell, I don't know. But neither do they." Reader smiled and raised the same gnarled finger he'd used to threaten the Shady Acres staff. "I'll tell you this, though. I bet your mama doesn't have any problems for the rest of her stay."

Owen and Reader had dinner and a few beers at Wilde's diner, so that Owen didn't return home until well after dark. He'd loosened the porch-light bulb when he'd installed the surveillance camera, so there was no light available and he had to feel for the door lock with his fingers and guide the key to the lock with his free hand. He missed the lock with his first try, but the key itself pushed the door open.

He didn't remember leaving the door unlocked. Standing in the doorway, he said, "Is anybody home?" When no one answered, he reached in and flipped on the light switch in the hallway. It brightened the porch enough to show him that the surveillance camera he'd hidden in the porch light now lay on its side under the fixture. Someone had smashed its lens.

He stood in the doorway, straining to hear some sound inside the house. When he heard none, he rushed to his office, where he switched on the overhead light, climbed on a folding chair, and grabbed the hollowed-out dictionary that held the camera trained on his file cabinet. Someone had smashed that camera as well.

Frustrated, Owen jerked the ruined camera free and hurled the dictionary at the file cabinet.

And the room exploded.

9

IF THE BOOT FITS

The explosion knocked Owen off the chair. He landed on his right wrist and lay crumpled under an avalanche of falling books, bookends, and collapsing shelves. When everything stopped falling, he crawled free of the debris and shook his head to clear the pain and stop the ringing in his ears.

The top drawer of the filing cabinet blew out with such force that it broke through the opposite wall and lodged itself there. The next drawer down left skid marks on Owen's desk and landed flaming on the office floor. Flames consumed the contents of the two lower drawers, turning the metal cabinet into an open kiln.

The fire from the lower drawer spread to the window blinds as Owen crawled through the office door and stumbled to the phone in the living room. His right hand was an unresponsive load of pain, so he punched in 9-1-1 and raised the phone to his ear with his left. He sensed the woman on the phone was saying something, but he couldn't tune out the ringing in his ears. Instead of waiting for her to stop, he shouted "Fire!" and his address into the mouthpiece. Then he shouted it again. And again.

He left the phone off its cradle and half stumbled, half ran to the garage, where he grabbed the fire extinguisher they'd been using as a doorstop for as long as he could remember. He lifted the extinguisher with his left hand and pinned it against his chest with his right forearm as he ran back to his office, praying that the heavy tube with the flaking red paint hadn't been pressed into doorstop duty because its useful days had passed.

A wall of heat greeted him at his office door. Flames from the upper drawer had crawled the wall and now licked at the ceiling, while the window blinds continued to burn.

He stumbled toward the drawer on the floor, pulling the safety pin on the extinguisher while clutching it against his chest. With one functioning hand, the only way he could aim the extinguisher was to push his chest as close to the fire as he could and bend over the flaming drawer. He squeezed the lever and was relieved to see yellow spray explode from the extinguisher nozzle, covering the flaming papers in the file drawer.

When the drawer stopped spewing flames, he turned to the blinds, aiming the spray at the base of the window. He swept the spray from side to side by rotating his torso and aimed it higher by leaning backward as he closed in on the flaming blinds.

Smoke stung his eyes and singed his lungs. When the blinds no longer burned, flames still licked at the ceiling from the top file drawer embedded in the wall. The flames in the two bottom drawers appeared to be contained by the cabinet itself, so Owen climbed onto his desk to get a line of fire above the top drawer.

The need to keep the extinguisher pressed to his chest kept him from getting it high enough to aim the spray down into the burning drawer, so he had to attack the flames from the side. From that lower angle, much of the yellow spray shot right through the fire without retarding it, and by the time he'd reduced the flames to a few glowing embers, he felt light headed.

Damn, he thought. Too much smoke. I should have been holding my breath. Or covering my mouth. Or something. He dropped the fire extinguisher, which thudded onto the floor.

Owen's legs wobbled. He sank to his knees, fell forward onto his stomach, and rolled off the desk onto the floor, landing on top of the fire extinguisher. Fighting to stay conscious, he clawed and crawled toward the office door, dragging his useless right arm.

His head and shoulders had just cleared the door when he took a deep breath and everything went black. The last thing he heard before he passed out was the distant sound of sirens.

The next morning, Owen was sitting in a wheelchair in the staging area of St. Vincent's Hospital answering questions posed by a white-coated attendant when Thad Reader caught up with him. "Here to offer you a ride home," Reader said.

Owen raised his right hand, which was encased in a cast. "Great. Do I still have a home to go to?"

"It's a little the worse for wear," Reader said. "But it's still standing."

"We'll have him signed out in a few minutes." The attendant tapped the questionnaire on his clipboard. "Just need to make sure he wasn't the victim of domestic violence."

"Well, there was certainly violence involved. And it was domestic," Reader said. "But as near as we can tell, he was the only person involved. How is he?"

"Should be okay," the attendant said. "Broken wrist and a few facial lacerations."

Owen touched the bandage over his swollen left eye. "A real horror show."

"You're lucky to be alive," Reader said. "If you'd been in front of that file cabinet, the explosion would have blown you halfway through the opposite wall."

The attendant scribbled something on his questionnaire and handed it to Reader for his signature. "I'm releasing you to the sheriff. You're good to go."

Owen started to rise, but the attendant stopped him by putting a hand on his shoulder. "You'll have to stay in the chair until you're out of the building." He grasped the handles of the chair and turned to face Reader. "Lead the way."

The attendant pushed the wheelchair out through the hospital doors to Reader's waiting patrol car. When he tried to take Owen's arm to help him into the car, Owen waved off his assistance. As they drove away, Owen asked, "Did the fire spread?"

"Not beyond your office. You had most of it contained by the time the fire trucks arrived."

"How does the room look?"

"Like a war zone."

"Think I can get it repaired before mom comes home?"

"Depends on how long she stays away. You sure you want to bring her back home? It's pretty clear whoever wired that bomb wanted to destroy you as well as your records."

Owen rubbed the bandage above his left eye. "But why? I don't know anything."

"Somebody must think you do."

Reader coasted to a stop in front of Owen's mailbox. Two patrol cars were parked in his driveway. "I've had my guys going over the scene of the crime," Reader said.

Owen ducked under the yellow CRIME SCENE tape linking the porch railings. The smell of smoke met him at the front door and accompanied him to his office. The exploding drawer had left a jagged hole in the interior wall opposite the file cabinet, as well as a smaller hole in the exterior wall beside it. Flames had singed the wall and ceiling and left an acrid smell in the room.

Owen sniffed the air. "God help me. I'll never get rid of that smell."

Reader fanned the air in front of the larger hole with his Mounties hat. "Give it time to air itself out. A little plaster and paint will work wonders. Your insurance should pay for the cleanup."

Deputy Blatt stuck his head through the office door. "We're ready with the video, boss."

"Great," Reader said. "Come on, Owen. Let's look at what your surveillance cameras picked up."

"You mean some cameras survived?" Owen said.

"All but two. You lost the one in here and the one on the front porch," Reader said.

"What about the mailbox?"

"Didn't touch it. Probably figured he'd done all the damage he needed to and didn't bother looking for more cameras."

"So we've got a picture of the guy."

"Oh, yeah." Deputy Blatt smiled and led the way upstairs.

"Did you recognize him?"

"Looked a lot like Richard Nixon."

Owen, Blatt, and Reader gathered around Ken Kaylor's surveillance monitor, which Blatt had set up on the edge of Owen's bed. "Show him the office first," Reader said.

Blatt cued up the office camera, which showed a blank screen. He used the remote to backtrack to 4:45 pm, when the screen showed the view captured by the camera hidden in the hollowed-out dictionary.

"Four forty-five," Owen said. "We were at Shady Acres. Think they knew that?"

"Could be," Reader said.

On the screen a man wearing a black leather jacket and baseball cap strode into the office. The dictionary camera picked up his back as he headed straight for the file cabinet. He started to open it, then stopped and glanced at a thin plastic device in his right hand.

"What's that?" Owen asked. "Looks like a TV remote."

"It detects surveillance cameras," Reader said. "Watch."

The intruder held his detector overhead, moved it in slow circles, and then turned and looked up at the bookshelf holding the camera.

"You were right," Owen said. "It is Richard Nixon."

"Knew it had to be somebody with break-in experience," Reader said.

The man in the Nixon mask approached the bookshelf, checking his detector as he waved it in front of him. Finally he stopped, looked straight at the camera, and reached for it with a gloved hand. A fleeting image of the office floor flashed on the screen before everything went black.

"Back it up a little," Owen said.

"Mask covers his whole face. Can't see much of anything," Blatt said, reversing the image.

"It's the cap insignia I want to look at," Owen said.

"R.C." Blatt read. "Royal Crown?"

"No," Owen said. "That's a baseball the cat in the logo is holding. It's the Sacramento River Cats."

"So he's a Republican from Sacramento," Reader said. "Can't be too many of those around."

"The Nixon mask doesn't make him a Republican any more than the River Cats hat makes him a baseball player," Owen said. "But the guy that talked to Ray Washburn's daughter gave her a phony Sacramento phone number."

"And there happen to be a few folks around right now with Sacramento connections," Reader said.

"And one of them is running for president," Owen said. "Did we catch anything on the other cameras?"

"Front-porch camera looks a lot like this one," Blatt said. "He located it with his detector and stomped on it. We got a little more from the camera you hid in the mailbox. His detector never picked it up."

"Too far away, I guess," Owen said. "Let's have a look."

Deputy Blatt brought up the view from the mailbox camera and backed it up until the time read 4:40 pm. At that time the man in the black leather jacket walked diagonally across the front lawn and climbed the porch steps. The distant view provided by the mailbox camera showed that he was wearing a carpenter's belt, blue jeans, and leather boots below the jacket.

He rang Owen's doorbell at 4:41. When no one answered, he moved his detector around the door frame, found the camera in the porch light fixture, unscrewed the fixture's globe, stomped the surveillance camera underfoot, and then returned the globe to the light fixture.

With the camera disabled, he went to work on the front door and was inside the house at 4:45 pm. Deputy Blatt fast forwarded to 5:20 pm, when the door curtains moved and the intruder reappeared on the porch and retraced his steps across the front lawn.

"That's all we got on this camera until you came home and the house blew," Blatt said. "It's not much to go on."

"We know a few things," Owen said. "Besides the Sacramento connection, we know how tall he is. And when he was reaching up to work on the porch light, you could see a watch on his right wrist."

"So he's probably left-handed," Reader said.

"Can you get a close-up of that watch?" Owen asked.

"We can try," Reader said. "I'll get my guys on it."

"And we know he came out of the house empty-handed," Owen said. "So he probably didn't find what he was looking for."

"Then why booby trap the house?" Blatt asked.

"Just in case," Reader said. "And to keep Owen quiet."

"The way he stomped my camera," Owen said. "Think that might leave glass or plastic on the heel of his boot?"

"Could be," Reader said.

"So all we have to do is find a boot with camera debris on the heel. Just like Cinderella's prince," Owen said.

"At least the prince had a slipper to start with," Reader said. "Without a warrant and some way of narrowing the field, we're not likely to find anything but a lot of ugly stepsisters."

"The California connection could help us limit the field," Owen said.

"But that's not enough for a warrant," Reader said. "Not yet, anyhow. Maybe my guys can take a look at the perp's boots when they're enlarging his watch. Could be there's something distinctive about his footwear."

One of Reader's deputies knocked on the open door to Owen's bedroom. "You better come have a look at what we've found," he said to Reader.

Reader, Owen, and Blatt left the computer monitor to follow the deputy, who stopped at the head of the stairs and raised a shushing finger to his lips. The deputy led the group downstairs to the living room, where he raised his finger to his lips again, then knelt and shined a penlight under the coffee table holding Owen's home phone. The light beam picked up a small black circle about the size of a quarter stuck to the underside of the table.

Owen's eyes widened. He was about to speak when the sheriff clapped a hand over his mouth. "We've already looked on the porch, deputy," Reader said. "Are you saying we missed something there?"

The deputy rose and pocketed his penlight. "Just follow me. I think you might be surprised."

Reader kept his hand over Owen's mouth as they rose. Then

Owen nodded and shoved the hand away as they followed the deputy to the front porch. When the front door closed behind them, Owen said, "I can't believe it. How long have they been listening to my phone calls?"

"Might have just put the bug in yesterday," Deputy Blatt said.

"Not likely," Reader said. "They wouldn't expect Owen to do much talking after the bomb went off."

"But if they put the bug in earlier, why wouldn't they have planted the bomb at the same time?" Owen said.

"Could be something interrupted them," Reader said. "Or maybe they got by your mom pretending to be with the phone company and had no excuse for being in your office."

"There's over a half hour between the time the guy planted the bomb and the time he left the house, maybe that's when he planted the bug," Blatt said.

"Wouldn't have needed that much time to bug the phone." Reader scratched at his chin stubble. "Could be he spent some time looking for your monitor."

"Good thing I hid it well." Owen's knees felt wobbly, so he sat down on the top porch step. "Oh my God. I used that phone to call Judith. We talked about the files I left at her house. If they heard that, they'll go after her."

"If they heard that, though," Reader said, "why would they go after you?"

"I'd kept some of the files," Owen said. "It makes sense to go after me first. Like you said, they're worried I might know something. They probably wanted to get me as much as the files." He stood up. "I've got to warn Judith."

"You can't do it from that phone, you know," Reader said.

"I know that," Owen said. "I'll use my cell."

"No. Wait." Reader held up his hand. "They may have bugged her phone too. And she's going to need protection. We can't be sure when they hid that bug in your living room. But now that it's there, we might as well use it. Let's plan to call Judith from that phone. But only after you talk to her on a safe phone first. She's in Palo Alto, isn't she? What county is that?"

"Santa Clara."

"I'll call the sheriff there. Have him bring her to a secure phone."

"Would he do that?" Owen asked.

"We're dealing with murder, arson, and attempted murder," Reader said. "That ought to be enough to get his attention."

"All right," Owen said. "But make it quick."

The sheriff took out his cell phone. "I will. In the meantime we can discuss what you ought to say to her."

"I was thinking of something on the order of 'Run like hell.'"

"Not the best idea," Reader said. "You can do better than that. Much better. I'll go help set it up."

While the sheriff talked on his phone, Owen walked around the outside of his house to check the exterior damage. The explosion had blown a hole the size of a basketball in the wall next to the file cabinet and singed the broken shingles surrounding the opening. Owen pulled off half of a blackened shingle. His mind told him the sheriff was right. He'd been awfully lucky. He just didn't feel very lucky.

Thad Reader joined him at the side of the house. "Let's drive to my office. The Santa Clara sheriff will have Judith call us there. Meantime, I want to make you a full-time deputy. At least until we can make some sense out of this."

"Deputizing a crime victim? Isn't that a little unusual?"

"I'm going to need more manpower until the election is over. And I'd feel better if you were carrying a gun."

"You might feel better, but I wouldn't."

Reader ran his hand over the singed and broken shingles. "Better get used to it. This hole could have been circling your navel."

When Owen and Reader arrived at the sheriff's office, a call was waiting from the Santa Clara County sheriff. Reader took the call, spoke briefly with his California counterpart, and then handed the phone to Owen. "He's putting Judith on the line."

Judith's words were jumbled, as if her mind were working faster than her mouth. "Owen. My God. The sheriff here … pulled me out of my office… What's going on? I was afraid …

113

Are you all right? What's going on?"

Owen couldn't remember her being so nonplussed. "I'm all right," he said. He told her about the explosion. When he listed his injuries, Judith broke in to say, "You were lucky. It could have been much worse."

"I haven't told you the worst part."

"Your mom," Judith said. "Was Ruth at home?"

"No. Mom wasn't around. But the sheriff's men swept the house afterwards. Looking for clues. They found out my phone had been bugged."

The other end of the line went silent for a short time. When Judith's voice broke the silence, it was calm and composed. "For how long?"

"No way of knowing. But they might have heard me asking you about my Tranalytics files."

"I found them, you know. Right where you said they'd be. I've started copying them, but it's a pretty big job."

"All right. Here's what I want you to do. Turn those files over to the sheriff there. He will finish the copy job and send us the originals. I don't want you anywhere near them."

"Will he do that?"

"The sheriff here will arrange it. They could be evidence in a murder case."

"Not to mention arson."

"Then there's something else we need to do. How long will it take you to get back to your office?"

"About twenty minutes. Why?"

"I'll call you in a half hour and ask you if you've located those files I wanted. You'll tell me you haven't been able to find them."

"So you've left the bug on your phone."

"Exactly. You shouldn't be too specific about the files. Pretend you've never seen them. They're just another damn thing I've asked you to look for."

"We ought to talk enough so you can say you don't know what the files are all about," Judith said. "Maybe argue a little about whether you actually left them with me."

"Argue a little. That's a good idea. Make it more realistic."
"Just like old times."

Thad Reader drove Owen home and they sat on opposite sides of the coffee table staring at the phone and talking about the office damage. Owen checked his watch every two minutes. When it was time to phone the call, he felt his muscles tense.

Reader mouthed the word "Easy" and slowly lowered both his hands, palms downward, like a conductor muting an orchestra. Then he said, "Maybe you better call Judith."

Owen took a deep breath and dialed Judith's number. "Judith? It's Owen. How are you?"

"I'm fine, thanks. But I've got a client coming in about five minutes. Is everything all right?"

"Not really. Something important has come up. I'm wondering if you've been able to find those files I asked you about."

"I'm sorry Owen. I just don't have them."

"You mean you can't find them."

"I mean I don't have them. I looked where you said to look. And everywhere else I could think of. They're not in the house. I don't think you ever left them with me."

"I'm sure I left them with you. When I came east. You must have thrown them out."

"I'd remember if I'd thrown them out. You left town ten years ago. You said your old Tranalytics files weren't important to you then. Maybe you threw them out."

"I never throw anything out. You're the one that was always throwing stuff out."

"Why are you being so disagreeable? What's so important about some old business files?"

"Dan Thornton was killed by someone looking for those files. Last night, someone tried to kill me by booby-trapping my file cabinet."

"My God. What was in those files?"

"I don't have any idea."

"How can you say that? It cost Dan his life. You must have

some idea."

"I just told you I don't. All I know is I left them with you."

"If you'd left them with me, I'd still have them. I never saw them. You must have taken them with you."

"You threw out everything that belonged to me when we got divorced. Didn't want any reminders, you said. Why don't you just admit it? Those boxes went with everything else. Maybe you just forgot."

"Wiped it from my mind? Like a bad accident, you mean? Believe me, there's lots about our marriage I'd like to forget."

"This is getting us nowhere."

"I'm sorry. About Dan. About everything. I know you've had a bad day. But there's nothing I can do to help you."

"All right. Let me know if the files turn up."

"Have you even been listening? I've looked all I can. All I'm going to. They're just not here. You never left them here. That's all there is to it. Goodbye."

The click of her receiver echoed like a shot in Owen's ear. He stared at his own phone, then hung it up.

"From the sound of this half of your conversation, that didn't go too well," Reader said.

"She can't believe I have no idea what this is all about."

"Maybe you better call your friend Washburn."

"What for? He doesn't know what this is all about either."

"To warn him," Reader said. "They blew up the records in his garage when he was out of town. But they tried to blow you up along with your records. He may not know any more than you, but he doesn't know any less, either. Whoever tried to kill you is likely to target him as well."

"We've talked about it. He has no idea what this is all about. His records have been destroyed. There's absolutely nothing to be gained by targeting Ray, and there's always the risk of being caught in the attempt."

Reader nodded toward the bug under the table. "You know that, but whoever blew your office doesn't. Better call your friend."

"I want to get started on some repairs first. I'll call him later."

116

Reader gestured toward the door with his thumb. "I've got to get back to the office."

"I'll walk you to your car."

When they reached Reader's car, Owen asked, "Do you think whoever was listening got the message that there was nothing to be gained in targeting Ray?"

"Might have laid it on a little too thick, but it didn't hurt to spell it out for them. Why not call him now? Use my cell phone. We're pretty sure that's not bugged."

Owen climbed into the passenger's seat and dialed Ray Washburn's number on the sheriff's phone. "Ray, it's Owen."

Washburn's voice sounded concerned. "You're lucky I picked up. I didn't recognize the calling number."

"I'm using the local sheriff's phone."

"Then you must be calling about something important."

"I am. Somebody blew up my file cabinet yesterday. It was rigged to blow when I opened it."

"Holy cow. Are you okay?"

"Yes. But my office is a mess."

"How'd you manage to stay out of the mess?"

"Blind luck."

"Good grief. First Dan, then me, and now you."

"Problem is, I don't think it's over. Somebody wants me dead because they think I know something I don't know. They must have the same concerns about you."

There was a long pause at the other end of the line. Finally, Washburn said, "Jesus Christ. What have you gotten us into?"

"You make it sound like it's my fault."

"I didn't mean to make it sound like an accusation. I've been thinking about it though. Nothing Dan and I did before you joined us was likely to trigger explosions. He was planning roads and I was laying out transit systems. Your jobs brought in the cops. Accident reconstruction. DUI studies. Motorcycle fatalities. This has to be about some study you led, not Dan's road networks or my bus routes."

It struck Owen that there could be a kernel of truth in Ray's analysis. But he felt the need to defend himself. "There was

117

good money in those jobs."

"I know. We were happy to have the jobs and the money. But that was then. Look where they've gotten us now. Dan's dead. And you're calling to tell me we've got killers after the two of us. What are we supposed to do?"

"I haven't figured it out yet myself. I've got work that needs to be done. But you're a retiree. Take a vacation. Hide out somewhere. Don't tell anyone where you're going. Not even me."

"Believe me, you're the last person I'd tell. But where am I supposed to go? How long am I supposed to stay?"

"I don't know. I'm hoping whoever's after us will figure out we're no danger to him with our files gone." Especially if they listened to the conversation Reader and I staged earlier, Owen thought.

"But how are we supposed to know that? Jesus Christ. You're telling me I've got to spend the rest of my days hiding out and looking over my shoulder?"

"Ray. I just called to warn you. I'm not telling you to do anything. We're in the same boat. They're after me too."

"But they're after you because of something you must know. Even if you can't figure out what it is. At least I'm pretty sure I don't know anything."

"Listen to yourself," Owen almost laughed. "That doesn't make any sense at all."

"None of this does. How could anything in our files be worth a man's life?" After another long pause, Ray said, "Okay. You've done your job. You've warned me. Let me know if you figure out anything we can do that doesn't involve running and hiding." Then he hung up.

Owen stared at the silent phone, then returned it to the sheriff.

"Trouble with your ex-partner?" Reader asked.

"He thinks this is all my fault."

"It's important to assign blame. It's the fastest human reflex."

Owen opened the passenger door and was about to climb out when Reader caught his left elbow. "Why don't you come back to the office with me? We've got to find some place for

118

you to stay tonight. You're not safe here."

"It's my house," Owen said. "I'll have to come back sometime. Besides, I've got to start cleaning up."

"Somebody just tried to kill you. I just heard you warn your ex-partner to be careful. You need to take your own advice."

"I've got to get the house in shape before Mom comes back home."

"You've got to get yourself in shape. And stay that way."

"Whoever planted that bomb probably has eyes as well as ears on me. I'm as safe here as anywhere."

"You're about as safe here as a fly in a Cuisinart."

"What do you suggest?"

"If you're hell bent on staying, I'll post Phil Blatt here until eleven and then assign someone from the night shift to park out front."

"I appreciate your concern, but it's a waste of personnel."

"They're my personnel. I get to decide whether they're wasted or not."

"Then have Phil pick up two large pizzas on his way here."

The three men shared the pizza before Reader left and Blatt posted himself in Owen's driveway. Then Owen made an appointment to meet with an insurance adjuster the next morning, cleared the burnt records from his dented file cabinet, and went to bed early. He woke from a deep sleep to answer his jangling phone and hear Reader's rushed voice asking, "Can you be ready to hit the road in fifteen minutes?"

The bedside clock read two in the morning. "Guess so. What's going on?"

"Remember that hot little assistant from Davison's campaign office? She's turned up missing."

10

THE EARLY WORM

The economic downturn had closed half of the hotels and motels in Barkley, but the tight primary fight had been a boon for those that remained, along with local rooming houses and bed-and-breakfast establishments.

Betty Sue Gardner had rented one of two upstairs rooms in a frame house belonging to Maude Jenkins, a widow who had turned her home into a rooming house when her husband died. When Sheriff Reader and Owen pulled up in their patrol car, Maude was standing under her porch light clutching a faded pink housecoat to her chest as if the night were chilly instead of seventy-five degrees and humid.

A thin brunette wearing a backward baseball cap, a teal tank top, jeans, and flip flops sat on the porch steps. As Owen and the sheriff approached, she stood and joined her landlady under the porch light.

Reader touched the tip of his Mounties hat. "Evening, Maude."

"Morning, more like." Maude nodded toward the brunette. "This here's Alice Ann DePrie. She's the one called your office."

"Maybe I should have called you sooner," Alice Ann said, "but I kept thinking she would come home."

"It's not always easy to know what to do," Reader said. "How long has your friend been missing?"

"This will be the third night. And she's missed work two days. We both work at Senator Davison's campaign office."

"Has she stayed out all night before this?" Reader asked.

"Not that I know of," Alice Ann said. "She often comes in quite late, though, which is why I waited so long tonight before I called."

"Is she seeing anyone?" Reader asked.

"I think she must be," Alice Ann said. "I mean, no offense, but there's not much night life to speak of here in Barkley, so I just assumed she was seeing someone."

"Any idea who that might be?"

"No. She never seemed to want to talk about it."

"Did she seem worried or afraid?"

"Oh, no. Nothing like that. Just, you know, like I'd say, 'What are you doing out so late?' and she'd say, 'Nothing much.' Like that."

Reader raised his eyebrows and looked to Maude for verification.

"Don't look at me," Maude said. "I run a respectable house. It's all I can do to keep my rooms free of hanky panky. You can't expect me to keep track of what goes on outside."

"So you never saw anyone bringing her home late at night?" Reader said.

"Not me," Maude said. "I'm a sound sleeper."

"I'm a light sleeper," Alice Ann said. "And we share a bathroom. But so far as I know, she always drove her own car home."

"And the car is missing too?"

"Yes."

"What kind of car was it?"

"A Prius. Light tan, but she called it 'Desert Sand.' She brought the car with her from Pittsburgh. She's been with the senator's campaign all year."

"Do her parents live in Pittsburgh?"

"I don't know that. I just joined the campaign here in West Virginia. I'm sure the campaign office can tell you, though."

"Did she seem happy?" Reader asked. "Was she having any sort of problems?"

"No problems she talked about. But then, she didn't talk a lot. She pretty much kept to herself."

"Is her room open?"

"No," Alice Ann said. "It's locked. I've knocked and called several times, but no one answered."

"Can you let us in, Maude?" Reader asked.

"Of course." Maude hesitated. "Do you think she might be …well …in there?"

"Not likely," Reader said. "Not with her car missing."

Maude led the way upstairs, opened a dark wood door with a master key, and stepped aside without looking in to let Reader enter first. The room was large and furnished with antiques. A beveled mirror framed by a curved wood molding sat atop a mahogany dresser across from a quilt-covered bed whose headboard matched the dresser design.

"It looks like a comfortable room," Reader said.

"It was our master bedroom when the mister was alive," Maude said.

Reader handed out latex gloves and cloth booties to the rest of the group, then pulled on a pair of gloves and bent to cover his high-top shoes with booties. "Try not to touch too much," he said, "but I'd like you ladies to tell me if you think anything's missing."

"Besides Betty Sue, you mean," Maude said. Owen couldn't tell whether she was relieved or disappointed that there was no body behind the locked door.

While Reader looked through the dresser, Owen examined a marble-top writing desk that sat under a window on the rear wall. One corner of the desk held a framed four-by-six photo of Betty Sue and Senator Davison, posed in front of a campaign poster. The desk drawer held two duplicates of the photo, along with a few blank sheets of stationery from a local hotel.

"Not much here," Reader said, closing the bottom drawer of the dresser. "Underthings and two sweaters. Bottom drawer's empty."

"Got a picture here we can use for ID." Owen handed Reader one of the duplicate photos. "Only other thing in the desk is some stationery from the Union Hotel."

"Hotel's closed," Maude said. "I picked up that stationery

at a rummage sale."

"I was hoping there might be an address book in one of those drawers," Reader said.

"Everything's on smartphones now," Owen said. "Not much call for address books anymore."

"I tried calling her iPhone," Alice Ann took out her own cell phone. "Several times in the last two days. All I got was her voice mail. And she never called back."

Reader took out his own cell. "What's her number?"

Alice Ann showed Reader her cell and he punched Betty Sue's number into his own phone. After listening for a short time, he returned his phone to his pocket. "Evidently you weren't the only one trying to reach her. Message says her mailbox is full."

Owen looked out the window above the writing desk. In the dim light of the half moon he could see an open field leading to a clump of oak trees. "What's out there?"

"It's the edge of the state forest," Alice Ann said. "It's got some nice pathways. Sometimes when she got to bed early, Betty Sue and I would go running there in the morning."

"She ever go running by herself?" Reader asked.

"Not that I know of."

Reader opened the door of the lone closet. It was empty except for two dresses and a pair of jeans hanging to one side and sandals sitting alongside a small red roll-aboard suitcase on the floor.

Reader turned to Alice Ann. "She seems to have traveled light."

"She kept a lot of stuff in her car," Alice Ann said. "She'd been moving from primary to primary with Senator Davison."

Reader lifted the small suitcase onto the bed and opened it. "Nothing but dirty laundry." He held up a handkerchief with a few dark dots that looked like dried blood. "Not exactly the work of a mad slasher, but we can use a DNA sample." He put the handkerchief in a plastic evidence bag and labeled it.

"You say you shared the bathroom?" Reader asked Alice Ann.

The young woman nodded and led him down the hall to the

123

bathroom. A search of the room turned up nothing more than a toothbrush, toothpaste, safety razor and hairbrush belonging to Betty Sue. Reader recovered a few strands of hair from the hairbrush for DNA purposes, took the master key from Maude, locked the bedroom door, and returned the key to the landlady.

"Don't let anyone in the room. And let us know the minute you hear anything from or about Betty Sue."

"Do you think she's all right?" Alice Ann asked. "She didn't seem like the kind of person who'd just run off."

"There's nothing here to alarm us," Reader said. "But she's still missing. Until we find out more about her life and habits, there's just no way of knowing."

Maude and Alice Ann accompanied Owen and the sheriff out the front door. As the men reached the driveway, a black sedan pulled up and parked alongside the sheriff's patrol car.

Owen squinted against the headlights as the tall figure of Tom O'Day emerged from the sedan.

"It's almost 4:30," Reader said. "Isn't that a little early to start your reporting rounds?"

"It's the early bird that gets the worm," O'Day said.

"Doesn't say much for the early worm, though, does it?" Reader shielded his eyes against the gleam of the headlights. It looked as if O'Day was carrying a passenger. "What brings you out at this hour?"

"It's been a slow news day so far," O'Day said. "I understand a young woman has gone missing."

"And how'd you hear that?" Reader asked.

"Police scanner's a wonderful device. What can you tell me about the woman?"

"Got no comment right now," Reader said. "Try me later in the day."

"Can you at least confirm someone is missing?"

"I don't know how you translate it in New York, but down here in West Virginia, 'No Comment' means no comment."

O'Day walked past Reader to the porch, where Maude and Alice Ann stood watching. "I hope you won't mind if I talk to these two private citizens."

"Remember ladies," Reader said. "Nobody gets into that locked room."

Maude clutched her robe around her and nodded grimly.

"It's a free country," Reader said to O'Day. "Knock yourself out."

O'Day waved toward the sedan. Its headlights went off and a bearded man wearing a Yankees warm-up jacket and carrying a camera left the passenger seat and joined O'Day and the two women on the porch.

Reader swept into his patrol car and slammed the door. Before Owen could fasten his seat belt, the sheriff backed angrily out of the driveway, spewing gravel and raising a cloud of dust in his headlights. He screeched to a stop in the roadway, then burned rubber and drove hell-bent for about half a mile before pulling off to the side of the road.

The sheriff snapped on his caution light and stared at his steering wheel, trying to bring his breathing back to normal. Then he grabbed his two-way radio and raised his dispatcher. "Claire Marie," he said, keeping his voice under control. "You called me on my cell to tell me about the missing girl. Did you go on the air with it at all?"

"Not exactly."

"What do you mean, 'not exactly?'"

"Well, I told Steve and Travis where you'd gone. They're the only ones on duty right now and I thought you might need back-up. Did I do something wrong?"

"No. That's all right. Did you mention the girl's name?"

"No. I just said we had a 10-57."

"Okay. You did just fine. Somebody was evidently monitoring our frequency."

"Not much to monitor this time of night."

"Not usually." Reader signed off and returned the radio to its cradle. "I think we're in for a real shit storm."

"You think the girl's dead?" Owen asked.

"Dunno. If she were local, we'd have a shot at figuring it out. We'd know the girl, know her family, know the kind of pressures she was under." Reader shook his head. "Here, though, what we've got is a young hottie working for a U.S. Senator who's running for president. And the senator has a history of trolling for hotties with his fly open."

"I thought there was nothing to those rumors."

"Got a friend on the force in Sacramento. Davison's daddy bailed him out of at least one jam with a big pay-off. Seems there were photos of the young senatorial candidate with an aide who was doing the Clinton curtsy. Daddy's bucks got the photos burned and stopped the damage at the rumor stage."

"But his boy still got elected, in spite of the rumors."

Reader shrugged. "Guess they go for that sort of thing in California. Shows you're at least as virile as the movie stars." He switched off the caution light and pulled back onto the road.

"Where are we headed?" Owen asked.

"Think I ought to talk to the candidate. He's staying at the old Rocker mansion."

"At this hour?"

"Press is going to be on this like flies on an open privy. I'd like to talk to Davison before he has a chance to confer with Daddy and his advisors. While he's still a little groggy with sleep." Reader glanced over at Owen. "Speaking of being groggy, you've had a rough couple of days. Maybe I ought to drop you at home."

"Are you kidding? I wouldn't want to miss this. I got to bed early. Had a good four hours before you called." He raised his cast. "If nothing else, the pain will keep me awake. So long as I stay free of any painkillers that might make me sleepy, I should be okay. Besides, I feel a lot safer with you than I would at home alone."

"Well, then. Let's not waste any time." Reader snapped on his siren and flash bars and sped down the empty highway.

The Rocker mansion sprawled across the top of a hill overlooking Barkley. Built nearly a hundred years earlier by coal baron Henry Rocker, it was currently owned by Rocker's grandson Lawson, who maintained the grounds and elegant wood interiors as a condition of his inheritance, but spent most of his time at homes in Palm Springs, Vail, and New York City.

Dawn was breaking over the shingled dormers on the mansion's third floor when Reader pulled his patrol car up next to the fountain at the center of the circular driveway. The black limousine that had carried the candidate to the Mason Hollow rally was parked in the driveway, along with Linton Barney's Harley.

A flight of stone steps led up from the driveway past a stone balustrade to a massive oak door. Reader rang the doorbell, then turned to look out over the apple orchard that sloped downhill into the valley. "Probably be a while."

He was about to ring the bell again when Linton Barney swung the door open. Barney was already dressed in his motorcycle leathers, his black jacket draped open to his waist.

"Is the candidate awake?" Reader asked.

"Got up at dawn to see the sun rise," Barney said.

"Couldn't have picked a better time for it. Can I talk to him?"

"He just left for a run." Barney's brow furrowed with concern. "Is something wrong?"

"One of your campaign workers has turned up missing. I'd really like to talk to the senator."

Barney stepped away from the door. "Come in. I'll call him."

Barney talked on his cell as he led Owen and the sheriff through an elaborate inlaid wood floor beneath a coffered ceiling to an oak-paneled library with floor-to-ceiling shelves holding leather-bound volumes that appeared to have been chosen with color coordination rather than reading in mind.

Handcrafted wood furniture was carefully arranged throughout the library. Morris chairs sat in two corners beside tables topped with Tiffany lamps, while the center of the room was dominated by a polished mahogany table surrounded by six ladder-back chairs.

"Jason will be with us in a few minutes," Barney announced. He nodded toward Owen's cast. "That looks new."

"Just a little blow-up," Owen said.

Barney gestured toward the ladder-back chairs with his cell phone. "Maybe you ought to sit and rest it." He turned his back to make another phone call.

After a brief conversation, Barney joined Owen and Reader at the mahogany table. "You say one of our campaign workers is missing?"

"Betty Sue Gardner," Reader said. "Her housemate reported her missing."

"I know she wasn't at work yesterday. I called her cell, but just got a recorded message. Do you think ... I mean is there any sign of ..."

"Foul play is the phrase you're struggling for, I think," Reader said.

"Actually I was struggling to avoid it. It sounds so hackneyed for something that could be so devastating."

"All we know right now is that she's missing," Reader said.

Jason Davison appeared in the doorway, wearing a navy blue Fila warm-up suit and wiping the sweat from his face with a white towel draped around his neck. "Who's missing?"

"The sheriff is here because one of our campaign workers is missing," Barney said. "Betty Sue Gardner."

Owen and Reader stood as Barney introduced them. Davison motioned for them to sit and said, "Better call Harrison."

"I already did," Barney said.

At the sound of his name, Harrison Marcus came into the room, wearing jeans and a tan polo shirt that bulged over his biceps. His eyes were heavy with sleep.

Barney started to introduce Marcus, but Owen waved him off, saying, "We've already met. At your office and we'd talked some time ago."

Marcus just grunted and joined them at the table.

"So, sheriff," Davison said. "How can we help you with this missing persons case?"

"Well, the girl wasn't from around here," Reader said. "We were hoping you could fill in the blanks on her background. Where she's from, who her parents are, things like that."

"We've got all that at the office," Barney said. "She's been with us ever since New Hampshire."

"When was the last time you saw her?" Reader asked.

Davison frowned and shrugged.

"It was at the Mason Hollow rally," Barney said. "Remember, Jason? She rode to the rally with me and then you took her back to the office in the limo."

"That's right," Davison said. "We were going over schedule changes."

"And have you seen her since that time?" Reader asked.

"No," Davison said. "Linton and I left for Indianapolis right after the rally. The Indiana election is coming up too. We didn't get back until yesterday evening."

"Do you know if she was seeing anyone?" Reader asked. "We've heard she had a secret boyfriend."

"If she did, it was a secret from us too," Barney said.

"There must be some reason you're here so early," Davison said. "This can't be your normal mode of operation."

"We don't usually have presidential candidates in our county," Reader said. "And I thought you might need a heads-up. There was a picture of you and Betty Sue on her writing desk."

Davison blanched at the word "picture," but recovered quickly and said, "I have my picture taken with all my campaign workers. It's good for morale."

"Still, the press could have a field day with any hint of a connection," Barney said.

"The press is already on it," Reader said. "They evidently used a scanner to tap into our broadcast frequency."

"Oh, God," Barney said. "Do we have another Chandra Levy case on our hands?"

"That would be a disaster," Davison said. "It ruined Gary Condit politically, and he had nothing to do with her death."

"Didn't have to," Marcus said. "Condit was diddling Levy. That was enough for the press."

"At least they can't hang that charge on me," Davison said. "I barely knew the Gardner woman."

"It's not clear that matters," Barney said. "One picture of you and her together is worth a thousand diddles."

"I'll tell you what is clear, sheriff," Davison said. "You've got to find that young woman. The sooner the better. Let us know if we can help in any way."

"I appreciate that," Reader said. "We'll need to talk to her co-workers later today. For now, though, all we need are her personnel records."

"If you head for our office right now," Barney said, "I'll follow you and give you everything we have."

"Sounds like a plan," Reader said. He and Owen stood up to leave. The candidate rose, shook their hands, and thanked them for coming. Harrison Marcus stayed in his chair, staring at the polished wood table.

As the sheriff wound his way down the hillside road with Barney's Harley following them, he asked Owen, "What do you think?"

"I think both Marcus and Barney wore watches on their right wrists."

"So do half the people in this car. And I'm guessing about twenty percent of the men in this county as well. At least, twenty percent of fogies like us who still wear wristwatches."

"But damn few of the men in this county have ties to Sacramento."

"You've got something there. But I was really asking what you thought about the senator."

"I think he wasn't going to tell us Betty Sue was in his limo after the Mason Hollow rally. Barney had to do that. Her flatmate said she hadn't been home for three nights and two days. That means she went missing the night after the rally. Davison could well be the last person to have seen her. And he turned white when you mentioned there was a picture of him and Betty Sue together."

"Can't hardly blame him," Reader said. "Man's had bad luck with pictures of him and his female workforce. And he's got hundreds of flash bulbs popping in his face every day. People taking lots of pictures. Easy to see why he was a little slow coming up with a plausible explanation."

"You think he might have seen the picture there in Betty Sue's bedroom?"

"That would surprise me. I think he's way too careful for

that."

"Probably not so careful he'd keep his fly zipped around a girl that attractive."

"No. By all reports, he keeps it oiled for just such opportunities."

Owen arrived home just before 9:30 am, stripped down to his underwear, and was about to take a quick nap when the doorbell rang. He looked out the front window. There was no patrol car guarding the house, just a blue Chevy where Phil Blatt had patrolled the evening before. The porch roof kept him from seeing who was at the door. The doorbell rang again. He hauled on his uniform pants, stuffed his revolver between the waistband and the small of his back, pounded downstairs barefoot, and opened the door to find an attractive brunette wearing a beige pantsuit and holding a clipboard.

The brunette seemed as startled by his appearance as he was to see her. "Mr. Allison?" she asked.

"Yes, what is it?"

She handed him a card. "I'm Anne Cheilek, your insurance adjustor. We have a 9:30 appointment."

Owen took his hand off his revolver and felt the butt catch on his beltline. "Oh, God. I'm sorry. I forgot all about it. I've been up all night."

She nodded as if that was no surprise. "We can reschedule if now is not a good time."

"No. I want to get this over with as quickly as possible." He opened the door and stood aside. "Please come in."

The adjustor stepped into the living room. "Are you the home owner?"

"No. My mother owns the house."

"Where is she?"

"She's in a rest home right now. But she'll be home in four or five days. And it's important that the repairs be completed by that time. Do you think that will be possible?"

"Well, first I'll have to see the damage."

"Of course." He led her through the house to the burned-out

remains of his office, with its charred drapes, crumpled file cabinet, singed paint, and the hole in the outer wall.

Anne clasped her clipboard to her chest as if she needed protection. "Good lord. What happened here?"

"A bomb went off."

"I've never seen anything like this. The only things that even came close were caused by kids playing with firecrackers and an arsonist trying to concoct a false claim."

"I don't have any children. And there's nothing false about this claim."

"So what were you doing with a bomb?"

"It wasn't my bomb. Someone tried to kill me."

"And how did you escape?"

"Blind luck. It went off prematurely."

"I see." Her tone implied she didn't see at all.

It occurred to Owen that the adjuster must have been hired for her poker face. And because it would be hard for male homeowners to argue with someone so attractive. "Sheriff Reader has investigated the scene. You can read the police report. The sheriff will tell you I'm no arsonist."

She photographed the hole in the wall with her iPhone and bent to examine the damage. "I'll be sure to contact him."

Owen felt the cold steel of the revolver shifting under his beltline. He wasn't sure how much longer he could keep it hidden. "Do you need me here? Is it all right if I finish dressing?"

Anne fingered the blackened remnants of the drapes and photographed them. "Whatever makes you comfortable."

Owen backed out of the office, hurried upstairs, laid his revolver on his nightstand, substituted a pair of jeans for his uniform pants, shrugged into a blue polo shirt, and pulled on socks and shoes. Then he splashed water on his face, combed his hair, and brushed his teeth.

Anne was writing on her clipboard when Owen returned to his office. "Well there's good news and bad news," she said. "Which do you want first?"

"I don't see how any of this could be good, so it doesn't much matter."

"Good news is, there doesn't appear to be any structural damage." She toed a curled fragment of linoleum with her brown loafer. "Bad news is, that's asbestos mastic under the linoleum. See the swirls in the exposed glue? Lots of old homes used asbestos glue as a fire retardant. You'll need professionals to clean that up."

"I have friends I want to do the repairs. I don't want people I don't know working in my house."

"Are your friends licensed to do asbestos removal?"

"No."

"Then you're in trouble. That's something you can't do yourself. I can give you a list of firms we approve of. We'll honor their estimates."

"What about the rest of the work?"

Anne checked her clipboard and rattled off a list of repairs that included new flooring, drywall, clapboard siding for the outer wall, and a floor-to-ceiling paint job.

"Can I hire friends to do that work?"

"I'll get you cost estimates for each element. So long as you don't exceed our estimates, we'll reimburse you. But we'll need to inspect the finished job. And you'll have to start with the asbestos removal."

"What's the chance it could all be finished in four or five days?"

"That depends on the people doing the work. But I'd guess the chances are slim to none."

"It'll kill my mother."

"She may be more forgiving than you expect. We usually hear worries like yours from teenage drivers who want dents repaired before daddy sees the car. It's been my experience that family members are usually understanding."

"My mother is in stage four dementia. There's an awful lot she doesn't understand. And I don't want to add to that list."

"I'm sorry. I guess I was a little glib."

"That's all right. Just give me the list of asbestos professionals and whatever I need from you to get them started."

"If you're trying to save money by using friends, it's only

133

fair to tell you that the asbestos removal will eat up your $1,000 deductible easily, so you're bound to be out-of-pocket at least that much."

"Thanks for your concern. But I want to use friends because strangers have been trying to kill me."

The adjustor's cheeks turned as red as her lipstick. "I really am sorry. Your situation is so … I just don't seem to be able to say anything right." She tore a sheet of paper from the rear of her clipboard. "Here's a list of asbestos professionals. To the best of my knowledge, none of them are killers."

PART III

THE MISSING MISTRESS

O'DAY'S DAYS

BARKLEY, WV — *Here in West Virginia, election news has been upstaged by the disappearance of a receptionist in the Jason Davison campaign. Friends of Betty Sue Gardner report that the blonde, blue-eyed, twenty-four year old beauty has been missing for more than three days. Ms. Gardner, who left a career as a model and actress to work for the Davison campaign in January, was last seen publicly sharing a limousine with the candidate following a voter rally in Mason Hollow, West Virginia.*

The missing woman's roommate, Alice Ann DePrie, told me that she delayed reporting her absence because "It wasn't unusual for Betty Sue to stay out late with no explanation." This behavior led Ms. DePrie to speculate that "... she must have had a mysterious boyfriend she couldn't or wouldn't talk about." A photograph of the missing woman with candidate Davison appears at right.

Raleigh County Sheriff Thad Reader reports that his office is following every lead, but so far has found no evidence of foul play. He encourages anyone with a knowledge of the missing woman's acquaintances or whereabouts to come forward as soon as possible. More interviews, photos, on Page 5.

Tom O'Day, for the New York Herald Dispatch

11

VOTE EARLY AND OFTEN

The evening TV news and next morning's newspapers were filled with coverage of the missing campaign worker. The photo of Betty Sue Gardner and Senator Davison posed in front of his campaign poster was above the fold in every West Virginia paper, as well as papers coast-to-coast and the nightly TV news. The Barkley Democrat also ran a photo of Maude Jenkins and Alice Ann DePrie alongside Tom O'Day's exclusive interview of the two women.

Owen spent most of the morning getting a crew of two workers in space suits started on the construction of a polythene tent to safeguard the removal of asbestos from the floor of his damaged office and didn't arrive at the sheriff's office on the town square until a little after eleven o'clock. Reporters and TV crews milled around the square and courthouse steps, but there was no sign of Tom O'Day.

Reader met him at the door of his office. "Seen the news?"

"Just the Democrat," Owen said. "If they got that picture of Betty Sue and Davison from the girl's bedroom, it looks like Maude Jenkins ignored your order not to let anyone in."

"Not hard to see why. O'Day gave her time to change out of her housecoat and put on makeup before he took her picture for posterity and the New York newspapers."

"A picture for a picture, then. Straight player-for-player trade."

"I'm guessing some cash changed hands as well," Reader said.

"From the look of the crowd outside, the storm you predicted is already building. What's next on our agenda?"

"We've got our hands full. It's exactly fifteen days before the election, so no-excuse voting starts today. Polls are open at the courthouse, and I've been sending deputies over every so often to keep an eye on things. Then there's Betty Sue's mother. She's driving down from Pittsburgh. Should be here in an hour or so. I'd like you to talk to her with me. You're good with people, and an extra pair of eyes and ears would be helpful."

"Better tell her to come in the back way. That gang out front can be brutal. It took me five 'no comments' just to get to the front door."

"I've already done that. I'll send Lucy out back to watch for her."

It was a little after noon when Officer Luceda Bring led Betty Sue's mother up the rear stairs to Sheriff Reader's office. A short, slim brunette, she was barely inside his office door when she started peppering him with questions. "Have you found her? Is there any news? What's your next step?"

"Nothing's changed since we last talked, ma'am," Reader said.

"I don't know whether that's good or bad."

"Why don't you sit down?" Reader introduced Owen and offered a folding chair to the woman. "So far there's no indication she's been harmed in any way. But she has been missing for over three days. Anything you could tell us about her life and friends would be most helpful, Mrs. Gardner."

"Call me Ethel, please." The woman draped the wrinkled jacket of her gray pantsuit over the back of the offered chair but didn't sit in it. Instead, she paced the floor, tugging at the ends of the black scarf knotted around her neck. "What would you like to know?"

"Did she have any special boyfriends?" Reader asked.

Ethel stopped pacing long enough to answer the question. "None she talked about. I'm afraid we weren't very close recently. She'd been pretty busy ever since she started working for Senator Davison."

"Where did she work before joining his campaign?" Owen asked.

"She'd been in New York for the last two years. Ever since college. Trying to get acting and modeling jobs. She did a few commercials and had a small part in an off-Broadway play."

"Doesn't sound like much for two years," Reader said.

"That's actually pretty good for a newcomer," Owen said. "Were you surprised when she went to work for Davison?"

"A little, yes. She never showed much interest in politics. But she expected to get back into show business after the election. She was sure the contacts she made during the campaign would help her get work."

"How about any special girlfriends? Someone she might confide in?" Reader asked.

"Not that I recall her mentioning. She always got along better with men. But like I said, there was no one special that I knew about." Ethel rubbed the knuckle of her right index finger hard across her lips. "I wish I could be of more help."

"You're doing fine," Owen said. "What about her father? Was she close to him?"

"Her father lives in California. He's remarried. She has very little contact with him. It's not that they don't get along. More like loyalty to me, I think."

"When was the last time you talked with her?" Owen asked.

"About a month ago. She visited me during the Pennsylvania primary."

"How did she seem then?"

"Happy. But a little on edge. Like a kid that expects something big for Christmas but isn't sure she'll get it. 'Big things are happening.' That's what she told me. Those were her exact words. 'Big things are happening.'"

"But she didn't say exactly what those big things were?"

"No. I thought she meant the presidential campaign. Being a part of something like that, it could be pretty heady stuff."

"We'd like you to take a look at Betty Sue's room," Reader said. "You might see something that could help us understand what happened."

139

"But surely, if there was no sign of a struggle . . ."

"Anything you might notice could be helpful," Owen said.

"Of course. I'd be happy to look at her room."

Maude Jenkins met Ethel Gardner, Thad Reader, and Owen on the porch of her boarding house.

"Nice picture of you in the Democrat, Maude," Reader said.

Maude smiled broadly, showing a missing tooth. "Thank you."

"Nice picture of Betty Sue, too. Did O'Day get that from her room?"

Maude stopped smiling. "Well, yes, but . . ."

"I thought I made it clear no one was to enter the room," Reader said.

"No one did. Well, I mean, I was the only one. I went in alone. I remembered you saying there was a duplicate picture in the drawer."

"So Mr. O'Day and his photographer didn't go into the room?"

"No." Maude hesitated. "Well, his photographer did take a picture from the doorway. But he didn't go in."

"Goddamn vultures," Reader said. "But I guess there's no real harm done. Can you show us the room now, please?"

While Owen and Sheriff Reader watched, Ethel Gardner went through her daughter's drawers, closet, and medicine cabinet. When she finished, she seemed drained by the effort.

"It's almost as if she didn't expect to return," Ethel said. "She always had a closet full of clothes. There are just two pairs of slacks in that closet. I remember the navy blue pair. I gave those to her. She hated them and let me know it. Said she'd never wear them in public. And I didn't recognize any of the makeup in the bathroom. Her favorite brand was L'Oreal, and there was no sign of it."

"She shared the bathroom with another girl," Reader said.

"Still, there's not much sign Betty Sue had ever been here."

"That may be what happens when you go from state to state following the primary schedule," Owen said. "You live like a nomad. Her housemate told me she kept a lot of things in her car."

"I really hoped I'd find something that would lead us to her," Ethel said. "But there's just not that much of her here."

"Well, thank you for trying," Reader said.

Thad Reader dropped Ethel Gardner off at her car and he and Owen returned to the sheriff's office to find most of the staff watching TV coverage of an earlier Davison press conference on the 2:00 p.m. news.

On the TV screen, a crowd of reporters surrounded Davison, who stood alone at the microphone. Tom O'Day asked, "Senator, how well did you know this woman?"

"I make it a point to get to know all my campaign workers. Betty Sue had been with us since our New Hampshire victory. I knew her to be a talented and resourceful young lady, and my heart goes out to her parents."

Off-camera, a reporter's voice asked, "Senator, when did you learn of Betty Sue's disappearance?"

"Sheriff Reader informed us that she was missing yesterday morning. We've given the sheriff our full cooperation, and I have the utmost confidence in him."

Reader's staff turned away from the TV to applaud the sheriff in the back of the room. He swept off his Mounties hat in a mock bow and everyone turned back to the TV, where the scene had shifted to the West Virginia Power's ballpark in Charleston. Davison was throwing out the first ball in the Power's game against the Asheville Tourists.

The senator lobbed a pitch to the Power's catcher and received a smattering of applause. As he left the pitcher's mound, though, the crowd began chanting, "Betty Sue, Where's Betty Sue?" over and over until a shampoo commercial interrupted the scene.

"Senator's getting pretty rough treatment," Reader commented.

Owen nodded agreement. "That newscast should have ended with a tag line saying 'I'm Sam Halstead and I approved this message.'"

As the TV watchers dispersed, the deputy staffing the reception desk drew Owen aside to tell him his mother had called. Owen hadn't seen Ruth since before his office exploded, and he returned her call as soon as he got to his desk.

"Owen, honey," Ruth said, "this scandal with the missing girl has got more people here interested in the election. Three of my bingo friends are ready to vote right now and the early voting window is still open at the courthouse. I wonder if you could drive by and take us all there."

Owen scratched at his wrist under his cast. He didn't want to have to explain his injury to his mother. "I don't know, Mom. I'd have to clear it with the sheriff. I'm working for him right now."

"I thought I was too."

"Of course you are. I'm sorry. I'll talk to the sheriff and come right over." Owen realized she'd have to see his cast sooner or later, but he hoped at least to avoid discussing the explosion.

"Better hurry. I'm not sure how long their interest will stay high."

When Owen related his mother's call to Reader, the sheriff said, "Never can tell what that might turn up. Take a patrol car. And have Deputy Blatt ride along."

"It's pretty close to being personal business. Why do I need to take a patrol car and an extra deputy? All I'm doing is escorting four elderly ladies to the courthouse so they can vote. Deputy Blatt will just make the trip more crowded. And with all those reporters outside you're likely to be pretty busy this afternoon."

"All right, leave Blatt here. But we're still investigating voter fraud, so make it an official trip. Take a patrol car. And your gun. It's your first time alone since your office blew up."

"Is that why you asked me to help interview Mrs. Gardner this morning? So I wouldn't be alone? Hell, I was alone all last night at my house."

"You may have thought so. But I had Steve and Travis watching your place. They must have done a pretty good job

142

if you didn't see them."

"You're taking two deputies off the street to watch my house? Isn't that like buying fire insurance after the barn has burned? Whoever planted that bomb thinks they got what they wanted. All the records in that file cabinet went up in smoke."

"Whoever planted that bomb evidently wanted you dead and that didn't happen. Steve and Travis have been spelling each other, so there's still a street presence. And they're not just watching you. I've got them looking for the receiver that's picking up your phone calls while they're in the neighborhood."

"Look," Owen said. "I appreciate what you're doing, but until we find that missing girl and the election is over, you've got bigger fish to fry."

"It's my county," Reader said. "So I'll decide what fish get fried. And right now you're working for me. So take a patrol car. And your gun. And be careful."

When Owen pulled the patrol car up in front of the Shady Acres Care Center, his mother was waiting on a bench under the front portico with two women. One wore red tennis shoes and a bright pink dress. Her heavily rouged cheeks stood out like twin stoplights under thinning auburn hair that spiked in all directions. The other woman wore black slacks and a cream-colored blouse. Her streaked gray hair curled softly above her shoulders and framed an attractive face that looked vaguely familiar to Owen.

Ruth rose from the bench as her son left the patrol car. "Why Owen, what happened to your hand?"

"I was standing on a chair reaching for the top shelf of my bookcase when I lost my balance and fell. It's just a sprain. Nothing to worry about."

Ruth hugged Owen. "You poor boy. You've got to be more careful." She broke the hug and turned to her two companions, who had risen from the bench. "We've lost one of our ladies already, but the rest of us are rarin' to go."

Ruth took the hand of the woman with spiked hair and drew her forward. "Pluma Johnson, this is my son Owen." Then she nodded to the other woman, who had hung back. "And Owen, you already know this lady. It's Marie Hager. You remember her daughter Robin."

"Of course." Robin Hager had been his steady date through most of high school.

"It's good to see you, Owen," Mrs. Hager said.

Ruth stepped back and surveyed her son. "I've never seen you in that uniform. With a gun and all."

"It was the sheriff's idea," Owen said. "I'm working with him full time now. At least until the election is over."

"It looks good on you," Ruth said. "Doesn't it, girls?"

"Smashing," Pluma said.

"It's good to see you, Owen," Mrs. Hager repeated.

Someone had once told Owen if he was serious about a woman he should check out her mother to see what the daughter would be like as she aged. Robin Hager was the first girl he'd been serious about, and her mother had been a striking beauty. Tall and self-assured, with a regal carriage, high cheekbones, and piercing blue eyes. You could still see traces of that beauty, but you had to look hard. The cheekbones were still there, but the eyes were dull and watery, and age had left her slightly stooped.

"How is Robin?" Owen asked.

Marie Hager stared straight ahead. It seemed to take all her energy to respond. "She married Rudy Slater. Big mistake. She should have married you."

"Rudy left her well fixed, though," Ruth said. "Owen, I signed us out. Told them you were taking us shopping. But they want to see you personally to make sure I'm not wandering off again."

Owen went to the reception desk and signed his name next to his mother's. Back outside, the three women had gathered near the door of his patrol car.

"Ruth, you sit in front with your son," Pluma said. "Marie and I will sit in the back. Where the perps sit. That's what you call them, isn't it, Owen? Perps?"

"Doesn't matter what I call them," Owen said. "They rarely come when I call."

Pluma loosed a loud "Haw!" that brought a grim smile to the face of Marie Hager.

"Well, you rarely came when I called, either," Ruth said, sliding into the passenger seat. "So I guess you're getting a little payback."

Pluma held up all four ends of the conversation as they drove. "It's really good of the state to let folks vote as early as two weeks in advance of election day," she said. "I can't wait to vote against that philandering womanizer. My sister in California says he tries to dunk his dick into anything that moves. Have you met him, Owen?"

"Yesterday morning. I moved a little, but he didn't try anything."

Pluma's "Haw!" nearly pierced the Plexiglas that separated the front and back seats. "You're not his type," she said. "His taste runs to big-breasted blondes. Like that poor missing girl."

"So he has a history of running around?" Ruth asked.

"Oh, yes," Pluma said. "This isn't the first time. Won't be the last, either. His daddy, the ex-governor, has bailed him out of a lot of trouble. My sister says daddy is on his way to West Virginia to do it again."

"I hadn't heard that," Owen said.

"Oh, the Davisons are big news in California," Pluma said. "They can't move anything but their bowels without getting press coverage. Wouldn't surprise me if the candidate's wife don't come too. She'll make a show of standing by her man. She's had lots of practice doing it."

Owen parked his patrol car in a handicapped zone next to the wheelchair entrance to the courthouse so that the three women wouldn't have to manage the stone steps leading to the main entrance. In the elevator on the way up, Pluma said, "It's real nice of you to do this, Owen."

"Yes," Marie Hager said. "It's good to see you, Owen."

On the main floor, Owen led the women across the central hallway under the rotunda to a teller's window with an EARLY VOTING sign over it. The young woman behind the window greeted them and asked to see their IDs.

"Cecilia, honey," Pluma said, reading the woman's name tag. "I can assure you I'm over eighteen. In fact, I can't even remember how long it's been since anyone wanted to check my age."

"I'm not worried about your age. I just need to make sure you're eligible to vote in this county." Cecilia smiled, examined their IDs, and jotted down their names. "It's all part of the formal procedure."

She flipped open a computer printout and used a ruler to help her read across the rows of names and addresses. Her smile vanished and she backtracked through the printout, checking and rechecking. Finally, she shook her head and said, "That's very strange."

"Is something wrong?" Ruth asked. "I'm sure we're all registered voters."

"It's true, you're all properly registered," Cecilia said. "But it appears Mrs. Johnson and Mrs. Hager have already voted. We have absentee ballots on file from both of them."

12

GOING VIRAL

The news appeared to deflate Marie Hager. Her knees buckled and both Owen and Ruth rushed to support her, each taking an elbow.

"Had you already voted?" Ruth asked.

Marie stared at the rotunda floor. "I can't remember. I guess I must have."

"Well, I sure as hell didn't," Pluma said. "You check that list again, Missy."

Cecilia ran her finger along the straight edge she'd laid on the computer printout. "No. We have your absentee ballot on file."

"I'm so sorry," Marie said. "I do remember signing an absentee ballot. But I thought it was last time. My memory … it plays tricks."

"Somebody's playing tricks on both of us," Pluma said. "I came here to vote and, by God, I'm going to vote."

"I'm sorry to be such a bother," Marie said.

"You haven't done anything wrong." Owen turned and addressed Cecilia at her teller's window. "These women have come here to vote in person. Wouldn't that nullify their absentee ballots? There must be procedures to handle cases like this."

"We're not allowed to nullify any ballots," Cecilia said. "But your ladies can cast provisional ballots. They will be opened along with the absentee ballots after election day and the Board of Canvassers will decide which to accept."

"And if there's fraud involved?" Owen asked.

"The Board of Canvassers will decide that too. Any

suspected wrongdoing will be reported to the proper authorities."
Cecilia scanned Owen's uniform. "Sheriff Reader will certainly
be informed."

"I sure as hell don't want to wait until after the election.
I'm here. Right now. I can prove I'm here." Pluma stomped
her red tennis shoe on the rotunda floor. "I want to vote. Right
now. You just tear up any ballot you've already gotten with
my name on it."

"We can't do that," Cecilia said. "We can't destroy any
ballots and we can't open any until election day. But if you fill
out a provisional ballot, I'm sure the canvassers will respect
the fact that you filed your ballot personally."

"All right, then. Give me one of them provisional ballots,"
Pluma said.

Ruth and Owen helped Marie to a long wooden bench
against the curved wall of the rotunda. "You should fill out a
provisional ballot too," Ruth said.

"I'm sorry to be such a bother," Marie said.

"You hush that kind of talk," Ruth said. "I don't want to
hear that from you ever again."

Owen couldn't match the cowering figure on the wooden
bench with the strong, assertive woman whose daughter he'd
once dated. He wondered if she were a preview of what lay
ahead for his own mother. "You're no trouble at all," he said.
"Whoever filed a ballot in your name is the real trouble here.
And we're going to find out who that is." He went to the Early
Voting window and requested a provisional ballot for Marie.

Cecilia pushed a blank ballot through the teller's slot at
the bottom of the window. "They used to call them 'challenge
ballots,' but somebody decided that wasn't politically correct."

Owen took the ballot back to Marie and sat with her as she
unfolded it and smoothed it out on the wooden bench. "I forget,"
she said. "Who did Pluma say I should vote for?"

Pluma stood at a high wooden table filling out her own
ballot. "Vote for Sam Halstead, honey," she boomed. "He keeps
his dick zipped up."

The rotunda's acoustics broadcast Pluma's voice throughout

the lobby. Heads swiveled in the direction of the women, causing Marie to blush. But she managed a grim smile as she marked her ballot and said, "Now there's a fine campaign slogan."

The three women left their ballots with Cecilia and Owen took them to the local mall for the shopping trip they'd used as an excuse to leave Shady Acres. While they dawdled over the sale racks at Macy's, he excused himself, called Thad Reader, and reported on the afternoon's activity.

"Sounds like you ought to get your mom to take a few more of her fellow residents on shopping trips to the courthouse voting window," Reader said. "The more evidence we have, the more likely we are to get a fraud conviction on those Shady Acres folks."

"I'll do that," Owen said.

"Meantime, I'd like you to hurry back here to the office. I've got a visitor coming at six that I think you'll want to meet."

"Who's that?"

"Your old California governor, Red Davison. Wants to make sure our investigation will bear fruit and clear his son's name. I know you and he have some history together."

"We have some history apart. He ruined my consulting business, but we've never met."

"Well, now's your chance."

Owen bought the ladies coffee at the mall's food court, deposited them at the rest home in time for dinner, and got back to the sheriff's office just in time to meet the visitors.

The former California governor was still as trim and fit as when he'd held office. His signature red hair had thinned to a sandy blond, but the only other signs of his age were a few lines on his face and the bifocals that split the image of his slate gray eyes.

It was the first time Owen had ever been in the presence of the man who had squashed his consulting business with as much attention and effort as it took to swat a fly. He found it easy to summon up the toxic mixture of contempt and hatred he'd nursed through the years, but he reminded himself that he needed to stay out of swatting range.

Harrison Marcus, who had worked for Red Davison and now helped with Jason Davison's campaign, had accompanied the ex-governor to Reader's office. He stood beside his old boss, scowling like a tiger with a toothache.

"What can I do for you, Governor?" Reader asked.

"I want to know how your investigation of this Gardner woman's disappearance is going."

"I'll tell you the same thing I've told the press. She's still missing. There's no evidence of foul play. We're pursuing every lead. And we encourage anyone with a knowledge of her acquaintances or her whereabouts to come forward."

"I was hoping to learn more than you've told the press," Davison said.

"I'm not in the habit of telling private parties more than I've told the press."

"I'm not just any private party. I've spent my life in public service. My son is running for president."

"As someone who has spent your life in public service, I'm sure you understand the need to guard against leaks," Reader said. "And your son has been linked to the missing woman. Which is all the more reason why I shouldn't be talking to you."

"My son's link to the missing woman is tenuous and troublesome. He's dropped five points in the polls just because he happened to have his photograph taken with a campaign worker."

Davison took off his bifocals and fixed Reader with a piercing stare. "I'm in a position to get you the help you need to solve this case quickly. Your state's governor, Dusty Rhodes, is a personal friend. He is willing to see to it that state police are assigned to the job of finding the Gardner woman."

"Governor, this is my jurisdiction. This office must seem pretty shabby by your lights, and you probably figure we're woefully understaffed. And you'd be right. But the people I have working for me are good at their jobs and I trust them. I don't want to have to wet nurse a bunch of staties and wonder which one is going to be leaking details to you, Dusty Rhodes, or the press." Reader measured out his words carefully. "So you can thank the governor for me and tell him I'd prefer to do without his help. But let him know that if he insists on sending officers down here, I'll just put them on traffic details to free up people I trust to help with the investigative work."

"You're making a big mistake," Davison said.

"Been a long time since that happened," Reader said. "I'd best mark my calendar. Help me remember."

"I'd scrap that attitude if I were you," Harrison Marcus said. "This case has gone national overnight. If you go it alone and come up empty, you're likely to be sucking hind tit come election day."

"That's not a picture I like to contemplate," Reader said. "But then, sucking front tit doesn't sound any more appetizing. Guess it all depends on the tit."

"I'm sure you're aware Harrison was speaking metaphorically." Davison put a minimum amount of effort into a thin smile. "You'll be up for reelection in November. Obviously, your chances will be better if you crack this case. Money and publicity will also improve your chances. We could help you with both."

"I want to crack this case for the sake of the missing woman," Reader said. "Not because I might get reelected or your son might get to be president."

"I've been in politics all my life," Davison said. "It always comes down to getting reelected."

"I don't know," Reader said. "I've got a long list of things I want to do before I die. If I'm not reelected, I could get started on that list."

"You'll need time to enjoy that list," Marcus said. "A lot could happen before you start on it."

"Are you still speaking metaphorically?" Reader asked. "Or was there a threat somewhere in those words?"

"I think Harrison is just suggesting we could help you with some of the items on your list."

"Not unless you happen to know Jacqueline Bisset or are willing to bankroll me in the World Series of Poker," Reader said. "Your man does raise a good point, though. I probably ought to make the most of whatever time I have left. I think I'll start by bringing this meeting to a close so Owen and I can get back to work."

"You're way out of line," Harrison Marcus said. "This meeting is over when the governor says it's over."

"No, Harrison," Davison said. "We're guests here. This meeting is over when the sheriff says it's over." Davison rose from his chair and shook Reader's hand. "I think we understand each other. Just remember that I want to know what's happened to the Gardner woman and am willing to provide whatever resources you need to find that out." He handed Reader a card. "That number will reach me day or night."

Reader took the card without comment as Davison shook the fingers that extended from Owen's cast. "I remember your name, Mr. Allison. You used to have a consulting firm in California, didn't you?"

"I did," Owen said. "Tranalytics."

"I'd heard good things about it. Whatever became of it?"

Owen wanted to shout, "You scuttled it, asshole," but remembered he'd resolved to stay out of swatting range. Instead, he said, "We lost a few big bids. One to Mr. Marcus here. The founding partners decided it was time to shut the doors."

"That's a shame," Davison said. "But you seem to have found a second career in law enforcement."

"Actually, Dr. Allison still has an active consulting business," Reader said. "I hire him when I need help with crash reconstructions and some of our tougher investigations."

"I misunderstood," Davison said. "The uniform suggested law enforcement."

"If I need his help over an extended period," the sheriff said, "it's easier just to deputize Owen. Gives him all the power of my office."

"And you certainly need all the help you can get right now." As he left the office, Davison nodded to Owen. "Glad to see you landed on your feet."

As soon as Davison and Marcus were out of earshot, Owen

loosed a barrage of profanity. "Landed on my feet? What kind of shit is that? I landed on my butt. And those two assholes put me there."

"Steady, big fellow. You're on your feet now. And I thought you showed remarkable restraint in dealing with those two assholes."

"More than I can say for you," Owen said. "You jerked their chain every chance you got. It's like you couldn't stand the thought of having friends in high places."

"Neither of them was ever likely to send me Christmas cards, no matter what I said. And I didn't like them thinking they could barge in and muck with the investigation."

"No danger of them thinking that now."

"Didn't you tell me you'd never met the ex-governor?"

"Never did. I was just a fly for his minions to swat when I lived in California. Why do you ask?"

"It's funny he'd know your name, is all."

"It's a politician's trick. He has his people look up a name and brief him before he meets the person. Like you asking people 'How's your bad back?' when you can't remember their names."

"Damn near everybody in the state has had a bad back at one time or another, so it's a safe bet. But Davison didn't know you'd be here. And the fly his minions swatted was labeled Tranalytics, not Owen Allison."

"What's your point?"

"Just wondering why he happened to know your background."

"That guy Barney that works with his son put my name together with Tranalytics. Because of our motorcycle study."

"Governor just flew in from California. His son's swirling around a political drain. What's he doing talking about a thirty-year-old research study?"

"He knows Dusty Rhodes. He must have talked to him if he's promising the state police. Maybe that's how he got my name. I'm on Rhodes' shit list."

"That speaks well for you. But it's a pretty long list."

"But I'm near the top. I'm not surprised he knows Dusty

153

Rhodes, though. Those two must lead the nation in kickbacks and corruption."

"Lots of competition from D.C. and Illinois. But those two guys would be right up there in the top five, no matter who they were up against. Still doesn't explain how he knew your name."

"Know what I think?" Owen said. "You're just jealous because I got on so well with the great man, while you managed to piss off both him and his henchman."

"In politics, you've got to know when to fuck 'em and know when to suck 'em. Don't let those smiling faces fool you. While you're busy making friends in high places, I'll keep trying to figure out who's trying to kill you. And based on what I just heard, those two pissed-off people who just left bear watching."

The next morning, the asbestos workers took down their polythene tent and left, carrying away plastic bags filled with contaminated debris, and the second shift of repairmen arrived. Bill Muth, a handyman friend from Owen's high school days picked up the Barkley Democrat from his front steps and brought it into the house with him, saying, "You gotta see this, man. It's really hot stuff."

A photo of Betty Sue Gardner covered half of the front page above the fold. Blonde hair disheveled, she smirked at the camera. She was not alone. Her left arm was draped around the neck of Linton Barney, while her right hand snaked around the neck of Jason Davison and rested on his right shoulder. The candidate's right hand held a beer mug, while his left hand disappeared in the vicinity of Betty Sue's backside, just below what appeared to be a pink tank top. A good portion of the top was covered by the black bar that newspapers use to protect the sensibilities of their readers.

The caption read SUPER TUESDAY VICTORY CELEBRATION.

Muth wagged the hammer dangling from his tool belt suggestively. "Man, I'd sure like to celebrate that."

After leaving the workers, Owen arrived at the sheriff's office to find Reader and three deputies crowded around a desk covered with scattered newspapers and a laptop.

Reader waved his hand over the papers. "Seen the news?"

"Just the Democrat," Owen said. "Looks like the candidate may have been a little more friendly with Betty Sue than he let on."

"Democrat didn't show the whole picture," Reader said. "The New York Herald Dispatch has it online without the censor's bar."

"No big deal," Deputy Blatt said. "All you see's about half a nipple."

"Newspaper picture's a freeze frame taken from a video." Reader turned the laptop screen so it faced Owen. "Video's already gone viral."

13

A BULLET FOR THE BOSS

The video opened with a close-up of a Jason Davison campaign poster, then drew back to take in a raucous celebration in a dimly lit room. Streamers shot through the air, propelled by poppers whose intermittent bangs mixed with the clinking of glasses, snatches of conversation, and the throbbing beat of a rock song that Owen didn't recognize. Heads bobbed in front of the camera as Betty Sue bounced into view, snapping her fingers to the beat, her breasts jiggling under the tank top. She threw her arms around Jason Davison, clinging to his chest as she delivered a long, lingering kiss.

Evidently surprised, the candidate staggered backward one step as beer sloshed from his mug onto the rear of Betty Sue's tight pants. She clung a little too long to Davison, then broke the kiss as Linton Barney appeared in the picture. He tried to draw her away from the candidate, who patted her wet behind with his free hand.

Betty Sue left her right arm around Davison's neck, threw her left arm around Barney, and smirked at the camera as her right nipple fought to be included in the photograph. It was the pose that had appeared in hundreds of newspapers.

Linton Barney succeeded in prying Betty Sue away from Jason Davison, but not before the candidate reached out and pulled her pink tank top up over her half-exposed nipple. The video ended as Barney and Betty Sue disappeared off the right side of the frame.

"That's all folks," Reader said, closing the laptop.

"Not exactly X-rated," Owen said. "But the candidate and Miss Gardner didn't exactly appear to be strangers."

"He plucked that tank top right over her titty," Deputy Blatt said.

"They sure seemed familiar," Owen said. "I mean, how many times in your life can you remember trying to cover up a pretty girl's nipple?"

"Seems like I maybe tried to uncover a few," Reader said. "But I can barely remember those."

"But you wouldn't have tried it with a stranger," Owen said.

"No. I'd remember that, for sure."

"Seems like Betty Sue was the only one of them aware of the camera," Owen said. "Who took the video?"

"Don't know," Reader said. "Tom O'Day's byline was on the story in his New York paper. He's the one who got them the still photo."

"Man's been Johnny-on-the-spot," Owen said. "Maybe we ought to talk to him about his sources."

"I've been trying to reach him," Reader said. "His office has promised to put him in touch with us. We need to talk to the candidate again, too. It's pretty obvious he's been holding out on us."

"He looked a little surprised by the kiss," Owen said. "He could explain the nipple tampering as an attempt to protect the public morals."

"But could he do it with a straight face?" Reader said.

"Why not? He's been a politician all his life."

"Actually, we've got a little more than the video as evidence he's been a tad more than friendly with Betty Sue."

"How's that?"

"Bus Stabler of the Moss Valley Garage was in to see me early this morning. He's got the AAA concession in this end of the county. Told me he fixed a flat for Betty Sue Gardner up on Ritter Road about a week ago."

"Ritter Road's that winding approach to the Rocker mansion where the candidate's staying," Owen said.

"Doesn't lead anywhere else," Reader said. "Dead ends

at the mansion."

"She could have been making a delivery from campaign headquarters," Owen said. "Nothing unusual about that."

"It was three-thirty in the morning. Stabler came forward because he'd seen the press conference where Davison said he didn't know Betty Sue personally."

"Still, the evidence that he knew her in the biblical sense is circumstantial," Owen said. "Other members of the senator's staff are staying with him at the mansion."

"I'll grant you the evidence is circumstantial," Reader said. "But there's more and more of it and it's starting to form a smelly pile. Be interesting to hear what the candidate has to say about it."

The intercom on Reader's desk buzzed and the deputy staffing the reception desk announced that Tom O'Day was in the outer office.

"Speak of the devil," Reader said. "Bring him back here." Then, to the deputies crowded around his desk, he added, "Fun's over, boys. Everybody get back to work. Except you, Owen. I want you to stick around. O'Day's likely to be too slippery for one person to pin down."

O'Day appeared at the door to the sheriff's office as the last of the deputies departed and asked, "How's the Gardner investigation going?"

"You tell me," Reader said. "Seems like you know at least as much as we do."

"All I know is our polls show Davison's dropping like a Mafia squealer with concrete overshoes."

Reader picked up one of the newspapers on his desk and tapped the front-page photo. "I'd say you know quite a bit more than that. You know who took this picture, for instance."

"Now, Sheriff. You know I can't reveal my sources." O'Day nodded toward the laptop on Reader's desk. "You've seen the video. It speaks for itself. What good would it do to know who made it?"

"Your source might know what went on after the camera went off," Reader said. "Can you at least tell us whether that source is likely to provide you with any more gems like this?"

"That's all I've been shown," O'Day said.

"So far," Owen said.

"So far, yes. But I asked, and I don't think there's likely to be any more coming from that particular source."

"You say that as if something might be coming from other sources," Owen said.

"Never can tell. I've been working hard to uncover a few more. A reporter's life isn't easy. Keeps you on the go."

"This office is on the go, too," Owen said. "But you seem to be running neck and neck with us. You damn near beat us to Maude Jenkins's boarding house when Maude's other roomer reported Betty Sue missing."

"I told you. I was listening to your police radio."

"Funny thing about that," Owen said. "You showed up asking about a missing woman, but the dispatcher says she just passed along a 10-57. Nothing gender-specific in that communication."

"I must have heard your deputies discussing it."

"The only information the guys in the field got was the 10-57 dispatch number," Reader said. "We checked to be sure."

"I don't really remember what made me think the missing person was a woman," O'Day said. "Maybe it was just seeing you talking to two women on Maude Jenkins's porch."

"I'd hate to think one of your sources might be in my office," Reader said. "If I find that out, it will go hard on you and harder on your source."

"I can assure you I don't have any sources in your office," O'Day said. "Look, if you want a lead, I'll tell you who you should talk to. Bus Stabler of the Moss Valley Garage."

"Why would we want to do that?" Reader asked.

"I talked to him yesterday. He had quite a story to tell about fixing a flat for Betty Sue Gardner in the wee hours of the morning. On Ritter Road. Wanted to sell it to me."

"Sounds like you weren't buying."

"Oh, I believed him. Wasn't worth spending money on, though. It didn't really forge any direct links between Betty Sue and Davison. More like back-fence gossip than hard news."

159

"Not like your video," Owen said.

O'Day smiled. "Exactly. Now that was worth everything we paid for it. Anyhow, I suggested Stabler take his story to you."

"Funny. He didn't mention you when he talked to me," Reader said.

"Probably wanted you to think he came straight to you of his own accord."

"You seem to be a jump ahead of us on a lot of things," Owen said. "If you won't tell us the names of your sources, can you at least tell us what tomorrow's lead story will be?"

"Don't know yet. A lot depends on what Davison has to say at his press conference."

"Press conference?" Reader said.

"He's scheduled a press conference to address the Gardner girl's disappearance. Three o'clock this afternoon."

"Guess that's why he's been too busy to get back to us. Too busy even to advertise his conference."

"Well, you're not exactly a member of the press," O'Day said. "Maybe he didn't want to risk being cross-examined by experts, or feel that he was under oath. Lying to a bunch of reporters is a lot easier than lying to the law."

Reader arched his eyebrows. "You saying he's likely to lie at his press conference?"

"Why break with tradition?"

The press conference called by Jason Davison was scheduled to be held on the steps of the Barkley courthouse, catty-corner across the town square from the sheriff's office. The square began to fill with TV crews at one o'clock, two hours in advance of the conference. By two o'clock, a lectern backed by red, white, and blue bunting had been set up on the top courthouse step and wired for sound. By 2:30, the square was packed with people.

Owen decided to watch with Thad Reader from the steps of the sheriff's office. Just before the appointed time, Tom O'Day joined them. O'Day nodded toward the four deputies patrolling each edge of the square. "Finally got the official word about the press conference, I see."

"They needed our guys for crowd control," Reader said.

"Nice touch, using the courthouse steps," O'Day said. "Makes it seem like he's got the force of the law behind him."

"Actually, we're across the way," Owen said. "Be interesting to hear what he has to say, anyhow."

The candidate came out through the courthouse doors, followed by Linton Barney, and took his place at the lectern. He smiled grimly to acknowledge the smattering of applause, then raised both hands to quiet the crowd.

"Thank you for coming," he said, and paused as the last word of his greeting echoed off the surrounding hills. "I've called you here to address the slander and innuendo that have appeared in the media following the disappearance of my campaign worker, Betty Sue Gardner. We are deeply saddened by Betty Sue's disappearance and want to assure you that we are cooperating fully with the local police in their search efforts."

"Good thing he finally invited you to this little shindig, so you could learn all about his cooperation," O'Day said.

Two men standing below O'Day on the sidewalk turned to glare at him.

At the lectern, Davison continued, "Since Betty Sue's disappearance has given rise to ugly rumors concerning me and my staff, I want to make a clean breast of our relationship with the unfortunate young woman."

"Clean breast," O'Day whispered. "Nice choice of words. Must have written it himself."

"To do that," Davison said, "I want to introduce the man who usually introduces me at these events, my chief of staff, Linton Barney."

"What the hell?" O'Day said, generating more glares.

Linton Barney grasped the lectern as Jason Davison stepped aside, taking care to stay within range of the TV cameras. Barney smiled at Davison and thanked him, then blinked against the afternoon sun and said, "There's been a lot of ugly speculation in the media since Betty Sue disappeared, but I'm here to set the record straight. For the last three months, ever since the New Hampshire primary, Betty Sue Gardner and I have been involved in a personal, private relationship."

The crowd fell silent.

O'Day said "Fuck" so quietly only Owen and Reader could hear him.

Barney blinked again. "We tried to be discreet, to keep our affair a secret from other campaign workers. And from Jason." He glanced over at his boss, who responded with a short, curt nod.

"When Betty Sue disappeared," Barney went on, "I continued to keep our affair secret. I was afraid it might hurt Jason's candidacy. But it quickly became apparent that I was hurting him more by keeping quiet. When I went to him this morning and confessed our affair, he insisted I go public with the information, regardless of the cost."

"Cost, hell," O'Day said. "It's a publicity bonanza."

"I want to stress that I have no knowledge of Betty Sue's whereabouts. I was campaigning with Jason in Indianapolis when she turned up missing, and we have shared this information with the local police."

O'Day raised his eyebrows at Reader, asking a silent question.

"He told us he was in Indianapolis," Reader said

"Nothing like half-truths to make you sound totally trustworthy," O'Day said.

"In conclusion," Barney said from the lectern, "I want to say I regret any confusion my silence has caused and reaffirm that we are cooperating fully with the local investigation."

"Full cooperation," Owen said. "Half-truth, hell. That's not even a quarter truth."

Jason Davison reclaimed the lectern and announced that they would take a few questions from representatives of the media.

A young blonde woman in the front row asked, "Any progress on the investigation?"

"That's a question you'll have to ask the authorities," Davison said.

"You'll notice he didn't ask you to come up and answer that question," O'Day said. "No wonder you guys were invited late."

A man on the edge of the crowd asked something Owen

couldn't hear, and the candidate repeated the question.

"You ask if I was surprised when Linton told me of his affair with Betty Sue," Davison said. "The answer is, very much so. But let's get something clear here. Neither of the two parties is married. They were two consenting adults. Under other circumstances, I would have been delighted to hear that they had found each other. As it turns out, when I learned of the affair, I insisted that Linton bring it to the attention of the proper authorities."

"I'm guessing he planted that question himself," O'Day said. "Just to minimize the affair and maximize his alleged cooperation."

A reporter sitting on the hood of the NBC-TV van called out, "Do you plan to keep Mr. Barney on your staff?"

"Linton Barney is my oldest, dearest friend," Davison said. "In the eyes of the law, he is innocent until proven guilty. In my eyes, there is no doubt he is innocent of any wrongdoing. As he said, he was with me in Indianapolis when Miss Gardner disappeared."

O'Day and a few other reporters waved their hands to get Davison's attention.

The candidate raised his right hand. "That's enough questions. I want to thank you for coming and stress again that we are cooperating fully with the local authorities. With them, we hope and pray that the mystery of Miss Gardner's disappearance will be solved quickly and that she will turn up unharmed."

"What bullshit!" O'Day was red-faced and angry. "Linton Barney just took a bullet for his boss."

"He's just made himself the prime suspect in what could be a murder case," Owen said. "That seems well beyond the call of duty to one's boss."

"I don't know why he did it," O'Day said. "But I know he's lying about the affair."

"You sound pretty sure of that," Owen said.

"Rumor has it Barney's ex-wife divorced him because he was having an affair," O'Day said.

"Seems like that just reinforces his story."

"The affair was with another man." O'Day took his cell phone and ran through some addresses. "I'm going to track down someone who can verify that."

14

OVER THE EDGE

Owen and Reader watched as O'Day disappeared inside the county office building, cell phone to his ear. "What do you make of that?" Owen asked the sheriff. "I would never have guessed Barney might be gay."

"Don't see that it matters much one way or the other," Reader said. "If he had a wife, he must at least be a switch hitter. So we can't rule out an affair with Betty Sue."

"Switch hitters usually have a higher average from one side or the other."

"Long as he had even one single from the straight side, I don't see that a higher average from the gay side proves anything."

"We really don't need proof in this case. Just a reasonable doubt."

"Let's say he is covering for his boss," Reader said. "That may have a bearing on the election. But not on our job. Whether she was sleeping with Barney or Davison, the girl is still missing."

"Does seem like she must have been overly friendly with one or the other. Maybe even both."

"That's as may be. But even if she'd had more pricks than a second-hand dartboard, our job is to find her, not judge her."

The crowd in the square began to dissipate. Reporters turned away from the courthouse steps to face the sheriff's office. The NBC-TV van began to ease its way around the square toward Owen and Reader.

"Shit," Reader said. "They're going to want an official statement. I'll take care of it. You go inside and stick with

O'Day. He already seems to know a little more than he ought to. Maybe you can find out if he learns anything new from his phoning. Keep him from getting too far ahead of us."

Owen went through the revolving doors of the county office building. O'Day stood at the end of the central hallway, bent into his cell phone. As soon as he saw Owen approaching, the reporter held up one finger in a "just a minute" signal.

Owen stopped and held his ground, blocking O'Day's way out.

O'Day put away his cell phone, scribbled something in his pocket notebook, tore out the sheet and walked over to Owen. "Barney's ex won't talk to me. Or to any reporter. I don't think she'll talk to anyone by phone. Too suspicious. But she might talk to a law enforcement officer in person."

He handed Owen the sheet of paper. "There's the information on her. She's living in Cincinnati now. Maybe you can get something out of her. It's worth a try. When I told her about Barney's speech, she sounded concerned, even frightened. Your uniform might have a soothing influence."

A cluster of voices from outside carried into the hallway. O'Day cocked an ear toward the revolving door. "What's going on out there?"

"Reporters want a statement from the sheriff."

"He doesn't have anything new to say, does he? It's pretty clear Barney's announcement took him by surprise."

Owen shrugged. "Your guess is as good as mine."

"I better join my fellow reporters anyhow," O'Day said. "Can't risk anyone getting the jump on me."

"Doesn't seem likely," Owen said.

O'Day nodded toward the sheet of paper he'd given Owen. "You might do it if you follow up with Michelle Barney."

When Reader finished with his impromptu press conference, Owen filled him in on O'Day's suggestion that they contact Barney's ex-wife.

"Call her," Reader said. "Let's see what she has to say. Cincinnati's not that far if she wants to talk in person."

Owen made the call. Michelle Barney seemed nervous and reluctant to talk about her ex-husband. But she was even more reluctant to stand in the way of a police investigation. She was adamant, though, about not responding to questions on the phone.

Owen made the drive to Cincinnati the next morning. He remembered making the same trip as a teenager with his older brother to see the Reds play. Those trips on the winding road hugging the Ohio River had been filled with happy anticipation. The road had since been straightened and upgraded to a superhighway with cuts through the inland hills, but Owen's mood on this trip was closer to apprehension than anticipation. He didn't look forward to questioning a woman about her ex-husband's sex life.

Michelle Barney opened the front door without unlocking the screen door. The face behind the screen featured a high narrow forehead above a nose that was a shade too long and a mouth that was a shade too wide. Not the face of a fashion model, but not bad, either. Her blue eyes darted back and forth, taking in the street and neighboring lawns as she examined Owen's credentials.

Finally, she unlocked the screen door and invited him to follow her through the house. She was nearly as tall as Owen's six feet, with athletic legs and a figure that was just short of being boyish. She paused in the kitchen and turned toward Owen, sweeping her auburn hair across her shoulders. "We can talk out back."

The kitchen door opened out onto a flagstone patio with two wrought iron tables surrounded by matching chairs. Michelle led Owen to the table farthest from the house, sat, and pulled a pack of cigarettes from the pocket of her beige cardigan.

"It's better we talk out here." She lit a cigarette and inhaled deeply. "Davison has ears everywhere. Besides, I can smoke out here. It's my parents' house. They don't like my smoking inside." Exhaling a thin stream of smoke, she added, "Don't like my smoking at all, actually. But I'm here to take care of them, so they try not to complain."

She stood her pack of cigarettes on end. "I'm sorry. Would you like a cigarette?"

When Owen shook his head, she said, "Of course. Nobody smokes anymore." She waved the cigarette in tight circles. "I hope you don't mind if I do."

Owen shook his head again. She pulled a glass ashtray closer to her. "I'll try to answer your questions. To help you find that poor girl." She tapped a thin sliver of ash into the ashtray. "But what I tell you mustn't go any further. Do you understand? Can you promise me that?"

"I'll do whatever I can to keep our meeting confidential."

Her eyes surveyed the yard, as if she wanted to extract a similar promise from the birdbath and rose bushes. "How can I help?"

"Your former husband has confessed to having an affair with the missing woman."

"Yes. I saw it on TV."

The cigarette smoke burned Owen's eyes. "There are rumors. That your husband was a homosexual."

"I wouldn't say that."

"Then it's not true that your marriage broke up because he had a homosexual affair?"

She looked down at her pack of cigarettes. "I guess it's fair to say that had something to do with it."

"But you wouldn't call him a homosexual?"

"No." A short laugh escaped her closed lips. "If anything, he was asexual. What you are calling a homosexual affair was a one-time fling. I'm fairly sure of that."

Her hand trembled and she nearly missed the ashtray with a leaning tower of ashes. "I wasn't feeling well. I came home early. Found Lin in our bed. With another man. Like some cheap melodrama." She stopped and took a deep, nicotine-free breath.

"I'm sorry," Owen said.

"The man jumped out of bed. He pulled on his pants and hurried out. Left everything else behind. Except his undershirt. He tried to shield his face with it as he went by me. But I recognized him. Pathetic. A closet queer." She stubbed out her cigarette. "You don't need his name, do you?"

"Not if you don't want to tell me."

"Oh, what the hell. You probably wouldn't recognize it anyhow. Larry Lewis. He was a reporter. Very big in Sacramento. Not that well-known outside the state. His columns had been exceptionally hard on Jason. When he was running for the Senate." She lit another cigarette and inhaled deeply. "Lin claimed it was just a one-time thing. Claimed he did it for Jason."

"For Jason? Why? To get the reporter to let up in his columns?"

"Or to get evidence to blackmail him. I don't know. I didn't want to know. But the affair didn't last. Neither did the negative columns. And the reporter was out of a job within a month."

Her lower lip trembled. Her eyes scrunched shut, but not in time to stop the tears from flowing. "I mean, we hadn't had sex in years. And here Lin was servicing this … this queer. And claiming he was doing it for Jason."

She bent forward, trembling. Owen left his chair to put his arm around her.

"For Jason," she sputtered. "Imagine that. It was the last straw."

She straightened, wedging Owen's arm between her back and the wrought iron chair. "I divorced him. And Jason. I'd had enough of the two of them. What a pair. They went way back. All the way to college at USC. Lin was a lot closer to Jason than he ever was to me."

Owen extracted his trapped arm and returned to his chair. "So I'm guessing you found it hard to believe Linton's confession that he'd been having an affair with Betty Sue Gardner."

She shook her head. "I can't imagine it. But not because he was homosexual. Sex of any sort was never high on his list. My guess is, he was covering for Jason. It wouldn't be the first time."

She took a handkerchief from her cardigan pocket and dabbed at her eyes. "I'm sorry. I must look terrible. But an affair with a campaign worker just isn't Linton's style. Jason, though, that's another matter."

She took a deep drag on her cigarette. "I don't know what else I can tell you. I hope you find the missing girl. If it's any consolation, Jason has a long history of buying them off. Not killing them off."

"Do you have any specific knowledge of buy-offs?"

"Just rumors, I'm afraid. I've no proof of any of it. And I'm trusting you to keep everything I've told you private. You will do that, won't you?"

Owen stood to leave. "Of course. Thank you for your time."

She extended her free hand without getting up. "Don't make me regret it."

"How'd things go with Barney's ex?" Reader asked when Owen showed up at the sheriff's office the next morning.

"Pretty well. She was all but certain that Barney was covering for his boss."

"How'd she seem?"

"Paranoid. But fairly positive there was nothing going on between her ex-husband and Betty Sue."

"You believe her?"

"No reason not to. She indicated Barney had covered for Davison in the past. And Davison evidently has a history of bedding campaign workers." He told Reader about the meeting, quoting the wife as much as he could from notes he'd dictated in the car after leaving her house.

"Well, whoever was bedding Betty Sue evidently left a little something behind."

"What do you mean?"

"Guess you haven't seen today's papers."

"No. I helped the repair crew install drywall in my office before I came in. That's what made me late."

Reader unfolded a copy of the Barkley Democrat and handed it to Owen. "Take a look at this."

The headlines read "BETTY SUE PREGNANT?" While Owen read the accompanying article, Reader summarized it for him. "A patient at the local Planned Parenthood clinic came forward. Seems she had a long talk in the waiting room with another patient that matched Betty Sue Gardner's description just two days before Betty Sue disappeared. The woman didn't come forward at first because she hadn't gotten the patient's name. But with all the press coverage, she recognized Betty Sue's photo. Seems the patient who fitted Betty Sue's description wanted to talk to someone about abortions."

Owen finished reading the article and looked up from the paper. "Is she sure the patient was Betty Sue?"

"There's not exactly any DNA evidence. But the story must be true, don't you think?" Reader arched an eyebrow. "After all, Tom O'Day reported it."

"O'Day again? How'd he get onto it?"

"The patient took the story to him."

"Well, there you are then. If it's O'Day's story, it must be true. Maybe we ought to leave the whole investigation to him and go back to worrying about election fraud."

"I'm not quite ready to go that far. In fact, I was so concerned about O'Day's accuracy, I dropped in on Planned Parenthood as soon as I read the story this morning."

"I'm guessing the staff wasn't very cooperative."

"Invoked doctor/patient privilege. Can't blame them. But a nurse I know got me a list of the patients they saw that day."

"Betty Sue's name on it?"

"No. But there was an Elizabeth Sowers."

"In that case, there's no need for DNA tests. Or for questioning O'Day's accuracy. Sowers was Betty Sue's mother's maiden name."

"So Betty Sue was pregnant," Reader said.

"I don't know," Owen said. "There's something fishy about the whole story. Betty Sue rarely shared anything personal with her flatmate at Maude Jenkins' place. Doesn't make sense that she'd suddenly bare her soul to a stranger at a Planned Parenthood Clinic."

"Hard to figure, I agree. If she was pregnant, though, she was under a lot of stress. And if she was pregnant, that's a pretty good reason for disappearing."

"Or for being made to disappear."

171

"Think she told the father?"

"What does O'Day say?"

"Says he got 'no comment' from the Davison campaign. Maybe they'll have a comment for us, though." Reader punched his intercom and said, "Essie, honey, get me Linton Barney at the Davison campaign headquarters."

"Will do, boss."

The intercom went dead for a while and then Essie came back on to say, "The candidate and Linton Barney are in the panhandle today. They're not expected back until tonight, but their office is patching us through."

"Thank you, Essie." Reader left the intercom on so that Owen could hear both ends of the conversation. After some static, Linton Barney's voice came on the line.

"Linton, this is Sheriff Reader back in Raleigh County. I imagine you've seen the news that Betty Sue Gardner was pregnant. We wanted to ask if you could corroborate that report."

"God, no. I had no idea. Do you think it's even true?"

"All we know so far is what we read in the papers."

"Well, if it is true, that's all the more reason that you should find her as soon as possible."

"We're doing our best. Is the candidate available to speak to us?"

"He's here now. But he's addressing the Chamber of Commerce in ten minutes."

"Would you put him on, please? We won't keep him long."

Jason Davison came on the line with a voice skilled in conveying both his impatience and his acknowledgement that the caller deserved a modicum of his busy schedule. "What is it, sheriff? I hope you're calling to say you've located Miss Gardner."

"I'm afraid she's still missing, Senator. We were following up this morning's news report to ask if she'd confided the news of her pregnancy to either Linton Barney or yourself."

"Certainly not. Why should she confide in me?"

"Well, Senator, as her employer and Linton Barney's boss, we thought you might have been a father figure in her eyes."

172

Reader winked at Owen. "And, quite frankly, although I didn't share this with Mr. Barney, there are rumors circulating that he might not be the child's father."

"My God. I would hope your office would deal in facts rather than rumors."

"I'm sure you understand, sir, that we have to follow every lead."

"Just find the woman, sheriff. Every day that she's absent, we slip in the polls."

"I thought Mr. Barney's public confession had stemmed that tide."

"Thank God for that. Now I just pray that you find the woman and that she is unharmed. If you don't feel up to that task, my father's offer to call in state help still stands. We can even get you federal assistance if it looks like kidnapping was involved."

"Thank you, sir. But we're progressing quite nicely on our own. And when we do find Betty Sue, I'm confident that a paternity test will be able to establish the facts of the case and put an end to these troubling rumors."

"I hope it won't come to that. I have to leave for a speaking engagement now, sheriff. But I hope that the next time we talk you'll have better news for me."

The abrupt click of the disconnection resonated through the office.

"Well, that should stir things up a little," Reader said. "It's not every day you get to fuck with the mind of a U. S. senator."

"Somebody once told me it's important to know when to do that."

Reader smiled. "And when not to do it."

The receptionist's voice came over the intercom. "Boss, Maude Jenkins called in while you were on the other line. She says some staties have been out to her place asking questions about the missing girl. Just thought you ought to know."

"Thank you, Essie." Reader shut off the intercom. "Shit. It looks like Dusty Rhodes has called in the state police even though I declined his offer of help."

"What'll you do?" Owen asked.

"What the hell. The more the merrier. Long as we don't trip over each other, they might even find something we missed."

Reader cinched on his Mounties hat. "Guess I better follow up on it, though. Some coordination is in order here. Can't have them trampling on evidence." He stopped in the doorway. "In some ways it's a positive sign. If Rhodes is obliging his friend Davison by using staties to search for the girl, it must mean his friend Davison thinks the girl is still alive. Otherwise, he'd just let sleeping dogs lie."

After a take-out Chinese dinner, Owen painted the baseboard in his office. He couldn't manage the rest of the room easily with his wrist in a cast, so he left that job for the workers the next day and went to bed early.

His bedside phone rang at one in the morning. Thad Reader rushed his words against a background of shouting voices. "Owen, I need you to get out to Ritter Road. Right away. About halfway up to the Rocker mansion. Linton Barney just dropped his motorcycle over the edge. They're bringing him up now, but it doesn't look like he'll make it."

15

HALF A PITCHER OF WARM SPIT

Halfway up Ritter Road, two patrol cars and a tow truck blocked traffic as their headlights pierced the gloom beyond a sharp downhill curve. The patrol cars played their spotlights over the side of the curve, outlining a steep drop to a tree-covered slope where Linton Barney's Harley lay crumpled at the base of a large scarred oak.

Thad Reader met Owen at the edge of the curve. "Ambulance just left. The tow truck was going to bring the motorcycle up, but I told them to wait for you."

"How's Barney?"

"D.O.A."

"Not too surprising." Owen's eyes followed the searchlights to the crumpled bike. "He picked a bad place to leave the road. If the drop doesn't kill you, the trees will."

"Yeah. He got the worst of both."

"How'd you get him back up to the ambulance?"

Reader pointed to the uphill side of the curve. "Slope gets more gradual up the hill. Paramedics took a stretcher down that way."

Owen patted the shoulder bag containing his camera equipment. "Show me that way down, and we'll take a closer look."

Reader led Owen around the curve and up the hill about four hundred feet before stepping off the road. The slope was more gradual than the drop at the accident site, but both men still had to fight to maintain their footing before reaching the tree line. Then Owen followed Reader's flashlight to the tree that interrupted the motorcycle's flight.

"Where did the body land?" Owen asked.

Reader shined his flashlight back along the tree line. "Back there about fifteen feet. Under that big overhanging branch. Looked like the branch caught Barney right around his Adam's apple. Separated him from his bike and damn near tore his head off his shoulders."

Owen shuddered, then turned his attention to the crumpled Harley. He took several medium-range shots to establish its position before moving in to snap close-ups of the twisted chrome and bent metal. He finished by taking several photographs of the dented metal saddlebags on either side of the rear wheel.

"See something?" Reader asked.

"Bring your flashlight closer." Owen pointed to the side of the left rear saddlebag. "See that?"

Reader squinted at the beam's target. "Not really."

"There's a streak of black paint that doesn't quite match the black of the saddlebag. More metallic."

"Think he scraped something?"

"Or something scraped him. Trying to run him off the road, maybe."

"Any way of telling whether that streak is fresh?"

"Not for sure. But we can have it analyzed to find out what type of vehicle it might have come from. And Barney had his bike at the press conference a couple of days ago. Maybe some of the TV footage or photographs could tell us if that streak was on his bike then."

"It's pretty hard to see up this close," Reader said. "I doubt if a random photograph would pick it up."

"Can't hurt to try. We're looking at the streak in the dark right now. The press conference was held at high noon."

Owen stood and dusted off the knees of his khaki slacks. "Let's get some guys to bring the bike up to the road. Maybe rig a stretcher or put it on a skid. Then tie it down on a flatbed. I don't want to see it dragged and dangling on a tow-truck hook. That could give us new dents and paint smears and compromise what we've got."

Reader took out his cell phone. "I'll get on it."

"Barney must have been pretty familiar with this road. What time did the accident happen?"

"People at the foot of the hill reported hearing a crash a little after midnight."

"Trajectory suggests he was coming downhill from the mansion. Wonder where he might have been headed at that hour?"

"Maybe somebody at the mansion can tell us. I sent word up about the accident."

Jason Davison, his face haggard under thatches of pale hair, cradled a mug of coffee in the kitchen of the Rocker mansion. "I just can't believe it. We were talking ...right here ...just a few hours ago."

"It must be quite a shock," Owen said. "I know the two of you went way back."

"All the way back to college. USC."

"You say you talked to him earlier this evening," Reader said.

"We watched the late news together. Talked some afterward."

"How did he seem?"

"Same old Lin. He seemed fine. We shared some bourbon. Had a few laughs."

"So he'd been drinking?" Owen said.

"Just one glass with me. I don't know what he had earlier or later."

"No need to speculate," Reader said. "The autopsy will settle that question."

Davison drew his rumpled bathrobe around him as if he felt a chill. "An autopsy? Is that really necessary?"

"Standard procedure," Reader said. "We autopsy all our traffic fatalities."

Davison stared down into his coffee mug. "I just don't like to think of Lin's body being ...manhandled."

"Don't worry, he won't feel a thing." Harrison Marcus stood in the corner of the kitchen, wearing a T-shirt and blue jeans. Aside from a few ritual grunts when Owen and Reader entered, these were the first words he'd spoken.

"That's hardly necessary, Harrison," Davison said.

Reader ignored the exchange between Davison and his campaign advisor. "What was Barney doing going out that late?"

"I have no idea," Davison said.

"Did either of you see him leave?"

Davison barely shook his head and Marcus grunted "uh uh" without moving his lips.

"I saw your black limo in the driveway," Owen said. "If he'd been drinking, why wouldn't he take that instead of the motorcycle?"

"Lin didn't like driving the limo," Davison said. "Too big and clumsy."

"Were there any other cars up here he might have used?" Owen said.

"No. Harrison drove me home in the limo. His car is at campaign headquarters. But Lin much preferred riding his Harley to driving a car."

"So the three of you were here with just one car," Owen said.

"True. But Harrison drives me wherever I want to go," Davison said. "Why is that important?"

"Just trying to get a picture of the situation," Owen said.

"I should think the situation of most interest would be at the crash scene," Davison said.

"We were looking at that before we came here." Reader stood up. "We'll get back to it now." He touched the tip of his Mounties hat. "I'm sorry for your loss, Senator."

The sun was coming up over the neighboring hills when Owen and Reader came down the front steps of the mansion. Owen walked past their patrol car and stopped at Davison's limousine, which was parked ahead of them on the circular drive.

He knelt to examine the limousine's right front fender. "Wanted to look at this in the light of day."

"You think they might have used their own limo to run Barney off the road?" Reader asked.

"I think somebody in a black vehicle ran him off the road," Owen said. "It might have been a stranger, but I doubt it. Not much reason for a stranger to be on this end of Ritter Road. Especially at midnight."

Owen checked the other side of the limo, then stood and dusted off his hands. "Doesn't look like it was this vehicle though." He saw Harrison Marcus watching them through the mansion's front window and waved to him before returning to the patrol car.

"Before we leave, let's drive around the property, see if there are any other vehicles up here," Owen said.

Reader chuckled. "Davison said there weren't. Don't you trust his word?"

"He's a politician in full campaign mode. He probably lies just to keep in practice."

Reader followed the driveway around the side of the mansion, where it ended in a three-car garage. Owen got out, peeked through the garage window, and returned to the patrol car.

"Garage is holding a bright red Porsche, a brown Olds, and a cream-colored Caddy," Owen said. "Davison didn't mention those in his account."

"The Porsche belongs to the mansion's owner," Reader said. "Davison may not have access to the cars in the garage."

"Guess it doesn't matter anyhow. None of those cars left that black streak on Barney's motorcycle."

Reader pulled out of the driveway and started back down the hill. "Let's say you're right. Why would Davison want to run his buddy off that cliff?"

"Maybe Barney had second thoughts about putting his neck in a noose for Betty Sue's disappearance. If she stays missing, he's a prime suspect. If she returns, he's a target for a paternity suit. It's a lose-lose proposition."

"If it's true he was covering for Davison, I assume the Senator made it worth his while."

"Barney's ex-wife seemed certain it was a cover-up. Said he'd covered for Davison before."

Reader stopped at the accident site to drop Owen off at his car. Two deputies and two tow-truck operators were rigging a skid to bring Barney's wrecked motorcycle back up to the roadway. "I'll help these guys to make sure they don't create any more dents than already exist," Owen said. "Then I'll head into the office."

"I'm stopping at home for a shower and shave first," Reader said. "Maybe you ought to do the same."

"They're still repairing the hole in my office wall at home," Owen said. "I feel a lot safer at your office. I'll just head straight in."

Owen helped the four men get the battered motorcycle onto the bed of a pickup truck and into the county impound lot, where he scraped a sample of the paint streak off the bike's saddlebags. Then he went to the county office building, submitted the sample for laboratory analysis, shut the door of the sheriff's private office, and promptly fell asleep on Reader's couch.

Early in the afternoon, the office receptionist buzzed Owen's desk. "Somebody here to see you."

"Who is it?"

"Won't give her name. Says she talked with you two days ago. In Cincinnati."

Michelle Barney. "Send her back."

The figure that followed the receptionist through the maze of desks and low cubicle walls was barely recognizable as Linton Barney's ex-wife. She wore shapeless blue jeans at least two sizes too large and a bulky gray jacket with a hood that covered most of a Cincinnati Reds baseball cap. Dark sunglasses hid her eyes.

When she arrived at Owen's desk she took off her sunglasses and surveyed the room like a deer sniffing for the scent of hunters.

"Can we go somewhere private?" she whispered. "I need police protection. And you're the only policeman I think I can trust."

"Let's go to the sheriff's office."

When Michelle saw that the office was already occupied by Thad Reader, she put her glasses back on and tried to back out of the doorway.

Owen slipped his hand around her wrist. "It's okay. If you

can trust me, you can trust him."

"All right. But close the door, please."

Owen closed the door and introduced Reader to Michelle, who pulled back her hood, took off her sunglasses and baseball cap, and shook out her auburn hair. "I feel so silly," she said.

"No need to apologize," Reader said. "Tell us how we can help you."

"I think I need police protection. And I want that protection from police I can trust not to betray me."

"Betray you to whom?" Reader asked.

"Jason Davison. He has eyes everywhere."

"Why should you feel threatened by Jason Davison?"

"Not by him personally," she said. "Well, maybe by him personally. By his campaign …his people."

"Has something happened since we talked?" Owen asked.

"Oh yes. You asked me if I thought Lin might have had an affair with the missing Gardner woman."

"And you said you doubted it," Owen said.

"I doubted it, but I couldn't be sure. But there's one thing I can be sure of. Lin's not the father of that woman's child."

"How can you be sure of that?" Reader asked.

"Two years after we were married, Lin had a vasectomy."

"And as far as you know, he never reversed the operation?" Reader said.

"He didn't while we were married. And he would have had no reason to after we were divorced."

"And you feel threatened because…" Reader said, leading her.

"Because very few people knew about Lin's vasectomy," Michelle said. "And strange things have been happening to those who did."

"You mean your ex-husband's death," Owen said.

"There's that, of course. Lin was a careful biker. As careful as anyone could be on those infernal machines."

"Is there anything else?" Reader asked.

"The doctor who performed the vasectomy was an old friend of Lin's family. He's been dead for a few years now, but he passed his practice along to his son. Until my parents needed help, I'd been living with my sister in California. She called this morning to say the son's office was fire bombed last night."

"My God," Owen said. "Was anyone hurt?"

"No. But all the practice's records were destroyed. So, don't you see? Just as soon as news surfaced that the Gardner woman was pregnant, Linton was killed and the records of his vasectomy went up in smoke. And that's not all."

"There's more?" Owen said.

"My sister said a man had called asking for me. Said he was an old college friend who wanted to pass along his condolences for Lin's death. It sounded odd to her, so she didn't tell him I was in Cincinnati with our parents. Just asked him for a phone number. He said he'd call back."

Owen put his hand on Michelle's arm. "You were right to come to us."

"So you don't think I'm being paranoid?"

"Even paranoids have real enemies," Owen said.

"Don't worry," Reader said. "We won't let anyone hurt you. But right now, Owen and I need to discuss this situation. Can we get you something? Food? Drink?"

"Water would be nice."

Reader buzzed the reception desk and asked for a glass of ice water. "You just relax here," Reader said to Michelle when the water arrived.

"Thank you." Michelle took the glass in both hands. Her hands shook and the ice cubes clinked against the glass. She looked about as relaxed as someone facing a firing squad.

"Don't worry," Reader said. "Owen and I will be right outside this door. Don't hesitate to come out if you need anything or think of something more we should know."

Reader closed the office door behind them, leaving Michelle alone with her water and her worries. "Well, it fits. You said it looked like somebody forced Barney off the road."

"It just seems so incredible, to think they might have killed him over a vasectomy."

"If word of his operation gets out, it blows the story of

Barney as Betty Sue's lover sky high," Reader said.

"Not necessarily," Owen said. "We're not even sure Betty Sue was pregnant, and she might have had more than one lover."

"From their standpoint, though, the world thinks Betty Sue was pregnant, and Davison has vouched for his buddy's affair. If Barney wasn't the father, they look like liars and suspicion shifts to Davison."

"Barney could have realized that, told them about his vasectomy, and tried to back out."

"Still it seems like they would have been better off trying to bluff it out. If his ex-wife is right, not that many people knew Barney was shooting blanks."

"She knew, though," Owen said. "I think she's right to be worried. They're playing for pretty high stakes."

"Presidency of the United States," Reader said.

"And there's no consolation prize. What vice president was it that said, 'The vice presidency isn't worth a pitcher of warm spit?'"

"At that rate, losing out in the primary can't even be worth half a pitcher of warm spit."

"And if you lose because you're suspected of porking a missing girl, you don't even get to keep the pitcher."

"So we agree we've got to protect that woman in there," Reader said. "Trouble is, I'm not quite sure how to do it."

"Why not?" Owen said. "Just make her comfortable in one of those cells down the back hallway."

"We've got Dusty Rhodes' staties poking around. That's just like having Davison's people coming in and out. It's too risky. And I can't be sure one of my own people might not spring a leak."

"What about renting a motel room?"

"Same problem. I'd need round-the-clock guards. Right now, nobody knows she's come to us. I'd like to keep it that way."

"I know a place where she'd be safe. Mom's live-in nurse, Trish Elkins, grew up in Devil's Hollow with three brothers. She's living with them now while mom's in Shady Acres. I guarantee nobody would think of looking for Michelle out there."

"I can't lay this off on civilians."

"Those civilians include two Iraq vets and a coal miner. Nobody messes with the Elkins boys in Devil's Hollow. They're tough as woodpecker lips. And Trish can hold her own with any of them. If you need an official presence, I could spend my evenings out there. It's better than being a sitting duck at home. And if I'm out there, it would free up the guys you've got watching my place."

"You're not exactly trained for that kind of duty."

"The Iraq vets are. Pick a deputy you can trust and have him spell me. Blatt seems like a good man."

"I guess it might work. I could spring a little from my travel budget to cover room and board."

"That would help. Jobs have been scarce in that part of the county."

"You'll have to check with them, of course. It should be a short-term deal. Michelle ought to be safe after the primary."

"Unless Davison wins and ends up being his party's candidate for president."

"God help us," Reader said. "Maybe we can hurry up the process by closing out the investigation of Barney's death. You get on the lab boys and have them speed up the paint sampling."

"Already done," Owen said. "And I'll check on stolen car reports too. If we're right, the killers wouldn't have wanted to use a car that could be traced or that Barney might have recognized."

"I'll call the coroner and have him check whether Barney's tubes are still snipped."

"If word leaks out that Barney was sterile, and we could back it with the coroner's report, Michelle should be home free. There's no point in silencing her once the news is out."

Reader shook his head. "I've never liked leaking to the press. And we'd be meddling in a national election."

"Well, let's get our facts straight first. We always know where we can take a leak."

"I'll try to forget you said that. I gather you're thinking of O'Day, but he's another reason I'm press shy. This is all happening too fast. And he always seems to be a jump or two ahead of us."

"We're ahead of him on this," Owen said. "Both on the cause of the crash and the vasectomy. And some other things are coming together in strange ways."

"Like what?"

"Well, somebody in California just firebombed an office to destroy some past records. Does that remind you of anything?"

16

ROOM FOR ONE MORE

The hills surrounding the hollow where Trish Elkins was staying with her brothers were so steep that direct sunshine only reached their house between ten in the morning and four in the afternoon. The sun had already left the valley floor and was shining on the serrated edges of the surrounding ridges when Owen pulled his patrol car up between a blue Ford pickup and a red Taurus on the wide swath of gravel at the edge of the Elkins's front lawn.

A barrage of barks came from the screened-in front porch of the frame house as Trish appeared at the front door. "Hush, now, Bruiser," she said to the source of the barks, which was hidden behind the low porch wall.

When the barking stopped, Trish stepped through the screen door and waved to Owen and Michelle. She was wearing a tank top and a pair of cutoff jeans. Her bare feet gripped the planks of the porch steps like talons as she came down them to wrap a comforting arm around Michelle. "Don't you worry none, Hon," she said, "we're gonna take good care of you."

Owen followed the two women up the porch steps, through the screen door, and past a large brown and white boxer crouched on the plank floor. The dog blinked and growled as they passed.

Trish ushered Owen and Michelle into the living room and held the screen door open while she fixed the dog with a commanding stare. "I told you to hush, Bruiser. Hush and stay."

Bruiser shook his hindquarters and stretched out on the porch.

Inside the house, Trish led Michelle to a wood-framed sofa

186

whose long cushions were covered with a yellow floral pattern. "You'll be safe here," she said.

A broad-shouldered man in a T-shirt entered through a side door, pushing a chunkier version of himself in a wheelchair. "Double safe," he said. "Our grandpap built this place big enough to handle six kids and strong enough to discourage revenuers."

Both men had buzz cuts that left the hair on their heads barely longer than their chin stubble and sported lightning tattoos of the Army's Stryker Brigade on their right arms. The man in the wheelchair held a shotgun on his lap, which was covered with a quilt that fell straight over the front of the chair, revealing no outline of legs or feet.

The man behind the wheelchair left it to shake hands with Owen and Michelle. "I'm Trish's brother Vern."

"You can just call me Mary Ann," Michelle said.

The man in the chair lifted his hand from the shotgun in a half wave. "And I'm Vern's brother Virg. We're twins. The way you tell us apart is, Vern's the one with blue eyes."

Owen laughed. "That's easy enough to remember."

"Can I offer you folks some of our home brew?" Vern asked. "Best 'shine in the state."

"Vern," Trish said. "This man's a police officer."

"Man's under our roof," Vern said. "Just bein' hospitable."

Owen waved him off. "I'm not worried about either concocting or consuming liquor right now. But I am surprised to learn you've still got an operational still."

"There's a small one out back where pap's big still used to be," Trish said. "We make enough for private consumption, and nobody bothers us."

Virg patted the shotgun on his lap. "Nobody dast bother us. Ever."

"But your dad made enough for public consumption?" Owen asked.

"Oh, yeah," Vern said. "Time was, you could wring out our doormat and get enough liquor to put the whole damn family in jail."

"But nobody had the guts to try," Virg said. "Only one road

in and we could hear 'em comin'. Nobody wanted to chance a crossfire."

"Well, truth to tell," Vern said, "there was a couple of times we had to hide out back in the mine while the law broke down our still. But we always put it back together."

"So there's a mine out back too," Owen said.

"Oh, yeah," Vern said. "Like the still, it's still up and runnin'. Brother Vic's out there now, workin' a seam."

"Didn't know there were any of you independents left," Owen said.

"Ain't many of us. Can't keep up with them mechanized mines. But there's still a market for what we bring out."

"So the mine gives us a fallback position along with our access control and our firepower." Virg patted his shotgun again.

"And for added protection," Trish said, "there's Bruiser out front."

Responding to his name, Bruiser thumped his tail twice on the porch.

"Fightinest dog you'll ever see when he's defending our front porch," Virg said. "So, like we told the sheriff, you don't have to worry none about bein' safe here."

"And you're welcome to stay as long as you like," Trish said to Michelle.

"Absolute maximum stay would be twelve days," Owen said. "That's how long it is to the election, and there shouldn't be any need to stay beyond that."

"Does this have something to do with that missing girl, then?" Trish asked.

"We can't tell you why Mary Ann's here," Owen said. "And you can't tell anyone you have a visitor."

"Don't worry," Vern said. "We'll keep your whereabouts as secret as Trish's real hair color."

Trish's face turned almost as red as her hair. "Vern Elkins, you know perfectly well this *is* my real hair color."

"Didn't say it wasn't," Vern said. "Just meant to say this lady's secret is safe with us."

A slammed door at the rear of the house caused Michelle to

jump and Owen to reach for his pistol, but none of the Elkins moved a muscle.

"That'll be Vic, done with the day's minin'," Vern said.

A figure black with coal dust from his lanterned helmet to his work boots paused in the doorway. White circles surrounded his eyes, which had been protected by the goggles dangling from his neck.

"Don't get up on my account," he said. "You don't really want to shake my hand right now. I'll just head downstairs for a wash-up and come back up to socialize."

"We were just going to offer our guests some before-dinner drinks," Vern said.

"Unless I'm mistaken, one of our guests is wearing a sheriff's uniform," Vic said. "Might be best not to compromise his working day with a drink offer."

"We done explained about our private stock," Vern said. "And how we keep it private."

"You're doing our office quite a big favor," Owen said. "I'd have to be an ungrateful fool to look too closely at the labels on your liquor."

"You'd have to look real hard to find any labels," Vic said. "Us Elkins figure liquor is a little like bread. If it's legal to buy it, it ought to be legal to make it."

"Sounds reasonable to me," Owen said. "Particularly if you're not selling it."

"Not since Pap died," Vern said.

"Save a little for me. I'll be back in time for dinner," Vic said, disappearing down the steps to the cellar.

While they waited for Vic, Vern offered samples of the Elkins latest batch of sour mash. Owen accepted a jar out of politeness, but barely sipped it. The batch smelled like iodine but tasted a little like scotch. He'd never developed a taste for moonshine, and wanted to keep a clear head for guard duty later in the evening.

When Vic finished washing up, Trish served a dinner of fried chicken, okra, and mashed potatoes. After dinner, Michelle helped Trish clean up the dishes and retired early. Owen watched a wavering TV broadcast of the night game between the Reds and Cardinals. Vern apologized profusely for the poor reception and went to bed after the seventh inning stretch, saying that he had the early shift in the mine the next day.

When the game ended, Trish set Owen up with blankets and a pillow for the metal glider on the screened-in porch.

"No need to stay awake all night," she said. "No way anyone knows your friend is here. And if someone did know, they wouldn't be fool enough to rush us. And even if they tried, Bruiser there would sense them before they got very close."

At the sound of his name, Bruiser thumped his tail twice on the porch and wiggled his hindquarters.

Owen removed his shoulder holster and wedged it and his revolver between the cushions of the glider. Then he gathered a blanket around him and settled in to listen to the crickets chirping around a distant creek. The soothing sounds of the late spring night were soon obliterated by the squeak of the metal glider and Bruiser's snores, which alternated like an out-of-sync metronome to lull him to sleep.

He woke suddenly, jolted by some inner alarm. Beside him, Bruiser was up and alert, sniffing the night air. Something rustled at the side of the house. Bruiser bolted off the porch and headed for the sound.

Owen grabbed his gun and flashlight and followed Bruiser down the steps. A great clatter came from the side of the house. Owen rounded the corner, gun drawn, to find two tin garbage cans rolling toward the rear of the house. Bruiser outdistanced Owen's flashlight beam, chasing something into the dark.

Vern Elkins appeared at the rear corner of the house wearing skivvies and a T-shirt. He stopped the rolling cans, hoisted them upright, and raised both his hands over his head.

"Whoa there, Sheriff," he said. "Best put that gun away. It's only coons. We try to keep the garbage lids on tight, but they're crafty little devils."

Owen masked his embarrassment with a nervous laugh and stuck his gun into his belt.

"Even if Bruiser don't catch 'em, they'll be too scared to

190

return," Vern said. "Either way, that's likely all the excitement we'll get for tonight."

"That's all the excitement I need."

Owen returned to the porch to find Virg Elkins sitting in his wheelchair beside the glider, wearing the same plaid shirt he'd worn earlier with the same shotgun and quilt resting on his lap.

"Coons, huh?" Virg said. "We've tried everything to keep 'em away from the garbage, even lashing down the can tops. But nothing seems to work."

"Might try combination locks," Owen said. "Raccoons are crafty, but they've got no head for figures."

"You're funnin' me," Virg said.

"No, I'm pretty sure I read that somewhere."

"Joke book, most likely." Virg ran his tongue around the inside of his mouth. "Bruiser's a good watchdog, but he's prone to false alarms. We don't need to know every time a coon comes calling. Maybe tomorrow we'll lay some thread."

"Lay some thread?" Owen asked.

"Old moonshiner trick. Pap used it back when he was running hooch. You circle the house with black thread a little ways out. Keep it a couple of inches above the ground, in the underbrush. Tie in some tin cans every so often. Four-legged varmints lift their paws when they walk, so they don't usually disturb the thread. Men, though, tend to shuffle their feet, 'specially if they're sneakin' along, and trip the thread. Lets us know they're comin'. Little extra protection."

"I'm sorry to put you to all this trouble," Owen said.

"You kiddin'? Ain't had this much excitement since Pap took the west county trade away from the Akers boys."

"Well, I just want you to know we appreciate it."

"Beats cashing disability checks." Virg sighted down the barrel of the shotgun. "Why don't you get some sleep? I can watch the rest of the night."

Owen woke to the sizzle and smell of bacon. The sky was light blue and cloudless, but the sun hadn't yet cleared the surrounding hills. Virg Elkins still sat beside the glider, his eyes focused on the incoming road. It looked as if he hadn't moved since Owen dozed off.

"Morning," Owen said. "Did Bruiser make it back?"

"He's in the kitchen, begging for bacon. Reckon you'd best hurry if you want to beat him to it."

Owen washed up, had breakfast, and called Thad Reader. "Anything new on Barney's death?"

"Nothing. No word yet on the paint sample. And nobody reported a black car missing any time in the past three days."

"The accident happened around midnight. Whoever clipped Barney could have borrowed a car after the owners were asleep and returned it before they woke up. Something's been bothering me about the whole setup, though."

"You think he might not have been run off the road?"

"No. I'm pretty sure he was. I just can't believe his vasectomy was the motive."

"Why not?"

"Suppose Davison and his crew were responsible for Betty Sue's disappearance," Owen said. "Then she's under their control, dead or alive, and they'd have no reason to worry about paternity claims."

"But what if they didn't have anything to do with her disappearance?"

"Then they do have to worry about word of the vasectomy leaking," Owen said.

"Could be the news of the possible pregnancy was the straw that broke Barney's back. Maybe he wanted out."

"Or maybe he realized they'd try to silence his ex-wife and he wouldn't hold still for that."

"In any case," Reader said, "I think you're right that Barney's death makes it seem less likely that Davison's responsible for Betty Sue's disappearance. But we still can't rule out that possibility."

"Still, it's more likely that they'll be trying to find Barney's ex-wife and make sure no one knows about his vasectomy."

"So how are things out there?" Reader asked. "How is Michelle holding up?"

"She seems to be settling in. She'll be safe so long as we can keep this place a secret." Owen looked out the back window at the way the hollow narrowed down to the mine face. "Even if word leaks out, the Elkins place would be tough to storm without an army."

"I don't like to think about that. Maybe you ought to stay out there for the rest of the morning. I'd like to minimize our comings and goings. I'll send Phil Blatt out to spell you this afternoon. We need a presence there."

"You're the boss." Owen thought of Virg on the front porch with his shotgun. "The Elkins boys have taken a personal interest in Michelle's safety. How much trouble would it be to deputize one of them?"

"You're telling me they're armed. Is that it?"

"Virg has been carting a shotgun around."

"Virg is the twin who lost his legs in Iraq?"

"Yes."

"Is he likely to be trigger happy? I don't want any blowback on my office."

"If anything happens out here, it'll blow back whether or not you deputize Virg. And it'd be better for the Elkins boys if they had some sort of legal sanction. Better for their morale too. We're asking a lot of them."

"I know Vic. He's a good man. And you've always spoken highly of Trish. But the twins were always wild hares. Why don't I drive out myself this afternoon? I'll spell you a little myself and size up all of the Elkins siblings."

"Sounds like a plan."

Owen spent the morning helping Vic lay thread as a booby trap for anyone approaching the house through the wooded fields on either side of the approach road. They strung lengths of black thread two inches above the ground and attached them to nests of tin cans that would rattle if intruders tripped the strands.

"Pretty primitive," Vic said. "But it worked for Dad."

"I've got some surveillance cameras at home we can put to work on the approach road," Owen said. "Be a little more up to date."

"Can't hurt," Vic said. "If the sheriff is really expecting trouble, though, seems like it would be easier just to put the lady up in his jail."

"He considered that. Better for all concerned if nobody knows she came to us or where to look for her."

"So somebody is really after her." It was more a statement than a question.

"I know she sounds paranoid at times," Owen said. "But she has real reason to be afraid."

Vic attached a length of thread to a nest of tin cans and tied it off. "She'll be safe with us."

Thad Reader arrived at the Elkins house in Devil's Hollow a little before three o'clock that afternoon. Owen met him in the driveway.

"I see what you mean about this place being well protected," Reader said to Owen. "I wouldn't want to attack it. But I wouldn't want to be here if it was being attacked either."

"With any luck, that's not going to happen," Owen said. He took Reader inside and introduced him to Trish, Vern, and Virg Elkins.

"Where's Vic?" Reader asked.

"Out back in the mine," Trish explained.

"I appreciate what you folks are doing for us." Reader glanced at Virg's shotgun. "I can see that your guest should feel quite safe here."

"Except for some clatter last night, I feel quite safe," Michelle said.

"Coons got into the garbage cans," Vern said. "We chased them off."

"I hope that's as noisy as it gets." Reader turned to Owen. "I'll spell you for a while. Take a break and come back this evening, but make sure nobody follows you."

As Owen started to leave, Reader added, "Your ex-wife has been trying to reach you. Said she tried your home and cell numbers without any luck."

"There's no cell phone reception out here," Trish said.

"I told her I'd pass along the message when I saw you," Reader said. "She sounded a little upset."

"Call her right now," Trish said. "You can use our land line."

Judith answered Owen's call right away. "Owen, thank God," she said. "I was expecting to hear from you when you got my package. I put a note in it asking you to call."

"I haven't gotten it yet," Owen said. "It's been a while since I've been home."

"Are you sure? I've been tracking it. The express mail service said you got it this morning."

"I wasn't home last night." Owen felt the first stirrings of panic. "Maybe they left it on the porch."

"They were under orders to get your signature. And nobody else's."

Owen struggled to keep his voice calm. "Well, they didn't. What was in your note?"

"I told you I'd made two copies of the files. I thought I could help with your search."

Think, Owen told himself. Keep it together. "Where are you right now?"

"In my car. On my way to lunch."

"And where's your copy of the files?"

"In my trunk. All four boxes. Something's gone wrong, hasn't it?"

"I don't know. Have you left the other copy with your friend the sheriff?"

"Yes."

"All right. Listen to me. I want you to drive straight to the sheriff's office. Wait there until I find out what's happened. Don't go back to your office. And whatever you do, don't go home."

"Owen, you're scaring me."

"I want to scare you. There's a good chance the people who blew up my office have got your package. And your note."

"But how could they? They'd need your signature."

"These people haven't stopped at murder. I'm thinking forgery wouldn't present much of an obstacle."

195

"But they'd need some ID, at least."

"Maybe it's a false alarm. Maybe one of the guys working on my office signed for it."

"They shouldn't have been able to do that. This should never have happened. Why haven't you answered my calls?"

"I'm sorry. It's my fault. I should have been paying more attention."

"And why weren't you home last night?"

"I've been guarding a woman in protective custody. In a place with no cell phone reception."

"I'm sorry. The sheriff told me about the cell phone problem. I guess it's all a case of rotten timing."

Not the first time with us, Owen thought. But he had to keep his mind on the subject at hand. "Look. You made an extra copy of the files, so there's no lasting harm done. Not yet anyhow. I'm going to try to figure it all out. But I want to be sure you're safe while I'm doing it. Just get to your sheriff's office as quick as you can. I'll contact you there."

"I'm on my way."

"Problem?" Reader asked when Owen hung up the phone.

"Big problem," Owen said. "Sounds like someone intercepted those Tranalytics files Judith sent me. If that's the case, they not only have the files, but know she kept a copy."

"How'd that happen?"

"The express service must have left a delivery notice on my door while I was gone. The actual delivery required my signature, but someone evidently managed to have the packages released without it."

"Are you sure someone at your house didn't sign for the release?"

"That's what I'm going to find out." Owen dialed the cell number of Bill Muth, the handyman overseeing his office repair, and found that Uniflo Express had left a delivery notice on the door yesterday when the crew was on its lunch break. Since the notice was gone this morning, they assumed Owen had picked up the packages.

Owen slammed down the telephone receiver. "The packages

are gone. Picked up. Got to assume the people who picked them up are the same ones who killed Dan Thornton, burned down Ray Washburn's garage, and blew up my office. And now they'll be gunning for Judith."

"See what Uniflo Express has to say," Reader said.

Owen called the Uniflo Express office in Barkley and gave his name, address, and Judith's tracking number to the clerk who answered the phone.

"According to our records," the clerk said, "you picked up those packages as soon as our office opened this morning."

"Well, your records are wrong. I never picked up those packages."

"So you say. But someone with the proper identification picked them up."

"What identification was that?"

"I'm sorry, sir. I can't give out that information over the phone."

"Wait a minute. You can't give out a simple detail over the phone to the person the packages were addressed to, but you can give out the packages themselves to an imposter. Don't you think that's a little silly?"

"I'm sorry, sir. But I have no way of knowing you are who you say you are."

"And who do you say you are?"

"I'm Michael J. Burns. I'm the assistant manager in charge of this office."

"Well, Michael J. Burns, I'm Owen Allison, a deputy to Sheriff Thad Reader. The office you help to manage has given away important evidence in an ongoing murder investigation. I'll be in your office in a half hour expecting you to tell me exactly how that happened. And I'll expect better answers than you've been giving on the phone. Do you understand me?"

Owen hung up without waiting for a response, left Devil's Hollow, turned on his siren when he hit the main roads, and left it screeching all the way to the Uniflo Express office. He stormed into the office in his deputy sheriff's uniform, slammed his driver's license and deputy's ID on the counter, and demanded, "are you satisfied now that I'm Owen Allison?"

Michael J. Burns wilted like a week-old corsage. "You certainly appear to be Owen Allison."

"Then why did you give packages addressed to me to someone else?"

Burns ran his finger under his starched white collar. "The man had the delivery notice from your door and proper ID."

"What ID?"

"Your passport and a copy of your latest electric bill. He said his driver's license had been stolen."

"Actually, it was my passport that has evidently been stolen." Owen hadn't needed his passport in months and hadn't missed it. But it could have been taken any time since he'd last used it. Most likely by the man who bombed his office.

"There was no way for us to know that."

"The man with my passport. Did he look like me?"

"He didn't have a beard."

"So he didn't look like my passport photo."

"Not many people do look like their passport photo."

"So you must not have looked very closely."

Sweat stains started to blossom under the assistant manager's arms. "I guess not."

"Would you recognize the man again? Can you describe him to me?"

"He was a little shorter than you. Broader. With a crew cut and a bent nose."

"How old would you think he was?"

"Forty, I guess. I really don't know."

"Did he touch anything?"

"He signed the release form."

"I'll need to take that with me. I'd like you to initial it, make a copy, and give me the original. Can you do that?"

"I'm not supposed to do that."

"You're not supposed to give the sheriff's evidence to murder suspects, either." Owen took out his evidence kit and handed Burns a pair of latex gloves. "Wear these while you're making the copy."

The assistant manager disappeared into a back room. When he returned with a copy and the original release form, Owen sealed the original in a plastic folder, took a sample of the assistant manager's fingerprints, and asked him to call if he remembered anything else about the person who had picked up the packages.

A late spring downpour had started by the time Owen left the Uniflo Express office. As soon as he reached his car, he wiped the rainwater from his eyes and called the Elkins home. When Trish answered, he asked if she had room for one more refugee.

17

THE PICK-UP

Judith's voice on the phone came across as an even mixture of annoyance and anxiety. "I can't just run to some hideaway in West Virginia. I've got a life here in Palo Alto."

"You might not have a life anywhere if you don't hide somewhere," Owen said. "If you're here, we can protect you."

"Who's *we?*"

"Myself. Sheriff Reader and the rest of his deputies. We're already guarding one woman who's in hiding through the election."

"So is there some sort of two-for-one discount on shared rooms?"

"You won't have to share a room. There's plenty of space in the place I have in mind."

"I was kidding. I don't require deluxe accommodations. It's the distance and disruption that have me worried."

"We can get you here. And provide round-the-clock protection. I'm afraid there's nothing I can do about the disruption. I'm sorry I got you into this."

"Whoever killed Dan Thornton got us both into this."

It had been a long time since Judith had used the word "us" to link them as a couple. Or since Owen had thought of them that way. Too bad it only happened because of his screw-up. "No," he said. "It's my fault. I thought copying the files would be a safe job. I should have been paying more attention."

"Don't beat yourself up. When I sent the package you just happened to be in the backwoods with no cell phone service.

200

Is that where you intend to stash me?"

"It's not so bad as it sounds. Remember Trish Elkins, who's been taking care of Mom? She has a good-sized house in the northern corner of the county. Right now she's living there with her three brothers."

"I thought she was living with you and your mom."

"I gave her some time off and put Mom in a rest home."

"Oh, Owen. You promised Ruth you'd never do that."

"It's only temporary. So long as somebody was gunning for me and my files, I thought it best to get her out of the house. Did it just in time. She doesn't know a whole room of her house blew up."

"Your room blew up. Right. You haven't even been able to protect yourself. How do you expect to protect me?"

"I told you. Deputies are watching the Elkins house around the clock."

"How do I get from here to there?"

"Southwest Air has an early flight from San Francisco to Chicago and on to Pittsburgh and Columbus. We'll get you a ticket. I've already covered it with Sheriff Reader."

"Is that as close as you can get me to Barkley?"

"It's as close as we want you to get by plane. One of Reader's deputies will bring you your ticket. She'll be on your flight as well, with a ticket to Pittsburgh. You'll get off at Pittsburgh, where the sheriff will meet you. The deputy will continue on to Columbus, pretending to be you. I'll meet her in Columbus."

"Won't the airline check my ticket?"

"Only when you get on in San Francisco. Southwest doesn't have assigned seats. They'll just do a head count of passengers staying on from Pittsburgh to Columbus. By that time you'll have switched tickets with the deputy. The count will come out right because you'll be getting off at Pittsburgh while she stays on the plane."

"So the deputy will be taking my place."

"Her name is Mary Galardi. She'll bring you luggage and a change of clothes so you won't have to go home. We can get anything else you need after you arrive."

"I haven't said I'll make the trip."

"It's not safe for you to go home. Or to your office. There's no telling how long you'll be safe with your local sheriff. This isn't his fight. You'll be safe with us."

"I still have to get there in one piece. You're almost all the way across the country."

"Your local sheriff can protect you on the way to the airport. Sheriff Reader will pick you up on this end. Even if the details of your flight leak out, nobody will be expecting you to get off in Pittsburgh. Any trouble will happen in Columbus."

"With you and my doppelganger deputy."

"It would help if the deputy looks as much like you as possible. Can you have someone in the sheriff's office there take your picture and send it to us right away?"

"Where is the deputy now?"

"She's home packing. If everything works out, she should be in San Francisco tomorrow afternoon, so you could take the first flight out the next day."

"Pretty sure of yourself, aren't you? What if I say no?"

"Then Mary will pick up the files and bring them back here on the return flight."

"And leave me here with the sheriff."

"For as long as he'll have you. There'd be no time limit on your stay here."

"That could be a problem. I have a job, you know. And clients. How long do you think I'd have to stay in West Virginia?"

"It shouldn't be too long. You and the deputy will be bringing the Tranalytics files with you. If we find out what's in the files that makes them worth people's lives, we can make that information public. Once it's out in the open, the people who are trying to keep it secret will have no reason to come after you."

"But what if we can't figure out why anyone would want the files?"

"If we can't figure it out, there's a good chance whatever they're after went up in smoke with Ray Washburn's garage. Since they already have the copies you sent to me, they'll know there's nothing in them."

"In that case, I'm safe right now."

"There's a fifty-fifty chance you're safe right now. But those aren't good odds if you're gambling with your life. I wouldn't want to bet on them."

"So I shouldn't have to stay any longer than it takes to examine your files."

"No. We can get you back home as soon as we feel you're safe."

"I looked through some of those files when I was having them copied. Nothing jumped out at me."

"We'll both be looking through the files this time. Together. If you like, we can get you a return ticket right now. Suppose we say you'll be here four days. It's easy enough to switch your Southwest ticket if we finish early."

"I still haven't said I'll do it. Who's paying for this, anyhow?"

"The sheriff's office."

"How does he justify that?"

"He's a good friend. But all this is a part of his investigation of an attempted murder."

"Whose murder?"

"Mine."

"Oh, God. Of course. I keep making this all about me, but they're your files. You're still in someone's crosshairs."

"Don't worry about me. Think of this as a four-day vacation. You used to take crossword puzzles to solve on our vacations. We'd work on them together, remember? Those files are just another kind of puzzle."

"With our lives as prizes. That's a little too much pressure for a vacation. But if your deputy is willing to take the risk of traveling as my double, I ought to be willing to make the trip myself. All right. I'll give you four days."

Owen was pulling into the parking garage of the Columbus International Airport when Thad Reader called. "We're on our way from the Pittsburgh airport to the Elkins place," Reader said. "I've got Judith and the files with me."

"So everything went off okay."

"So far. If there's any trouble, it's likely to be at your end."

"I'm just pulling into the airport garage right now. Mary's plane is due to arrive in about a half hour."

"Pick a parking spot where you can't be shot from behind. Are you wearing your vest?"

"It was a little hot on the ride up. I've got it with me."

"Get it on. It's not going to do you any good in your trunk. Mary will be wearing hers. What about the welcome package?"

Owen patted the dozen red roses sticking out from the package on the passenger seat. "Right next to me."

Judith came on the phone. "Owen, everything went really well. I've got all the files with me."

Owen was always surprised at how happy he was to hear her voice. "That's great."

"Mary was a big help. I'm counting on you to protect her."

"If anything goes down, she's likely to be the one protecting me. She's the professional."

"Well, be careful. Both of you. I want to see you tonight."

"Don't worry. I want to see you too." Owen signed off and found a parking place next to the back wall of the garage. If there was trouble, at least he wouldn't have to watch his rear.

Owen stood by the Information Desk in the baggage claim area watching the carousel that had been announced for the arriving baggage on the Southwest flight from San Francisco by way of Chicago and Pittsburgh. Although the plane had landed, neither the passengers nor the bags had arrived at the carousel yet.

Passengers from another flight were picking up the last of the bags from the next carousel over. After it had been picked clean, a tall man in a dark suit stood staring at the empty maw where the conveyor belt had stopped delivering bags.

The three carousels nearest to Owen were empty now, and the only people nearby were the man watching the stalled carousel, a janitor pushing a broom, and the elderly woman behind the Information Desk. No one appeared to be watching him. He shifted the spray of roses in his arms, trying to look unconcerned.

Arriving passengers started to trickle in and cluster around the designated carousel. He didn't see Mary Galardi at first, but then heard a voice call, "Owen. Over here."

The woman who called didn't look like his ex-wife Judith or deputy Mary Galardi, but some mismatched amalgam of the two. She had the deputy's stocky build, a bulky beige jacket that Owen knew was hiding a Kevlar vest, and Judith's short dark hair and bangs. Large round sunglasses with chartreuse rims completed the disguise.

Owen hurried to meet Mary and hand over the conical spray of flowers. She said, "How nice," and cradled them in the crook of her left arm, grasping the tip of the cone in her right hand. Then she threw her left arm around Owen's neck and planted a lingering kiss on his lips.

The kiss surprised Owen, who was just starting to enjoy it when some instinct told him to pull away. "Easy there," he whispered. "We're divorced, you know."

Mary smiled. "What I hear, there's still some spark there."

"Where did you hear that?"

"Where do you think?"

A buzzer sounded and a rotating red light announced the arrival of baggage as the carousel began its slow rotation. "Better get a baggage cart," Mary said. "I've got three big suitcases."

"I thought the files came off in Pittsburgh," Owen whispered.

"They did, but we thought it should look as if they came all the way to Columbus so we checked a batch of old files all the way through."

Owen tracked down a baggage cart and returned to find Mary pointing at a large suitcase revolving on the carousel. "There's the first one," she said.

Owen grabbed the handle of the suitcase, which was so heavy it nearly pulled him onto the carousel. He finally wrestled it into submission and transferred it to the baggage cart.

"Not much heavier than a loaded coal hopper," he said.

Mary just smiled. "You said you wanted files."

"I was expecting paper, not carpenter's tools."

Owen loaded two other large suitcases and Mary's roll-aboard onto the baggage cart and started pushing it toward the parking garage. Mary walked beside him, cradling the roses. When they left the baggage claim area and no one could hear, he asked, "What's in those bags, anyhow?"

"Old phone books, dead files, shredded memos, scrap paper. You'd be surprised at the amount of spare paper you can find in an office that's supposed to be computerized."

Owen pushed the cart into the parking garage and headed for the row of cars against the back wall where he'd parked his patrol car. The only other signs of life in the garage were an attendant in the exit booth and a black Mercedes entering from the opposite corner. Owen had just turned the baggage cart up the back row when the black Mercedes turned down the parallel row to their right and headed slowly toward them.

"That Mercedes has passed up two parking spaces and he's not in an exit row," Owen said.

"Could be he just wants a space closer to the terminal," Mary said. "He's going pretty slow. See if you can roll this baggage cart just fast enough to keep that concrete pillar between them and us."

Owen picked up his pace slightly so that the Mercedes was hidden behind the wide support column as it approached.

"Could be nothing," Mary said. "If it looks like trouble, I'll yell and you dive under the nearest parked car."

Owen kept his speed even with the oncoming Mercedes so that it stayed hidden behind the pillar. "What'll you be doing?"

"Don't worry about me. I've got all those suitcases to hide behind."

The Mercedes lurched forward, leaving the cover of the column with an ominous looking barrel thrust out of its passenger window.

"Duck!" Mary shouted.

As Owen dove for the garage floor, a burst of flame spurted from the muzzle in the Mercedes window. Above him, a dozen roses scattered in the air as the Glock he'd hidden in the tip of the floral arrangement barked four times.

Owen rolled on his side under a white van, unholstered his revolver, and fired at the tires of the accelerating Mercedes. The car veered and swerved, crashing into a row of parked cars. Two more shots rang from Mary's Glock and the crashed auto answered with a popping noise and a screeching horn.

Mary rolled the baggage carrier forward, keeping it between her and the Mercedes. Owen crawled out from under the van, and they both advanced on the crashed car, using the luggage as a shield.

The garage attendant poked his head out of the exit booth as a crowd collected at the garage entrance. Mary called out "We're police! Everyone stay back!"

Owen peeked over the luggage and trained his revolver on the Mercedes. The snout of an Uzi poked through the passenger window, pointing skyward. Gasoline dripped from the car's rear and the horn continued to honk.

They rolled the baggage carrier closer to the passenger side of the car. The passenger with the Uzi leaned forward involuntarily as the air bag pinioning him collapsed. From the look of the wound in the side of his head, he wouldn't be moving much more on his own.

The driver's door swung open and more shots rang out. Owen and Mary both ducked behind the baggage carrier as bullets thunked into the luggage. Owen slid around the side of the carrier in time to see the driver disappear through the door leading to the terminal. He gave chase with his revolver drawn, but skidded to a stop inside the terminal when uniformed men holding guns confronted him with a human barrier. He laid down his revolver and raised both hands in the air as the barrier closed around him. The driver was nowhere to be seen.

The local Franklin County sheriff interviewed Owen and Mary, then sequestered them in a car rental office for two hours while he checked their stories. The office window looked out on the parking garage, where photographers snapped pictures, officers interviewed witnesses, and an EMT team transferred the Mercedes passenger into a body bag.

207

Mary trembled as she watched paramedics load the body bag into a waiting ambulance. "I may have been too quick on the trigger."

"He was leveling an Uzi at us," Owen said. "If you hadn't acted, we'd both be dead now."

"But I killed a man."

Owen took her hands in his to stop the trembling. "Better him than us."

The Franklin County sheriff, a ruggedly handsome man built like a fireplug with a nametag that read Bettencourt, entered the room. Stroking his brown moustache with his index finger, he said, "Looks like you two are exactly who you claim to be."

Owen released Mary's hand. "Took you a while to come to that conclusion."

"We're funny that way. When people shoot up our airport and cause a panic, we like to be sure what's going on. You've been deputized recently, right? You're not a career cop. I hope you're not trying to tell us how to do our job."

"He's not," Mary said. "We're both still a little shaky."

"I can understand that," the sheriff said. "We needed time to sort out the crime scene. And I wanted to talk directly to your boss. Never met him, but he's got a good rep that reaches beyond your state borders. He vouched for the both of you."

"Are we free to go, then?" Owen asked.

"Before you do, we need to get some jurisdictional matters straight. Transportation Security Administration will want a crack at all this. They need to assure themselves that neither you nor those guys in the Mercedes are terrorists."

"Oh, for Christ's sake," Owen said. "My boss has vouched for us. And those men weren't terrorists. Like I told you, they were after some files they thought we were bringing in."

"But you don't know what it is in those files that makes them valuable?" the sheriff asked.

"I haven't had a chance to examine them. But we do know somebody has already killed one person, burned down another's garage, and booby-trapped my office trying to destroy them."

"How'd they know you were bringing the files into this

airport this evening?"

"We don't know that either. These guys seem to keep one jump ahead of us."

"Well, TSA will be impounding the Mercedes," the sheriff said. "They'll probably want to take charge of your suitcases as well."

Owen smiled at the thought of federal agents examining outdated phone books for evidence of conspiracy. "They're welcome to them. But I don't think they'll find the contents very enlightening. The real files got off at Pittsburgh. Those suitcases are just decoys."

"Like you and the lady here."

Owen put his hand on Mary's arm, which had stopped trembling. "Yeah. Like that."

"So that guy in the body bag and the one that got away weren't exactly one jump ahead of you."

"Not exactly, no. Not this trip."

"Assuming those two guys weren't terrorists, I'm next in line to investigate. This county is my jurisdiction, and I want to find the guy that got away." The sheriff pointed at Owen. "Your boss said you could be available to help us."

"I'll do what I can," Owen said.

"Off the top of your head, is there anything special we should be looking for?"

"Well, if one of those guys bombed my office, the bomber looked to be left-handed. And he stomped my surveillance equipment underfoot, so we were thinking there might still be traces on the soles of his shoes."

"Like a nail in a tire," the sheriff said.

"It's worth looking for. Who knows whether the guy would be wearing the same pair of shoes, but we could get lucky, and it could tie him into earlier crimes."

"We'll look into it. Have you thought any more about IDing the missing driver?"

"I can't ID him," Owen said. "All we saw was his back. I was about ten steps too slow."

"Don't worry about it. So were the TSA guys." The sheriff

started for the door, then stopped and addressed Owen. "Your boss says you're pretty good with accident scenes. Would you like to check this one out before they haul the Mercedes away?"

"Nothing very mysterious about what happened here," Owen said. "But I'd be happy to take a closer look at the car."

"Good. Follow me." The sheriff led the way out of the car rental office into the parking garage. "I'm afraid the front seat's kind of messy," he said as they approached the wrecked Mercedes.

"That's okay." Owen knelt to look at the two rear tires, which had been pierced by his shots from under the van. As he rose, a scratch on the left rear fender caught his eye. "Could you have your photographers take some shots of this?" he asked.

"The fender? You see something there?"

"This horizontal scrape is about the height of a motorcycle's saddlebags." Owen traced his finger along the scar. "There's a chance this car was a part of at least one other murder attempt."

18

A BLOWN COVERLET

The TSA and the Franklin County Sheriff's Office didn't release Owen and Mary Galardi until well after midnight. Mary slept through most of the drive to her home in Barkley, and it was nearly four a.m. when Owen pulled his patrol car into the parking lot behind Sheriff Reader's office. The sheriff was waiting for him.

"How's Mary?" Reader asked as soon as Owen closed his car door.

"Tired and frazzled. Still shaken up. I think she'll be okay."

"And you. How are you?"

"About the same as her. Even though I didn't kill anyone."

"Shoot-outs were never a part of your job description. Got time for a little debriefing?"

"So long as we can keep it brief. I still have to get out to the Elkins place."

"I've got Phil Blatt out there. You can spend the night here in Barkley. Where I can watch you."

"You think I need watching?"

"Somebody just tried to kill you."

"They were after the files. Not me."

"You've been in the way both times they tried for your files. They didn't seem to care whether they got you or the paperwork."

"Well, I don't have any files with me now. You've got the real ones and the fakes are in Columbus with the TSA."

"Whoever's after them doesn't know that."

"Maybe we should point them to the TSA."

"I've got a few thoughts about that." Reader put a hand on Owen's shoulder. "Let's go inside." Inside his office, Reader poured himself a steaming mug of coffee, got Owen a Coke, and then lowered himself into his swivel chair, opened his bottom desk drawer, and propped a boot on it. "Been on the phone with Franklin County. Dead man's name was Sanford Towle. Muscle for hire out of Cincinnati."

Owen shrugged. "Name means nothing to me. What was left of his face didn't look familiar either."

"Sheriff Bettencourt is tracking down his known associates. Turns out the Mercedes was reported stolen a week ago in Cincinnati."

"No surprise there. I guess Mr. Towle didn't want to risk scratching up his own Mercedes."

"Speaking of scratches, the lab came back with a report on the paint sample we took off Linton Barney's saddlebags. The Mercedes you shot up in Columbus is on the list of models using that paint."

"I had the Columbus cops take a sample from a scratch on the fender of the Mercedes. I'm guessing it will match Barney's motorcycle. It's just too much of a coincidence otherwise."

Reader blew softly over the rim of his coffee mug. "But if it matches, what's the connection between the two incidents?"

"I've been racking my brain over that all the way from Columbus. Why would the same guys who killed Barney come after me and those Tranalytics files?"

"Maybe they were really after you and not the files. Maybe they're worried you'll figure out how Barney was killed."

Owen shook his head. "Doesn't make sense. If Barney's killers were following me and not the files, the open road between Barkley and Columbus was a lot easier place to stage a hit than an airport parking garage. They had to be following the files."

Reader sipped his coffee. "I came to that same conclusion. So what we need to do now is let them know TSA has the files they want."

"How do we do that? Rent a billboard? Take out a personal

ad? Fit me out with a stenciled T-shirt?"

"I've been working on that with Sheriff Bettencourt. I assume the people who want your files are still listening to your home phone. You and I are going to spend the rest of the night at your place. At ten-thirty tomorrow morning, you're going to call Sheriff Bettencourt on your home phone to ask how his investigation of the shooting is going. He'll tell you he hasn't made much progress, but he's close to getting an ID on the dead man. He'll also tell you TSA is sitting on your luggage."

"I like it," Owen said.

"Naturally, you'll argue that you need the luggage badly. That they hold files you need that may contain the key to a murder case. But he'll say he's sorry. There's nothing he can do. The TSA is making a federal case out of it."

"So we sic the bad guys onto the TSA."

"I doubt that they'll be foolish enough to try to get the files from the TSA. Much more sensible to wait until they're released to you. Sheriff Bettencourt will tell the TSA what we're up to. And suggest they hang onto the luggage for a while."

"In spite of my continued protests."

"Your plaintive requests will go unanswered. For a while at least. If it works, it should buy us a little breathing room. You'll still need to be careful, but they probably won't make a move until you're back in contact with the files."

"Pretty slick. Assuming they're still listening to my phone."

"No reason why they wouldn't be." Reader set his mug down on his desk. "All right. Let's get you home so you can be fresh for your ten-thirty call to Sheriff Bettencourt."

"I'd been looking forward to catching up with Judith at the Elkins place. But it's way too late for that. It'll be good to be sleeping in my own bed for a change."

Owen slept until nine-thirty the next morning, pulled on jeans and a work shirt, and came downstairs to find Thad Reader sipping coffee and chatting with the workers replacing the window in his office. He fixed a cup of tea and joined the sheriff in his living room as a marked patrol car passed slowly down the street.

"They've been cruising by about four times an hour at random intervals," Reader said.

"Sounds like overkill," Owen said.

"You better get it through your head somebody's trying to kill you. That's not going to happen on my watch."

They shared the newspaper and sipped their drinks in silence until it was time to call Sheriff Bettencourt in Columbus. Bettencourt answered on the first ring, and explained on the speakerphone that the Transportation Security Agency had taken charge of the luggage involved in the previous evening's shootout.

Owen laughed off the implication that the luggage might be connected to any sort of terrorism, while Reader insisted that the suitcases contained files that were vital to an ongoing murder investigation.

Bettencourt was sympathetic, but made it plain that the issue was out of his hands. Finally, he said, "Look guys, I understand you need the files. I'll let you know as soon as TSA releases the luggage to my office."

"I hope so," Reader said. "I've got several people on my staff itching to look at them." He wanted to let anyone listening know that Owen wouldn't be the only person examining the files.

"I hear you," Bettencourt said. "But you've got to understand we're dealing with the federal government here, so I wouldn't hold my breath."

"Anything new on the shooter?" Owen asked.

"Car was stolen. Wiped clean of prints, so that's pretty much a dead end. Driver got away clean. Shooter wasn't local, but I expect we'll have a firm ID later today."

"Well, keep us informed," Reader said.

"Will do."

Reader gave a "thumbs up" sign as Owen hung up the phone. "Bettencourt seems like a good man."

"Funny. He said the same thing about you."

"Well, that settles it."

Owen had barely taken his hand off the phone when it rang.

He picked up the receiver to hear his mother's voice.

"Owen, are you all right?" Ruth asked. "The TV this morning said local deputies were involved in a shooting in Columbus."

"I'm all right, Mom."

"They didn't give the names on the TV. But Pluma said she recognized you."

"I was there, but I'm all right. Really. I'm here with the sheriff now. You're on the speakerphone. He'll tell you there are no holes in me that I wasn't born with."

"That's right, Mrs. Allison," Reader said.

"Look," Owen said. "I'll stop by and visit you. Let you see for yourself."

"When? When will you stop by?"

"As soon as he gets his uniform on, Mrs. Allison," Reader said.

"That's good. Because I've got things to tell him. About the election. Only I keep forgetting."

"I'll want to hear about the election too," Reader said. "So I'll come along with Owen. We'll hang up now. See you soon."

Reader reached across Owen to hang up the phone, then put a warning finger to his lips. "Get your uniform on. We'll go see your mom together." He pointed to the front door, indicating that he wanted to talk outside, out of the range of any listening devices. Owen nodded and followed him out.

As soon as they cleared the front porch, Owen said, "I've been planning to go to the Elkins place. Maybe we ought to take two cars."

"I've been thinking about that," Reader said. "You're a hot item right now, and I want to be sure no one follows you out there. So go get your uniform on and take a change of clothes with you. We'll go see your mother together. Then I'll arrange to have Phil Blatt trade places with you."

"How will that work?"

"He's at the Elkins place right now. I'll set it up so that he drives an unmarked car to your mom's rest home. He'll park it out back in the employee's lot and come inside wearing civilian clothes. Then he'll change into his uni and leave with

215

me, while you change into street clothes and take Phil's car out to the Elkins place."

"Sounds complicated. You think that's really necessary? I thought we'd taken some of the heat off me with that Bettencourt call."

"We don't know for sure whether anyone was listening to the call. And even if they were, we don't know that you'll get a free pass so long as the feds keep your luggage. Besides, you're not my only worry. We've got two important women stashed at the Elkins place. I don't want anyone following you out there."

"You're right. I should have thought of that myself."

Owen changed into his uniform and packed a duffel bag with a change of clothes and his overnight kit. Thad Reader drove them both to Shady Acres, where he parked his patrol car in the loading zone in front of the main entrance to minimize the exposure of his passengers on their way in and out.

Ramona, the Shady Acres manager, came out from behind the reception desk and started to issue a warning about parking in the loading zone. She stopped abruptly and retreated when she saw Thad Reader, who had threatened to decertify the rest home on the day Ruth had wandered off the grounds unattended.

"We'll only be a short time," Reader said, edging past Ramona.

"Is anything wrong?" she asked.

"That's what we're here to find out," Reader answered, heading for the residents' quarters.

Ruth threw open her door almost before Owen had a chance to knock and hugged him fiercely.

Owen lifted his mother off her feet and walked her back into her room to allow Reader to enter. Finally breaking her embrace, he said, "It's all right, Mom."

"But what happened?" Ruth asked. "The TV accounts weren't clear."

"We didn't want them to be too clear," Reader said.

Ruth kept one hand on Owen's arm. "But someone was shooting at you."

Owen spread his arms wide. "As you can see, they missed."

"But why were they shooting at you in the first place?"

"It's complicated, Mom. They wanted something they thought was coming in on the evening flight."

"Someone was killed." Ruth stopped, searching her memory for the details of the story. "Someone else got away."

"That's right," Owen said.

"Will that person still be trying to kill you?"

"We don't think so, Mrs. Allison," Reader said. "Owen doesn't have the materials they were after. But just to be sure, we're taking him to a safe house for a while."

"A safe house? Where? Will I be able to see you?"

"It's not far, Mom. I'll stay in touch."

Ruth's face clouded. "How long will this be?"

"It should all be sorted out by election time," Owen said.

"Election time? But that's more than a week away." Ruth frowned. "Oh my goodness. I've been forgetting so much lately. I've been trying to reach you. You remember Pluma, don't you, Owen?"

"Of course. One of the women I drove to the courthouse to vote."

"Well, Pluma blabbed about our trip. Told everyone we'd been to vote. Not shopping like we said we'd been doing. But someone had already voted in her place. So you see, she exposed my…" Ruth stopped, searching for an elusive word. "…my coverlet."

"Blew your cover, you mean," Owen said.

"Oh, Owen. You know I've been having problems with nouns. Let's just call it a coverlet. It sounds more feminine."

"It's whatever you want it to be, Mrs. Allison," Reader said. "How did the staff here react to the news?"

"They've been perfectly nice about it. I think they must have remembered your little speech about keeping me happy. But they've made it plain they will order absentee ballots for anyone else that wants to vote."

"They don't want anyone else finding out somebody has already cast their ballot," Owen said.

"Yes. I understand," Ruth said. "But with my coverlet in

tatters, there's not much reason for me to stay here. Maybe it's time for me to go home."

"That's not a good idea, Mom." Owen scrambled for a reason, knowing his still unrepaired office would upset her. "I won't be at home to look after you."

"There's Trish."

"I promised Trish a paid vacation. Through the election. I could check with her, I guess."

"Maybe there's still some work you could do here," Reader said. "Are you sure you can't find anyone else who'd like to take a voting trip to the courthouse?"

"It's difficult. I invited a few of my bingo buddies, but they ordered absentee ballots when the staff here said they'd do it for them."

"They just want to cover their behinds," Owen said. "They'll collect all the completed ballots and you can bet they'll scrap any they've already submitted."

A knock on the door interrupted Owen's speech. Reader opened it and Phil Blatt entered, wearing jeans and a windbreaker and carrying a duffel bag that matched Owen's. He nodded to Owen and Reader and said, "It's good to see you again, Mrs. Allison."

Confusion covered Ruth's face. "I'm sorry. Have we met?"

"It's Phil Blatt, Mom," Owen said. "He's the deputy who found you wandering on Jefferson Street."

"You probably didn't recognize me without my uniform," Blatt said.

"I know a lot of Blatts." Ruth blinked, still uncertain. "But my memory… I can't remember their names. Are you related?"

"You probably know Barbara Blatt, ma'am. She's my cousin. Lives out German Ridge."

Ruth smiled. "Oh, yes. I know Barbara."

Reader took Blatt's duffel bag and showed him to the bathroom. "Maybe you ought to change."

As Blatt closed the bathroom door, Reader explained to Ruth, "He'll be changing into his uniform so he can leave with me. Anyone watching will assume he's Owen. Then Owen can slip out later in his civilian clothes."

"But that man doesn't look at all like Owen," Ruth said. "He's blond. And thin. And shorter. And he doesn't have a beard."

"I've parked close to the entrance," Reader said. "He'll be wearing his Mounties hat. And a beard."

"And walking on tiptoe, I hope," Ruth said. "If you're taking all these precautions, you must believe Owen is still in danger."

"We're taking no chances," Reader said. "Owen will visit with you a little longer and then change out of his uniform and go out the back way."

"Maybe we can work out something with one of those friends of yours with absentee ballots while I'm here," Owen said. "Maybe mark their ballots so we can challenge later if they don't show up in the primary results."

Phil Blatt emerged from the bathroom, wearing his uniform and sporting a greasepaint beard and moustache.

"Oh my God," Ruth said. "That beard wouldn't fool a blind man."

Blatt raised and lowered his eyebrows rapidly. "Worked for Groucho."

"We only have to cover a short distance to my car," Reader said. "Anyone watching will be far away. Best case, they'll just figure Owen is having a bad hair day. Worst case, they'll figure he's still inside. He still should be able to sneak out the back."

"Don't see we have much to lose," Owen said as Reader left with Blatt. "Mom, why don't you contact one of your friends and we'll see what we can do with their absentee ballot."

Owen wasn't prepared for the bingo buddy who appeared in response to his mother's call. Balding and unshaven, with a stump of a left leg that poked out ahead of his wheelchair, he smelled of stale whisky and bed sweat and was evidently just as surprised to see Owen as Owen was to see him.

"Ruth, honey, when you invited me to your room, I expected we'd be alone." His eyes bulged under wiggling eyebrows as he raised and lowered his stump suggestively.

"Warren, you old goat, this is my son Owen. Owen, this

is Warren Stanton."

"Well, son Owen," Stanton said, "I see by your uniform you're a lawman. It's a good thing you can't arrest me for what I've been thinking."

"I don't want to know what you've been thinking," Owen said, although anything approaching the fringes of the man's thoughts made him uneasy. "Unless it involves the current election."

"Ruth asked me to bring my absentee ballot." Stanton squirmed in his wheelchair so he could remove a creased and wrinkled ballot from his hip pocket. "Want to buy my vote for sheriff?"

"I'm afraid I'm not on that ballot. And neither is my boss. And since buying and selling votes is a criminal offense, I'll pretend I didn't hear that offer."

"So, what's the catch?" Stanton asked.

"No catch," Owen said. "I just want you to vote your ballot. Then you and I will initial it so we can identify it later."

"You think it might not make it through the system?" Stanton asked.

"I'll deliver it myself. I want to make sure it gets counted. And I want to know if it doesn't. And I'd like you to keep quiet about all of this."

Stanton grinned. "So if you won't buy my vote, maybe you'd like to buy my silence."

Ruth was outraged. "Warren, I'm surprised at you."

Stanton continued to grin. "No need to be. Your boy here don't look surprised."

"All right," Owen said. "What will it take for you to cooperate and keep your mouth shut?"

"Vote for sheriff usually goes for around ten dollars. I reckon twenty should do me right fine."

"Owen," Ruth said. "I'm so sorry. I thought the sleaze was all an act."

Stanton pouted. "Like I don't have no feelings."

"It's okay, Mom." Owen took out his wallet and was about to extract a twenty when his mother stopped him.

220

"I'll get this Owen. As a police officer, you shouldn't be buying either votes or silence." Ruth fished a twenty from her purse and gave it to Stanton. "I'll win it back from him at Bingo within a week."

Owen thanked Ruth and asked Stanton, "How do you happen to know the going rate for a vote for sheriff?"

"Got a cousin in Mingo County who votes the obit pages."

"Sounds a lot like voting the graveyard," Owen said.

"Safer. You know nobody will have time to take fresh obit names off the voter rolls."

"Something to think about," Owen said. What he thought about was scanning obituary notices for the past two months, sorting them by precinct, and posting an alphabetized list at each polling place. "For now, though, I'd just like you to vote your own ballot."

"Just normal like?"

"Just like normal. Except I'd like you to pick one of the positions with a space for a write-in candidate and write your own name in."

"Hot damn, now that sounds like fun." Stanton scanned the ballot quickly. "What the hell, might as well go all out. I got no strong feelings for Halstead or Davison. Davison took shit because everyone thought he was screwing a woman his best friend was actually bonking. Now that his best friend is dead, I guess I could give him a sympathy vote. But hell's fire, I'd make a better president than both of them guys put together." He entered his own name in the space reserved for a write-in presidential candidate. "Maybe I ought to campaign."

"Too bad there's so little time left before the primary," Owen said.

"Hell, I'd wrap up the cripple vote just by throwing my crutches in the ring." Stanton scanned the rest of the ballot. "Sure you don't have a favorite candidate you want to recommend?"

"No. Just vote however you want. And remember to keep quiet about all this."

Stanton tapped the breast pocket where he'd stashed Ruth's twenty. "No need to worry about me. If I'm bought, I stay

221

bought." He bent over his ballot, filled in a few squares, looked up, and said, "All done."

"That was quick," Owen said. "Now initial it and I'll do the same."

Ruth's phone rang as Owen bent over Stanton to initial his ballot. Her face clouded over as she listened to the caller. She said, "Just a minute," put her hand over the mouthpiece, and turned to Owen. "It's Ramona at the front desk. There's a man in the lobby who says he's been sent to take me to see you."

Owen tried not to show the alarm he felt. "Stall. Have Ramona ask him if anything's wrong."

As Ruth repeated the question into the mouthpiece, Owen punched Thad Reader's number into his own cell phone.

"The man says he doesn't know if anything's wrong," Ruth said. "He's just been sent to pick me up."

"Have Ramona tell him you're dressing and will be out in five minutes," Owen said, then added, "tell her she should not, I repeat *not*, give him your room number."

"Oh, she'd never do that." Ruth's expression cycled from confused to fearful. "Owen, what's going on?"

"I don't know, Mom. Just deliver the message."

While Ruth promised Ramona she'd be out in five minutes, Owen described the situation to Reader. "I don't know what's happening, but I think you ought to get a couple of squad cars over here right away. Seal off the entrance and send somebody in."

"Sounds like the guy's got your mom measured for a hostage outfit," Reader said. "Stall him. Hunker down and don't do anything foolish. We'll be there in five minutes."

Ruth hung up her phone. "I don't understand."

"Thad Reader's coming to check it out." Owen turned to Warren Stanton. "In the meantime, I'd like to borrow your wheelchair."

Stanton shrunk visibly, leaking bravado like a punctured balloon. "I'm sorry. I can't get up without help."

Owen put his arms around Stanton's waist and pulled him upright against his chest. Then he pivoted like a clumsy dancer and sat the one-legged man on Ruth's bed.

Stanton shook his head. "Forty years in the mines without a scratch, and I lose a leg to diabetes. How fucking dumb is that?"

Owen sat in Stanton's wheelchair and shucked his shoes and socks. Then he took off his uniform jacket and rolled his pant legs above his knees. "Mom, did you bring that hooded robe of yours?"

"Owen, what on earth are you doing?" Ruth asked.

"I'm going to make sure that guy doesn't get away before the sheriff arrives," Owen said.

Ruth handed Owen a quilted robe emblazoned with yellow daisies. "You're not going to do something foolish?"

Owen stood to put on the hooded robe, draped a white towel around his neck, and then sat in the wheelchair and used Stanton's lap robe to cover his bare knees.

"Sure looks foolish to me," Stanton said.

Owen removed his gun belt and hid his revolver under the lap robe. "Foolish enough not to seem threatening. That's the idea at least."

"Owen, you're not going out there," Ruth said. It was half a question, half a command.

"Don't worry, Mom. This business has got to stop." He propelled the chair out of his mother's room and down the hallway, stopping at the door to the reception area. Five minutes had passed since he'd called Reader. Where was the sheriff?

Owen maneuvered the chair through the door. The only person besides Ramona in the reception area was a man reading a newspaper in an easy chair across the room. The man glanced up as Owen wheeled in, evidently took him for a patient, and returned to the paper. Owen recognized him immediately. It was the same man who had been waiting at the baggage carousel the previous night for luggage that never arrived. Most likely, he'd been the driver of the Mercedes.

Owen wheeled the chair along the opposite wall and pretended to examine a rack of pamphlets. Where the hell was Reader?

"Excuse me. Do I know you?" Ramona addressed Owen from behind the reception desk.

The man in the chair looked up.

Shit. Owen gave his chair a mighty push toward the center of the reception area, threw off his lap robe, and leveled his revolver at the man's stomach. "Just keep both hands on that newspaper and sit still."

Ramona gasped.

With his free hand, Owen threw back the hood of his robe. "It's all right, Ramona. The sheriff is on his way."

The man in the chair suppressed a chuckle.

"Just keep both hands on that newspaper or I'll shoot," Owen said.

"Oh, I don't think you'll shoot," the man said. "You're a temp agency rent-a-cop without the training or the stomach for what you're into."

"Just keep your hands where I can see them. At this range I can hardly miss."

The man held the newspaper in front of him and stood up slowly. "I'm holding the newspaper. Just like you said. But I'm also going to walk toward that door. Slowly. Just don't do anything you'll regret."

"That's far enough," Owen said. "What makes you think I'd regret shooting you?"

The man took another step. Now he was in front of the door. "You don't know me. I've done nothing wrong. There's no reason to shoot."

The man turned his back on Owen. Still holding the newspaper, he put both hands on the door, just above the PUSH lettering. "I'm going through this door now. You're not going to shoot. And I don't think you'll follow me. Not in that ridiculous get up."

Owen's voice tightened. "I'm telling you. Don't open that door."

The man's right hand released the newspaper as he pushed the door open with his left.

Owen fired off two rounds at the back of the man's knees.

Ramona screamed.

The man stumbled forward through the door. He fell on his

right elbow, his left hand clutching his left knee. The snout of a Beretta appeared under the newspaper, level with the ground.

"Point that gun at me and you're a dead man," Owen said.

The man released the gun and fell back against the tiled entryway. "Fucking amateur."

Sirens sounded in the distance, growing louder.

19

BINGO!

Owen and Thad Reader stood in the Shady Acres parking lot watching an ambulance pull away with the wounded gunman. "You sure that's the same guy you saw at the airport last night?" Reader asked.

"No doubt about it. When the tests come back on the slugs in my luggage, I'll bet they match the ones in his Beretta."

"That was pretty good shooting you did." Reader patted Owen's shoulder. "For an amateur."

"I wanted to kill the son of a bitch," Owen said. "It was all I could do to aim low."

"Sounds like you're taking this personal."

"These guys have killed my ex-partner, bombed my house, shot at me, and tried to kidnap my mother. Damn right it's personal."

"Maybe you could use a little R & R." Reader nodded toward Owen's feet. He had rolled down his pants legs but was still barefoot. "Better get your shoes on and change out of that uniform. You've still got to get out to the Elkins place."

"I thought I could help question our friend in the ambulance."

"He'll be in surgery for a while. I want you someplace safe from killers," Reader said. "And reporters," he added as a TV van turned into the Shady Acres driveway.

"Maybe I ought to take my Mom with me to the Elkins place. Somebody evidently wanted to use her for leverage."

"The Elkins place will be bulging at the seams."

"Trish loves my Mom. She'll make room for her."

"At least call in advance." Reader headed for the door of the rest home as two men emerged from the TV van and started unloading camera equipment. "Your mom must be getting anxious. Let's go show her you're safe."

Inside the Shady Acres reception area, a team of deputies photographed the bloodstains in the doorway and the wheelchair Owen had abandoned. Ruth had worked her way to the front of the crowd of residents pressing against the yellow crime scene tape that stretched diagonally from the reception desk to the pamphlet rack in the front corner of the waiting room. When Owen and Reader entered the room, she ducked under the tape and hurried to her son.

"Owen. Thank God. Who was that man? What did he want?"

"He was trying to get to me through you, Mom."

"But why? Why did he want to get to you in the first place?"

"It's complicated. Someone is afraid I might have some damaging information."

"And do you?" Ruth asked.

"That's what's complicated. I don't know. But I do know you can't stay here any longer."

"Good. I'm ready to go home."

Owen had a vision of his bombed-out office. Repairs would take at least another day. "I'm afraid it's not safe there either."

"Then where will I go?"

"I have a place in mind. The sheriff has been guarding it. If you get your things together, I'll take you there." Owen put his arm around his mother's shoulders. "It'll be all right."

"I just don't understand." Ruth's eyes swept the room, as if she didn't know where she was. "Oh, my. There's Warren Stanton's wheelchair. I'd forgotten all about it. We've got to get it back to him. He's helpless without it."

Reader addressed the deputy taking pictures. "Got everything you need on the wheelchair?"

When the deputy nodded, Reader grabbed the chair's handles and told Ruth, "Lead the way."

Owen lifted the crime scene tape for his mother and Reader, and the crowd parted to let them get to the double doors leading to the residential area. "Did I understand you to say this wheelchair belongs to Warren Stanton?" Reader asked as he pushed the chair down the residential hallway.

"Yes," Owen said. "He was filling out an absentee ballot for us when the call came announcing Ruth's visitor."

"So you were going to use his ballot to uncover any local voting shenanigans." Reader laughed. "That's really sending a thief to catch a thief."

"How so?" Owen asked.

"Stanton and his brothers and cousins have been buying and selling votes in Mingo County for as long as I can remember. It's a family tradition."

Owen chuckled. "I should have figured that out when he quoted us the going price for a vote for sheriff."

"His family sets the price."

"He was telling me about a family who scanned recent obituary columns to get names that would still be on the voter rolls."

"Sounds like insider knowledge," Ruth said.

Owen nodded. "Struck me that we ought to scan recent obituaries ourselves, sort them by voter precinct, and provide every polling place with an alphabetical list of potential frauds."

"Good idea," Reader said. "Better not let Stanton near any of the lists, though. Last election, when Mingo County's voters exceeded its entire population by five hundred souls, two hundred of the suspect ballots were cast in alphabetical order."

Owen couldn't suppress a grim smile. "Simple as ABC."

Reader stopped the wheelchair just short of Warren Stanton's good leg, which stuck out into the hallway from the door to Ruth's room. Stanton sat with his back propped against the doorframe.

"Warren. Whatever happened to you?" Ruth asked.

"Heard them shots and crawled as far as this here door. Folks kept runnin' right by without stopping. Needed that chair you're wheelin' there."

Owen and Reader grabbed Stanton under his arms and hefted him into his wheelchair. "That's more like it," Stanton

228

said. "Looks like them shots managed to miss you two lawmen."

"That's right," Reader said. "Owen here fired them."

"Did Owen here tell you he paid me twenty bucks for my vote?" Stanton asked.

"That's not quite accurate," Owen said. "My mom paid you twenty dollars to keep quiet about casting your absentee ballot."

"Maybe you'd like to pay me another twenty. Just so's I can keep that distinction fresh in my mind. Wouldn't want nobody thinkin' I sold my vote for money. Especially not to a lawman."

"I can see that," Reader said. "Vote selling being a felony and all."

Stanton rubbed his thumb and fingertips together. "So what do you think? A little more grease for my palm?"

"I think you're lucky I don't arrest you for what you've just admitted," Reader said.

"Ain't that just the way of it though," Stanton said. "You try to do the law a favor, votin' the way they want and loanin' 'em your wheelchair, and all you get is grief."

"You're lucky that's all you're getting," Reader said. "I could add attempted extortion to voter fraud charges."

"Extortion? Hell's bells, twenty bucks don't even constitute a good tip."

"Here's a good tip," Owen said. "Wheel that chair back to your own room right now. With my thanks."

"Your thanks don't fill my wallet," Stanton said, wheeling his chair out into the corridor.

"But they'll keep you out of jail," Owen said. "For now."

As Stanton wheeled down the corridor, Ruth said, "I'm sorry, Owen. I just didn't realize he was so ... so venal."

"It's all right, Mom. He was actually quite helpful. Can I give you a hand with your packing?"

"Better get your shoes on and get out of that uniform first," Reader said. "We'll set up another diversion. I'll take a deputy with me when I leave again, try to make him look like you. The unmarked car Phil Blatt left is still out back. Take your mom and circle a couple of blocks to make sure you're not being followed. If there's any chance someone is on your tail, head straight for our office."

Owen changed into street clothes and called Trish Elkins to make sure there'd be room for his mom at her place. "Grandpa added a bedroom each time grandma got pregnant," Trish said. "We've still got room for a couple more in your little witness protection program, and you know we'll take good care of Ruth."

When Ruth was packed and ready to go, Owen led her out the back way to the waiting car. The second time he started to circle the block, she said, "Owen, I'm the one in our family with memory issues. Do you have any idea where you are going? Maybe if you told me where we're headed I could help."

"Where we're going is a surprise, Mom. I'm just trying to make sure no one is following us."

"And why would anyone want to do that? Did that man you shot have friends?"

"He didn't seem very friendly. But he wasn't acting on his own. It's likely he had an employer somewhere who wants to see me dead."

"But why?"

"I told you, I'm not entirely sure. Someone thinks I may have some damaging information."

"So this all goes back to that shooting at the airport."

"The man today was one of the shooters at the airport. They wanted some files they thought I was picking up. Files from my days at Tranalytics." He told Ruth the story of Dan Thornton's death and Ray Washburn's garage burning, without mentioning the destruction of the room in her house or Judith's role in bringing in the targeted files. He still hoped to be able to finish repairing the room without Ruth's knowledge, and Ruth still hoped he and Judith would get back together. It would be a lot easier to repair the room than the broken marriage, but he wanted Judith's presence at Trish Elkins's home to be a surprise for Ruth, and he was looking forward to seeing his ex-wife as well.

Owen stepped on the gas, whipping around uphill curves, both to elude any pursuers and reach the Elkins place more quickly. Ruth grabbed the dashboard. "For heaven's sake, Owen, slow down. If you crash on these roads you'll save anyone following us the trouble of killing you."

"I made sure nobody was following us."

"Then there's no need to be in such a hurry."

They crested a scrub-covered hill and wound their way down into the valley that held the Elkins house. It was just a little past four in the afternoon, but the sun had already disappeared behind the pine-topped ridge to the west as they approached the valley floor.

"I have a feeling I've been on this road before," Ruth said.

They reached the valley floor, followed a meandering stream, and then turned down a gravel road leading to the Elkins home.

"My goodness," Ruth said. "It's Trish's mother's house."

"It's Trish's house now, Mom. Her and her brothers."

As they approached the house, Bruiser barked and hurtled down the porch steps, churning up gravel as he ran to meet the car. Owen parked and tried to calm Bruiser as two women left the shadowy porch and descended into the fading valley light.

"Oh, my land," Ruth said. "Is that Judith?"

Judith wore a beige jacket and blue slacks that matched the outfit Mary Galardi had worn at the airport. She and Trish headed straight for the passenger door of the car, helped Ruth out, and enveloped her in a group hug. Then Judith took Ruth by the hand, went around the front of the car, looped her free arm around Owen's neck, and kissed him firmly on the lips. It wasn't the same lingering kiss Mary had given him while passing for Judith the night before. Still, it was a kiss, and the half hug she ventured with Ruth in tow took Owen back to happier days.

"What's happening here?" Ruth asked. "Are you two getting back together? I've always said absence makes the heart grow fonder."

"Fonder for somebody else, I'm afraid," Owen said. "Judith isn't here to see me, Mom. She's here for the same reason you are. People were trying to get at me through her and this is a safe haven."

"But if there's nothing between you, how can people hope

to reach you through her?"

"A good question," Trish said.

Owen leapt in with an answer before Judith had a chance to deny that there might be any feelings between them. "She was holding the files people are after. She brought them with her. And now that I have them, I'm going to find out what makes them so important."

"After dinner," Trish said. "I've got pork chops on the stove and shelves full of applesauce canned from our own crop."

After dinner, Owen, Ruth, Judith, and Michelle Barney sat on the floor in Trish Elkins's living room with the fireplace behind them and the eight file boxes Judith had brought from Palo Alto in front of them.

"All right," Owen said. "We'll each go through two file boxes. If nothing suspicious turns up, we'll switch boxes and try again."

"What are we looking for?" Michelle asked.

"I wish I knew. Something that would be damaging if made public. Something worth killing for." He held up a bound report entitled "Mobile Phone Risks and Benefits." "Whatever it is, it's probably not in a formal report like this, because lots of copies of these reports have already been circulated to the public. Aside from them, though, we should examine every piece of paper in these boxes."

No one spoke for a while. Owen's first box contained year-by-year files of business correspondence. He was halfway through the letters he'd written during his first year with Tranalytics when his mother held up a thick file folder.

"Here's a folder marked TIME SHEETS," Ruth said. "Looks to be about ten years' worth of monthly records of projects and hours signed by you and somebody whose name I can't make out. Do I really need to go through all of these?"

"My God, Owen," Judith said. "You really were a pack rat. Why on earth would you keep those records?"

"We needed them in case we were audited."

Judith took a handful of sheets from Ruth's folder. "Some

of these records go back thirty years. The statute of limitations on any audits must have run out long ago. Only God cares what you were working on then, and he or she doesn't need time sheets as a reminder."

"I guess I thought it might be fun to look back on old projects some day," Owen said.

"But these files don't contain anything anyone would likely want to kill for," Ruth said.

"Unless you had a wife that needed storage space," Judith said.

"All right. All right. I hear you," Owen said. "You don't need to look through those time sheets, Mom."

"Does that mean I can feed them into the fireplace?"

"Nothing goes into the fireplace until we've found what we're looking for," Owen said.

Judith held up a manila folder. "Here's a file labeled PERSONAL STUFF."

"I doubt there's anything in there worth killing for," Owen said.

Michelle raised her eyebrows. "Maybe we should be the judge of that."

Judith pulled a printed sheet from the folder. "Oh, look. Here's an old menu from the Bella Vista Restaurant."

"Where's that?" Michelle asked.

"In the hills overlooking Palo Alto," Judith said.

"Sounds romantic."

"It was," Owen said. "It was our first date, so I kept a souvenir."

Judith smiled. "Owen. How sweet." She dug deeper into the folder. "Here's a bunch of old internet jokes. Looks like people sent you a lot of redneck humor."

"They thought I'd laugh because I'm from West Virginia."

"They must have been right," Judith said. "You took the trouble to print them out."

"Unfortunately, it's the image of our region," Ruth said.

Judith read aloud from the joke file. "A West Virginia state trooper stops a redneck who's been weaving all over the road.

233

Trooper says, 'Got any ID?' Redneck says, ''Bout what?'"

Ruth groaned. "Much as I'd like to, I doubt anyone would kill over that. But maybe we ought to revisit the rule about when things can go into the fireplace."

"Here's another Bella Vista menu," Judith said. "Dated before we ever met."

Michelle laughed. "Owen. You sentimental devil."

"Here's a folder filled with old eight-by-ten photographs." Ruth held up a picture of a softball team. "You're in this one, Owen. Before you grew your beard."

"Is that you leaning on the bat?" Michelle asked. "You were one handsome dude."

Owen's eyes fastened on the broad shouldered blond kneeling beside him in the picture. Dan Thornton, holding the ball he used to baffle opposing batters. Young. Healthy. And alive.

"You *were* handsome then," Ruth said. "Why did you quit playing softball?"

"Other teams kept getting younger and faster."

"Here's another Bella Vista menu," Judith said. "I can see why someone might want to kill over this."

"That was before we were married. I only had eyes for you after that." Owen stopped himself from pointing out that he wasn't the one who had been unfaithful.

"Still," Judith said, "I see lots of mementos of old girlfriends, but not a single wedding photo."

"I took the wedding photos with me. They've always been in my office." Where they went up in flames a week ago, Owen thought. "Look, I appreciate your help, but you guys are starting to make me wish I was doing this on my own."

"You're right. We're having entirely too much fun," Judith said.

They worked in silence for a while. Then Judith closed the folder marked PERSONAL STUFF, set it aside, and pulled another thick folder from her box. "Here's one labeled M/C ACCIDENT REPORTS (1-400). What's this all about?"

"It's the raw data from our motorcycle accident study," Owen said. "We tracked eight hundred motorcycle accidents in

Los Angeles. Sent teams to the crash scene as soon as we could. Took photos. Followed up with interviews and got hospital reports when injuries were involved. It was a landmark study in its day. The feds are updating it now."

Judith began leafing through the pages in the file and the others went back to their own boxes. Owen was finishing the correspondence from his second year at Tranalytics when Judith said "Bingo!"

"Got something?" Owen asked.

Judith waved a page over her head. "Accident report. Almost thirty years old. Couple of blotto teenagers turned left in front of a motorcyclist on Los Feliz Boulevard. Put him in a coma."

Ruth, Owen, and Michelle crowded around Judith, who pointed at the name of the errant driver listed on the police report. "Driver's name was Jason Davison."

Michelle gasped. "And Linton Barney was in the car with him."

20

ACCIDENT RECONSTRUCTION

The first thing the next morning, the group that had uncovered Davison's accident report surrounded Thad Reader in Trish Elkins's living room as he scanned the record.

"So this is what all the fuss is about?" Reader said.

"Has to be," Owen said. "Davison has a near-fatal DUI accident on his driving record. It's not something he'd want publicized."

"I don't see it," Reader said. "He wasn't even eighteen when it happened. Voters tend to overlook youthful indiscretions. And I say thank God for that. I've got a few of those on my own record."

"But you're not running for president," Owen said.

"George Bush had a DUI on his record," Michelle Barney said. "And he still got elected."

"But he didn't hit anybody," Owen said.

"And Chappaquiddick pretty clearly kept Teddy Kennedy out of the White House," Judith said.

"Or at least kept him from running," Ruth added.

"But that was different," Reader said. "The girl in Kennedy's car died, and he ran away from the accident scene without reporting it."

"And even tried to cover it up," Judith said.

"Maybe that's what happened here," Owen said. "Maybe this accident was covered up somehow."

"And that's why nobody knows about it," Judith added.

"But how would you cover up something like this?" Michelle

236

Barney asked. "The biker was in a coma."

"From a legal point of view, maybe they plea-bargained," Judith said. "Or maybe the DUI evidence was suppressed."

"That doesn't seem like enough," Owen said. "The accident would still be on Davison's record."

"But what else could have happened?" Judith said.

"What we've got here isn't the official report," Owen said. "It's a copy of the original report from the accident scene. We just happen to have it because we had a research team on the scene. Maybe the official report was changed after the fact so it never went on Davison's record."

"But how?" Judith said. "A man was injured. Maybe even killed. There would still have to be a report."

"Maybe someone changed it to a hit-and-run," Owen said. "Or maybe the official report named Linton Barney as the driver."

"Oh, God," Michelle Barney said. "That makes sense. I told you I always thought there was something in Jason's past that bound him to Linton. Something they never wanted to talk about."

"Barney did step up and take the heat for Davison over the Gardner girl's disappearance," Reader said.

"But why would he step up thirty years ago?" Ruth asked. "A drunk driving accident that results in injury was just as serious then as it is now."

"Money," Michelle said. "Linton was always guarded about his income. His family was far from rich, and USC wasn't cheap, but they managed to pay the full tuition. And he always had more money than you'd expect for someone with a government job."

"But how would they doctor the records in the first place?" Judith asked.

"Thirty years ago, Davison's dad would have been lieutenant governor," Owen said. "He'd have had the clout to get the records changed."

"Be like fixing a traffic ticket," Reader said. "You could do it with a single phone call if you knew the right person to contact at the local level."

"So the lieutenant governor would have to contact the CHP?" Judith asked.

"Not in this case," Owen said. "The accident happened on a Los Angeles street, so the reporting jurisdiction would have been the LAPD. Their officers' names are on the accident report."

"This is all just speculation." Reader tapped the report he held. "Even if you're right, it still doesn't seem like this piece of paper is worth all the killing that's gone on."

"They may never have intended to kill anyone," Owen said. "It all started when someone pretending to be a local journalist named Alex Matthews contacted Dan Thornton. They must have thought it would be easy to get Dan to lead them to his old Tranalytics files. It might have worked, too, if Dan hadn't discovered that the real Alex Matthews was a woman. He must have confronted the man using that name. Backed him into a corner that left him no way out."

Reader tapped the report again. "But how would they know this report even existed?"

"We had to register the fact that we had copies of the on-scene reports," Owen said. "The local police would have known. They had to account for all the copies."

"But if someone did change the record," Reader asked, "why would they wait thirty years to track down the one missing copy of the original?"

"Presidential campaigns attract dirt diggers the way dung heaps attract flies," Owen said. "Bush's DUI didn't surface until he started rising through the political ranks."

"So who would have known this original even existed?" Reader asked. "If there was a switch, who would have known about it?"

"Whoever changed the records locally," Owen said. "Both the Davisons, father and son, of course. And Linton Barney. The first time we met, he complimented me on the Tranalytics motorcycle study. At the time, I thought nothing of it. He was a biker and the report is well-known in biking circles. But now I think he must have known about the surviving accident record."

"Too bad you can't interrogate him," Judith said.

"That record may be one reason he can't be reached," Owen said.

Reader raised his hand, palm outward, giving the traffic cop's STOP signal. "That's a topic for another day. Right now all we've got is a copy of an original accident report and a lot of speculation."

Owen understood that Reader didn't want to discuss the details of Barney's death publicly, but he was convinced they were on the right track. "The first thing we need to do is find out whether there really was a cover-up. If we can track down the official report that went to the CHP and the DMV, we'll know whether the record was altered along the way."

"Would the official record still be on the books thirty years later?" Judith asked.

"I don't know," Owen said. "But it was a serious accident. Maybe even a fatal one. There must be a record somewhere."

"That's your department," Reader said. "You're the one who knows the most about tracking California accident records. Meantime, I'll see what we can learn by sweating the gunman you shot."

Judith nodded toward the array of file boxes left on the living room floor. "Maybe the rest of us can go back over those files. See if we missed anything."

"I think it's a safe bet we've already found what everyone's been looking for," Owen said. "It's right there in Sheriff Reader's hands."

"That may be," Judith said. "But I'm curious to know how many more Bella Vista menus are in those boxes."

As soon as government agencies were open on the West Coast, Owen called the California Department of Motor Vehicles. After several false starts, he was directed to a woman named Li Choo in the Information Services Branch.

"We can get you driver records," Ms. Choo said. "It will cost five dollars for each paper record. Take at least a month."

"Is there some way to expedite the process?" Owen asked. "I'm with the Raleigh County sheriff's office in West Virginia and the information is crucial in a murder investigation."

"So you wish to see a third party record? Not your own?"

"Yes. That's right."

"There are forms to fill out. We must notify the third party."

"Is there some way to avoid the month's wait?"

"Others are ahead of you. We'll need an official letter from your agency."

"We can do that. Will that hurry the process along?"

"We still have to follow procedure, sir. Budget cuts have caused big backlogs."

Owen felt as if he needed a course in bureaucratese as a second language. "I should have asked this earlier. How far back do your records go?"

"Three years."

"It's likely that the accident I'm interested in was fatal. Wouldn't you keep fatal accident records longer?"

"We keep fatal records four years."

"The accident I'm interested in happened thirty years ago."

After a short silence, the woman said, "Files here are no older than five years. We must purge to make room for new records."

"There must be backup memory somewhere in the system."

"I can check with the computer people. But they're busy upgrading the system. If older files exist, you'll have to pay for programming and computer time."

"How long will that take?"

"Can't say. Long time."

"Could you please ask your computer people?"

"Before we start anything, we'll need an official letter."

Owen took down the woman's work address, promised to send a letter, and slammed the phone back into its cradle.

Across the room, Judith looked up from her crossword puzzle. "Trouble?"

"The DMV," Owen said, as if that were explanation enough. "No matter what state you're in, dealing with them is like swimming in quicksand."

"At least you didn't have to stand in line."

"No. But I still got shunted from person to person until I finally wound up with someone who tried hard to be no help at all. And she made it plain any future request will be sent to the end of a long line."

"Can you try working your way up the bureaucratic ladder?"

"Won't do any good. They don't keep any driver records longer than five years and purge most after three. Finding a thirty-year-old accident record at the California DMV would be like searching a haystack for a needle that somebody took out twenty-five years earlier."

"If the records exist, you'll find them. But now that I've helped you turn up Davison's accident report and figure out what your needle looks like, I think it's about time I got back to Palo Alto."

Her statement surprised Owen. He'd been hoping they could spend some time together. "Your four days aren't up yet, and it's still not safe. The bad guys don't know we've found the accident record. They think we're still waiting for TSA to release the files."

"Why not just go public with the accident report?"

"You heard Reader. He doesn't think the report is enough. If you go back thirty or forty years, drunk driving wasn't taken so seriously. When I was a kid, it was just a joke on the Dean Martin Show. Unless we can prove there was a cover-up, the report's not a credible motive for murder. It's not even likely to change many voters' minds."

"The bad guys may not know whether you have the report, but they know I don't. Can't we at least talk about shortening my stay?"

"They've threatened Mom, trying to get at me through her. They might try the same thing with you."

"Trying to get at a man by threatening his ex-wife is a little like trying to get at B'rer Rabbit by threatening to throw him in the brier patch."

"That's not fair. You know I still care for you."

Judith put down her crossword puzzle, crossed the room, and put her hand on Owen's shoulder. "And I still care for you.

But there's no reason the bad guys would know that. And we've both got separate lives now."

Owen dipped his cheek and nuzzled the hand on his shoulder. "No matter what the bad guys think, they don't know about this place. You're safe here. The sheriff has deputies watching us. I've installed Ken Kaylor's surveillance cameras on the entrance road and the porch. And the Elkins boys seem to have cut their teeth on gun barrels."

"Somehow the Elkins boys' teething habits don't make me feel any safer."

"If you won't stay for me, do it for Mom. You saw her face light up when she realized you were here."

"Playing the Mom card. That's really low. You know I've always liked her. And the way she is now…" Judith sighed. "Well, okay. I'll stay on a few more days."

"Stay until the election is over. Everything ought to be cleared up by then. One way or the other."

"That's almost a week. Let's just take it a day at a time."

Owen patted the hand on his shoulder. "I can live with that."

After lunch, Owen made a list of all those who might have more knowledge of Davison's accident. In addition to Davison and his father, it included Linton Barney, Barney's parents, the parents of the injured motorcyclist, the head of the Tranalytics crew that responded to the accident alert, and the LAPD officers named in the report.

Michelle Barney was playing Scrabble with Ruth, Trish, and Judith in the Elkins living room. Owen asked Michelle whether Linton Barney's parents were still alive.

"His father died about five years ago," Michelle said. "His mother's still alive in a San Fernando Valley nursing home. It's my impression she's not doing too well."

"Would she be likely to remember whether Linton was charged as a driver in a serious accident when he was a teenager?"

"I understand her memory is failing, but I could phone and ask."

"My memory's failing," Ruth said. "But that's the kind

242

of thing I'd never forget. I remember when you took out the Mocarski's mailbox with our Dodge Dart, Owen. The Hager girl was with you."

"Ah, yes. The Hager girl," Judith said.

"You'd been drinking and there was lipstick on your collar," Ruth said.

"If Mrs. Barney's memory is half as good as yours, it could solve a lot of my problems." Owen turned to Michelle. "It would be interesting to know if the family came into any large sums of money around that time, but I don't know how you'd approach that question."

"I can ask how Linton managed to pay for USC," Michelle said. "I'm curious about that myself. If you want to take my place here, I'll go make some calls."

Before Michelle could get up from the Scrabble table, the living-room phone rang and Trish answered it. She said, "Yes, he's right here," and brought a cordless handset to Owen, saying, "It's Sheriff Reader."

Owen took the handset into the kitchen and closed the door.

"I just talked to Sheriff Bettencourt in Columbus," Reader said. "TSA released our luggage and he's got his guys working on ballistics."

"I'm sure the bullets will be a match for the Beretta we got from the guy I shot yesterday. How's he doing?"

"He'll limp for life. Got a lawyer threatening to sue us for using unwarranted force."

"That's bullshit. He went for his Beretta."

"The lady at the reception desk didn't see him pull his gun. She just saw you threaten him with your revolver and shoot him in the back of his leg when he turned to leave."

"But we've got his Beretta."

"He's got a permit for it. Claims he works for a security firm. If we don't charge him soon we'll have to release him."

"You've got to be kidding me. He's the same guy who shot at us in Columbus. I recognized him. Doesn't that count for something?"

"I don't think we have much to worry about. We'll charge

him with the Columbus shooting for starters. It'll help if the bullets in the luggage turn out to be from his Beretta."

"They will. Unless he was such a lousy shot he missed the luggage altogether."

"Hired guns aren't usually lousy shots. Strikes me this might be a good time to make another fake call from your home phone to Sheriff Bettencourt in Columbus. If the bad guys are still listening, it will keep them off balance. They think the files they're worried about are still with the TSA in Columbus. We want them to go on thinking that. And we don't want them to know we've connected your gun to the Columbus shooting."

"When do you want to make the call?"

"I'll set it up with Bettencourt right away. Meet me at your place at three o'clock."

Owen was listening to phone messages when Reader arrived at his home that afternoon. He met the sheriff at the door, motioned him in, punched a button on the phone, and returned it to its cradle.

"Didn't jump the gun on me and call Bettencourt already, did you?" Reader asked.

"Message machine was full," Owen said. "Haven't been home for a couple of days and hadn't bothered to check it."

"Anything good?"

"Couple of reminders to register and vote. CVS pharmacy is holding one of Mom's prescriptions for pick-up. Three people want me to refinance. Recorded message says there's a home in our county broken into every fifteen minutes."

"Sounds like a pretty busy home. Thieves must meet themselves coming and going."

"Sounds like the sheriff's office could stand a budget increase."

"Never happen. But we do seem to have our hands full."

"Anything new from Columbus?" Owen asked for the benefit of anyone listening.

"Haven't heard since yesterday. Maybe we ought to call them."

Owen called Sheriff Bettencourt in Columbus, who followed the script laid out by Reader, saying that the TSA was still examining the luggage that had been used for target practice in the airport shootout.

When Owen and Reader protested that the luggage contents were vital to a murder investigation, Bettencourt was sympathetic but reminded them that he would need to go through the luggage as well when the TSA released it, since the shootout occurred in his jurisdiction.

"Just let us know when you get your hands on those files," Reader said and ended the call.

As soon as Reader hung up the phone, Owen unleashed a barrage of profanity. "Goddamn bureaucratic circle jerk. There's something in those files that will lead us to Dan Thornton's killer, and we can't get at them."

Reader motioned for Owen to follow him outside, where they could talk without being overheard.

Owen was still ranting and swearing when they cleared the porch. "You can quit now," Reader said. "No one is listening out here."

"We're still clearing bureaucratic hurdles when we ought to be crossing the finish line," Owen said. "I've seen the files. I know who had Dan Thornton killed, and I still can't get at the bastard."

"It's all speculative right now. Unless we can show Davison had some compelling reason to suppress that accident report, like a cover-up, it's not enough to hang him."

"The bastard has pulled even with Halstead in the polls. Why don't we just leak the accident report to the media? Let the voters draw their own conclusions."

"All we have is a copy of a copy of a thirty-year-old accident report. And a preliminary one at that. We need the official document. Or some other proof there was a cover-up. If we release the report now, they'll circle their wagons and we may never find that proof."

Owen pounded a fist into his thigh. "There had to be a cover-up. They wouldn't have been shooting at me if there weren't a cover-up. If that accident had been reported properly, news of it would have spread all over the minute Davison announced his candidacy."

"Not necessarily. Davison was underage. His name wouldn't have been made public."

"They've killed to keep that record secret. That's reason enough to take it public."

"A DUI at age seventeen isn't damaging enough. It's only half the story. We need to be able to prove the other half."

"Let's just leak it to Tom O'Day. He's got a hard-on for Davison. He'll make up the other half. And know how to spin it to tie Davison in knots."

"As it stands, the story might just generate sympathy for Davison. But this is bigger than the primary election. Whether or not Davison carries West Virginia, we need to lay the groundwork for a murder charge." Reader looked at his watch. "Shit. I forgot O'Day. I'm supposed to meet him at my office in fifteen minutes."

"What for?"

"Don't know. He called me. Sounded upset. Said he wanted to talk."

Tom O'Day was sitting in the waiting room when Owen and Reader arrived at the sheriff's office. Reader led the way past the desk sergeant and the three men took chairs around the table in the interrogation room.

"You called this meeting," Reader said. "What's on your mind?"

"Betty Sue Gardner is missing."

Reader raised his eyebrows. "Hotshot reporter like yourself should know that was old news a week ago."

"That may be true," O'Day said. "But until two days ago I knew where she was."

21

THE HONEY TRAP

"So you've been holding out on us," Reader said.

"I know a little more than you do," O'Day said. "But I want you to promise me immunity before I bring you up to speed."

"You know I can't do that. That's for the DA to decide." Reader took out his cell phone. "Want me to call him?"

"No. Not just yet. The fewer people who know about this, the better. Can you at least promise me you'll argue for immunity with the DA if push comes to shove?"

"If you've been withholding evidence, I'd say push is pretty damn close to shove right now."

"I'm here because I think Betty Sue's life is at risk," O'Day said. "I'm hoping you'll see my side of things."

"Only way to find that out is to show us your side of things," Reader said.

"All right." O'Day inhaled deeply and cleared his throat. "Betty Sue was planted in Davison's campaign headquarters."

"Who did the planting?" Owen asked.

"A group of Halstead supporters," O'Day said. "Halstead knew nothing about it."

"Like Nixon knew nothing about Watergate," Reader said. "So was Davison's seduction in her job description?"

"At first, they just wanted her to keep her eyes and ears open. Report back on strategy." O'Day paused. "But everybody knew Davison had a reputation for trolling with an open fly among female campaign workers."

"And in this case the fly-fishing expedition was successful,"

Owen said.

"Didn't take long," O'Day said. "Hard to tell who seduced who. Betty Sue joined the campaign in January. They were in each other's pants before the month was out."

"So the honey trap worked," Reader said. "What was in it for the girl?"

"Hefty paychecks. Notoriety. An extra fifteen minutes of fame. The way it was planned, Betty Sue was going to tell Davison she was pregnant a couple of weeks before the election and then disappear. There'd be big headlines. Pictures in all the papers. TV specials. Speculation. Articles on Davison's past peccadillos. The press playout was all planned. A headline a day: 'Betty Sue in the mansion after hours,' followed by 'Betty Sue pregnant,' …"

"That all worked," Owen said. "What went wrong?"

"The way it was supposed to play out, Betty Sue would show up the day before the election saying she'd told Davison she was pregnant, he'd erupted, and she feared for her life."

"So that explains her disappearance," Reader said.

"At least two things went wrong," O'Day said. "Betty Sue fell hard for the guy. He made a lot of promises and she started seeing herself as the first lady. Or at least a senator's wife. So she really did get pregnant. I guess she thought that would help seal the deal. But when she told Davison he really did erupt. Blew sky high. Insisted on an abortion. Threatened her life if she told anyone."

"So the script turned real," Owen said.

"She had trouble handling reality, but she still disappeared on schedule," O'Day said. "Trouble was, Davison countered by pushing Lin Barney front and center. When Barney claimed he was her lover, Betty Sue didn't know what to do. His story would take her right out of prime time. Reduce her to fodder in an office romance. She saw her fifteen minutes of fame shrinking."

"But she could still come back and set the record straight," Owen said. "Point the finger at Davison. Claim he frightened her into disappearing."

"That's what I told her," O'Day said. "But then Barney was killed. That really spooked her."

"Spooked her how?" Reader asked.

"She saw how far Davison was willing to go. Barney's death was no accident."

"Can you prove that?" Reader asked.

"I was hoping you guys will be able to," O'Day said. "Ten to one, Jason or his father ordered the hit."

"But why?" Owen asked, wanting to test his reasoning against O'Day's knowledge.

"Who knows? Linton knew too much. Maybe he and Jason had a falling out. Maybe Linton's conscience bothered him. Jason would have paid him to lie about the affair. Maybe he decided he hadn't been paid enough." O'Day shrugged. "Anyhow, Betty Sue panicked when Linton died. I was her go-between. I could tell she was going off the rails. But I couldn't help her."

"Where was she?"

"Little motel in the panhandle. Off the beaten path. Dyed her hair brown and wore baggy flannel shirts over scruffy jeans. You'd never have recognized her."

"Did somebody recognize her?" Owen asked. "Is that what spooked her?"

"Nobody recognized her. She was in a 7-11 in Moundsville, though, when a pair of state cops came in looking for her, flashing photographs, offering a reward. She knew the governor's cops were in league with Davison, and she knew what had happened to Barney. She called me two days ago to say she wanted out."

"So she really did fear for her life," Owen said.

"Like I told you," O'Day said. "And she really has disappeared. Next day, she checked out of her motel. Didn't call in and wouldn't answer her phone."

"And you've no idea where she went," Reader said.

"No. She clearly didn't want me to know."

"Woman had sucked in more than she could swallow," Reader said. "Can you take me to the motel?"

"Of course."

"I'm curious," Reader said. "What made you decide to try

249

manufacturing the news instead of just reporting it?"

"Davison is pond scum. He's got no ambition beyond holding office, no vision beyond what it takes to get elected, and no scruples about what he'll do to get the votes he needs."

"And how does that set him apart from the general run of politicians?" Owen asked.

"Most politicians don't sanction murder and slander as campaign strategies," O'Day said.

"Sounds like you're taking all this personal," Reader said.

"Damn right it's personal. Larry Lewis was a good friend."

When Reader didn't react to the name, Owen explained, "Lewis is a California reporter who was stifling Davison's first Senate race until Linton Barney outed him as a homosexual."

"*Was* a reporter," O'Day said. "Barney had photos that cost Larry his job. Seduced Larry himself to get them. That's how I knew Linton wasn't a likely candidate for Betty Sue's bed."

"Just because he slept with your friend doesn't mean he couldn't have been balling Betty Sue as well," Reader said.

"I don't care whether Barney was homo-, hetero-, or ambi-sexual," O'Day said. "What he did to Larry was despicable. And it cost him more than his job. After two years without work, Larry killed himself."

"All right, I get the picture," Reader said. "From now to the election, I don't want you out of my sight."

"Does that mean you're arresting me?" O'Day shot up from his chair. "On what charge?"

Reader stood and extended his right hand, palm down, like an umpire giving the safe sign. "Calm down. If I wanted to arrest you, I'd have a whole smorgasbord of charges to choose from, starting with obstruction of justice. So long as I can keep an eye on you, though, I'm willing to wait and see how this all plays itself out. And right now, I want you to take me to the place where you were hiding Ms. Gardner."

A grim-faced O'Day nodded without saying anything.

"You know," Reader said, "if this little scheme of yours ever got out, it could scrap your career and do your candidate a lot of harm."

"Halstead's not exactly my candidate," O'Day said. "He just happens to be running against Davison."

"Doesn't matter," Reader said. "If the public finds out about your little honey trap, then Davison becomes a sympathetic victim and your Ms. Gardner is nothing but a garden variety bimbo."

"I tell you, the seduction was mutual," O'Day said. "And Davison threatened her when she told him she was pregnant."

"Too bad there's not an equivalent word for male bimbo," Reader said.

"Try 'Senator,'" Owen said. "Or maybe 'Governor,' depending on what state you're in."

"So is there some chance we can find Betty Sue alive, beat Davison, and keep all this quiet?" O'Day asked.

"Those are three different issues," Reader said. "That's a tough trifecta. Offhand, I'd say it's about as likely as drawing three cards to an inside straight."

After Reader and O'Day left the office, Owen made several copies of the accident report that had already cost at least two lives. He put one copy in the office safe, along with the master, and kept two for himself. In addition to the names of the auto occupants, the injured motorcyclist, and the local police, the lower right-hand corner bore the initials of the Tranalytics team leader who had responded to the accident call. The initials were D.T., for Dave Thom. When Tranalytics folded, Dave had moved on to work as an expert witness for a small consulting firm in Los Angeles. Owen called the firm and spent a little time filling in the blanks since they'd last talked before getting to the point of the call, saying, "Dave, I'd like to test your memory. How much do you recall about the accidents you covered for our motorcycle study?"

"That was at least thirty years ago. I can barely recall the details of last month's witness gigs."

"I know it's been a long time, but the accident I'm interested in put the motorcyclist in a coma and involved some recognizable names."

"Only one that comes to mind involved a kid named Jimmy Easter."

Owen pumped his fist. "Yes! You're amazing. That's the accident I'm interested in. What made it stick in your mind?"

"Had to keep following up with the kid's parents to know whether to code the accident as an injury or a fatal. Pretty grim business. He stayed in a coma past our report deadline. Finally died, but we'd already coded it as an injury accident in our analysis."

"What else do you remember about it?"

"Driver was drunk as a skunk. Rich kid in a red Corvette. Kept claiming it wasn't his fault, even though he'd turned left in front of Jimmy. Officers had to calm him down."

"But you don't remember the driver's name?"

"No. Should I?"

"It was Jason Davison."

"Holy cow. You're kidding me."

"No. I'm not. Are you saying his name didn't register with you at the time?"

"He was just a kid."

"But his father was lieutenant governor."

"Well, that explains why his name didn't register. I couldn't tell you who the lieutenant governor is today."

"The accident report says there was a passenger in the car."

"Might have been. I only remember the driver. Kept screaming at the cops, telling them to call his father. Seemed weird at the time. Makes sense now that I know who daddy was. What's this all about?"

"If I tell you, someone will want to kill you."

"I think the saying is supposed to go, 'If I tell you, I'll have to kill you.' You don't get to fob the job off on somebody else."

"Somebody else is already involved. Somebody else killed Dan Thornton because they thought he had our copy of the accident report. When they found out he didn't, they burned down Ray Washburn's garage and blew up my office trying to destroy it."

"I'd heard Dan died. I thought it was natural causes. Where's the report now?"

"I've got it. Or at least, I've got the copy that was in our files."

"So what makes it worth killing for?"

"If I tell you, you'll be a target too."

"It's just you and me on the phone. Who's to know you told me anything? If you're worried about it, don't tell me everything. Tell me just enough so the bad guys will only want to threaten me with a severe lecture. I'd be willing to risk that."

"I'm serious, Dave. We're dealing with dangerous guys."

"I'm serious too. Look, you called me for help. You wanted to know about a particular accident. I was on the scene. I remember a few things, but maybe I can help more. If it means finding Dan Thornton's killer, count me in."

"All right." Owen filled Thom in on the mayhem surrounding the accident report and his speculation that the official report had been altered to clear Davison, probably by naming Barney as the driver.

"The kid who owned the Corvette was the driver. I was there. If the report in our files lists Davison as the driver, what makes you think there was a cover-up?"

"Somebody has placed a high value on our report. A cover-up is the only thing we could think of that might make a difference in the presidential race if it were made public."

"Makes sense."

"Did you ever follow up on the initial accident reports to get the official DMV records?"

"Rarely had a reason to. We tried to get everything we needed while we were on the scene. We were interested in the motorcyclist, not other drivers. That's why I had to follow up with Jimmy Easter's parents."

"So you'd have no way of knowing whether the official DMV report had been altered?"

"By changing the driver's name? We wouldn't have cared. We didn't need drivers' names in our report. Just the physical accident description and a lot of details on the rider."

"You must see a lot of accident reports now that you're

doing expert witness testimony. Who would have a chance to change them?"

"Any of the officers on the scene, I guess. Or somebody higher up the food chain at the LAPD."

"What about somebody at the CHP or DMV?"

"Can't see the CHP altering a report that originated with the LAPD. Chippies are mostly interested in raw statistics. How many injuries? How many fatalities? They purge driver IDs once they've passed the data on to the DMV. Maybe somebody at the DMV could make the switch, but it would have to be done before the report starts to circulate. You'd have to involve the LAPD in any case. If there's a trial, their officers could be called to testify. What are the names of the officers that signed the preliminary accident report?"

Owen read the names of the two officers, then wished he hadn't. "Look. If either of these two guys had a hand in switching the records, they're likely to be really dangerous."

"Don't worry. I don't intend to confront them. But a couple of my best riding buddies are LAPD motor officers. I'll see if they know either of the two guys whose names are on your report. Find out what they're up to now."

"Even that sounds dangerous. Be careful. Don't ask anything that might get back to the officers themselves. If you get any kind of a lead at all, let us know and we'll send in some real policemen."

"That what you are now? A real policeman?"

"No. I'm just helping the sheriff out part-time. I've still got a few consulting jobs going." He was embarrassed to think how few there were.

"If your part-time job is getting you shot at and bombed, it sounds like you're the one who needs to be careful."

Owen drove from the sheriff's office to Trish Elkins's home, taking a circuitous route calculated to throw off anyone attempting to follow him. He was so intent on confounding potential tails that he forgot to pick up his mother's medicine at the CVS pharmacy. When he arrived, he found Trish playing

254

Scrabble in the living room and asked her to take care of the errand, reasoning that she wouldn't have to worry about shaking off followers.

Trish agreed and invited him to take her place in the Scrabble game with Judith and Michelle Barney. As Owen sat down at the table, Michelle looked up from her game tiles to tell him, "I called Lin's mother. She said people had visited her rest home to inquire about my whereabouts. When I asked who they were, she sounded muddled. Finally, she said she thought they were police."

"Probably were police. The Davisons must have a lot of favors they can call in all around California," Owen said. "What did Lin's mother have to say about his USC tuition?"

"She was even more muddled about that. Finally, though, she told me he had a full scholarship. All four years."

"So much for the possibility of a tuition payoff for services rendered," Owen said.

"Her memory is one of the reasons she's in the home," Michelle said. "There's a good chance she might not have known how Lin's tuition bills were covered, and I'm pretty sure he didn't have either the grades or the SAT scores to rate a full ride. So I called USC. Told them I was a grieving widow trying to pull together a memorial booklet in Lin's honor and wanted to get a few facts straight."

Owen nodded appreciatively. "Good thinking."

"Once I proved who I was, they confirmed my suspicions. There was no full ride. Someone paid Lin's tuition in full at the start of each semester."

"I think we can guess who did that," Owen said. "Amazing, isn't it? You can find out how Barney's tuition was paid over thirty years ago, but I can't find out whether there was a fatal DUI accident on his driving record at that same time."

"Why not?" Judith asked.

Owen shrugged. "DMV purges its records after three to five years."

"Did you try the Department of Justice?"

"No. Should I?"

"If there was a hearing, they'd still have a record of the results," Judith said. "And a fatal DUI would probably rate a hearing. Your friend the sheriff could get them to expedite a search of their records. As a police officer he would have access to the rap sheets."

Owen kissed Judith on her forehead. "It pays to have married a lawyer."

"What about me?" Michelle said. "You said I did good. Don't I rate a kiss too?"

Owen laughed and planted a kiss on Michelle's forehead. Then he excused himself and used Trish's landline to call Thad Reader, who was still on the road to Betty Sue Gardner's last-known hiding place with Tom O'Day. The sheriff agreed to call the Department of Justice as soon as it opened in the morning to institute a search for any records of court cases involving Linton Barney.

Owen hung up and rejoined the women at the Scrabble table. The case was finally breaking his way.

Reader called shortly after lunch the next day with the results of his Department of Justice query. "We were right. The accident went on Barney's driving record. He was charged with DUI but it got bargained down to reckless driving. Should have thought of the DOJ ourselves."

"So now we've got a clear motive for the death of Dan Thornton and the shoot-out at the Columbus airport. Davison has been trying to cover up his cover-up."

"Sure looks that way. But we've still got more speculation than hard evidence. There's nothing connecting Davison to Dan Thornton. And as for the cover-up, all we've got of the original accident report is a copy of a copy. They can claim it's been altered. Or was wrong to begin with. Maybe Davison claimed to be the driver at first to shield his friend."

"Jason Davison hasn't had an unselfish instinct since he was sucking his mother's breast. He probably didn't even share in kindergarten."

"That's as may be," Reader said. "But he's got a staff full

of spin doctors that can paint him as pure as Snow White if there's the slightest doubt about our facts. We need to put him securely in the driver's seat of that Corvette and track the way he wriggled out."

"We've got the report they've been killing people to suppress. Why not just release it?" Owen said. "Our report and Barney's DOJ record should be enough to sink Davison at the polls."

"Our job is to nail down a murder case, not meddle in politics. Premature press leaks can only hurt that job."

"But he's getting away with murder. And leading in the primary polls."

"Right now we've got no hard evidence linking Davison to either of the murders we know about, or the accident cover-up. If we show our hand too early, we may never get that evidence. We're not even sure Davison was driving the car that hit the motorcyclist."

"I've contacted the leader of our on-site team. He says Davison was definitely the driver of the car."

"But your man wasn't there when the accident happened."

"No. But he was there when they were mopping up. He says Davison kept bawling that they should contact his father."

"That's a switch."

"My guy offered to track down the LAPD officers whose names were on the report."

"That could be a help. Could be dangerous, though, if one of them switched the records and finds out he's being tracked."

"I told him that. He said he could make discreet inquiries through friends on the force."

"The more we can lock down, the more likely we are to nail Davison. We're almost there. Just be patient."

"Patience is hard. We've only got a week to the election. How are things going with O'Day? I never had a chance to ask you what you made of his story."

"It's a little like stale popcorn. Takes lots of grains of salt to make it palatable. Claims he wasn't around when they planted Betty Sue, but got recruited to spin the news when the affair came to light. He's serious about wanting to find the woman, though. And I think we're getting close. She's been using a credit card with a false name that her handlers set up. According to her recent charges, she crossed over into Pennsylvania and now appears to be headed back toward Barkley."

Owen spread out a road map on the kitchen table. "Her mother's in Pittsburgh. Maybe she contacted her. Although that would be pretty risky. But so is using a credit card. She must realize it can be traced."

"She probably didn't think O'Day would dare go to the police with the phony name. She's no dummy."

"I agree, but smart or dumb, she's in over her head."

"O'Day's been texting her and leaving messages on her cell phone trying to get her to turn herself over to my office. He claims we can protect her from Davison and the state cops. I'm betting O'Day will talk her in. We're getting close. I can feel it."

"Davison engineered the murders of Dan Thornton and Linton Barney. That should be what sinks him. Not dallying with a campaign worker who was paid to seduce him."

"Thornton and Barney can't talk. Betty Sue can. She's fearing for her life. That's what she'll say if and when she surfaces. And it's God's own truth. It should be enough to sink Davison's campaign."

"Dammit, Thad. You were right the first time. It's not enough that Davison can't get elected. I want him behind bars."

"We'll get there. One step at a time."

Owen was working on his laptop after dinner when an email came through from Dave Thom. "Have tracked down your LAPD officers. Call me."

Owen used Trish's kitchen phone to respond. Dave sounded impatient. "I've been calling your cell without any luck."

"We've got no reception where I'm staying," Owen said. "Everything comes in and goes out the old fashioned way. Back roads and land lines. What's up?"

"My riding buddies knew both of the LAPD officers listed in the accident report. One, Ignacio Porras, was killed in a high-speed chase ten years ago."

"Too bad," Owen said. "For him more than for us. What about the other officer?"

"Robert Reed. He's dead too. But you'll be interested in how he died. Killed when his home burned down earlier this year."

"Sounds suspiciously familiar. What caused the fire?"

"Newspapers said it was an accident. Traced it to a gas leak in the living-room fireplace. Sound of the explosion carried three or four blocks."

"Your buddies have anything of interest to say about either of the two officers?"

"Nothing about Porras. They didn't know him too well. Said Reed really knew how to work the system. He'd gotten pretty high in the force before he retired two years ago. LA Times gave his obituary two full columns. I'll send you a link to the article."

"Appreciate it."

"Quite a coincidence, don't you think? I mean, Reed's home exploding just when Davison was breaking away from the pack in his run for president."

"I don't believe in coincidences."

22

THINGS THAT GO BUMP IN THE NIGHT

"I don't believe in coincidences either," Thad Reader said when Owen called to fill him in on Dave Thom's findings.

"I looked at the LA Times story of Reed's house fire," Owen said. "Front-page news that day was the outcome of the Ohio presidential primary. When Davison was leaving the rest of the field in the dust."

"What do you make of that?"

"Here's a hypothesis that fits the facts. Reed was paid to rig the original accident report and name Barney as the driver of record. But he kept copies of all the paperwork. When Davison looked like a serious candidate, Reed figured he'd been underpaid for his paper shuffling and tried for a bigger payday."

"Greed reared its ugly head."

"And bought him an exploding fireplace."

"Makes sense. Hard to prove though."

"It also explains why Tranalytics' records were targeted after sitting in a file for thirty years. After one blackmail attempt, Davison decided to tie up any loose ends."

"It's still all speculation. But those loose ends do tie up neatly."

"Where are you now?" Owen asked.

"Back at the office. I put O'Day in a cell overnight."

"So you've charged him officially?"

"Not yet. Don't know that I will. But until this mess gets cleaned up, I want to be able to show I took appropriate action with a confessed lawbreaker."

"And O'Day's okay with that?"

"Don't see he's got much choice. I've put a safe roof over his head. And we'll go after Betty Sue again tomorrow. If we find her unharmed, things may turn out okay for everyone."

"Everyone except Davison."

"Couldn't happen to a more deserving fellow."

That evening, Owen and the women played hearts on the dining-room table while the three Elkins brothers watched *Ocean's Eleven* on the living-room TV. Trish interrupted the card game momentarily to help Ruth get ready for bed. When she returned from Ruth's bedroom, she asked to speak to Owen privately.

"Is something wrong with Mom?" Owen asked, following Trish into the kitchen.

"No. But something's screwy with her meds." Trish held up a plastic pill container. "I stopped at CVS like you asked to get Ruth's Namenda. When I trotted it out tonight, she said she still has plenty on hand. There's almost a two-month supply in her night kit."

"So she didn't need the refill. Does she remember ordering it?"

"Well, you know what her memory's like. But she says she didn't order it. There'd be no reason for her to order her own meds anyhow. The pharmacy keeps track of her dosage and orders her refills automatically."

"And she's been taking her medications regularly?"

"Whenever I've been with her."

Owen took the pill container from Trish and looked at the label. "And there would have been a container like this at our house."

"Probably. Ruth liked to keep her trip medicine separate."

"Where did you go when you left the pharmacy?"

"I came straight home."

"Did anyone follow you?"

"Not so far as I know. I was careful. But if somebody thinks I'm harboring witnesses, they already know where I live."

Owen went to the living room, called Vic Elkins away from

261

the TV and led him back to the kitchen. "It's possible someone followed Trish home from the pharmacy."

"It's not certain," Trish said.

"Best not to take chances." Vic turned to Trish. "You know grandpa's drill. Womenfolk and children go to the mine. I'll break out the ammo."

Trish didn't look convinced, but she nodded. "I'll take care of it."

"I'll call Thad Reader," Owen said. "We'll need reinforcements." He dialed the sheriff's number on the kitchen phone.

When Reader answered, Owen said, "There's a chance our location has been compromised." Before he had a chance to explain, the phone went dead and the house lights went out.

The kitchen was pitch black.

From the living room, Virg Elkins shouted, "What the fuck?" and Owen heard Trish's quieter voice saying, "Just stay calm."

Owen sensed movement to his right, heard drawers open and shut, and felt someone brush past him on his left. By the time his eyes adjusted to the dark, Vic Elkins switched on a flashlight. The beam swept past Vern Elkins, whose hand clutched the cellar doorknob, and settled on Trish, who stood in the dining room passageway.

"That tears it," Vic said. He handed Trish a revolver and a second flashlight. "Get the ladies into the mine. And don't come out until you hear from me."

As Trish followed her flashlight beam toward the living room, Vic trained his light on the cellar door and led his brother Vern and Owen down wooden steps into a dank room lined with shelves of canning jars. A footlocker and gun rack filled with shotguns and assault rifles had been squeezed into the open area under the stairs.

Vern Elkins grabbed an AK-47 from the gun rack while Vic opened the footlocker. "You take the shed," he said, handing his brother a flashlight and a yellow ammo box. "I'll get to Uncle Dooley's dugout and light things up when they trip the alarm. Don't fire unless they do. Now go!"

262

As Vern pounded up the cellar steps, Vic pulled an AR-15 assault rifle from the gun rack and handed it to Owen with a box of ammunition. "Ever use one of these?"

"No, but I've got my revolver upstairs."

"Take this too," Vic said. "It's scarier than a revolver."

"Sure scares me," Owen said.

"You take the front porch with Virg. He'll be waiting there with his own rifle. If there's time, we'll grab a mattress to give you guys some cover."

"Seems like you've done this before."

"Grandpa was still fighting off robbers and revenuers when I was a kid. After the dust settled, us boys would cover the same ground with cap pistols and BB guns."

"Not quite the same thing," Owen said.

"Vern and Virg went through the real thing in Iraq. They've got enough experience for all of us." Vic took an AK-47 from the gun rack, lifted a flare gun and outsized ammo can from the footlocker, and led the way upstairs with his flashlight.

The two men passed quickly through the darkened house to the front porch, where Virg Elkins balanced an AR-15 on his lap and tightened his hold on Bruiser's leash, which was tethered to Virg's wheelchair. The dog strained against the leash, jumping and barking at the gloom outside.

"See anything yet?" Vic asked.

"Not me," Virg said. "But Bruiser knows they're out there, even though they ain't tripped the alarms."

"If they're not past the alarms, we've probably got time to get you guys some cover." Vic led Owen to the master bedroom. Through the back window they could see Trish's flashlight dancing as she led Michelle, Judith, and Ruth to the mine entrance. The women disappeared inside the mine as Vic and Owen stripped the king-size bed of sheets and wrestled the bed's mattress to the front porch.

As the two men propped the mattress against the posts on either side of the porch steps, Vic asked Owen, "Did you get through to the sheriff?"

"I told him I thought we'd been compromised. But the line

263

went dead and I'm not sure how much he heard."

Standing on the porch steps, Vic switched off his flashlight and said to Virg, "You know the drill. Vern is in the shed like pap. I'll be in Uncle Dooley's dugout. That puts you in grandpa's place here on the porch. Don't fire unless they shoot first." Then he backed down the porch steps and disappeared in the darkness to the left of the house.

Owen and Virg took positions behind either end of the mattress. Owen was tall enough to see over the top of the makeshift barrier, but Virg had to wheel his chair alongside it to peer out into the gloom. Bruiser barked whenever the wheelchair moved and jerked his short leash.

"Vern's in the shed on our right," Virg said. "Him and Vic will catch anybody coming at us in a crossfire. Make them wish they'd stayed to home."

"We don't know how many are out there," Owen said.

"Don't matter none. If they think turnin' off the electric will spook us, they got some surprises comin'."

Bruiser barked sharply. Virg tugged on the leash, pulling the dog tight against the wheelchair, and stroked his side. "Shh, big fella. We know they're out there."

The dog trembled. Saliva dripped from his lips.

Owen strained to hear or see something in the blackness beyond the porch, but the only sound was Bruiser's labored breathing.

Cans clattered in the field. "That's it," Virg whispered. "They tripped the wire."

Bruiser howled. A single shot sounded to the left of the house and a flare arced upward from Vic's dugout. It peaked and parachuted down, lighting the field and woods in a fluorescent glow.

Three men in black stood in the open field between the last row of trees and the house, their faces hidden by goggles and greasepaint. Caught in the fiery glare, the two men with assault rifles dropped to the ground, while the third stood still as a statue, pointing a flamethrower at the house.

Vic's voice boomed from the dugout as the bright flare

floated to earth. "You men. We're deputy sheriffs. Throw down those guns and put your hands in the air."

Just before the flare hit the ground, the gunman on the left fired off several rounds in the direction of Vic's voice, while the man on the right sprayed shots at the front of the house. Bruiser yipped as windows shattered and bullets thocked into the mattress.

Vic and Vern answered with shots on the intruders' left and right flanks, while Owen and Virg loosed volleys from either side of the mattress.

The flare sputtered and died, leaving the field in darkness. The shooting stopped, and a burst of orange flames leapt from the center gunman to the mattress shielding Owen and Virg.

The mattress exploded in flames, igniting the porch rug.

"Fucking flamethrower!" Virg wheeled his chair in circles, tangling Bruiser's leash as he beat the flaming rug with his lap robe.

Vic and Vern caught the flamethrower in a crossfire and the blazing muzzle dropped to earth, where the ground smothered its deadly spurts.

Owen kicked the burning mattress down the steps onto the flagstone walk, exposing both himself and Virg to rifle fire. He scrambled to take cover behind the porch columns as Virg flailed at the burning rug with his lap robe. When the robe itself caught fire, he flung it off the porch and released Bruiser, whose tangled leash was choking him against the wheelchair spokes.

Bruiser leapt from the porch and bounded straight at the trespassing gunmen.

Vic sent a second flare acing into the air, lighting up the field between the house and the woods. The center gunman lay crumpled over the snuffed flamethrower, while the man who had fired first writhed on the ground next to his assault rifle. Faced with Bruiser's attack, the third gunman broke ranks and ran for the woods.

Vic shouted "Stop!" and sprayed bullets into the trees beyond the man's head.

The gunman stopped in his tracks and laid his rifle down.

Bruiser yapped at the man's boots as the second flare floated to earth.

Bruiser's barking was the only sound in the darkened field. Owen kicked the smoldering rug off the porch and asked Virg to cover him as he followed it down the steps. As soon as he reached the flagstone walk, rifle fire rang out from the woods.

Bullets stitched the porch screen above Owen's head as he dove for the ground. Vern and Virg both returned fire, chipping the trees at the edge of the woods.

The gunman in the open field kicked at Bruiser and bent to pick up his rifle. Vic yelled, "Let it be," and loosed another volley over the man's head. The man raised his hands in the air, then collapsed to the ground as more shots came from the edge of the woods.

All three Elkins boys returned fire as Owen ran in a half crouch to join Vic in the dugout, which ran from the side of the house about halfway to the woods. "Whoever's shooting from those trees doesn't want to leave any witnesses," Vic said. "Cover me and I'll try to flush him out." He hunched over and crabwalked to the end of the dugout nearest the woods.

Bruiser wheeled to join Vic when a shrill whistle from Virg started the dog backtracking toward the porch. He stopped about halfway to sniff at the fallen flamethrower, drawing more fire from the woods. Vic answered with shots from the end of the dugout, silencing the shooter. A second whistle from Virg brought Bruiser scampering back to the relative safety of the porch.

Owen crabwalked to the end of the dugout, which was about ninety feet from the edge of the woods. "Son of a bitch was firing at Bruiser," Vic said.

"Looked more like he was aiming at those bodies in the open field," Owen said. "Like you said, he doesn't want anybody left alive to talk."

"Either way, I'm going in after him," Vic said. "Keep the bastard occupied with rifle fire until I get to the woods."

Owen poked his head above the dugout and shot at the trees that had shielded the shooter. Vic reached the tree line without drawing any return fire and waved to Owen as he disappeared into the woods.

Gunfire erupted so deep in the woods that Owen couldn't see any muzzle flashes. He ran across the open space between the dugout and the tree line and caught up with Vic, who was picking his way from tree to tree toward the source of the shots.

"Bastard's trying to make it back to the access road," Vic said. "Cover me while I cut him off." Using the trees as cover, Vic advanced about thirty yards in the darkness, then flicked his flashlight on and off and motioned for Owen to join him. They had covered about half the distance to the access road when an engine roared and a pair of headlights flashed on. Through the trees they could make out a black van backing up the access road toward the state highway.

"Damn," Vic said. "That guy is getting away." He fired off a volley at the van, but most of his shots thocked harmlessly into tree trunks.

The echo of Vic's shots had barely died when it was replaced by the screech of police sirens. Two patrol cars with flashing red lights blocked the access road before the retreating van could reach the highway.

Owen and Vic picked their way through the woods toward the flashing lights. By the time they reached the patrol cars, Thad Reader had handcuffed two of the van's occupants and was reciting their Miranda rights. Both of the handcuffed men wore the uniforms of the night: black jeans, black windbreakers, and greasepainted faces under black baseball caps.

Owen didn't recognize the first of the van occupants Reader shoved into his patrol car. But even with the blackened face, there was no mistaking the sturdy form and trimmed goatee of the second man. It was Harrison Marcus, the Jack-of-all-trades for Jason Davison and his father.

PART IV

UNCOVERING THE COVER-UP

O'DAY'S DAYS

BARKLEY, WV — *Over the past three months, a series of violent incidents ranging from arson to murder have apparently been launched in an effort to cover up evidence potentially damaging to Jason Davison's campaign for president.*

The most recent of these incidents, an armed assault on the home of a West Virginia resident, was overseen by a high-ranking member of the Davison campaign and has left two men dead and one wounded. This reporter has learned that the apparent purpose of this assault was to destroy evidence of a long-ago cover-up, when the candidate's responsibility for a fatal DUI accident was shifted to a passenger in his vehicle, Linton Barney. We have obtained a copy of the original, undoctored accident report, which appears at the right.

Tom O'Day, for the New York Herald Dispatch

23

WEST VIRGINIA JUSTICE

The operator of the flamethrower and the gunman felled by shots from the woods were both dead on the scene. The third gunman was bleeding from wounds in the arm and abdomen and was driven to St. Vincent's Hospital for treatment. Thad Reader took Harrison Marcus and the van driver into custody and insisted that they have their booking photos taken in blackface before allowing them to wash up and have another set of pictures made. After the second set of photographs had been taken and the prisoners were fingerprinted, Reader ushered Marcus and the driver to separate interview rooms. Then he let Marcus stew while he and Owen interviewed the driver, Brewer Stevens, who had identified himself as a state police captain.

"This is all a colossal mistake," Stevens said. "Mr. Marcus and I were acting as observers on official state business. I would expect more cooperation from a fellow law enforcement officer."

"As a fellow law enforcement officer," Reader said, "I'm surprised that official observers would find it necessary to disguise themselves with greasepaint. Maybe you haven't heard that minstrel shows have been politically incorrect for some time."

"Stow the sarcasm," Stevens said. "The governor will vouch for me and my mission."

"I'll be sure and check with him," Reader said. "Before I do, though, maybe you could fill me in on the exact nature of the mission you and Mr. Marcus were observing."

"We'd received reliable information that the Elkins were

operating an illegal moonshine still on their property."

It was all Owen could do to keep from leaping out of his chair. "What a load of crap."

Reader waved a calming hand. "And acting on this reliable information, you found it necessary to attack the Elkins home with assault weapons and a flamethrower?"

"We understood that the three Elkins males were armed and dangerous," Stevens said. "Our men had orders not to fire unless they were fired upon. They followed those orders."

"Really?" Owen nodded toward the recorder on the center of the interview table. "Is that your official statement?"

"I was there," Stevens said. "That's what I saw."

Owen bit his tongue to keep from telling Stevens he was there as well. Instead, he said, "Moonshining is a federal offense. So I assume those men assaulting the Elkins home must have been federal agents."

"We proceeded with federal approval," Stevens said. "Using undercover agents to root out and destroy illegal liquor production."

Reader pinched his nostrils as if he'd smelled something vile. "Pretty deep undercover, I'd say. None of those men carried identification to indicate they were any kind of federal or state agent. And it's my understanding they failed to identify themselves as law enforcement officers before they started shooting."

"Before they returned fire, you mean," Stevens said. "The Elkins gave them no chance to identify themselves."

Reader swiped at his nose with his handkerchief and returned it to his pocket. "No. I said before they started shooting and I meant before they started shooting. And could you tell me how a civilian like Harrison Marcus happened to be observing a raid on moonshiners?"

For the first time, Stevens appeared uncertain. He answered in slow, measured tones, as if he were examining the facts himself before explaining them to a slow child. "When Betty Sue Gardner went missing, the governor assigned me to work with Mr. Marcus and the Davison campaign people. As a result,

I've spent a lot of time in the Barkley area recently. So when a state patrol presence was required on the Elkins matter, I was ordered to provide that presence. Mr. Marcus happened to be with me when I received the order and asked if he could come along. I saw no reason not to honor his request, so long as he stayed out of harm's way."

"And you just happened to have enough greasepaint for the two of you," Reader said.

"I suggest you contact the governor before you do something that could cost you your career," Stevens said.

"I serve at the pleasure of the citizens of this county, not the governor," Reader said. "And if there's any career at risk here, I'd say it's yours. That story you just told stinks like a stopped-up septic tank. And as a fellow police officer, I'm insulted you think I might buy any part of it."

Stevens shook his head. "Just contact the governor."

"And what do you think the governor will say when I tell him at least one of his official observers joined in the shooting spree?" Reader asked.

"That's absurd," Stevens said. "We were asked to observe and that's what we did."

"Somebody fired on the Elkins from the edge of the woods," Owen said. "Odds are it was somebody in your van. I'm guessing a residue test will show you've fired a weapon recently."

Stevens folded his arms across his chest. "I'm not talking any more until I see a lawyer."

Before interrogating Harrison Marcus, Owen and Reader stopped in Reader's office to compare notes.

"It's all bulllshit," Owen said. "Every word of it. Even 'the' and 'and.'"

"I know," Reader said. "He was making lots of it up on the fly. Couldn't bring himself to admit that Marcus was calling the shots."

"He can't hope to make that story stick."

"He may think he has a chance. After all, our story is a little more preposterous than his. Everybody knows the Elkins brew

273

their own whiskey. Stevens there claims he was just helping to enforce the liquor laws. On the other hand, we claim we were defending an accident report that's more than thirty years old."

"Surely the governor won't back Stevens' story."

"I'm guessing the governor won't want to talk to me tonight. He'll need some time to circle his wagons and confer with Davison. No way of knowing how tight they are. Or who owes what to whom. If Davison doesn't have something powerful on the governor, though, I can't see Rhodes putting his name on the story we just heard. If nothing else, supporting an armed raid on a moonshine still would put him on the short end of popular opinion in this part of the state." Reader opened his office door and stepped out into the hallway. "Let's see what your friend Marcus has to say."

Marcus had been joined in the interrogation room by his lawyer, a tall, thin man with a smile that went no deeper than his lips. The lawyer handed cards to Owen and Reader that identified him as Sinclair Brown, LLD, and demanded that his client be released immediately.

"Not going to happen," Reader said.

"My client is an upstanding citizen who was merely observing a valid police action."

"Your client rode in a van along with thugs carrying assault weapons who fired on innocent residents of my county. He's wearing the same outfit as those thugs. At least two men are dead."

"Police officers, killed in the line of duty by lawbreakers," the lawyer said.

"If those men were police officers, I'm Wyatt Earp," Owen said.

"There do seem to be some questions regarding the legitimacy of the men who attacked the Elkins home," Reader said. "Perhaps your client could help clear up a few of those questions."

Marcus leveled a sneer at Reader and appeared to be about to respond when Brown put a hand on his arm. "I've advised my client not to respond to any questions regarding the incident," the lawyer said.

"Well, until those questions are cleared up, I'm sure you'll understand that we can't release your client," Reader said.

"This is outrageous. My client was on the scene as an observer. He had nothing to do with what transpired."

"Then your client has nothing to fear from the law," Reader said. "But until I'm sure that what you say is true, your client will remain a guest of the county."

Marcus sat stolidly through this exchange, as if it didn't concern him. A thin ring of greasepaint circled his neck like a noose. Whatever satisfaction Owen gleaned from seeing the man in custody was mitigated by the fear that his claim to be nothing more than an observer might hold up in court.

Sinclair Brown snatched his briefcase from the interrogation table and headed for the door. "I'll be back tomorrow with release papers. Until then, Harrison, don't say a word to these gentlemen."

Reader was right about Dusty Rhodes's reluctance to get involved with the Elkins raid. The governor's office reported that he was unavailable to take calls for the remainder of the evening. Some hint of his official position came in the morning edition of the Barkley Democrat, which reported that "...a state raid on a suspected moonshine still on the property of Victor Elkins of Raleigh County left two men dead when the suspects resisted arrest." A state police spokesperson expressed confidence that "...arrests would be forthcoming."

Owen stormed into Thad Reader's office the next morning and slammed a copy of the Democrat down on his desk. "Can they make this bullshit stick?"

"The governor's still not taking my calls," Reader said. "Somebody pulled that news story together in a hurry without even consulting me. I'm guessing it was prepared in advance and fed to the newspaper. It's all pretty general. They promise arrests will be forthcoming, but they don't say who's likely to be arrested."

"You can bet they're not talking about arresting the

governor's buddy Harrison Marcus," Owen said. "And where the story is specific, it's leaking lies. It claims the Elkins boys fired without provocation on officers who were dispatched to investigate rumors of illegal whiskey production."

"The Democrat won't piss unless the governor is holding its cock," Reader said. "They must have had that cover story ready to go in case the raid turned out badly."

"It's ludicrous," Owen said. "You'd deputized the Elkins boys. They were the real police officers on the scene. Not those gun thugs."

"They may claim those thugs were deputized as well. Then we'd have ourselves a Mexican standoff with the staties. It should sort itself out eventually. Trouble is, right now they're saying the Elkins boys fired first."

"That's bullshit. Vic Elkins floated a flare and issued a warning. That's when the thugs opened fire."

Reader shook his head. "Too bad we can't prove that."

Owen smiled. "Maybe we can."

Tom O'Day knocked on the sheriff's door and entered without waiting for an answer. "Is that Harrison Marcus in your holding cell?"

"It is," Reader said. "But he's got lawyers working to spring him."

"Did somebody finally make campaign lies a federal offense?" O'Day asked. "I must have missed that memo."

Owen and Reader exchanged glances. Then Owen banged his fist so hard on the edge of Reader's roll-top desk that his copy of the Democrat bounced. "What the hell, why not tell him? If they're using the media to spread lies about us, maybe we should use it to tell the truth about them."

They closed the office door and filled O'Day in on the history of Jason Davison's teenage DUI accident from the forging of the initial report through the death of the suspected LAPD forger to the assault on the Elkins homestead.

When they'd finished, O'Day slapped his hands together and said, "Boy oh boy, when this gets out, Davison won't be able to outpoll your average serial killer."

"It's clear we need some ground rules here," Reader said. "I don't care how many votes the guy gets. I want him behind bars. So anything you take public has to go through me first. If you have any doubts about doing that, remember that I can always bring you up on charges of obstructing justice. You're nowhere near out of the woods yet."

O'Day extended his hand to Reader. "It's a deal." Then he shook Owen's hand as well. "You say you can prove the Elkins boys didn't fire first last night. Let's start there."

By two o'clock that afternoon, a video went up on YouTube. Titled "West Virginia Justice?", it displayed footage from the surveillance cameras Owen had borrowed from Ken Kaylor and installed on the Elkins property. Murky at first, the video sprang to life when Vic Elkins' flare lit up the field in front of his home. Although there was no sound to record Vic's warning, the black-faced marauders caught in the flare's glare clearly opened fire on the house before muzzle flashes from the Elkins' guns answered their volleys. The video showed the first gunman dropping under the homeowners' fire and ended just after the fiery blaze leapt from the flamethrower and scorched a path to the house.

By three o'clock the video had gone viral, and by four o'clock Governor Dusty Rhodes issued a statement disavowing any connection with the assault, branding it a "rogue operation" and promising a thorough investigation.

Thad Reader and Owen took a copy of the governor's statement into the interrogation room, where they showed it to Brewer Stevens, the state police captain who had driven the black assault van. Harrison Marcus's lawyer, Sinclair Brown, who announced that he was also representing Captain Stevens, joined them in the room.

"Governor is calling last night a 'rogue operation,'" Reader said. "Your buddy Harrison Marcus claims he was only there as an observer. Looks like you're being thrown under the bus."

Stevens tried to look as if he weren't worried, but his left foot beat an uneven tattoo on the concrete floor. "We'll see about that."

"Nothing to see but the bus's undercarriage," Reader said. "Tell the truth now. Marcus was leading that little expedition. You were the observer, not him."

Sinclair Brown cleared his throat loudly before saying, "I'd advise you not to answer that, Brewer."

When Stevens didn't answer, Reader said, "You realize that this man advising you has a vested interest in seeing that Harrison Marcus goes free."

"I have a vested interest in seeing that both Captain Stevens and Mr. Marcus go free," Brown said.

"It makes sense that Marcus was calling the shots," Reader said to Stevens. "They took you along in case they needed to put an official face on everything. What did they tell you they were doing?"

"Moonshine raid. Like I told you."

"With no feds and a flamethrower in tow?" Owen said. "You're smarter than that."

Stevens shrugged. "They said those good ol' boys were harboring a fugitive. They didn't name names, but I assume it was Betty Sue Gardner. Her disappearance was the reason I was assigned to the Davison campaign."

"So Harrison Marcus was calling the shots," Owen said.

"Again, I'd advise you not to answer that," Brown said.

"What if you were asked that question under oath?" Reader said. "What would you say?"

Stevens paused before answering, but his left foot kept right on tapping. "I might plead the fifth. Depends on whether I'm still looking at the bus's undercarriage."

Reader shoved the governor's statement across the table to Stevens. "I don't think your view is likely to change anytime in the near future."

The next day, Tom O'Day launched the first of a planned series of articles on the West Virginia primary. In his nationally syndicated column, he asked and answered the question, "WHAT WAS THE DAVISON CAMPAIGN AFTER?"

Two days ago, a group of masked marauders launched an armed assault on the home of Raleigh County resident Victor Elkins that left two raiders dead, one wounded, and a high-ranking member of the Davison presidential campaign behind bars, along with a state police captain. Governor Dusty Rhodes has characterized this raid as a 'rogue operation' and promised a thorough investigation. To date, however, their investigation has failed to provide any answers, or even to address the basic question of what the raiders hoped to gain from their armed assault on private property.

This reporter believes that the misguided operation was the most recent in a series of violent assaults designed to recover evidence potentially damaging to Jason Davison's campaign for president. Evidence that over thirty years ago, Davison's responsibility for a fatal DUI accident was covered up by shifting the blame to a passenger in his car, his friend Linton Barney.

A copy of the original accident report naming Davison as the driver accompanied O'Day's article, along with a copy of the plea-bargained Department of Justice case against Linton Barney for this same accident. The article went on to cite the deaths of former LAPD officer Robert Reed and Dan Thornton, along with the firebombing of Ray Washburn's garage and several attempts on Owen Allison's life as examples of

... Seven violent incidents, ranging from arson to murder, in the last three months that can be linked to the original accident report listing Jason Davison as the driver in a fatal DUI accident. One such instance might be written off as a random event. Two could possibly comprise a coincidence. But seven in three months suggest a concerted effort to destroy evidence that could prove damaging to the Davison campaign. Both the initial shifting of blame for the fatal accident

and the ruthless attempts to cover up that shift provide
a damning comment on the character of the current
presidential candidate.

O'Day's article ignited a media firestorm as TV announcers, radio commentators, internet bloggers and newspaper reporters rushed to verify his story and find a fresh angle on it. Several political analysts drew obvious parallels between Linton Barney's role as a foil in the long-ago accident case with his recent role in helping Jason Davison dodge any blame for the disappearance of Betty Sue Gardner. Commentators routinely attached the adjective "mysterious" to all mentions of Barney's death and Betty Sue's disappearance. Senator Davison's office issued a response observing that " …a teenage DUI offense should have no more bearing on the presidential election than Sam Halstead's college experiments with marijuana," just before Davison shifted his campaign activities to nearby Indiana.

A plague of reporters and TV newsmen descended on Barkley, packing the courtroom the next morning to hear Judge Rowan McKee set bail for both Harrison Marcus and Brewer Stevens at fifty thousand dollars. The two men posted bail and emerged from the courtroom flanked by four state troopers who led the way through a barricade of TV cameras and microphones as their lawyer Sinclair Brown followed, answering all interview requests with a terse " No comment."

Owen and Thad Reader had to run the same gauntlet of reporters as they made their way from the bail hearing to the sheriff's office, and Reader mimicked the lawyer's response, mouthing "No comment" every few feet. Once they reached the sheriff's office, Owen threw his body into a chair and asked, "How the hell could this happen? How could that judge turn those two murderers loose?"

Reader settled into the swivel chair behind his desk and said, "First thing you've got to know is that those white specks on Judge McKee's robes were lint from the governor's pocket."

"So he's the governor's man. There still ought to be some semblance of justice. We caught those two at the scene of the crime."

"Like their lawyer said, there was no evidence that either man was involved in the shooting. And the three Elkins boys did have an illegal still on their property." Reader offered Owen a stick of gum. "In fact, if it weren't for your video, those three boys would likely have been the ones facing the judge."

Owen refused the offer of gum. "Stevens had to have been the one shooting at us from the woods."

Reader unwrapped a stick of gum and put it in his mouth. "Tests showed his hands were clean."

"Then he must have been wearing gloves."

"We never found any. And there weren't any traces of gunpowder residue on his clothes either. It's just as likely there was another gunman who got away on foot when we stopped the van. From what you saw, the shooter in the woods was aiming at the raiders, not at you and the Elkins boys."

"Trying to make sure nobody was left alive to point their fingers at Marcus and Stevens," Owen said. "Even if those two didn't fire any weapons, they were running the show."

"By the time we go to court, we've got to be able to prove exactly who was running what," Reader said. "Having the two of them out on bail doesn't change that. I think the judge was right on one point. Neither of them is likely to skip town. They'll both be around for the trial."

"The judge today bought their moonshine raid story. Is that likely to stand up when they go to trial?"

"It's pretty thin. But there's no question the Elkins were operating a still."

"For their own consumption. The moonshine story is so thin it's transparent." Owen shook his head. "How can Marcus and Stevens expect anyone to believe it?"

"They never expected they'd have to use it. Their plan was to leave everything burned to a cinder. No witnesses. No files. Nothing to explain. No blowback on the campaign or the state police."

"Guess I'm lucky to be alive."

"It's more than luck. You were ready for them. And you'd

handpicked the Elkins."

The receptionist buzzed Reader to say that the waiting area was full of reporters.

"Guess I'll have to elaborate on my 'No comment' comment." Reader stood. "We don't want you bothered by those dirt diggers though. Why don't you hang out here in my office for the rest of the day? I'll have my reception guys fend off press visitors and phone calls."

Owen barricaded himself in Thad Reader's office through most of the afternoon, until Phil Blatt cracked the door open and said, "Got a call you might want to take. Lady says she's a friend of yours."

Owen manufactured a half laugh. "Everybody's my friend today."

"Said to tell you her name was Theresa Thornton."

"What do you know? She really is a friend. Put the call through."

Theresa rushed her words as soon as Owen answered her call. "Owen. That man. The man on TV who was released today with that state trooper."

"You mean Harrison Marcus."

"That's the one. I'm pretty sure he's the man who was visiting Dan before he died. The man who called himself Alex Matthews."

24

AN ARRESTING FITTING

"Are you sure, Theresa?" Owen asked. "You told me you'd only caught a glimpse of the phony reporter who visited Dan."

After a short pause, Theresa said, "I'm not a hundred percent certain, no. But I think I could pick him out of a lineup."

"That may not be necessary. Didn't the local sheriff dust your house for fingerprints?"

"Yes, but that was over a week after Dan died. And over two weeks after he'd talked with the reporter. I'd cleaned the study at least twice between the first reporter meeting and the sheriff's dusting. I told the sheriff that."

"I'll talk to the sheriff and send him copies of Marcus's prints. Maybe we'll get lucky."

"He's the man. I feel it, even if I did only catch a glimpse of him."

As soon as he'd hung up, Owen called Sheriff James McDonald of Washington's Whatcom County and forwarded copies of Marcus's prints. Then he filled Thad Reader in on Theresa's suspicions.

"It's great, isn't it?" Owen said. "Shouldn't that be enough to get the bastard back behind bars?"

"Better wait for the fingerprint results before you start celebrating," Reader said.

"But that seems like a long shot."

"So's Theresa's ID. You said she sounded tentative."

"Couldn't we arrange for her to view a lineup? Or a set of photos with his mug shot mixed with others?"

"Wouldn't hold up in court. The way Marcus has been all over the evening news, the defense would have the results of any lineup ID thrown out. The judge who let Marcus and Stevens out on bail is in Dusty Rhodes' pocket. We'll need something stronger than Theresa's ID to get Marcus back under our roof. He's a public figure."

"A public figure who's been tied to at least one murder and one attempted murder."

"The judge bought his story that he was just along as an observer on the Elkins raid."

"He was the one behind it. He was calling the shots."

"But he wasn't one of the ones shooting. We just need to be patient. We'll get him. So long as he's involved in Davison's campaign, he's not a flight risk."

"I'm not convinced of that."

"So long as Marcus doesn't know we want him for the Thornton killing as well, he's not likely to run. We don't want to show that hand until we've got stronger evidence. In the meantime, we can try to prove he was more than just an observer on the Elkins raid."

The second of Tom O'Day's series of West Virginia articles came out the next morning. It focused on the Elkins family and the "rogue" assault on their private residence and was accompanied by photos of the family members. Vern was shown kneeling in the field and holding a string of tin cans from their jerry-rigged alarm system, and Virg was depicted in his wheelchair cradling an AR-15 on his lap and holding Bruiser's leash as the dog sniffed at the charred remains of the mattress that had provided temporary cover on the Elkins' porch. Both brothers wore camouflage caps embroidered with the circled star emblem of the American Legion.

But the highlight of the article was the account of the experience of the women hiding in the mine while the attack on their homestead raged outside. The report of their ordeal was accompanied by a photograph of Trish in her nurse's uniform with her arm around Ruth in front of the craggy mine entrance. Even sitting, Ruth's head barely exceeded the height of the mine opening. O'Day quoted Ruth's report of the sounds of gunfire resonating in the echo chamber of the mineshaft. "But the worst of it came after the shooting stopped. We didn't know what had happened, and Trish turned off the lamp on her miner's hat so we wouldn't be found if our menfolk didn't … well, it was too awful to contemplate, hunched over in all that blackness. Waiting and worrying. It was a hellish eternity before Vern Elkins found us with his flashlight and told us it was all right to come out."

O'Day was careful not to mention the other women hiding in the mine, since it wasn't certain that the whereabouts of Michelle Barney and Judith Allison were known to "Davison's crew of paid assassins," as the newspaperman characterized the raiders, repeating his accusation that the object of the assault was the continued coverup of a fatal DUI accident in the candidate's past.

As soon as the thug who was wounded in the Elkins raid had recovered enough to be questioned, Owen and Reader visited his hospital room. The same lawyer who had represented Harrison Marcus and State Police Captain Brewer Stevens was at his bedside. The thug, Danny Bridgeman, was a young man with curly black hair and a protruding jaw that ruined an otherwise handsome profile. He fidgeted in his hospital bed, but his movements were constrained by the cast on his right arm and the handcuffs on his left wrist.

Reader, who remained standing while Owen took a seat next to Bridgeman's lawyer, opened the questioning. "All right, Danny. You want to tell us what you were doing at the Elkins place the other night?"

Bridgeman glanced nervously at the lawyer and said, "I was part of a police raid on their moonshine still."

"So you're a state policeman?" Reader said.

"No. Not exactly."

"Not even close," Reader said. "You had no identification to show you were an officer of the law and you failed to mention it when you were arrested."

"My client was unconscious when he was admitted to the hospital," the lawyer said.

"He's had plenty of chances to mention it since he's been awake," Reader said.

"Captain Brewer Stevens deputized me," Bridgeman said.

"And why have you waited this long to tell us?" Reader asked.

Bands of sweat formed under the armholes of Bridgeman's hospital gown. "I was scared."

"But you have no papers documenting your alleged appointment," Reader said. "Didn't it strike you as strange that you wore no uniforms, disguised yourselves with greasepaint, and advanced on the Elkins home with flamethrowers and assault rifles under the cover of night?"

"I trusted Captain Stevens."

"And how do you know Captain Stevens?"

"I met him at the state police academy."

'Before you washed out. So Captain Stevens recruited you for the job?"

"That's right."

"And how much were you paid?"

The lawyer interrupted. "You don't have to answer that."

"Son, let's be clear here," Reader said. "Strictly speaking, you don't have to answer any damn thing at all. We've already told you that, just before we told you anything you do say can be used against you. But let me add this to that warning." Reader nodded to the lawyer. "This man would rather you didn't say anything at all. He's representing the people who got you into this mess. Two of those men are already out on bail. I'm here to tell you, though, there's precious little chance you'll be getting out. We have videotape of you firing on innocent citizens."

"I was returning their fire."

"That's not what the video shows," Owen said.

Reader made a calming gesture with his open palm. "Son, your lawyer here has bigger fish to take off the hook. Your best chance for leniency is to cooperate with us and tell us what we want to know. So I'll ask you again. How much were you paid?"

Bridgeman picked at the cast on his right arm with his handcuffed left hand. "Two thousand dollars."

"And since this was official state business, I assume you had to submit time cards and fill out a withholding form," Reader said.

Bridgeman grimaced. "No. We were paid in cash. Half before and, well, we were supposed to get half after."

"Doesn't seem like a lot of pay for getting shot at," Reader said. "Who paid you the up-front money?"

"The man with Captain Stevens."

The lawyer bolted to his feet. "I'm afraid I must insist you stop badgering my client. He's much too weak to continue this interrogation."

"Is that right, son?" Reader asked. "Do you feel like you can't continue?"

Bridgeman slumped back against his pillow. "Whatever."

"We'll stop for now," Reader said. "But we'll be back when you're feeling better."

As they left the hospital, Reader said, "Kid must have thought he was just being paid for playing cowboys and Indians."

"With real bullets," Owen said. "Do you think that deputizing claim was real too?"

"Even if they did deputize him, it's not likely to stand up in court. The other two gunmen were real scumbags. Ex-cons with rap sheets as long as King Kong's dong."

"At least you managed to get it on record that Marcus was more than just an observer," Owen said. "He bankrolled the operation."

Reader smiled. "There's that, for sure."

Owen had barely settled in at his desk when Reader and Tom O'Day pounded into his office. Reader's face was flushed with excitement. "We've got a fresh lead on Betty Sue. She used her phony ID and credit card to pay for a visit to a Planned Parenthood clinic near Zanesville. There's a good chance she's still in the area."

"How soon can we leave?" Owen asked.

"I've got a court date in a half hour. No telling how long that will run."

"We shouldn't be wasting time." Owen stood up. "I can go alone."

"Not a chance," O'Day said. "I'm going with you. If you find Betty Sue, she'll need to see someone she knows and can trust."

"He's right," Reader said. "And take Mary Galardi as backup."

"Isn't that overkill? If Betty Sue trusts O'Day, the two of us should be able to handle her."

"It's not just Betty Sue we have to worry about. In the past month you've had to dodge bombs, bullets, and a flamethrower because someone thought you had files that could endanger Davison's candidacy. What do you think those people will do if they know you have Betty Sue in custody?"

"You're right. I should have thought of that myself."

"Plus, Betty Sue may find a female officer to be reassuring. Mary's scheduled for the afternoon shift. She's likely to be at home now. Arrange a pick up and tell her to bring an extra uniform."

"You thinking we'll be in Ohio overnight?" O'Day asked.

"I think if you find Betty Sue, you'll need a disguise to bring her in safely."

"It's about a four-hour drive," Owen said to Tom O'Day. "How soon can you be ready?"

"I'm as ready as I'll ever be."

Owen picked up his desk phone. "Then let's get to it." He called Mary Galardi, and then he and O'Day drove by her house to pick her up.

"Haven't seen you since Columbus," Owen said as he helped Mary transfer her duffel bag to the trunk of his patrol car. "How have you been?"

"Sheriff's got me on a reduced schedule. I'm not sure I'll ever be able to fire my gun again. I hear you've had to use yours a couple of times since Columbus. Did it bother you?"

"Didn't have a lot of time to think about it at the Elkins house." Owen slammed the trunk lid down. "Don't believe I hit anything. Of course, I didn't hit anything in Columbus but the tires of that black Mercedes."

"That Mercedes. I won't soon forget it. Or its passenger."

Mary slid into the back seat of the patrol car and Owen introduced O'Day. "Mary saved my life in that Columbus airport shoot-out," Owen said. "Guy was aiming an Uzi at us. And she shot him."

"Good to know we're well protected," O'Day said.

Mary grimaced as she fastened her seat belt. "I hope I never have to go through anything like that again."

Owen pulled away from the curb. Instead of making a left onto Robert Byrd Drive, he drove a block beyond his turn, stopped to let two cars pass him, and, when nothing appeared in his rear view mirror, he made three successive right turns and picked up Byrd Drive that way. Satisfied that no one was tailing him, he headed for I-77 northbound.

"So. Was Columbus the first time you ever fired your gun in the line of duty?" O'Day asked Mary.

"First time off the range."

O'Day took a small notebook from his pocket and held it up so Mary could see it from the back seat. "Mind if I take down a few notes?"

"Ask away and I'll let you know if I mind."

"How long have you been with the sheriff's office?"

"Two years."

"Are you a native of Barkley?"

"Grew up there. Went to college in Huntington. Marshall."

"Married?"

"Divorced."

"Any children?"

"None. Decided right quick my ex wasn't a good bet as a father."

"What drew you to law enforcement?"

"Not a lot of jobs around. My best friend from college died of an overdose and I thought I might be able to save some lives."

"How'd that work out?"

"Saved mine," Owen said.

"Any others?" O'Day asked.

"Pried a couple of high school kids out of a wrecked Chevy and got them to the emergency room on time. Same with a motorcyclist who couldn't handle our switchbacks. Not much luck with druggies, though."

"How's that?" O'Day asked.

"Oh, we save them all right. But it's a short-term deal. Find them near death. Shoot them with naloxone. They come around, swear at us for interrupting their high, and are back again the next week. We can't always get to them in time."

Owen didn't need to be reminded about the opioid problem. His adopted son had been hooked on OxyContin for a harrowing period during his junior year in high school. "It's worse here than anywhere in the country," he said. "In Huntington last August, there were twenty-eight heroin overdoses and two fatalities in the space of four hours."

O'Day jotted figures in his notebook. "I think I remember reading that. It was national news."

Owen marveled at O'Day's interview technique. In the space of ten minutes, he'd learned more about Mary than Owen had gathered in the two years she'd worked for Thad Reader.

The freeway was almost free of traffic as it wound through tree-lined slopes, creek-side valleys, and exposed sandstone cuts that had been blasted out of the hillsides and were seamed with dark streaks that looked like a map of the heart's arteries.

As they left West Virginia and crossed the Ohio River at Williamstown, Thad Reader called to say they had an update on Betty Sue's location. She'd used her credit card to pay for a motel room just outside of Zanesville. Owen punched the address Reader gave into his GPS. "We're a little more than an hour from that motel right now. If she's there, she's ours."

"Keep me updated," Reader said before signing off.

"My turn to ask questions," Mary said to O'Day from the back seat. "What's your relationship to Ms. Gardner?"

"I've been covering the campaign in your state. Interviewed

her a couple of times."

"But you think she'll trust you to bring her back. Why's that?"

"My last few columns have been critical of Davison. She contacted me just after Linton Barney claimed to have been her lover. Said it wasn't true."

"I don't recall reading about that," Mary said.

Owen knew O'Day shouldn't be elaborating on his real relationship with Betty Sue Gardner. "O'Day told us about the call," Owen said. "We weren't sure it was bona fide. If it weren't, reporting it would make Davison out a liar and could upset the election."

"And get me sued," O'Day said.

"But if it were true…" Mary began.

"If it were really Betty Sue, we hoped she would call back when the story didn't appear in the news. We put a trace on O'Day's phone so we could locate her and bring her in if she did call back."

"So she didn't call back," Mary said.

"No. But now we're pretty sure the call was bona fide," Owen said. "We know Barney didn't get Betty Sue pregnant. Autopsy results showed he'd had a vasectomy."

"So Davison really was her secret lover."

"Looks that way," O'Day said.

"So why won't she just turn herself in?"

"I'm guessing she's afraid," Owen said. "And she has a good right to be. We haven't released news of the vasectomy, and there's every indication that Barney was killed to make sure he didn't recant on his claim to be Betty Sue's lover."

"To paraphrase your sheriff," O'Day said. "She realized she'd bit off more than she could swallow."

"So what do we do if Betty Sue won't open her motel room door to Mr. O'Day here?" Mary asked.

Owen tightened his grip on the steering wheel. "Then you and I will have to bring her in kicking and screaming."

A canopy of mid-afternoon thunderclouds hid the sun when

Owen approached the Comfy Inn Motel on Sixth Street in Zanesville. He drove past the motel's VACANCY sign and parked a block down the street to avoid a stir that might attract the attention of motel residents and alert Betty Sue. He left O'Day and Mary in the patrol car and walked back to the motel office. The stout woman behind the registration desk wore matted gray hair over a "What is it this time?" look.

Owen showed his badge and asked if she had a Margaret Blair registered. It was the name that went with Betty Sue's phony credit card.

The woman lifted her glasses from the cord around her neck, examined Owen's badge, and asked, "She done something wrong?"

"We just need to ask her a few questions. Is she in one of your units?"

"Unit Fourteen. In the back row. Came in around noon."

"Is there a man with her?"

"Wasn't when she checked in. Can't rightly say about now. I can't see the unit from here."

"Do you have a plan of the unit?"

The woman pulled a stack of yellowing drawings from a creaking file drawer, laid them on the registration desk, and disturbed the dust on the top drawing with her index finger. "All them rear units got the same plan."

Owen examined the drawing and nodded. "All right. Thanks for your help. Just stay right here at your desk, please. There shouldn't be any commotion."

Owen walked down the street to the parked patrol car where O'Day and Mary waited. "There are two rows of units," he reported. "Betty Sue is in Unit Fourteen in the back row, using the name that goes with her credit card. There's a window in the rear of the unit. I'll go behind the motel and watch through that window. I'll let you know when I'm situated. When I am, the two of you leave the patrol car and go knock on her door. With any luck, O'Day should be able to talk her out."

O'Day nodded once, his face as grim as the darkening skies.

The rear of the motel ran parallel to a pair of abandoned

railroad tracks and served as a dumping ground for used pizza boxes, crushed beer cans, empty coffee containers, and other debris that tumbled from the overstuffed garbage cans at either end of the row of units. Owen picked his way through the debris, counting the windows until he came to the back of Unit Fourteen. The rear windows were narrow and raised seven feet off the ground, either to keep the occupants from getting out or voyeurs from peeking in. An inverted wooden box under the window of the room next to Unit Fourteen suggested that at least one Peeping Tom had managed to overcome the architectural barrier.

Owen repositioned the inverted box under the window of Betty Sue's unit and used it as a stepping stool to peer into the room. The window opened into the bathroom, but with the bathroom door open the flickering light of a TV set illuminated two bare feet and a pair of legs on the edge of a twin bed.

Owen called O'Day to report, "I've got my eyes on her. She's lying on the bed watching TV. Time for you guys to go visiting. I'll stay on the line. If she lets you in, O'Day, you should go in alone and leave Mary outside to guard the door. Betty Sue is leery of police officers, but she should trust you and you can explain the situation to her. It's important she understands that Mary and I aren't threats before you let us in."

"I understand," O'Day said. "We're on our way."

The knock on the door brought the bare feet out of bed and sent their owner scurrying out of Owen's line of vision.

O'Day's voice overrode the murmur of the TV set. "Betty Sue, it's Tom O'Day. Please open the door."

Betty Sue reappeared with her back to the bathroom door. She held a revolver in her right hand.

"She's got a gun," Owen said into his cell phone.

After another knock, O'Day said, "Betty Sue, put the gun down. I'm here with friends."

Betty Sue stared at the motel door, then looked down at the gun in her hand as if she were wondering how O'Day knew she was armed. Finally she turned, looked straight at the bathroom window, and raised the gun barrel.

Owen jumped down from the wood box just before a pistol shot shattered the window.

"Betty Sue," O'Day shouted. "Put the gun down and open the door. We're here to help you."

Mary's voice came over Owen's cell phone. "Owen. Are you all right?"

"I'm okay," Owen said. He shifted his cell phone into its camera mode and held it just over the edge of the windowsill like a periscope, half expecting it to be shot away. Instead, he saw the image of Betty Sue on one knee in the bathroom doorway, laying her gun on the floor. Then she disappeared from the camera's view, but Owen could hear her say, "I've laid the gun down. I'm going to open the door. Please don't shoot."

Owen called O'Day to say, "It's true. I saw her put the gun down."

"Then I'm going in," O'Day said.

Owen heard the motel door open, then climbed back onto the wooden box in time to see Tom O'Day envelop Betty Sue in a hug.

By the time Owen had picked his way back through the debris to the front of Unit Fourteen, Mary was guarding the closed door and motel guests were poking their heads out of the doors on either side of the unit. He raised both hands in the air and said, "It's all right. Everything's under control. We're sorry to have disturbed you."

Half of the open doors closed, but the other half remained open as guests came out into the parking lot to watch. Owen gave Mary the keys to the patrol car and said, "Get your extra uniform and my baseball cap and jacket from the trunk and bring the car as close as you can get it to the motel room door." As Mary left, he told the remaining onlookers, "Nothing to see, folks. Show's over," and squeezed through the motel room door, trying to minimize the interior view available to the gawkers.

As Owen entered, Betty Sue stepped free of O'Day's encircling arms. "I'm so sorry," she said. "When I saw your hat in the window I thought you were one of the state troopers Jason sent to find me. That's why I shot at you."

"I'm glad to hear it was nothing personal." It was Owen's first close look at the remodeled Betty Sue. She was thinner than he had remembered, her hair had been dyed brown, and there were worry lines under her eyes. She was still an attractive woman, but no longer a knockout.

"You're safe now," O'Day said. "We're going to take care of you."

"I'm with another deputy who's bringing our patrol car around," Owen said. "She knows nothing about your deal to spy on the Davison campaign and it's important she be kept in the dark about it."

"I already told her that," O'Day said.

"The fewer people who know about it, the better," Owen said. "If word that you were planted leaks out, it could ruin a few careers."

"Mine included," Betty Sue said. "I understand. It would make me look less like a wronged woman and more like a scheming bimbo."

"And would generate a lot of sympathy votes for Jason Davison," Owen said.

"To be clear," Betty Sue said, "right now I don't much care about Jason's poll numbers. Or whether you think I'm a victim or a bimbo. I'm feeling like a hunted rabbit and am grateful for any help you can give."

Mary came into the motel room with a bundle of clothes under her arms. Owen introduced the two women and said, "We'll do our best to keep you safe. We're going to start by asking you to slip into something less comfortable. Mary's brought a deputy sheriff's uniform for you to wear on the way back to Barkley. We're putting you into protective custody, but we don't want anyone watching the roads or our office to know we have you."

Betty Sue sniffled and nodded as Mary took her hand and led her into the motel bathroom.

After ten minutes, Owen led the way out of the motel, followed by two female deputies. The two deputies flanked Tom O'Day, who wore a Cleveland Indians cap under a hoodie and kept his head bowed as the deputies led him to the back seat of the waiting patrol car. O'Day was handcuffed to Betty Sue Gardner, outfitted in a deputy's uniform that was at least one size too large for her. When the tall reporter had trouble ducking through the rear door of the car, Betty Sue pushed the top of his hoodie until it cleared the doorframe and then slipped into the rear seat beside him.

Owen paused in front of his patrol car and announced, "We're done here, folks," to the remaining gawkers. Then he lowered himself into the passenger seat and the onlookers parted as Mary backed out and drove to the motel office, where Owen gave his card to the manager, along with a promise to pay for the room damages.

Betty Sue sighed as the motel's VACANCY sign receded in the distance. "Don't worry," O'Day said, "things will be all right now."

"After listening to his campaign lies, I should have known better than to believe that louse would leave his wife for me," Betty Sue said. "When I told him I was pregnant, he was so mad I thought he'd strap me down and do the abortion himself. Or at least watch while one of his flunkies did it."

"Did you consider Linton Barney a flunkey?" Owen asked.

"No. Linton was lovely. Almost too nice. Like the platoon member that you know isn't going to make it through the war movie."

"So you weren't surprised by his death?" Owen said.

"God, no. I didn't mean that. I was not only surprised, I was scared. It was so convenient. I know Jason must have arranged it."

"I thought the two of them had been friends for a long time."

"They had. But Jason always took him for granted. Like he'd been bought and paid for." She paused. "He never let you forget who signed the checks."

Thunder rolled and rain pelted down as Mary turned off I-70 and headed south on I-77. The storm followed them to the West Virginia border, where they encountered a traffic back-up waiting to cross the Marietta-Williamstown Bridge over the Ohio River.

"Wouldn't expect to find rush-hour traffic outside of Marietta," Mary said.

"Looks like the problem is construction on the bridge approach," Owen answered.

Two lanes of traffic fed slowly into a single lane that stalled periodically as a backhoe took large chunks of earth from the berm of the existing bridge approach. Mary finally worked their way to the head of the line, waited while the backhoe swung its load away from the traffic lane, and crossed the bridge.

As soon as they made it across, Owen raised Thad Reader on the car phone to tell him about the tie-up on the bridge and update their expected arrival time.

"Now that you're in West Virginia, the state police might be curious about our out-of-county activities. They've all got their eyes open for Betty Sue, so you better keep yours open as well."

"Roger that," Owen said. As if on cue, a blue-and-gold state police car pulled in behind him with its flasher blinking and siren screeching.

Reader's voice came over the intercom. "What's going on?"

"State police just lit us up," Owen said.

"Leave your radio on so I can listen in," Reader said.

"What do you think?" Mary asked.

"Slow down and take your time stopping," Owen said. "I think we have to be prepared for anything. These guys could be wolves in cops' clothing. Unsnap your holster."

The snap resonated through the car. "I'm not sure I could use my Glock again," Mary said.

"It's not likely you'll have to. But we better be prepared." Owen unholstered his own revolver, held it in his lap, and covered it with his Mountie's hat.

"Oh God," Betty Sue said.

"Everyone stay calm," Owen said. "It's probably just a routine traffic stop."

A man wearing a yellow poncho with the triangular state

police logo appeared at Mary's window, circling his finger to indicate he wanted it rolled down.

Rain splashed into the car as Mary rolled down the window. "Something wrong, Officer Coggins?" Owen asked, reading the policeman's nametag for Reader's benefit.

"Noticed you crossing the bridge. You're a far piece from your jurisdiction. Thought you might need help."

"Got a tip some fugitives from a county breakout were spotted in Ohio," Owen said, ignoring the policeman's offer of help.

"Any luck?" Coggins asked.

"Nabbed one. Two got away. Lost them in the storm."

"Rain's been a bitch tonight." Coggins leaned down and shined a flashlight into the back seat. Betty Sue raised her handcuffed left hand, dragging O'Day's right hand up with it.

Coggins shifted his flashlight beam to Owen's lap. "Your hands cold there, deputy?"

Owen felt the cold steel of his revolver under his Mountie's hat. "No. Why?"

"You know the drill. We like passengers to keep their hands where we can see them."

"Oh. Sorry." Owen raised both hands, rotated them as if he were a magician showing he had nothing up his sleeve, and laid them on the brim of his Mountie's hat.

"That's better." Officer Coggins stood upright. "I'll let you get back on the road. Just thought you might could use a little help. Being so far from home and all."

"No, we're okay. But thanks for the thought." Mary rolled up her window and nosed the patrol car back into the traffic lane.

Reader's voice came over the intercom. "What was that all about?"

"Fishing expedition," Owen said. "Wanted to see if we were carrying anybody."

"Anybody like Betty Sue?"

"Be my guess. Doing a favor for Senator Davison. I think we passed muster, though. Betty Sue's in uniform, handcuffed to a perp."

"A perp?"

"O'Day. He looks appropriately sinister."

"Type casting," Reader said.

"I heard that," O'Day said.

When Owen signed off the call, Mary asked, "You think they bought our story?"

"I think so. Coggins barely looked at Betty Sue. And I think he was a legitimate officer. He had the stopping ritual down pat. All the same, I think we're better off if we stick to back roads the rest of the way home. Even if they do suspect us, they aren't likely to stake out anything but the major routes in this weather."

Mary nodded. "Country roads, take us home."

25

DEUS SEX MACHINA

Owen arrived at his office the next day to find two extra TV cameras in the sheriff's interrogation room. Tom O'Day was fussing with one of them while Reader watched.

"Did someone alert the media?" Owen asked.

"I'm the media this morning," O'Day said. "I'm recording an exclusive interview with Betty Sue."

"How's that going to work?" Owen asked.

"Betty Sue requested it. She wants to get her story out," O'Day said.

"The sooner she does, the safer she'll be," Reader said. "And we can all get back to work." The sheriff turned to leave the interrogation room.

"Stay," O'Day said. "You need to be a part of this."

"It's theater, not law enforcement," Reader said.

"It's a little of both," O'Day said. "Think of it as a campaign video."

"I'm running unopposed."

"In the primary. You'll have an opponent in November."

"Your interview's a put-up job," Reader said. "As rigged as a clunker's odometer."

"It was your detective work that located her," O'Day said. "Nothing rigged about that."

"We only found her because we could trace the credit card her handlers gave her."

"She needs your protection," O'Day said. "She's been in fear for her life. She still is. We're not making that up."

Betty Sue entered the room with a female deputy. Owen barely recognized the woman he'd rescued the previous night. Her brown hair had been cut, washed, and set so it barely grazed her right eyebrow and rested gently on her shoulders. He thought her makeup was a little heavy around the eyes and lips, but maybe that was necessary for TV, and the worry lines had vanished. She looked more like a poised fashion model than a scheming seductress.

O'Day looked up from the nearest TV camera. "You look great, hon. Just sit here with the sheriff and I'll ask a few questions. You've got nothing to worry about."

"Actually, I've got a lot to worry about."

"Well, it won't hurt to let that show a little," O'Day said.

"I don't need motivation coaching." Betty Sue held up her left hand, which was trembling. "I'm really frightened." She clasped her hands together and forced them onto her lap.

Reader shifted uneasily in his seat as O'Day adjusted the TV cameras and set them running. Then he sat at the table opposite Reader and Betty Sue, introducing them to the camera and explaining that Reader was instrumental in bringing Betty Sue out of hiding and that she had come forward voluntarily and asked to be placed in the sheriff's protective custody.

Out of respect for Betty Sue's wishes and concern for her safety, O'Day explained, they were taking the precaution of conducting this closed interview in the sheriff's office. The reporter promised that Sheriff Reader would be available for a press conference once the current interview had been distributed. Because the details of Betty Sue's protective custody were still being worked out, though, he could not say when or whether Betty Sue herself would be available for media interviews.

After disposing of the preliminaries, O'Day turned to Betty Sue. "Let's get right to the heart of it. You've been the object of a nationwide search for over two weeks. What made you go into hiding?"

Betty Sue looked down at her lap as if she were gathering her thoughts. "I was afraid."

"Afraid of what?" O'Day asked.

"I'd been having an affair with Jason Davison. When I found out I was pregnant, I went to him. He insisted I have an abortion and said that bad things would happen to me if I didn't, or if I even told anyone he was the father of my child."

"So you ran," O'Day said.

"I ran. I didn't know what else to do."

"And you hid out, even though you must have known that most of the country was looking for you."

"I hid. I hadn't expected all the fuss. When it started, I wanted to come out of hiding. But then Linton Barney came forward and was killed. That frightened me even more."

O'Day's face was the model of a concerned listener. "Why was that?"

"It showed me how far Jason's people were willing to go to protect their candidate."

"Are you saying, then, that you did not have an affair with Linton Barney?"

Betty Sue straightened in her chair. "I definitely did not have an affair with Linton Barney."

"What reason would Barney have to lie publicly about an affair?"

"To protect his boss. And then he was killed."

"You say that in a way that seems to link Linton Barney's statement with his death. Do you have any reason to believe his death wasn't an accident?"

"I have no way of knowing. But Linton was always a careful rider. And whether or not his death was accidental, it left me in even more trouble, since I was the only person outside of Jason's campaign who knew for sure Linton had lied about being my lover."

"So what did you do?" O'Day asked.

Tears brimmed in Betty Sue's eyes. "I decided to have an abortion." Her shoulders shook as she struggled to control her emotions. "It was what Jason wanted. And after everything that had happened, I didn't want to have his child."

"But since he'd denied having an affair with you, you were still a potential danger to him."

"Yes. Oh, yes."

"So what made you stop hiding and come forward?"

"I'd been afraid too long. Jason had men everywhere looking for me. A few had come close to finding me. I was in a convenience store when two policemen were showing my picture to the manager. They didn't recognize me, but I knew I couldn't stay hidden much longer. I just didn't know anyone I could trust." Betty Sue put her hand on O'Day's arm and took a deep breath before proceeding. "Then I read your article on the way Jason had blamed his teenage DUI accident on Linton. I knew the man who wrote that article couldn't possibly be in Jason's pocket."

Watching through the one-way glass in the adjoining observation room, Owen thought, uh oh, this is getting sticky. Those are all good points, but they feel a little too rehearsed.

"The article you wrote mentioned Sheriff Reader," Betty Sue continued, nodding toward the sheriff. "I'd met him and trusted him. So I contacted the two of you and asked to be placed in protective custody."

O'Day smiled. "And here you are."

Betty Sue squeezed O'Day's arm. "And here I am."

Thad Reader squirmed in his seat. To the casual viewer, it might seem that he was embarrassed when Betty Sue singled him out for acknowledgement. But Owen knew he was seething over the blatant pretense that Betty Sue had come forward voluntarily.

O'Day seemed to sense Reader's impatience, because he brought the interview to a close, announcing to the cameras that he would make the film available to TV news outlets immediately and that a transcript would accompany his newspaper column tomorrow morning. He also repeated his promise that Thad Reader would be available for a press conference the next day.

As soon as O'Day turned the TV cameras off, Reader tore off his lapel microphone and tore into O'Day and Betty Sue. "You've made me party to a bald-faced lie."

"What lie?" O'Day asked.

"You said Betty Sue gave herself up voluntarily."

Betty Sue's lower lip trembled. "But I did."

"Only after we tracked you down," Reader said. "And you fired a shot at my deputy."

"Your deputy frightened me. But I was ready to come in voluntarily. I wasn't lying. I really did fear for my life."

"You better start fearing me," Reader said. "Until I get to the bottom of this mess, I'm keeping you both under my roof. You can call it protective custody if you like, but if I need to charge you, I will."

"With what?" Betty Sue asked.

"There's a long list to choose from," Reader said. "Obstruction of justice, fraud, perjury, impersonating a brunette."

Betty Sue failed to laugh at Reader's attempt at humor. "That's just not funny. I really was going to give myself up." Then she broke down and gasped out a series of staccato phrases between sobs. "Tired of being hunted.... Gave myself up.... Trusted you.... Need protection." She choked back her sobs and hurried toward the restroom.

Reader got the female deputy at the reception desk to follow her, then turned to O'Day. "You don't dare let your press and TV buddies interview that woman. She's a walking time bomb. If she lets it leak that she was planted in Davison's campaign, it could ruin your career. And I don't want to be collateral damage."

"I agree," O'Day said. "But she's big news right now. If you can keep her under wraps two more days until the election, Davison is likely to drop out of the running and she'll be old news."

"I don't give a damn who wins the election," Reader said. "I'm trying to solve a murder case. And while I'm at it, I'd like to keep my job."

"I understand," O'Day said. "You throw up the protective shield, and I'll insist any press contacts with Betty Sue run through me. She'll agree to that."

"Let's hope that's enough," Reader said.

In the late afternoon, Owen got a call from Sheriff McDonald of Whatcom County. The prints Owen had sent him failed to match any taken in the living room and study of Dan and Theresa Thornton's home in the foothills of Mount Baker.

Owen didn't try to hide his disappointment. "Damn. I was sure we'd get a match."

"The house had been cleaned pretty thoroughly between the time the phony reporter was there and the time we dusted for prints," McDonald said. "Don't forget, until you put us wise, we thought we were dealing with a suicide and didn't bother to take any prints inside the house."

Theresa had said she wasn't certain about her identification, Owen thought. But it would have been so satisfying to nail Harrison Marcus for murder. "Did you check for prints at the storage facility Dan visited with his killer?" he asked.

"We'd dusted the file cabinet that had held the missing documents. No luck with a match there, either."

"Well, the killer may have already decided Dan had to die by the time they visited the storage facility, so he would have been careful about leaving prints there. But I thought sure we'd find a match in the Thornton study."

"Like I said, it had been cleaned up pretty good."

Owen closed his eyes and visualized the Thornton's study. "Do me a favor. There's a tall bookcase to the left of the TV in the study. One of the middle shelves has a bunch of old Tranalytics reports. There'll be one titled 'Motorcycle Accident Causes and Cures.' We talked about it at the wake. Bag it and check it for prints."

"You think the killer might have looked at it?"

"The phony reporter was really after the backup data that went into that report. He and Dan would have talked about the motorcycle study during his first visit. There's a chance they would have looked at the report. It's not likely our man would have been wearing gloves then."

"We'll give it a shot."

Owen thanked the sheriff, hung up, and stared at the silent black receiver. "Damn," he said aloud, "I thought sure we'd nail the son of a bitch with that set of prints."

*****

305

Ruth's move from Shady Acres to the Elkins' homestead gave Owen the extra time he needed to finish repairing his office. Following the siege of the homestead, however, Ruth began insisting that they move back to their own house. Once Tom O'Day released the news of the doctored accident report, Owen reasoned that neither he nor Ruth were likely to be targets anymore, and he finally agreed to the move.

Michelle Barney elected to stay with Trish Elkins through the election, so Owen asked Judith to accompany Ruth as a temporary caretaker.

"I promised four days and I've been away a week already," Judith said. "And it's been anything but a vacation."

When Ruth interceded, though, Judith agreed to stretch her stay an extra two days and leave on Election Day.

Owen, Ruth, and Judith had their first home meal together on the evening following the release of O'Day's interview with Betty Sue. Owen expected that the dinner conversation would focus on the interview and the election, but his mother had other ideas.

As soon as they sat down, Ruth said, "Did you think my memory is so far gone I'd forget the color of the walls in your office?"

"I repainted it, Mom," Owen said. "It's the latest color. It's called celestial latte."

"I don't care if it is the latest color. It doesn't match the rest of the house."

"It was as close as I could get. We could redo the rest of the house to match. This place could stand a new paint job."

"It's still my place, and I don't want something called celestial latte on my walls. Whatever happened to plain old white?"

"It's still around, but the paint stores had a hundred different shades."

"Well, I prefer shade number one."

"I'll have it redone."

"Why'd you change it in the first place?"

From the tone of her question, Owen guessed she already

306

knew the answer. Hoping he was wrong, he said, "There was an accident."

"An accident with a firebomb. My memory may be failing, but I can still read the newspaper. Your Mr. O'Day told the whole world about your little accident. Why hadn't I heard about it from you?"

"I didn't want to upset you."

"Just because someone firebombs my home and tries to kill my son? Why would you think I'd be upset?"

"You're upset right now."

"Only when I see that new wall color."

"I told you, I'll take care of it."

"And how will you take care of whoever is trying to kill you?" Ruth asked.

"I don't have anything they want anymore. There's no need for them to come after me. And they've got bigger worries now."

"What sort of worries?" Judith asked.

"We've found Betty Sue Gardner. O'Day's interview with her will be on the evening news."

Ruth checked her watch. "That's only ten minutes from now."

"Don't worry. I've set up the recorder."

"Finish your dinner. I want to see the news while it's still fresh."

Owen wolfed down his dinner and cleared the table while Judith rinsed the dishes and Ruth fixed tea for the three of them. They settled onto the living room couch just in time to see the WSAZ TV call letters announcing the evening news. The two news anchors had trouble concealing their excitement as they told of Betty Sue's safe return, hyped O'Day's interview, and promised to air Jason Davison's reaction to the news.

Following three commercials, the news anchors led up to O'Day's interview by summarizing the controversy surrounding Betty Sue's disappearance while displaying a photo collage of Betty Sue, Jason Davison, and Linton Barney. Then they played excerpts from O'Day's interview, showing Betty Sue denying any affair with Linton Barney and naming Jason Davison as her lover. The interview had been edited so that it closed with Betty Sue's tearful acknowledgement that she had dropped out of sight because she "feared for her life."

"The poor girl," Ruth said.

Wishing he knew either a little more or a little less about Betty Sue's experience, Owen responded with a noncommittal grunt.

After another three commercials, the male half of the anchor team introduced footage of Jason Davison responding from his Indiana campaign headquarters. Reading from a prepared script, Davison began by saying, "Ever since Betty Sue Gardner disappeared, her plight has been on our minds and we have prayed daily for her safe return."

"Jesus Christ," Owen exploded at the TV. "What a hypocrite."

"Owen," Ruth said. "There's no need to swear."

"I can just imagine God's response to any prayers from Davison. He'd start by saying 'Jason WHO?'"

Davison went on to say that he was "...dismayed that Betty Sue had cast aspersions on the veracity of my departed friend Linton Barney, who is no longer around to counter her claims. It's also unfortunate that her abortion leaves us no way to determine the paternity of her unborn child."

"She's calling you a liar, asshole, not Linton Barney," Owen shouted.

Then, over Ruth's shushing, he heard something that stopped him cold. He quickly backed up the video to the point where he'd shouted down Davison's words to see the candidate address the close-up camera and say, "Although we are distressed by this woman's false claims, we are not surprised by them, because only yesterday we learned that Betty Sue Gardner was planted as a spy in our campaign headquarters and received undercover payments for her clandestine services."

26

OVER THE HILL

As soon as the newscast ended, Owen headed for his car. His cell phone rang as he turned the key in the ignition. He glanced at the face of the phone, saw that the caller was Thad Reader, answered and said, "I'm on my way in," as he backed out of his garage.

Betty Sue Gardner and Tom O'Day were sitting at the long mahogany table in the sheriff's conference room when Owen arrived. He joined Thad Reader on the opposite side of the table.

"All right," Reader said as soon as Owen was seated. "We all saw the telecast. Can Davison have any proof Betty Sue here was planted in his campaign?"

Betty Sue stared at the floor and shook her head.

"He doesn't have any proof," O'Day said. "It's all a bluff."

"Think carefully," Reader said to O'Day. "Your career and this woman's freedom could depend on it."

Betty Sue let out a sound that started as a soft wail and ended as a whimper.

"They can't have found out," O'Day said.

"Why not?" Reader said. "You did."

"It wasn't like I discovered it all on my own," O'Day said. "I was brought in after the affair began. They needed someone with media connections. Someone who could guide the story when it broke. They knew I hated Davison's guts for what he did to Larry Lewis."

"Davison made it sound as if he had proof," Owen said. "Could they trace a trail of money from the Halstead campaign to Betty Sue?"

Betty Sue shook her head. "No. I was paid in cash. Fifty thousand up front and fifty thousand if it comes off and Davison loses the election."

"That's a slug of cash," Reader said. "What did you do with it?"

"I deposited it a little at a time."

"So there's fifty grand sitting in your bank account that you can't really explain," Reader said.

"Not in my account. At least not in any account with my name on it." Betty Sue raised her eyes and looked at Tom O'Day. "I used the account attached to the phony ID and credit card they set up. I was careful. I did everything they told me to do. Used a separate computer and iPhone for all my transactions. Used different ATM machines so I never had to go into a bank."

"It doesn't make sense," Reader said. "If they knew about your phony ID and credit card, they would have found you before we did."

"Why do you say that?" Betty Sue asked.

"We lollygagged around calling and trying to coax you out under your own steam. Took our time getting organized before leaving for Zanesville. They wouldn't have wasted any time. They would have gone right in. And I'm guessing you wouldn't be here now."

"Maybe it is a bluff," Owen said. "What's he got to lose? Election's only the day after tomorrow. And it's still close. If he can create enough doubt about Betty Sue's credibility, he could win enough electoral votes to wrap up the nomination."

"And if he does," O'Day said, "he could be magnanimous and forgive Betty Sue without ever having to show any proof."

"And if he doesn't climb back into the race, he'll drop out of the running and nobody will care whether you were a plant or a patsy," Owen said. "Either way, he doesn't have to show his proof."

"You're the investigator," O'Day said to Reader. "Call his bluff. You're holding Betty Sue. Offer to file criminal charges if he can prove his allegations."

"Now wait a minute," Betty Sue said.

"I've got as much at stake as you." O'Day turned from Betty Sue to Reader. "You've got a press conference tomorrow morning. It's the day before the election. Put them on the spot. If someone asks about Davison's allegation that Betty Sue was a plant, tell them you're looking into the accusation and invite Davison to share any evidence that he has."

"Sounds risky," Reader said.

"After tonight's broadcast, there's no dodging the subject," Owen said. "Davison made his accusation publicly. Some reporter is sure to follow it up."

"They've already started phoning," Reader said.

"Let's think about how we'd prefer to have the subject brought up," O'Day said. "I have friends who can spin the question any way we'd like."

"Why am I not surprised?" Reader said.

"It's tomorrow morning that we don't want you to be surprised," O'Day said. "I won't be able to control all the questions you'll be getting. Let's spend some time now brainstorming what you'll say up front, what you're likely to be asked, and what you ought to answer."

"I'm supposed to be keeping the peace and catching bad guys," Reader said. "News management isn't in my job description."

"Don't worry," O'Day said. "It's at the top of mine."

Thad Reader held his press conference the next morning on the courthouse steps. None of Barkley's public buildings had a room large enough to accommodate the crowd of reporters that had converged to cover Betty Sue Gardner's return. Owen recognized the few local newsmen, reporters from the Charleston and Huntington TV stations, and one or two national news figures, but most of the milling faces were unknown to him.

The sheriff opened the conference with a short statement announcing Betty Sue's request to be placed in protective custody, a request he was honoring while investigating the various aspects of her case. As soon as he offered to answer

311

questions, the crowd erupted with a waving of white notebooks that looked like a flock of seagulls scavenging in the morning sun.

Reader acknowledged the raised notebook of a reporter from the Charleston Mail, a paper that had backed Jason Davison heavily. O'Day had advised him to get the tough stuff out in the open early.

The reporter smiled. "Sheriff, Miss Gardner's unsupported allegations seem to be timed to affect Jason Davison's chances in the upcoming presidential primary. The candidate claims that these allegations are false and that Miss Gardner was planted as a spy in his campaign. I'd like to know what you are doing about these allegations and counter claims."

Reader nodded, trying to look as if he were considering the question for the first time. "I'm currently investigating all the allegations surrounding Miss Gardner's disappearance and reappearance. If Senator Davison has any evidence to support his own allegations, I invite him to bring that evidence forward so that I can take appropriate action."

Reader paused, then acknowledged the raised notebook of a young blonde woman whom he recognized as a correspondent on the CBS evening news. The woman favored him with a camera-ready smile. "When you say 'appropriate action,' sheriff, can you be more specific?"

Reader shaded his eyes against the low morning sunlight. "Miss Gardner is currently in my custody. If there is any evidence to support the accusation that her claims are fraudulent, I have forty-eight hours to charge her as a criminal. If no such evidence appears, she will remain in my custody until I am convinced that there is no threat to her well-being."

The questioner jotted something in her notebook and said, "Forty-eight hours takes us just past election day."

Reader nodded. "I'm not concerned with the outcome of the election. My office is investigating serious charges involving threats of bodily harm, armed assaults, arson, fraud, and possibly murder. In my mind, those concerns take precedence over the timing of the election."

Reader faced another flurry of waving notebooks and

acknowledged a balding man whom Tom O'Day had pointed out as a friendly questioner. "You say a possible murder," the man said. "Are you speaking of Linton Barney's death? Is there some reason to believe it wasn't accidental?"

Reader looked out at the crowd. "We are currently investigating the circumstances surrounding Mr. Barney's death. That's all I'm at liberty to say right now."

The balding reporter followed his question by saying, "You mentioned assaults. Plural. Can you be more specific?"

"The assaults are definitely plural," Reader said. "In the past month I've had deputies assaulted in their homes, in a convalescent facility, and in the Columbus airport. Just a few days ago, several deputies were under fire in an unprecedented assault on the home of a county resident."

A reporter sitting on top of a WSAZ-TV van shouted, "Is it true that a member of Senator Davison's staff was involved in that assault?"

Reader frowned. "I'd appreciate it if you would all wait to be acknowledged before asking questions. In response to this question, though, it is true that Senator Davison's campaign organizer, Mr. Harrison Marcus, was present at the assault on the local home of Mr. Victor Elkins. Mr. Marcus has been released on bail. I can't tell you any more than that."

Reader acknowledged the young Mail reporter who had led off the questioning, who asked, "How is it that you have granted one reporter, Tom O'Day, exclusive access to interview Betty Sue Gardner, but have denied that access to the rest of us?"

A number of heads nodded in the audience.

Reader sighed. O'Day had prepared him for this question, but it wasn't one he was comfortable answering. "Mr. O'Day was instrumental in bringing Miss Gardner out of hiding. When she sought protective custody from my office, she agreed to an interview with Mr. O'Day because she trusted him and wanted to get her story out. She is in my custody, but she is not a prisoner, and it is my understanding that she has said as much as she wants to publicly. I'm not in the habit of worrying about press access, but so long as the woman is in my custody, there will be no media contacts that she doesn't approve of in advance."

"She and Tom O'Day, you mean," the reporter said.

Anger flashed in Reader's one good eye. Then he appeared to relax, and the good eye became as tranquil as its glass mate. "Miss Gardner does appear to have selected Mr. O'Day as her spokesperson."

"So Miss Gardner is telling us one thing and the candidate is telling us another," the Mail reporter said. "All we have is this circular 'he said/she said' argument, and your investigations aren't able to shed any light on it."

Standing on the courthouse steps, Owen was close enough to feel Reader's uneasiness. He knew the sheriff didn't feel the two sides of the argument had equal weight, and wouldn't want to leave that impression with the audience.

"I understand your frustration," the sheriff said. "There is one fact we've uncovered that has a bearing on that very issue. I believe I can share it with you without compromising any of our investigations. Once I do that, though, I'll take no more questions and bring this press conference to a close. Do I make myself clear?"

Heads nodded. At the edge of the crowd, Tom O'Day smiled.

"I believe I can state with some certainty that Linton Barney was not the father of Miss Gardner's aborted child," Reader said.

The crowd's crosstalk stopped and scores of notebooks flipped open.

Reader continued. "The autopsy we performed on Mr. Barney revealed that he'd had a vasectomy at least five years ago and that its effects had not been reversed."

The reporters began to shout follow-up questions, waving their hands.

"That's all we have for you today. Thanks for coming," Reader said and turned away from the microphone.

As the crowd dispersed, Owen followed Reader back to his office. "I thought that went pretty well," he said.

"Could have been worse," Reader said. "Could have been better, too. Davison's claim that Betty Sue was a plant is still hanging out there. It's time to find out whether the candidate is bluffing or whether he really had evidence to back up his claim."

Reader punched a button on his intercom and asked the receptionist to get Senator Davison on the phone. Then he put his desk phone into speaker mode and said, "Why don't you listen in?"

"You think the senator heard your press conference?" Owen asked.

"This call will go a lot better if he didn't."

The receptionist buzzed to say she had Jason Davison on the line. Reader leaned over his desk phone. "Senator, this is Sheriff Thad Reader."

The voice on the phone was dry, noncommittal. "Yes. I was just listening to your press conference."

Reader rolled his eyes upward. "I saw clips from your talk last night as well. I'm calling because you said you had evidence that Betty Sue Gardner was planted in your campaign and that some of her claims are fraudulent."

"Not some. All."

"Betty Sue is currently in my custody, Senator. If you have evidence against her, I'd like to know what it is so I can file the appropriate charge."

"And keep all the headlines and glory for yourself."

"If you have evidence of a crime, sir, I'm asking you to turn it over to law enforcement. I'm just trying to do my job. There's precious little glory attached."

"Why should I trust you? I watched you doing your job yesterday and today. Between slanting the news of that woman's return and smearing Linton Barney's name, your job could be costing me my job. I'm lucky I'm still in the race."

Owen mouthed the word "good" and gave Reader a thumbs-up sign.

Davison continued. "So I'm sure you'll understand if I'm not anxious to burnish your image by giving you first crack at any sort of evidence. Instead, I'll tell you what I'm going to do. I'm going to give what I know to the state police and let them take over the case. They'll show you up for the over-the-hill, incompetent grandstander you are. You're going to regret meddling in my campaign."

"I'm sorry you feel that way, Senator. But Betty Sue is in protective custody, and it would take some pretty strong evidence to get me to turn her over to anyone else."

"Well, brace yourself, because it's coming."

The line went dead.

Reader stared at the silenced phone. "Man hung up on me. Called me over-the-hill and hung up on me."

"Look at it this way," Owen said. "We're in West Virginia. Everybody's over at least one hill. And once you're over that hill, you pick up speed."

Reader smiled. "You think he actually has any evidence?"

"I still think he's bluffing. If he's got any evidence at all, though, he's got to get it out right away if it's going to help his campaign."

"If he does have evidence, I could look pretty silly protecting Betty Sue. Be nice to know what he's up to. You've got friends on the state police, don't you?"

"I've helped them out with some accident investigations," Owen said.

"Know anybody who could tell us whether Davison has approached them with some hard evidence?"

"Know a few people I could try."

Owen returned to his office and called John Keller, a state police captain in charge of research at their Charleston headquarters. After a few brief personal exchanges, Keller was the first to bring up the current business of their two organizations. "You had one of our guys behind bars for a couple of days," Keller said.

"Brewer Stevens," Owen said. "Yes, I interviewed him. He was riding along on a crazy black ops assault near Barkley. Evidently doing a favor for the governor."

"Who was doing a favor for Jason Davison. I think you ought to know most of us with the patrol are none too pleased with the favors we've been asked to do for that guy."

"Then why do them?"

"Governor's at the top of our chain of command. He seems

to think cozying up to Davison will get him a friend in the White House."

"Way things are going, best he can expect from Davison is a buddy in the outhouse," Owen said. "It's a shame the patrol stands to come away with a black eye."

"We'll survive. We'll be around long after this governor's gone."

"Since you feel that way, maybe you wouldn't mind doing me a favor that could put you sideways with the governor. Or at least with his buddy Davison."

"What is it?"

"Betty Sue Gardner has come to us asking for protection from Davison. Claims he got her pregnant and threatened her. Davison says she's lying and that he has evidence she was a paid spy in his campaign headquarters."

"I got all that from the evening news."

"We're trying to get to the truth of the matter. We've asked Davison to give us any evidence he has. He's refused. Says he's going to share it with the patrol. So you guys can come forward with it and make us look silly for protecting Betty Sue."

"If that part made the evening news, I must have missed it."

"It's a threat he just made. Fresh this very hour. Here's the thing, though. I used up my year's quota of silly-looking days by March first. I'd rather not have any more. We just don't know whether Davison is bluffing about having evidence that Betty Sue was a plant. If he's running a bluff, we want to protect her. If he has proof she's a plant, though, we'd like to know about it."

"So you want to know if he's shared any of this so-called evidence with the patrol."

"And exactly what it is, if it's real."

"I certainly haven't heard anything. But I'll ask around."

"Appreciate it. Whether or not you find out anything, I owe you one."

"What for?" Keller said. "We never had this conversation."

27

FOOLING SOME OF THE PEOPLE
SOME OF THE TIME

John Keller called back a little after lunchtime. "I've managed to find out a little bit," he said. "But people here have clammed up about the details. Seems like all Davison had to offer were a few suggestions about where we might look for evidence. Like Betty Sue's bank accounts."

"Find anything?"

"Not there. But Betty Sue's mom deposited a couple of large slugs of cash in her own checking account recently."

"Do you know where they came from?" Owen asked.

"That's the problem. I gather nobody's sure of the source. Our guys are reluctant to move forward without that information. Unless we can prove the money came from Halstead's campaign chest, I don't think we'll move on it. The governor's already been stung once doing Davison favors. I don't think he wants to be stung twice. Particularly because Davison is looking more and more like a loser."

"Thanks, John," Owen said. "It's too bad we never had this conversation, because if we had, I'd owe you big time."

"If you get a chance, go easy on Brewer Stevens. He's not the brightest badge in the lineup, but he was just following orders."

"That excuse didn't go far after World War II, and I don't think it's gained any ground since."

"I don't like it either," Keller said. "But Brewer's young and you don't get far in our organization bucking the chain of command."

*****

"Let's get Betty Sue into the conference room. Right now," Reader said as soon as Owen relayed the information from John Keller.

"What about Tom O'Day?" Owen asked.

"This affects him too," Reader said. "Might as well make it a foursome."

Betty Sue was the last to arrive at the conference room. Reader ushered her in and sat her next to O'Day and across from Owen. Then the sheriff stood with both hands pressed down hard on the head of the table.

Betty Sue took one look at Reader and said, "Is something wrong?"

"Something's very wrong," Reader said. "Have you given your mother any large sums of money recently?"

"Why, no."

"Did you contact her when you were on the run?" Reader asked.

"No." Betty Sue looked at O'Day. "We agreed that Mom would be the first place Jason would look when I disappeared. Why are you asking about my mother? Has something happened to her?"

"She's evidently come into some large sums of money recently," Reader said. "Davison might be fixing to claim they were payments made indirectly to you in return for going undercover in his campaign."

"That's crazy."

"Maybe so. Maybe no." Reader put the conference room phone on speaker and shoved it down the table to Betty Sue. "I want you to call your mother right now. Find out if she's received any money recently."

Betty Sue dialed the phone, then leaned over to surround it with her body as if she could protect her mother from whatever was coming. When her mother answered, she said, "Mom. It's Betty Sue."

"Oh, honey. I saw you on the TV. You've lost a lot of weight."

"Mom, I'm here in Barkley with Sheriff Thad Reader, his

319

deputy Owen Allison, and Tom O'Day."

"I saw Sheriff Reader on TV too. And I remember talking to him and Deputy Allison. And isn't Mr. O'Day the man who interviewed you on TV?"

"That's right, Mom. He's a reporter. And a friend."

"Are you in some kind of trouble, hon?"

"I hope not, Mom. But these men have some questions to ask you."

"Mrs. Gardner, this is Sheriff Reader. I'd like to know if anyone has deposited large sums of money in your bank account recently."

The pause at the end of the line was so long that Reader asked, "Mrs. Gardner. Are you still there?"

"Yes. I'm sorry. An officer from your highway patrol was here this morning asking me that same question."

"And what was the answer?" Reader asked.

A sigh preceded her answer. "Yes."

Betty Sue clasped her hand to her forehead. "How much, Mom?"

"Two deposits of ten thousand dollars. In cash."

"And where did it come from?"

"I can't tell you that. I had to promise not to tell anyone. That was the deal. That's what I told the highway patrolman."

"Mom, you've got to tell us. Senator Davison is likely to claim that money was payment for my spying on his campaign."

"Senator Davison is going to say that?"

"Yes. I could go to jail."

"That son of a bitch."

Betty Sue jerked back from the phone, surprised at her mother's language. "Mom. What makes you say that?"

"The money came from Senator Davison," Mrs. Gardner said. "At least the first ten thousand did. I assume the second did as well."

Tom O'Day whispered, "Holy cow."

"Mom," Betty Sue said, "why did Senator Davison give you money?"

"His people came to see me right after you disappeared.

They asked me if I knew where you were. When I said no, they didn't believe me at first. But then they offered to give me ten thousand dollars if I promised to call them if you contacted me. And another ten thousand if they actually found you because of my call."

"And you took it?" Betty Sue said.

"Honey, I never intended to turn you in. It was found money. Tax free."

"Can you prove it came from Davison?" Owen asked.

"His people made me promise not to tell where the money came from. But I remembered you telling me the man couldn't be trusted. So I asked his people to have him call me personally. So I could make sure he didn't intend to harm you."

"And did he call?" Betty Sue asked.

"Oh, yes. A few hours after his people left. He praised you to the skies. Said all he wanted was to see you safely home. To make sure no harm befell you. Befell you. Those were his exact words."

"Mom, he was lying."

"Well, I didn't exactly trust him. He's a politician, after all. They're all phonies. But the first ten thousand came right after he called. Deposited straight into my account. Nothing phony about that."

"There may be a record of that call," Reader said. "Even if there's no way to prove where the money came from."

"Will I have to give the money back?" Mrs. Gardner asked. "I didn't keep my end of the bargain."

"They're not likely to know that," Owen said. "And if it ever goes public, all you have to do is tell where the money came from."

When the call ended, Owen asked Reader, "What do you think?"

"If that's Davison's best play, it's a pretty weak one. Even if the deposits can't be traced, he's got another 'he said/she said' argument on his hands. And money to Betty Sue's mom isn't exactly the same as money to Betty Sue. It's not only weak, it's risky."

"The man's desperate," Owen said. "Discrediting Betty Sue is the only play he has."

"The more the public hears that Betty Sue was a plant, the worse it is for all of us," Reader said.

"Still, it is hard to believe Davison would think he could pull it off," O'Day said.

"To quote Lincoln," Reader said, "It's easy enough to fool all of the people some of the time. And if a politician does it once it lasts for four years."

Owen smiled. "I don't think that's quite what Lincoln said. And Davison's staking his candidacy on a blatant lie."

"He's been getting away with blatant lies all his life," Reader said. "Being a lying lout doesn't disqualify a man from public office. And he may be lying about the twenty-grand payoff, but his claim that Betty Sue was a plant is actually true, even if he doesn't know it. Wouldn't it be funny if the one time he's telling the truth, nobody believes him?"

"Nobody forced him to seduce Betty Sue," Owen said. "It's a clear case of sexual harassment. I can't believe you're actually feeling sorry for the bastard."

"I'm just saying neither side has totally clean hands. There's never only one cockroach."

"It's certainly true neither of us was innocent," Betty Sue said. "We were both consenting adults. But I don't want my mother hurt by this."

"So far, there's been no mention of her in the news," O'Day said. "Davison is running out of time. If he tries one last 'Hail Mary' and mentions your mother, we'll have to be ready with a rebuttal statement. I don't think she'll be hurt. She's the only innocent party in this whole mess."

"I'm not buying this business that neither party has clean hands," Owen said. "Maybe Halstead isn't squeaky clean, but it's pretty clear Davison is the bigger bastard. And the bigger threat to the country."

"Clear to you," Reader said. "But you've got to admit you're biased."

"My bias has been building for over twenty years. I'll give

you that. But the bastard had my friend killed. That goes way beyond bias. We're talking open hatred. And I want to see him pay for Dan Thornton's death."

Following the meeting, Owen made a call to John Keller at state police headquarters. "Thought you might like to know that the sizable deposits in the bank account of Betty Sue Gardner's mother came from Jason Davison himself. He was trying to ensure that her mother would turn her daughter in if she learned of her whereabouts."

"You've got to be kidding."

"No. And that's the story that will come out if the patrol cites the deposits as proof that Betty Sue was planted in Davison's office."

"I think we'd pretty much decided not to go down that road, but I'll make sure we don't. Thanks for the heads-up."

"My pleasure." Owen hung up with equal measures of satisfaction and relief.

The rest of the day passed with no further claims or denials from the Davison camp and no messages from the state police. With the primary just a day away, polls continued to show a slight decline in the Senator's popularity, but many votes had been cast in advance of the cover-up revelations, and most experts said the election was still too close to call.

Because Judith had announced her intention to leave for California on election day, Ruth insisted that Owen take her out to dinner so that they could spend a little time together before she had to go. Owen was quietly pleased by the prospect, and made reservations at the Cordea Mira, one of the few restaurants in Barkley that advertised fine atmospheric dining rather than fast food or TV sports.

"It's not exactly the Bella Vista, but the food is good," Owen said as the hostess led them to a wood-paneled corner booth beneath an oil painting of a hilly Italian village.

"The Bella Vista isn't the Bella Vista anymore," Judith said. "It closed last year."

"I'm sorry to hear that. I guess nothing really good lasts forever."

"You should keep your old menus, though. Maybe they'll be worth something on the *Antiques Roadshow* some day."

Owen ordered a bottle of Chianti, and when the waitress had filled their wineglasses he toasted Judith, saying, "I'm really glad you decided to stay for a while. After what you'd been through, I was afraid you'd take the first plane out."

"I've got to admit you really know how to show a gal a good time. Flamethrowers, assault rifles, underground hideouts, battlefield flares, and flying bullets. It's better than Disneyland."

"Stick around. After the election I'll have plenty of time to make amends."

Judith shook her head. "Got to get back. Need to attend to my law practice."

"Have you thought any more about bringing your practice in this direction?"

"Owen, we've been through all that before. Have you seen the local billboards advertising legal services? 'THINKING ABOUT BANKRUPTCY?' or 'HAVE YOU OR YOUR LOVED ONES BEEN DIAGNOSED WITH MESOTHELIOMA?' That's not exactly the kind of practice I want. I don't belong here."

"Just thought I'd ask."

Judith reached across the table and covered his right hand with her left. "Owen, you don't belong here either. Not really. Not with people shooting at you. You're in the business of analyzing accidents. Not living through them."

Owen took a sip of Chianti with his left hand. "The accident business has been a little slow lately."

"But working for Thad Reader is dangerous."

"So's going without food."

"There are lots more people in California. Lots more accidents. You could make a living there without having to dodge bullets."

"I've been away too long. And Mom needs me here."

Judith squeezed his hand. "That's it. Play the Mom card.

She's in good hands with Trish."

"Trish isn't family."

"She takes better care of your mom than you could. And you know it. Besides, California is only a day away. And your brother George is here in Barkley."

"George has problems of his own."

"Can't blame a gal for trying."

"I thought you already had someone in Palo Alto."

"I do. But he's getting impatient. And he has every right to."

Owen covered Judith's hands with his own. "I guess I should apologize for the length of your stay, but I'm not sorry." He stared at the clasped hands in the center of the table and remembered when the parts of him most alive were those Judith touched.

A young woman with flowing black hair appeared at the side of their booth. "Excuse me," she said to Judith. "Do you mind if I ask you a personal question?"

"So long as it's not too personal."

"How long have you two been together?"

Judith seemed to recoil slightly, like a fighter dodging a jab. "Twenty-four years. Why?"

"My husband and I were watching you just now." She nodded toward her husband, who sat in the mirror image of their booth across the tiny room and immediately looked away. "It's so nice to see older people being so affectionate."

"My husband and I have been married two years," the woman continued. "Well, nearly two years. You give us something to look forward to." She looked to Owen for confirmation. "Twenty-four years."

Owen nodded. "Ten of the best years of my life."

Judith released his hand.

"It's still nice to see." The woman managed an embarrassed laugh and retreated to her own booth.

"What an asshole response," Judith said under her breath.

"You're the one who pretended we're not divorced."

"I didn't see any point in disillusioning her."

"Personally, I thought ten years was quite a generous estimate."

"Thanks a lot. Very funny, since we were married for twelve."

"I still think ten years was a fair estimate. Those last two years I spent in D.C. were a disaster."

"They weren't that bad."

"For you, maybe." Owen started to add, "You were the one having the affair," but thought better of it.

"We've been divorced as long as we were married, and you still can't let it go," Judith said, as if she'd read the thoughts he'd censored.

"Maybe ten years really was an underestimate," Owen said. "We have had some good times together since the divorce."

Judith dabbed at her mouth with her napkin. "Too little. Too late."

"I'm sorry," Owen said. "I never could resist the easy punch line, and sometimes my mouth runs ahead of my mind."

"Maybe your mind should exercise a little so it could run ahead of your mouth and shut it up."

"I said I was sorry. Even when I shut up in time you anticipate the worst."

They passed the rest of the meal in silence. As he paid the check, Owen glanced at the young woman in the booth across from theirs, who pretended to study her wineglass.

When they got home, Owen asked Judith if she'd like a drink.

"I'm pretty tired," she said. "I think I'll go straight to bed."

"Probably best," Owen said. "I've got to get up early tomorrow to help Thad Reader police the election precincts."

"You're right," Judith said. "It's probably best."

PART V

ELECTION DAY

O'DAY'S DAYS

BARKLEY, WV—*Here in West Virginia, today's forecasts predict bright blue skies throughout most of the state as voters make their way to the polls. Traditionally, good weather means that more undecided and low-income voters will take the trouble to cast their ballots. The outcome of this election, though, is more likely to be determined by the safe return of missing Davison campaign worker Betty Sue Gardner than the vagaries of the weather.*

When Ms. Gardner first went missing, Davison was able to counter slippage in the polls through increased spending and frequent denials of the rumors that he was involved sexually with his comely campaign worker. Since her return, Ms. Gardner has confirmed these rumors and identified Davison as the father of her aborted child. This revelation, coupled with the exposure of a fatal DUI accident cover-up, has led to still more slippage in the polls. However, most experts continue to rate the race as "too close to call," suggesting that Davison's increasingly implausible denials have kept enough of his followers faithful to deny Sam Halstead a runaway victory.

Tom O'Day, for the New York Herald Dispatch

28

THE BALLOT BOX BOOGIE

The sun rose on election day with pundits still insisting the West Virginia primary was too close to call. Polls opened at 6:30 in the morning, and at twenty past six Owen parked his patrol car alongside Thad Reader's in a turnout about a quarter mile down a winding road from the VFW hall that served as a polling place for the sixteenth precinct, one of the county's largest voting precincts.

Fog like cotton swabbing clung to the wounds where power lines and narrow fire roads had been cut through the mountains. "We'll walk from here," Reader said. "Don't want to be too conspicuous right off."

"What are we looking for?" Owen asked.

"I've got poll workers inside watching out for repeat voters. We've given them lists of the recently deceased residents in each precinct. You and I will go precinct to precinct checking with them for any signs of shenanigans around the ballot boxes, give them any backup they need. Mostly, though, we'll be outside watching for signs of the ballot box boogie."

"What's that?"

"It's a local dance popular on election day." Reader led Owen off onto a dusty fire road. "It should be pretty easy to spot from where we're going."

After a short walk, Reader left the fire road and picked his way along a footpath through a cluster of oak trees that ended at a grassy slope leading downhill to the parking lot behind the VFW hall. U.S. and West Virginia flags on the roof of the hall marked it as a polling place. Across the road from the hall, a diner, a beauty salon, a boarded-up storefront, and a Goodwill store backed onto a nearly dry creek bed.

Under the cover of the oak trees, Reader pulled binoculars and a camera with a telescopic lens out of the leather satchel slung over his shoulder. He handed Owen the binoculars and trained the camera's lens on a man in overalls emerging from a black SUV in the Goodwill store's parking lot. The man propped a DAVISON FOR PRESIDENT placard against the side of the vehicle and walked toward the VFW hall.

"It's one of the Stanton boys," Reader said. "He'll likely be leading the dance." Reader lowered the camera as the man in overalls entered the VFW hall. "It's his job to come away with a blank ballot. If he doesn't already have one, he'll sacrifice his vote by dropping a blank facsimile in the ballot box and bring his own ballot back to the SUV."

"What good will that do?" Owen asked.

"They'll rig it with votes for a predetermined slate and pay a different voter to deposit it. That way they can be sure the man they pay will vote the way they want."

"Whatever happened to honor among thieves?"

"Ward heelers figured out pretty soon that a man who'll sell his vote might not be altogether trustworthy."

"I get it," Owen said. "Then the voter who deposited the rigged ballot will bring back the blank ballot he's been given."

"That's when he gets paid," Reader said. "They'll rig the fresh ballot and the dance will go on all day."

"And the candidates supply the cash," Owen said.

"An old established custom," Reader said. "In the grand tradition of the Kennedys and Rockefellers and hundreds of lesser lights. A true bipartisan effort."

The man in overalls emerged from the VFW hall and headed back toward the black SUV he'd left in the Goodwill parking lot. He arrived just as a battered station wagon pulled up alongside the SUV.

"Good timing," Reader said. "The first batch of dancers has arrived."

330

The man in overalls climbed into the driver's seat of the SUV while the station wagon's four doors opened, disgorging three passengers and the driver, who stretched, yawned, and leaned on the open passenger window of the SUV. Two of the wagon's passengers, rawboned farm boys in jeans and denim jackets, lit cigarettes while the third disappeared around the rear of the Goodwill store toward the creek bed.

The driver of the station wagon accepted a sheet of white paper from the passenger window of the SUV, laughed, and handed it to the taller of the two smokers, who headed off toward the VFW hall.

"That paper's the rigged ballot," Reader said, snapping off photos of the exchange. "The boogie's begun."

"How much will the kid get for his vote?" Owen asked.

Reader shrugged. "Fifteen, maybe twenty bucks. Going rate will vary with the number of buyers. Sometimes even with the time of day."

"From the look of that placard propped next to the SUV, Davison is one of the buyers."

"Wouldn't surprise me. Most likely one of my would-be opponents for sheriff and a few state senate candidates have been sweetening the pot as well."

The young man returned from the VFW hall and handed a folded sheet of white paper over to the driver of the station wagon, who passed it through the passenger window of the SUV. Then the driver extracted a wad of bills from his hip pocket, rolled off a bill, and handed it to the young man.

"Looks like twenty is the going rate for the slate," Reader said, peering through the telescopic lens and snapping another photo. Then he put the camera back in his shoulder bag. "Let's go break up the boogie."

The men standing around the SUV scattered when Owen and Reader drove up in their patrol cars. The driver and passenger in the SUV stayed put, though, and Owen recognized the passenger as Warren Stanton, the hawk-nosed amputee whose wheelchair he had borrowed at the Shady Acres Care Center.

"Morning, sheriff," Stanton said.

"Morning, Warren," Reader said. "What's going on here that caused your buddies to take off in such a hurry?"

"Can't speak for them. Me, I'm exercising my right as a citizen to do a little electioneering."

"That electioneering wouldn't extend to vote buying, would it?"

"Ain't nothing illegal going on here, sheriff."

"Then why is that young man hovering across the street?" Reader pointed to the young man in denim who had returned from the VFW hall expecting to find his driver standing where the sheriff now stood.

"Have to ask him that," Stanton said.

"You, there," Reader called to the young man, "come on over here."

The young man made his way hesitantly across the street.

"I'd like you to give me that ballot you're carrying," Reader said.

The young man looked uncertainly at Stanton. "Will I still get my twenty?"

"Not from me." Reader held out his hand. "Now turn it over."

The young man reached inside his denim jacket and gave Reader the blank ballot.

"You're interfering with this boy's God-given right to exercise his voting franchise," Stanton said.

"I'm interfering with the buying and selling of votes, which is illegal," Reader said.

"No such thing going on here," Stanton said.

"I've just photographed an exchange of money," Reader said. "The driver of that station wagon paid this boy's friend twenty dollars for a blank ballot."

"The driver of that wagon is my cousin," Stanton said. "I paid him one hundred and fifty dollars to transport folks to the polls. What he does with that money is his own business. My payment to him, though, is all legal and aboveboard. Ask our current senators. When they're running, they outfit whole fleets of drivers at election time." Stanton handed his cell phone out the window. "Or maybe you'd like to call my lawyer."

332

Reader ignored the phone. "And just who is paying you to outfit your fleet?"

Stanton pointed to the placard leaning against his rear door. "Senator Jason Davison, for one. A friend of the workingman. And a real believer in getting out the vote."

"Senator Davison paid you himself, did he?" Reader said.

"No, he used a go-between."

"Would you be willing to swear to that in court?" Owen asked.

"'Course I'd swear to it. Ain't nothing illegal about it. Like I said, our own senators recruit poll drivers all the time."

"And do those senators pay you personally?" Owen asked.

"'Course not. They use go-betweens too. Hell, their go-betweens have go-betweens."

A Ford Escort rattled into the Goodwill parking lot. As soon as the driver spotted the two patrol cars, he threw the Escort into reverse and wheeled back onto the highway.

"Looky here, sheriff," Stanton said. "This is my peak earning season and you're interfering with my livelihood. There's nothing illegal going on here. I'm more than three hundred feet from the front entrance of the polling place. That means I'm within my rights to stump for my candidates."

"Looks to me like what you're doing is filling out blank ballots and hiring flunkies to hand them in. So you're buying more than your share of votes. That's flat-out illegal. I could run you in for that." Reader tore up the blank ballot. "At the very least, I can't let you go on doing it."

"Supposin' I just sit here and recommend how folks might like to vote?" Stanton asked.

"Long as you stay three hundred feet from the VFW hall, I can't stop you from making recommendations. But you can't keep on handing folks filled-out ballots to turn in."

"If I don't give them a filled-out ballot, how will I know they're following my recommendations?"

"That's your problem." Reader cinched his Mountie's hat tight under his chin. "We're done here. For now. But we'll be checking back from time to time to make sure you're not rigging any more ballots. If we catch you at it again, you're likely to miss a lot of the peak earning seasons you've got coming up."

"No need to hurry back," Stanton said. "I ain't going nowhere."

Owen and Reader checked on operations inside the VFW hall and then walked back to their patrol cars. The fog had been reduced to tiny puffs of smoke against the highest ridges.

"Would it do any good to trace the chain of go-betweens linking Davison's money to Stanton's vote buying?" Owen asked.

"Be as useless as a screen door on a submarine. Davison could always say he was just paying for drivers to bring people to the polls. All perfectly legal."

"There must be something we can do," Owen said.

"We could run Stanton in for the ballot scam I just photographed, but that's hardly worth the trouble. Best thing we can do is keep busting up the boogies wherever we find them. And check with the poll watchers in case they're having any trouble. I've got Phil Blatt working precincts one through five and Ginny Kaib working six through ten. I'll take eleven through fifteen, which leaves you sixteen through twenty. Lots of Stantons in precinct eighteen, so I wouldn't be surprised if there's a ballot box boogie running there right now."

Owen spent the rest of the morning working the remaining precincts on his list, breaking up a boogie in the eighteenth precinct and helping the poll watchers in the nineteenth discourage an elderly man who felt he should be able to cast a ballot in the name of a recently deceased neighbor because "I lived next to Herb for over twenty years and know just how he'd vote." A little after noon he returned to the sixteenth precinct, where Warren Stanton's SUV still sat in the Goodwill parking lot.

Owen watched from the tree-lined vantage point he'd shared with Reader earlier as the same battered station wagon that had delivered three passengers in the morning returned with three more. A young pregnant woman wearing a backward baseball cap left the station wagon, took a rolled-up paper from Stanton, walked to the VFW hall, and returned to pass something small and black through the SUV window to Stanton. Even with his binoculars, Owen couldn't quite make out what was passed through the window, but it evidently satisfied Stanton, because the driver of the station wagon peeled a bill from his wad of cash and handed it to the woman.

Owen continued to watch as a man wearing a Cincinnati Reds windbreaker took a rolled-up sheet of white paper from Stanton and set off toward the VFW hall. As soon as the man reached the polling place, Owen walked back down the fire road and drove his patrol car to the Goodwill lot, arriving at the same time the Reds fan returned from voting and handed a cell phone through the passenger window of the SUV. After a nod from Stanton, the station wagon driver handed a twenty to the man, who stuffed it in the pocket of his windbreaker.

When a woman with a baby strapped to her chest approached the SUV and took a rolled-up sheet of paper from Stanton, Owen stepped forward. "Let me see that, please."

"Something wrong, deputy?" Stanton asked.

"We warned you about handing out rigged ballots."

"Ain't doing no such thing. Show him, Mindy."

The woman handed her rolled-up packet to Owen. It contained a crudely lettered slate of candidates wrapped around a cell phone. Jason Davison's name led the slate.

"Mindy here's going to vote my slate and take a picture of her ballot with that there cell so's I'll know she done her electoral duty. Ain't technology grand?"

Owen handed the paper and cell phone back to the woman. "Couldn't be grander."

Owen continued to patrol his five precincts until the polls closed at 7:30 in the evening. Except for a few aborted attempts to vote graveyard residents, he encountered nothing that was blatantly illegal. Every time he visited the sixteenth precinct, though, a steady stream of voters flowed between Warren Stanton's SUV and the VFW hall. Votes for Jason Davison, bought and paid for legally. A strong reminder of Winston Churchill's observation that democracy was the worst form of government ever devised, except for all the others.

He arrived home exhausted by his thirteen-hour day. Ruth had laid out a turkey and bacon sandwich and a cold bottle of Stella Artois, but there was only one place set at the table.

"Isn't anyone joining me?" Owen asked.

"I ate earlier and Judith left for California," Ruth said. "Rented a car and drove to the Columbus airport."

"Did she say anything?"

"Nothing you'd care to hear. What happened last night, anyhow?"

"Nothing."

"Maybe that's the problem."

"We had a nice romantic dinner, Mom. Just like you intended. We were so wrapped up in each other that our attentiveness got rave reviews from at least one adjacent table."

"But not from Judith, evidently."

"Evidently."

Ruth sighed. "Well, you're welcome to join me in the living room if you want company."

Owen took his sandwich and beer into the living room and watched the local news reporters chew over the breaking election results. Counts were slow in coming at first, and the two WSAZ-TV anchors filled the airtime by debating whether Betty Sue Gardner's return had helped or hurt Jason Davison's chances.

"On the one hand," a blond and tanned anchorman observed, "the fact that Betty Sue is alive absolved the candidate of any suspicions of foul play."

"On the other hand," the anchorman's partner, a pert brunette with a perpetual smile, said, "her accusations won't set well with female voters and born-again Christians."

"Who would they set well with?" Owen asked the TV. "Serial killers and rapists?"

"Owen, that's not necessary," Ruth said.

The anchorman answered his partner's observation by saying, "Let's not forget we only have Betty Sue's word for what happened. There's no real proof. To me she sounds like a woman scorned."

336

"That's not fair."

"The woman's accusations have reduced the campaign debates to a 'he said/she said' spat. Halstead might even have planted her in Davison's campaign."

"There's no real proof of that, either," the brunette said. "And it appears Davison was responsible for any planting that occurred."

"Jesus Christ!" Owen exploded at the TV. "I can't believe that guy. 'Foul play,' 'woman scorned,' 'he said/she said.' He must get his dialog from old Agatha Christie books. Jason Davison is a stone-cold murderer."

"What do you mean? The girl is still alive," Ruth said.

Owen realized that he'd said more than he could reveal to his mother. "You're right, Mom, but those two on the TV screen are a stronger argument against democracy than a five-minute chat with the average voter."

"Careful, son," Ruth said. "You're talking to an average voter."

By ten p.m., results were coming in so fast that the commentators had little time to speculate and by eleven Sam Halstead had won West Virginia's presidential primary, defeating Jason Davison by a margin of fifty-six percent to forty-four percent. Halstead also carried the other eastern states holding primaries that day by substantial margins.

"Well, that pretty much does in Jason Davison," Ruth said. "That should make you happy."

It should, Owen thought, but it doesn't. Somehow, it's just not nearly enough.

By the next morning, Davison had withdrawn from the presidential race. Ruth set a mug of hot tea and two cinnamon buns in front of Owen, along with a handset from the home phone. "I'm sorry," she said. "You got a phone message yesterday afternoon. It must have come when I was napping. Anyhow, I missed it altogether until this morning."

Owen waved off her apology. "It's probably nothing important."

337

The message was from Sheriff James McDonald in Washington. He apologized for taking so long to get back with the latest fingerprint results, but he was shorthanded. He was leaving the message both on Owen's home and office phones to make sure he got it as soon as possible. Owen's hunch had been right. Prints on the motorcycle report in Dan Thornton's family room matched those of Harrison Marcus. McDonald had issued a warrant for Marcus's arrest, and he hoped Owen and Sheriff Reader would be able to bring him in.

Owen called Thad Reader immediately. "Better get out to the Rocker mansion right away," Reader said. "Take Mary with you. She'll be on backup this morning, and you shouldn't go alone."

"Will you meet us there?" Owen asked.

"I've got a meeting with the mayor. Seems he thinks we clamped down a little too hard on voter transactions yesterday."

"Damned if you do, damned if you don't."

"Damned if I care about the mayor's complaints," Reader said. "But I've got to hear him out. The good news is we've finally got something solid on that smug bastard Marcus."

"You're right," Owen said. "But the bad news is that Sheriff McDonald left his message on my home phone. I'd given him the number back before we knew anyone was listening to it. If it's still being monitored, that smug bastard has a half day's head start."

29

THE BULLET STOPS HERE

The office dispatcher told Owen that Mary Galardi had been called away to cover a domestic dispute, so he left messages for Mary and Thad Reader and drove straight from his home to the Rocker mansion without waiting for backup. He swung his mother's Chrysler into the circular drive in front of the mansion and parked behind the only other car in the front lot, a dark blue Cadillac coupe. The campaign's black limo was nowhere in sight, suggesting that Harrison Marcus had already flown the coop. The mansion's large oak door was slightly ajar, with no bodyguards around. Evidently someone figured the body wasn't worth guarding any more.

Owen rang the doorbell and waited. When no one answered, he pushed the heavy door open far enough so that he could poke his head in and say, "Hello in there. Anybody home?"

Still no answer. He pushed the door wide open and stepped into the wood-paneled reception hall, where he repeated, "Anybody home?"

The high-ceilinged room echoed the question, but no answer came until the echo died. Then a voice called out, "In the library."

Owen crossed the hall to the open library door. Jason Davison and his father sat at the far end of a mahogany conference table. "What can we do for you, deputy?" Red Davison asked.

Owen walked to the near end of the table. "I'm looking for Harrison Marcus."

"I thought we'd settled that matter," Red Davison said.

"Your governor admits he sanctioned the raid on the Elkins home. The results were unfortunate, but Harrison was only an observer and has been released on bail. If you need to see him, you should contact his lawyer."

"This is another matter," Owen said. "He's wanted for murder in Washington State."

"Murder? Whose murder?" Jason Davison asked.

"A former partner of mine. Dan Thornton."

"I've never heard of the man," Jason said. "What motive could Harrison possibly have?"

"The same motive that had people shooting at me in the Columbus airport," Owen said. "He wanted the original copy of your teenage accident report."

Jason clutched the edge of the conference table as if he needed it to keep afloat. "Believe me. I had nothing to do with that shooting."

"I hope that's true," Owen said. "Be a shame if you lost your freedom along with your run for the presidency."

"There's no need for threats," Red Davison said. "I'm sure we can clear this up." He turned to his son. "Has Harrison been around this morning?"

"I haven't seen him," Jason said.

"Where's the rest of your staff?" Owen asked. "There weren't any guards on the door."

"Rats deserting a sinking ship," Jason said.

"I'm sure Harrison wouldn't desert," Red Davison said. "He's been with me nearly forty years." He stood up, retrieved a handset from the sideboard, and laid it on the conference table in front of his son. "Buzz him."

Jason pressed a button and stared at the phone as if it were somehow defective. Then, without waiting very long, he pressed the button again and looked up at Owen. "No answer."

"Perhaps I was wrong about Harrison," Red Davison said. "He does have a tendency to be a bit overzealous."

Jason dropped the handset on the table and gaped at something over Owen's shoulder.

Harrison Marcus stood in the doorway. His blue suit was

dirty and rumpled, his drooping necktie revealed a red scar around his neck, and he was pointing a snub-nosed revolver at Jason Davison. "You didn't really expect me to respond to that buzzer, did you Jason? In fact, you expected me to be well out of reach of any buzzer."

"I don't know what you mean," Jason said.

"Sure you do. I hear the cellular reception in hell is a little spotty." Marcus turned the revolver on Owen. "I didn't expect to find you here, Doctor Allison. That must be your beater in the front driveway."

"It is," Owen said.

"Too bad for you, doctor," Marcus said, putting enough spin on the word "doctor" to bounce it sideways. "Leave your gun in your holster and drop your holster to the floor."

Owen unsnapped the flap on his holster, pulled it free of his belt, and laid it on the parquet floor.

"That's fine," Marcus said. "Now just slide that holster along the floor to me."

Owen took one step and kicked his holster about halfway along the wall toward Marcus.

"Now doctor, what brings you to this fine mansion?"

"I came here to arrest you," Owen said.

"Did you now?" Marcus said. "On what charge? Being overzealous?"

"For the death of my friend Dan Thornton. Maybe we should add Linton Barney's name to the list of charges as well."

"Linton's death was an accident," Jason Davison said.

"Barney's motorcycle was forced off the road by the same Mercedes sedan that fired on me in the Columbus airport," Owen said.

"That's impossible," Jason said. "Linton was my best friend. Harrison would never have harmed him."

"You always claimed to be my friend," Marcus said. "And you tried to have me killed."

"I did no such thing."

"The hell you didn't. The minute you learned I was wanted for murder in Washington, you hired two rent-a-thugs to drive me to Canada. We got a little north of Altoona when the driver announced he had to piss." Marcus grimaced. "Like I'd never seen *The Godfather*. I got my pistol ready and when the thug behind me looped a piano wire around my neck I blew his brains all over the back seat."

"I had nothing to do with that," Jason said. "I swear to God."

"You gave me money and a fake ID and put me in your limo with two thugs."

"That's all I did," Jason said. "I never told anyone to kill you."

"Somebody in this room did," Marcus said. "If it wasn't you, it's only because you can't go to the bathroom without daddy's permission. And he's still wiping your hind end for you."

"That's enough, Harrison," Red Davison said.

"I guess it had to be you, didn't it, Red?" Marcus said. "Murder would be too big a step for junior here. He's barely potty trained. My God. You and I have been together for forty years."

Red Davison fixed his slate-gray eyes on Marcus. "I said that's enough."

"How long do you think you'll have to clean up junior's messes?" Marcus asked. "This whole shit storm would never have happened if you'd made him take the blame for that DUI charge instead of shifting it to Barney. And that business with the Gardner woman. We could have gotten by that if Jason had just had the balls to stand up and say 'I slept with her. It was a mistake. I'm sorry. It won't happen again.'"

"You know we couldn't do that," Red Davison said.

"That's because we'd used up his last 'Get Out of Jail Free' card on that bimbo you bought off in his last senate race," Marcus said. "So we had to blame everything on Linton Barney again. But he crumbled when Betty Sue's pregnancy surfaced and he realized his claim to be her lover wouldn't stand up."

"Only a few people knew about his operation," Jason said. "We agreed it didn't matter."

"Will you two just shut the hell up," Red Davison said.

"You're not telling me anything I didn't know already." Owen felt his heart pounding, then realized it was the phone in his shirt pocket vibrating. He had to keep them talking. He took a step toward Marcus and held out his hand. "Look, Harrison, give me that gun. It's obvious the killing of Dan Thornton wasn't premeditated. And all they can really prove is that you were in his house looking for files. With a good lawyer, you might even get off."

"We'll get you a good lawyer, Harrison," Jason said.

"Fat chance." Marcus wagged the barrel of his revolver in the direction of Red Davison. "Daddy here knows if I went to trial the scandal would keep the Davisons out of public office forever. Think he's going to let that happen?"

"Think about yourself, not about them," Owen said. "If you kill a presidential candidate and a peace officer, there's no place you'll be able to hide."

"I've got to hide anyhow, one way or the other," Marcus said. "You're forgetting I killed another man just last night."

"From the looks of that scar on your neck, that was self defense," Owen said.

"If you only killed one man last night, what happened to the other one?" Jason asked.

"Danny Bridgeman. Did you even know his name? The wanna-be state trooper who you bailed out and hired to drive and pretend to piss while your other buddy wired my neck?" Marcus rubbed his neck with his free hand. "I'll tell you what happened to Danny. He's trussed up in the trunk of the limo. I'm guessing he wasn't supposed to make it to Canada either. Not after everything he'd seen at the Elkins place."

"I hired him to drive you. That's all."

"Shut up, Jason," Red Davison said. "Look here, Harrison. If it's more money you want, I can get it for you pretty quickly. Then tie us all up to give yourself a head start. The deputy here is right. If you take this any further, it will only make things a lot worse if you're caught."

"You son of a bitch," Marcus said. "You're still trying to buy your baby boy out of trouble."

Owen slid a step closer to Marcus. "He's right, Harrison. Take the money and run. While you've still got a chance."

"A chance to do what?"

"To get away," Owen said. "And to beat the rap if you're caught."

"I guess I just don't see it that way." Marcus leveled his gun at Jason.

Jason shielded his face with both hands. "This is not my fault."

The shots came without warning. The instant after the first one, Owen dove for Marcus's knees. Two more rang out over his head, and something stung his right shoulder as Marcus crumpled under his tackle.

Owen crawled up Marcus's shins and scrambled to grab his gun hand, which had gone limp at the wrist. Blood spread across the gunman's shirtfront.

Owen rolled off Marcus. Thad Reader stood in the doorway, covering the room with his Colt automatic.

Owen knocked Marcus's gun away with the cast on his right hand. The man groaned and rolled over on his side, clutching at his stomach.

Jason Davison lay on the floor, cradled in his father's arms. Reader checked the candidate's pulse, then shook his head. Red Davison moaned and clutched his son's body to his chest.

Reader stepped across Jason Davison's legs and bent over Harrison Marcus. He called 911, then pulled out his handkerchief and tried to staunch the bleeding stomach wound. "Looks like this one might live," he said as he turned to Owen. "How're you doing?"

"Something nicked my shoulder. I don't think it's very deep. Glad you showed up when you did."

"As soon as I found out you'd come up here alone, I tried calling you from the mayor's office. When you didn't answer, I thought I'd better get right over."

Red Davison raised his head. His son's blood covered his cheek. "He could have been president," Davison said. "Maybe not now, but the next time for sure. The voters love Jason."

Owen rose to his knees. "Too bad Linton Barney wasn't around to take the bullet for him."

ABOUT THE AUTHOR

John Billheimer, a native West Virginian, lives in Portola Valley, California. He holds an engineering Ph. D. from Stanford and writes the "funny, sometimes touching," Owen Allison mystery series set in Appalachia's coalfields. The Drood Review voted his first book, *The Contrary Blues,* one of the ten best mysteries of 1998. Four subsequent novels, *Highway Robbery, Dismal Mountain, Drybone Hollow,* and *Stonewall Jackson's Elbow*, explore a variety of Mountain State scams, scandals, and frauds. *Primary Target* is the sixth book in the series.

Billheimer has also written *Field of Schemes* and *A Player to be Maimed Later*, entries in a mystery series featuring sportswriter Lloyd Keaton, as well as *Baseball and the Blame Game*, a non-fiction look at scapegoating in the major leagues and *Hitchcock and the Censors*, a look at all forms of movie censorship and how Alfred Hitchcock coped with them.

www.johnbillheimer.com

CPSIA information can be obtained
at www.ICGtesting.com
Printed in the USA
LVHW080800290819
628849LV00004B/8/P